ALICE CAMPBELL
KEEP AWAY FROM WATER!

ALICE Campbell (1887-1955) came originally from Atlanta, Georgia, where she was part of the socially prominent Ormond family. She moved to New York City at the age of nineteen and quickly became a socialist and women's suffragist. Later she moved to Paris, marrying the American-born artist and writer James Lawrence Campbell, with whom she had a son in 1914.

Just before World War One, the family left France for England, where the couple had two more children, a son and a daughter. Campbell wrote crime fiction until 1950, though many of her novels continued to have French settings. She published her first work (*Juggernaut*) in 1928. She wrote nineteen detective novels during her career.

MYSTERIES BY ALICE CAMPBELL

1. *Juggernaut* (1928)
2. *Water Weed* (1929)
3. *Spiderweb* (1930)
4. *The Click of the Gate* (1932)
5. *The Murder of Caroline Bundy* (1933)
6. *Desire to Kill* (1934)
7. *Keep Away from Water!* (1935)
8. *Death Framed in Silver* (1937)
9. *Flying Blind* (1938)
10. *A Door Closed Softly* (1939)
11. *They Hunted a Fox* (1940)
12. *No Murder of Mine* (1941)
13. *No Light Came On* (1942)
14. *Ringed with Fire* (1943)
15. *Travelling Butcher* (1944)
16. *The Cockroach Sings* (1946)
17. *Child's Play* (1947)
18. *The Bloodstained Toy* (1948)
19. *The Corpse Had Red Hair* (1950)

ALICE CAMPBELL

KEEP AWAY FROM WATER!

With an introduction
by Curtis Evans

DEAN STREET PRESS

ALICE IN MURDERLAND

Crime Writer Alice Campbell, The Other "AC"

In 1927 Alice Dorothy Ormond Campbell—a thirty-nine-year-old native of Atlanta, Georgia who for the last fifteen years had lived successively in New York, Paris and London, never once returning to the so-called Empire City of the South, published her first novel, an unstoppable crime thriller called *Juggernaut*, selling the serialization rights to the *Chicago Tribune* for $4000 ($60,000 today), a tremendous sum for a brand new author. On its publication in January 1928, both the book and its author caught the keen eye of Bessie S. Stafford, society page editor of the *Atlanta Constitution*. Back when Alice Ormond, as she was then known, lived in Atlanta, Miss Bessie breathlessly informed her readers, she had been "an ethereal blonde-like type of beauty, extremely popular, and always thought she was in love with somebody. She took high honors in school; and her gentleness of manner and breeding bespoke an aristocratic lineage. She grew to a charming womanhood—"

Let us stop Miss Bessie right there, because there is rather more to the story of Alice Campbell, the mystery genre's other "AC," who published nineteen crime novels between 1928 and 1950. Allow me to plunge boldly forward with the tale of Atlanta's great Golden Age crime writer, who as an American expatriate in England, went on to achieve fame and fortune as an atmospheric writer of murder and mystery and become one of the early members of the Detection Club.

Alice Campbell's lineage was distinguished. Alice was born in Atlanta on November 29, 1887, the youngest of the four surviving children of prominent Atlantans James Ormond IV and Florence Root. Both of Alice's grandfathers had been wealthy Atlanta merchants who settled in the city in the years before the American Civil War. Alice's uncles, John Wellborn Root and Walter Clark Root, were noted architects, while her brothers, Sidney James and Walter Emanuel Ormond, were respectively a drama critic and political writer for the *Atlanta Constitution* and an attorney and justice of the peace. Both brothers died untimely deaths before Alice had even turned thirty, as did her uncle John Wellborn Root and her father.

Alice precociously published her first piece of fiction, a fairy story, in the *Atlanta Constitution* in 1897, when she was nine years old. Four years later, the ambitious child was said to be in the final stage of completing a two-volume novel. In 1907, by which time she was nineteen, Alice relocated to New York City, chaperoned by Florence.

In New York Alice became friends with writers Inez Haynes Irwin, a prominent feminist, and Jacques Futrelle, the creator of "The Thinking Machine" detective who was soon to go down with the ship on RMS *Titanic,* and scored her first published short story in *Ladies Home Journal* in 1911. Simultaneously she threw herself pell-mell into the causes of women's suffrage and equal pay for equal work. The same year she herself became engaged, but this was soon broken off and in February 1913 Alice sailed to Paris with her mother to further her cultural education.

Three months later in Paris, on May 22, 1913, twenty-five-year-old Alice married James Lawrence Campbell, a twenty-four-year-old theatrical agent of good looks and good family from Virginia. Jamie, as he was known, had arrived in Paris a couple of years earlier, after a failed stint in New York City as an actor. In Paris he served, more successfully, as an agent for prominent New York play brokers Arch and Edgar Selwyn.

After the wedding Alice Ormond Campbell, as she now was known, remained in Paris with her husband Jamie until hostilities between France and Germany loomed the next year. At this point the couple prudently relocated to England, along with their newborn son, James Lawrence Campbell, Jr., a future artist and critic. After the war the Campbells, living in London, bought an attractive house in St. John's Wood, London, where they established a literary and theatrical salon. There Alice oversaw the raising of the couple's two sons, Lawrence and Robert, and their daughter, named Chita Florence Ormond ("Ormond" for short), while Jamie spent much of his time abroad, brokering play productions in Paris, New York and other cities.

Like Alice, Jamie harbored dreams of personal literary accomplishment; and in 1927 he published a novel entitled *Face Value,* which for a brief time became that much-prized thing by publishers, a putatively "scandalous" novel that gets Talked About. The story of a gentle orphan boy named Serge, the son an emigre Russian prostitute, who grows up in a Parisian "disorderly house," as reviews often blushingly put it, *Face Value* divided critics, but ended up on American bestseller lists. The success of his first novel led to the author being invited out to Hollywood to work as a scriptwriter, and his name appears on credits to a trio of films in 1927-28, including *French Dressing*, a "gay" divorce comedy set among sexually scatterbrained Americans in Paris. One wonders whether in Hollywood Jamie ever came across future crime writer Cornell Woolrich, who was scripting there too at the time.

Alice remained in England with the children, enjoying her own literary splash with her debut thriller *Juggernaut*, which concerned the murderous machinations of an inexorably ruthless French Riviera society doctor, opposed by a valiant young nurse. The novel racked up rave reviews and sales in the UK and US, in the latter country spurred on by its nationwide newspaper serialization, which promised readers

> . . . the open door to adventure! *Juggernaut* by Alice Campbell will sweep you out of the humdrum of everyday life into the gay, swift-moving Arabian-nights existence of the Riviera!

London's *Daily Mail* declared that the irresistible *Juggernaut* "should rank among the 'best sellers' of the year"; and, sure enough, *Juggernaut*'s English publisher, Hodder & Stoughton, boasted, several months after the novel's English publication in July 1928, that they already had run through six printings in an attempt to satisfy customer demand. In 1936 *Juggernaut* was adapted in England as a film vehicle for horror great Boris Karloff, making it the only Alice Campbell novel filmed to date. The film was remade in England under the title *The Temptress* in 1949.

Water Weed (1929) and *Spiderweb* (1930) (*Murder in Paris* in the US), the immediate successors, held up well to their predecessor's performance. Alice chose this moment to return for a fortnight to Atlanta, ostensibly to visit her sister, but doubtlessly in part to parade through her hometown as a conquering, albeit commercial, literary hero. And who was there to welcome Alice in the pages of the *Constitution* but Bessie S. Stafford, who pronounced Alice's hair still looked like spun gold while her eyes remarkably had turned an even deeper shade of blue. To Miss Bessie, Alice imparted enchanting tales of salon chats with such personages as George Bernard Shaw, Lady Asquith, H. G. Wells and (his lover) Rebecca West, the latter of whom a simpatico Alice met and conversed with frequently. Admitting that her political sympathies in England "inclined toward the conservatives," Alice yet urged "the absolute necessity of having two strong parties." English women, she had been pleased to see, evinced more informed interest in politics than their American sisters.

Alice, Miss Bessie declared, diligently devoted every afternoon to her writing, shutting her study door behind her "as a sign that she is not to be interrupted." This commitment to her craft enabled Alice to produce an additional sixteen crime novels between 1932 and 1950, beginning with *The Click of the Gate* and ending with *The Corpse Had Red Hair*.

Altogether nearly half of Alice's crime novels were standalones, in contravention of convention at this time, when series sleuths were so popular. In *The Click of the Gate* the author introduced one of her main recurring characters, intrepid Paris journalist Tommy Rostetter, who appears in three additional novels: *Desire to Kill* (1934), *Flying Blind* (1938) and *The Bloodstained Toy* (1948). In the two latter novels, Tommy appears with Alice's other major recurring character, dauntless Inspector Headcorn of Scotland Yard, who also pursues murderers and other malefactors in *Death Framed in Silver* (1937), *They Hunted a Fox* (1940), *No Murder of Mine* (1941) and *The Cockroach Sings* (1946) (*With Bated Breath* in the US).

Additional recurring characters in Alice's books are Geoffrey Macadam and Catherine West, who appear in *Spiderweb* and *No Light Came On* (1942), and Colin Ladbrooke, who appears in *Death Framed in Silver*, *A Door Closed Softly* (1939) and *They Hunted a Fox*. In the latter two books Colin with his romantic interest Alison Young and in the first and third book with Inspector Headcorn, who also appears, as mentioned, in *Flying Blind* and *The Bloodstained Toy* with Tommy Rosstetter, making Headcorn the connecting link in this universe of sleuths, although the inspector does not appear with Geoffrey Macadam and Catherine West. It is all a rather complicated state of criminal affairs; and this lack of a consistent and enduring central sleuth character in Alice's crime fiction may help explain why her work faded in the Fifties, after the author retired from writing.

Be that as it may, Alice Campbell is a figure of significance in the history of crime fiction. In a 1946 review of *The Cockroach Sings* in the London *Observer*, crime fiction critic Maurice Richardson asserted that "[s]he belongs to the atmospheric school, of which one of the outstanding exponents was the late Ethel Lina White," the author of *The Wheel Spins* (1936), famously filmed in 1938, under the title *The Lady Vanishes*, by director Alfred Hitchcock. This "atmospheric school," as Richardson termed it, had more students in the demonstrative United States than in the decorous United Kingdom, to be sure, the United States being the home of such hugely popular suspense writers as Mary Roberts Rinehart and Mignon Eberhart, to name but a couple of the most prominent examples.

Like the novels of the American Eber-Rinehart school and English authors Ethel Lina White and Marie Belloc Lowndes, the latter the author of the acknowledged landmark 1911 thriller *The Lodger*, Alice Campbell's books are not pure puzzle detective tales, but rather broader mysteries which put a premium on the storytelling imperatives of atmosphere and suspense. "She could not be unexciting if she tried," raved the *Times Literary Supplement* of Alice, stressing the author's remoteness from the so-called "Humdrum" school of detective fiction headed by British authors Freeman Wills Crofts, John Street and J. J. Connington. However, as Maurice Richardson, a great fan of Alice's crime writing, put it, "she generally binds her homework together with a reasonable plot," so the "Humdrum" fans out there need not be put off by what American detective novelist S. S. Van Dine, creator of Philo Vance, dogmatically dismissed as "literary dallying." In her novels Alice Campbell offered people bone-rattling good reads, which explains their popularity in the past and their revival today. Lines from a review of her 1941 crime novel *No Murder of Mine* by "H.V.A." in the *Hartford Courant* suggests the general nature of her work's appeal: "The excitement and mystery of this Class A shocker start on page 1 and continue right to the end of the book. You won't put it down, once you've begun it. And if you like romance mixed with your thrills, you'll find it here."

The protagonist of *No Murder of Mine* is Rowan Wilde, "an attractive young American girl studying in England." Frequently in her books Alice, like the great Anglo-American author Henry James, pits ingenuous but goodhearted Americans, male or female, up against dangerously sophisticated Europeans, drawing on autobiographical details from her and Jamie's own lives. Many of her crime novels, which often are lengthier than the norm for the period, recall, in terms of their length and content, the Victorian sensation novel, which seemingly had been in its dying throes when the author was a precocious child; yet, in their emphasis on morbid psychology and their sexual frankness, they also anticipate the modern crime novel. One can discern this tendency most dramatically, perhaps, in the engrossing *Water Weed*, concerning a sexual affair between a middle-aged Englishwoman and a young American man that has dreadful consequences, and *Desire to Kill*, about murder among a clique of decadent bohemians in Paris. In both of these mysteries the exploration of aberrant sexuality is striking. Indeed, in its depiction of sexual psychosis *Water Weed* bears rather more resemblance to, say, the crime novels of Patricia Highsmith than it does to the cozy mysteries of Patricia Wentworth. One might well term it Alice Campbell's *Deep Water*.

In this context it should be noted that in 1935 Alice Campbell authored a sexual problem play, *Two Share a Dwelling*, which the *New York*

Times described as a "grim, vivid, psychological treatment of dual personality." Although it ran for only twenty-two performances during October 8-26 at the West End's celebrated St. James' Theatre, the play had done well on its provincial tour and it received a standing ovation from the audience on opening night at the West End, primarily on account of the compelling performance of the half-Jewish German stage actress Grete Mosheim, who had fled Germany two years earlier and was making her English stage debut in the play's lead role of a schizophrenic, sexually compulsive woman. Mosheim was described as young and "blondely beautiful," bringing to mind the author herself.

Unfortunately priggish London critics were put off by the play's morbid sexual subject, which put Alice in an impossible position. One reviewer scathingly observed that "Miss Alice Campbell . . . has chosen to give her audience a study in pathology as a pleasant method of spending the evening. . . . one leaves the theatre rather wishing that playwrights would leave medical books on their shelves." Another sniffed that "it is to be hoped that the fashion of plumbing the depths of Freudian theory for dramatic fare will not spread. It is so much more easy to be interested in the doings of the sane." The play died a quick death in London and its author went back, for another fifteen years, to "plumbing the depths" in her crime fiction.

What impelled Alice Campbell, like her husband, to avidly explore human sexuality in her work? Doubtless their writing reflected the temper of modern times, but it also likely was driven by personal imperatives. The child of an unhappy marriage who at a young age had been deprived of a father figure, Alice appears to have wanted to use her crime fiction to explore the human devastation wrought by disordered lives. Sadly, evidence suggests that discord had entered the lives of Alice and Jamie by the 1930s, as they reached middle age and their children entered adulthood. In 1939, as the Second World War loomed, Alice was residing in rural southwestern England with her daughter Ormond at a cottage—the inspiration for her murder setting in *No Murder of Mine*, one guesses—near the bucolic town of Beaminster, Dorset, known for its medieval Anglican church and its charming reference in a poem by English dialect poet William Barnes:

> Sweet Be'mi'ster, that bist a-bound
> By green and woody hills all round,
> Wi'hedges, reachen up between
> A thousand vields o' zummer green.

Alice's elder son Lawrence was living, unemployed, in New York City at this time and he would enlist in the US Army when the country entered the war a couple of years later, serving as a master sergeant throughout the conflict. In December 1939, twenty-three-year-old Ormond, who seems to have herself preferred going by the name Chita, wed the prominent antiques dealer, interior decorator, home restorer and racehorse owner Ernest Thornton-Smith, who at the age of fifty-eight was fully thirty-five years older than she. Antiques would play a crucial role in Alice's 1944 wartime crime novel *Travelling Butcher*, which blogger Kate Jackson at *Cross Examining Crime* deemed "a thrilling read." The author's most comprehensive wartime novel, however, was the highly-praised *Ringed with Fire* (1943). Native Englishman S. Morgan-Powell, the dean of Canadian drama critics, in the *Montreal Star* pronounced *Ringed with Fire* one of the "best spy stories the war has produced," adding, in one of Alice's best notices:

> "Ringed with Fire" begins with mystery and exudes mystery from every chapter. Its clues are most ingeniously developed, and keep the reader guessing in all directions. For once there is a mystery which will, I think, mislead the most adroit and experienced of amateur sleuths. Some time ago there used to be a practice of sealing up the final section of mystery stores with the object of stirring up curiosity and developing the detective instinct among readers. If you sealed up the last forty-two pages of "Ringed with Fire" and then offered a prize of $250 to the person who guessed the mystery correctly, I think that money would be as safe as if you put it in victory bonds.

A few years later, on the back of the dust jacket to the American edition of Alice's *The Cockroach Sings* (1946), which Random House, her new American publisher, less queasily titled *With Bated Breath*, readers learned a little about what the author had been up to during the late war and its recent aftermath: "I got used to oil lamps. . . . and also to riding nine miles in a crowded bus once a week to do the shopping—if there was anything to buy. We thought it rather a lark then, but as a matter of fact we are still suffering from all sorts of shortages and restrictions." Jamie Campbell, on the other hand, spent his war years in Santa Barbara, California. It is unclear whether he and Alice ever lived together again.

Alice remained domiciled for the rest of her life in Dorset, although she returned to London in 1946, when she was inducted into the Detection Club. A number of her novels from this period, all of which were published in England by the Collins Crime Club, more resemble, in tone and form, classic detective fiction, such as *They Hunted a Fox* (1940). This event may have been a moment of triumph for the author, but it was also something of a last hurrah. After 1946 she published only three more crime novels, including the entertaining Tommy Rostetter-Inspector Headcorn mashup *The Bloodstained Toy*, before retiring in 1950. She lived out the remaining five years of her life quietly at her home in the coastal city of Bridport, Dorset, expiring "suddenly" on November 27, 1955, two days before her sixty-eighth birthday. Her brief death notice in the *Daily Telegraph* refers to her only as the "very dear mother of Lawrence, Chita and Robert."

Jamie Campbell had died in 1954 aged sixty-five. Earlier in the year his play *The Praying Mantis*, billed as a "naughty comedy by James Lawrence Campbell," scored hits at the Q Theatre in London and at the Dolphin Theatre in Brighton. (A very young Joan Collins played the eponymous man-eating leading role at the latter venue.) In spite of this, Jamie near the end of the year checked into a hotel in Cannes and fatally imbibed poison. The American consulate sent the report on Jamie's death to Chita in Maida Vale, London, and to Jamie's brother Colonel George Campbell in Washington, D. C., though not to Alice. This was far from the Riviera romance that the publishers of *Juggernaut* had long ago promised. Perhaps the "humdrum of everyday life" had been too much with him.

Alice Campbell own work fell into obscurity after her death, with not one of her novels being reprinted in English for more than seven decades. Happily the ongoing revival of vintage English and American mystery fiction from the twentieth century is rectifying such cases of criminal neglect. It may well be true that it "is impossible not to be thrilled by Edgar Wallace," as the great thriller writer's publishers pronounced, but let us not forget that, as Maurice Richardson put it: "We can always do with Mrs. Alice Campbell." Mystery fans will now have nineteen of them from which to choose—a veritable embarrassment of felonious riches, all from the hand of the other AC.

Curtis Evans

CHAPTER ONE

SARAH MacNeil paused at Trafalgar Square to allow thirty-odd motor cars to whizz by her. She was vexed at the delay. Every moment must weigh against her; yet though something whispered that it might be simpler by far to cast herself into this dizzying traffic, she had no hankering to end existence while the loose change rattling in her purse gave her a gambler's chance of continuing it. Besides, motor accidents were not necessarily final. She had been in one, and all it had done was to unfit her for work.

Behind her rose the columns, sharply divided in black and white, of St. Martin in the Fields. Hadn't she heard there was a crypt beneath this church where waifs and strays like herself occasionally sheltered for the night? There was an idea . . . but no, it was the worst possible tactics to think of that now. Better fix her eyes on Nelson up there in front of her, for it was Nelson who said . . .

"Wrong," she corrected herself. "Nelson didn't say, 'Don't give up the ship.' What a sketchy education I've got! It was that thing about England expects—and I'm not even English! Oh, well, that's ten striking now. I may be in time, if it's only for another turn-down."

A white-cuffed policeman, who had been slapping his hands together with the cold, gave his royal permit to cross, which she did, holding her head high and skimming jauntily as though the coat she wore had been designed for English winter instead of Riviera spring. She skirted the fountains, ventured a less safe transit to the haven of Northumberland Avenue, and in another minute was speaking to a busy hotel clerk.

"Miss Venables?" the latter threw in her direction. "It's about the advertisement, is it? She has someone with her. Take a seat, I'll tell you when she's free."

So, after all her hurrying, she wasn't the first.

"Fool that I am! Why can't I get an early start? It was my one hope. Still, I seem to be the second arrival. Maybe the one she's interviewing will have adenoids or warts."

Light-headed from the super-heated atmosphere, she sank on to a deep sofa. A smooth-footed waiter bearing aloft a tray glided past, and slid like an eel into the lift, leaving behind an aroma of hot coffee. She sniffed in the scent. Real coffee, such as one gets in good hotels like this. For it was a good hotel. Miss Venables must have money. She could have her breakfast in bed, lying snug and luxurious between clean linen sheets, with a bath of her own to step into when she wanted it, instead of having to queue up for a dribble of lukewarm water which was perversely apt to dry up just as one was nicely soaped. Why should such a fortunate woman want a companion? Sarah could think of no reason, except that Miss Venables was not quite "all there." Come to think of it, this advertisement did have a peculiar sound. What exactly did it say?

From her purse she fished out the front page of the *Morning Post* and ran her eye down the Agony Column. Passing over the daily quotation from Scripture, the inevitable "Bitter-Sweet—Why long silence?—G.", the titled lady offering genuine Russian sables at forty-five shillings; and the imbecility which was probably code, "Oggly-Woggly—Pale Dawn Waits for Piddum-Widdums," she reached what she sought:

"Single lady desires well-bred young woman as travelling companion. Light duties, but requirements of a rather special nature. Ample remuneration for congenial person, suitably recommended. Apply Miss Venables, Metropolitan Hotel."

Yes, the single lady might well be a lunatic. Still that was not what Sarah was worrying about. It was the bit about recommendations that brought the sick feeling in the pit of her stomach—for what recommendations, suitable or otherwise, could she command? Only the words "congenial" and "travelling" held out a straw at which to clutch, while the reference to light duties suggested that this injured wrist of hers might not, as hitherto, prove an insuperable obstacle. Even so she knew to a bitter certainty that those with experience were likely to be preferred. . . .

A minute, apple-cheeked page poised before her.

"Beg pardon, miss—but was it you asking for Miss Venables? This way, please."

In the mirror of the lift Sarah surveyed her reflection, twitching her beret to a more rakish angle, and pulling out the pussy-cat bow of her brown spotted scarf.

"Heavens, but I'm hideous!" she thought. "All nose and eyes."

No use to remind herself that a certain dry-point artist, as recently as last May, had called her most prominent feature aristocratic, her eyes—grey-green they were, and fringed with black lashes—provocative. All that was ancient history, along with the drowsy sunshine of Portofino where these compliments had been uttered; and still more ancient the school-days in Paris when envious companions, banting on red cabbage and chicory, had sighed over her greyhound slimness, then well within the mannequin limit. There was little to envy now, she reflected. She looked skinny, half-starved, her olive pallor so pronounced that the merest trace of rouge was a risk. Only her hair remained unaffected, still curling into nut-brown waves as lustrous as ever. Tired as she had been, she had trimmed and shampooed it last night, and true to habit it suggested expensive luxury. One small mercy to be thankful for; and another blessing that even in old clothes she managed to preserve some remnant of smartness. No one would spot her for a down-and-out.

The lift halted. Buttons marched along a velvet-floored corridor, with Sarah behind, striving to emulate his casual importance. He showed her the door, but before she could knock a spectacled girl came out of it, blundering against her with the blind, defeated look she knew so well. "Pardon me," the latter murmured breathlessly and scuttled confusedly away. Poor creature—self-damned by a turn of phrase which all unconsciously set her down as sure to be either servile or defiant, helpless on a journey, troubled about her forks! No wonder she had failed.

And yet, maybe it was not class which was at fault. The voice which bade Sarah come in was so querulous, so stridently ill-bred, that a panic of misgiving seized her. If Miss Venables used a tone like that, she was not going to want anyone like Sarah MacNeil. For a second Sarah was tempted to turn tail and run.

Instead, she entered, and found herself in a spacious, cozy sitting-room, bright with pink and mauve chintz, with a blaze of electric light to atone for the dinginess of the day. Two middle-aged women confronted her. She gazed doubtfully from one to the other, thinking that if the owner of the voice—she knew at a glance that the tubby, short-legged person lolling with a false assumption of ease on the sofa was she who had spoken—turned out to be Miss Venables, then her errand would indeed prove fruitless. The long-chinned, leathery face with its shrewd, pale eyes so smilingly malevolent filled her with repulsion, as did the shrunken woollen spencer strained across the bosom with a diamond brooch, the cheap beads wound around the scrawny neck, and the stubby, beringed hands clutching a bursting shopping bag in a predatory manner. No, oh, no! Not this woman. If it were the other, now, there might be some chance.

The second woman, who had risen, was tall, of an angular and prim rigidity, but quite clearly a lady. Her wine-red frock if not fashionable was good, she wore no jewellery save a locket dangling over her flat chest, and a half-hoop of diamonds, very loose on her bony left hand. Her skin had that rosy freshness retained till late in life by so many English women, her hair, which was dark just tinged with grey, was neatly and monumentally arranged rather in the style affected by Queen Alexandra. What Sarah chiefly noticed were her eyes, large, luminous brown, and highly sensitive in expression.

"Won't you sit down?" she spoke in a precise, well modulated voice, her manner business-like but pleasant. "In one moment I will be free to attend to you."

Sarah sighed with relief. So it wasn't the tubby female after all! She heard the thin woman address the companion with quiet pointedness.

"Don't let me keep you, Gracie. I know you have shopping to do."

"Oh, well," retorted the other, somewhat huffily. "If you think you can manage without me, why, I'll be buzzing along." Rising with a flounce and wriggling the creases out of her tweed skirt she added with a crude tentativeness, "I daresay that young rogue Harry will be coming along for lunch?"

"If he's not too busy to get away," answered Miss Venables, her prim dignity slightly tinged with hauteur.

"Harry too busy to get a free meal?" The departing woman gave a scornful laugh. "Trust him! Well, by by."

In the doorway she paused with a pantomime of frowns and nods which Miss Venables stoically ignored, a second later heaving a barely audible sigh, and compressing her thin lips into a tight line.

"And now," said the latter, self possessed and direct. "Tell me who you are, and all about yourself."

Sarah recognized the origin of that authoritative tone. It came from being sole mistress of an ample bank account. So might she have spoken in the days when there was no need to ask favours, or bother about rebuffs. Its simplicity put her wholly at her ease.

"My name is MacNeil," she said with equal straightforwardness. "I'm afraid I haven't done any work before, but when I read your advertisement I thought—"

The thin lady had grown suddenly inattentive. Her features trembled slightly, and her brown eyes, meeting the girl's, held something which arrested the sentence in midchannel. Sarah felt a curious sensation pass over her. What was it she had seen hovering in that clear, steady gaze?

All at once she read its meaning. It was stark, undiluted terror.

CHAPTER TWO

THE impression was fleeting, and even as Sarah registered it Miss Venables spoke again hesitatingly but with the air of wishing to make some explanation on her own account before continuing with her caller's history.

"The lady who has just left us," she said, "is my sister-in-law, Mrs. Mark Venables, who lives in Huddersfield, and whom I invited to accompany me to London because, for a definite reason, I am unwilling to remain alone." She paused, moistened her lips, and continued, "I myself have no fixed abode. I am in the habit of spending my winters, indeed most of the year, at a small resort in the south of France. This year I did not go there, but it was a mistake to break my rule, and my health has suffered in consequence. Several attacks of an old gastric complaint—the English climate does not suit me—in short,"—with forced firmness—"I intend to return, as soon as possible. Only, I do not wish to go unaccompanied. To be perfectly frank, I feel it unwise to be left by myself for some time to come."

Again, more strongly than before, Sarah sensed that this woman was frightened—badly so—but too reserved to speak openly of her fear. She waited, burning to learn further details, only to find the tide of confidences stemmed, and the topic changed to her own qualifications. Ruefully she admitted she had none.

"I'm an American," she added. "Only I left home when I was so small I don't know anything much about my country. I've a smattering of languages, but beyond acting as my father's secretary I haven't done any work. Now my father's dead—he was killed last August in a motor smash in Scotland—I have to scramble round for my living as best I can."

Miss Venables surveyed her attentively.

"American?" she mused. "And you've done secretarial work? I wonder you don't try to get on with that."

"I can't," explained Sarah, "because I'm incapacitated. In the accident I mentioned I got a broken arm and a deep cut from the windscreen across my right wrist." Stripping off her glove she displayed a long, ugly scar. "You see, the muscles were severed. It means I can get no grip on anything, and can't even use a typewriter with any speed. It wouldn't have mattered, only the shares my father had always counted on to provide me with an income fell to nothing in the slump. I got out of hospital to find I had exactly thirty-five pounds, which I've been living on ever since."

"Had you thought of teaching?"

"I'm not good enough. I was educated in a scrappy way, in Switzerland, France, Germany, wherever we happened to be, but I've no certificates. There are too many who are fully qualified."

"And you've no family?"

"Only distant relatives I've never seen, most of them, from all accounts, very hard up. Even if I had passage money to America, I couldn't think of descending on them. No," Sarah went on philosophically, "this is my problem, I must solve it for myself; but it's only fair to tell you that with the best will in the world I shouldn't be much practical help to you. I can't so much as sew on a button."

"Well, well!" The kind eyes showed real concern. "It's a bad predicament, especially in these times—though the handicaps you mention wouldn't affect me. It's not a personal maid I want, but an intelligent person who *understands*. One I can live with agreeably, without fear of being—ridiculed." Miss Venables searched her companion's face with anxious embarrassment. "I suppose," she suggested, "you can furnish me some proof that what you say is all true?"

"I'm hoping you'll accept it as proof," answered Sarah diffidently. "The best I can offer without causing delay is the word of the American Consul-General. He knew my father, who was a journalist named Frank MacNeil. He will gladly speak for me. If you are willing to trust what he says—"

The telephone rang. Miss Venables gave a nervous start and grew pale and a little tense as she picked up the receiver.

"Yes, yes," Sarah heard her say quickly. "Send him up at once—and if any other young women have arrived, tell them to wait."

Taking a folded, spotless handkerchief from her bag she drew it across her lips, apparently to hide a spasm of quivering. In her sudden unaccountable apprehension she had evidently lost the thread of their remarks.

"Miss MacNeil," she said abruptly, "I am going to ask you to step into my bedroom till this visitor is gone. I must speak to him privately. It won't take long . . . There! That is he. Would you be so kind as to let him in?"

Sarah sprang to do as she was bidden, took one glance at a nondescript man carrying a bowler hat and a small attaché case, and slipped quietly through the bedroom door. Although the conference was plainly of a confidential, not to say mysterious nature, it puzzled her less than Miss Venables' manner and the vague hints so reluctantly given. All idea of mental disorder was banished from her thoughts, while she could not even picture this sensible north-countrywoman as altering her mode of life from trivial or imagined causes. What, then, was the reason for her fear? It seemed incredible that a woman in affluent circumstances, as she was certain Miss Venables was, should be afraid of anything.

Through the closed door only a low rumble of voices reached her. She looked about the luxurious, scrupulously tidy bedroom, taking note of the yellow crepe-de-chine nightgown laid primly across the unmade bed, the fur-bordered slippers placed together, not kicked about anyhow as hers would have been, the tortoise-shell brushes ranged in order on the dressing-table, the glass slab of which was not even dimmed by loose powder. Then her eye came to rest on the bedside table, where in company with a reading-lamp, a biscuit-box, and one of Priestley's novels stood the silver-framed photograph of an exceedingly good-looking young man. Who was he? He was a shade too handsome for her taste, now that she had ceased to thrill over *The Film Weekly*: and yet there was plenty of virility behind the regular features, frank, engaging humour in the eyes, and enough heaviness to the jaw to save the face from cloying perfection.

"English through and through," she thought. "What the magazine writers call clean-limbed—and very nice, too. Oh, dear! Not much chance of meeting his sort now, much as I'd like to . . . I wonder if I'll be lucky enough to land this job?"

How stupidly wobbly she felt! That was because she hadn't been able to eat her cold-storage egg at breakfast. There were biscuits in this box. Dared she—? Sarah always dared. Helping herself, she crunched a thin disk, brushed away the crumbs, and sitting down in a big, cushioned chair by the window watched the motor cars whirling by towards the embankment. She began to yawn, and the hands of the little travelling clock on the chest of drawers had marked ten-thirty before she was called back to the sitting-room, to find the visitor gone, and Miss Venables standing straight and resolute in her trim, dark-red frock, just putting a long manilla envelope into her bag. Absent though her air, the spinster looked troubled, too strung up to relax a muscle.

"I've rung up your Consul-General," she declared. "And I'm not surprised to learn that all you tell me is correct. I knew I could trust my judgment. What is bothering me now is whether, when you hear what is expected of you, you'll be prepared to take it on."

Pausing, she gripped her bag so tightly that her knuckles turned white.

"That person," she went on with determined hardihood, "is a detective. I consulted him over a strange and distressing affair which has been going on for nearly a year. He has just brought me his report, and as I feared he can do nothing to solve the mystery of certain alarming communications I have been receiving. Eleven letters—all in this envelope—and no means of stopping them. In short,"—with a despairing sigh—"I am just where I was before."

"Do you mean threatening letters?" asked Sarah incredulously.

"Exactly. My life is threatened. Now you see why I dread being alone. Only I've decided to go where I like, not be influenced any longer. To submit is cowardice, and I detest cowards."

Her flash of spirit commanded Sarah's respect.

"I quite agree, Miss Venables. Please go ahead and tell me where I come in."

"I—I'm ashamed to; but—well, the point is this: if these letters are to be taken seriously, at any moment I may be attacked. I realize how ridiculous that sounds, but without going into details just yet I may say that enough has happened to make me terrified of my own shadow."

"I don't wonder," replied Sarah with energy. "Particularly if you can do nothing about it."

"What can I do, when I've no idea what to guard against? It may be poison, accidental drowning, anything. I simply don't know, except that it will probably be made to look like chance. It's impossible to punish anonymous threats which can't be traced to their source. I shall have to be killed before the law can step in. My one safeguard is to have some responsible person in close attendance, mainly, I admit, to give me confidence: and that someone will have to agree to certain rather tiresome conditions, such as occupying an adjoining room with the door open between, going with me to places of amusement and so on, never, in fact, leaving me alone. I might even on occasions ask her to taste the food I eat, or the wine I drink. Should you consider such a demand too fantastically absurd?"

Sarah felt startled. Visions of mediaeval kings and their wine-tasters floated before her. It did not seem possible that in full day, surrounded by the security of a first-class London hotel, she could be listening to such a suggestion.

"Understand," the other hastened to add, "there would be little or no danger attached to such a service. The mere fact that you stood ready to perform it would protect you from harm, for who would dare risk killing you instead of me? Probably I should never ask it—and in any case I shall expect to compensate you by paying a larger salary than is usual. Also you will not always be tied to my apron strings. A nephew of mine, to whom I am greatly attached, will be joining us at Ste. Brigitte—that is the small place to which I am returning—and during the two months he is there you will be comparatively free. Now—does the prospect seem too dreadful?"

Sarah's grey-green eyes met the anxious brown ones with a smile. A look of sympathy passed between them.

"Not a bit dreadful," came the prompt reply. "If I hesitated, it was from astonishment, not alarm. I should adore to come to you. Do you really want me to?"

Miss Venables checked a spontaneous gesture. Perhaps she was reminding herself that after all this American girl was a total stranger. Her voice, however, held a quiver of relief as she answered simply, "Yes, Miss MacNeil, I knew instantly you were the sort of person who would suit me. You are frank, and I like frankness. There! Shall we regard it as settled?"

She held out her thin hand. Sarah clasped it warmly.

"Done, Miss Venables! I'm yours body and soul—and if these devils, whoever they are, succeed in getting you, they'll have to get me first."

At that moment a light tattoo beat upon the corridor door, and an agreeable, easy-going masculine voice called, "What ho? Am I allowed to barge in?"

"It's Harry, the nephew I spoke of," cried Miss Venables, her whole mien quickly irradiated with pleasure. "Don't on any account," she whispered, "mention the detective. I hate for him to guess how worried I am." Then, patting her high coiffure and straightening her dress she bade the caller come in.

The door opened, and there strolled into the room a tall broad-shouldered youth of about eight-and-twenty. He was immaculately but not foppishly clad, his crisp chestnut hair had a tendency to wave, his teeth were even and strong, his blue eyes serene with good-humour. One glance, and Sarah recognized him as the original of the silver-framed photograph she had lately admired.

CHAPTER THREE

"UP AND at it already? Good Work!"

The newcomer had a lazy voice, with a pleasant ring in it. His frank blue eyes rested on Sarah first with curiosity, then with approval, as slipping an arm around his aunt, he kissed her lightly and inquired how she had slept.

"Just thought I'd drop in on my way to the City," he explained with boyish diffidence, "but if I'm interrupting anything, I'll clear off."

"That was sweet of you, dear," replied Miss Venables, flushed with pleasure, suddenly grown young. "And you've chosen a good time, for now I can introduce you to Miss MacNeil, who is going to act as my companion. Only," here she lowered her voice—"In Ste. Brigitte we are not going to let people know she's my companion. You'll remember that, won't you? She's just a friend who's come with us."

"That won't be hard, will it?"

He had taken Sarah's hand in a warm grasp, and was smiling at her in so friendly a fashion that she felt instantly at home with him. Still eyeing her with flattering interest—was he relieved to find her not positively ill-looking?—he asked if she knew the part of the world they were bound for. "A little," she told him. "Not actually Ste. Brigitte."

He made a wry face. "Fishing-village, you know. Bit of a dump, not Monte Carlo, exactly, but I shouldn't wonder if we three could put some go into it. I'm jolly bucked you're coming. I say!" He brightened with an idea. "I do the thing by road. Why don't we all pack into the old 'bus and trundle along together? Just this once," he begged of his aunt. "I swear not to go above forty."

Sarah was a trifle disappointed that Miss Venables should refuse.

"No, Harry!" She laughed but held firm. "Long motor-journeys tire me, and it would tire you, too, if you weren't allowed to speed. We'll have plenty of jaunts when you arrive. I must say I'm quite elated over the prospect. Aren't you?"

It was not difficult to see why the somewhat prim and repressed old maid had become girlish in her enthusiasm. Under the influence of this joyous and healthy young Englishman hardly anyone could have harboured morbid thoughts. His smile alone, enveloping all it touched with an impartial warmth like sunlight, had a singular power to dissipate gloom, even though, behind it, Sarah sensed something puzzled and solicitous which told her its owner realized his aunt's situation and was anxious to relieve it by keeping to a light note.

"How's Gracie?" he inquired. "Done up with yesterday's shopping?"

"I'm afraid she is. You know she never can resist a sale."

"Gracie? Not half!" He gave a rapturous chuckle. "Particularly if it's in a bargain-basement, or the Edgware Road. Well, if that's what London means to her, what's the harm? Except that when she wears herself out and gets a pain in her tummy she's apt to take it out on you."

The two Venables exchanged twinkling glances.

"All the same, dear," murmured the spinster tolerantly, "we must make allowances for your stepmother, because between ourselves she is in a far more serious state of health than she imagines. One reason I persuaded her to come to London with me was to take her to a good specialist, but now she's turned very stubborn. As a matter of fact, my own doctor is calling by this morning, and I've begged her to let him give her his opinion. He has helped me so wonderfully with my gastric trouble, and although he won't have much time at least he can suggest the right man for her to see."

"Your doctor?" The nephew paused in the act of removing a cigarette from a thin gold case, and crinkled his brow inquiringly. "Whom have you got now?"

"I thought you knew. I'm referring to my Ste. Brigitte doctor, who has been spending a fortnight with his mother, and is going back to-day by the noon train. I've the utmost confidence in him. Indeed, I am determined to be under his treatment again."

"Oh, I see! The young chap."

A teasing light had come into Harry Venables' eyes. As he offered his cigarette case to Sarah, he seemed to be inviting her to share in a private joke.

"And what if Dr. Gilcrest is young?" defended Miss Venables, rising promptly to the bait. "I like young doctors. They have modern ideas. And you can never say Dr. Gilcrest is lacking in experience. The Hyères district is teeming with English people."

"Crocks, everyone of 'em," agreed Harry, catching Sarah's eye. "Can't say I know another such collection of the lame, the halt, and—but have we any blind? If not, it's about the only disability that's lacking. Oh, yes, that fellow of yours has good material to practise on!" Thoroughly enjoying his aunt's indignation, he laughed whole-heartedly, squeezed the arm he held, and continued, his eyes radiating merriment, "Go on, I love hearing you boost your particular pets! All your geese are swans, what? Gilcrest's one, I'm another—a black swan, I suppose but still a—"

"No, you're only a goose!" cried Miss Venables, giving him a little push, and looking delighted with his nonsense. "Still, the Baron isn't a goose, but a very clever man, and you know quite well what a high opinion he has of . . . s'sh! That's Dr. Gilcrest now. I recognise his knock. Let him in, will you, dear?" To Sarah she whispered, "Don't go, Miss MacNeil. This is another person I should like you to meet—the only one, incidentally, who knows what I have told you, except for my nephew and yourself."

She showed scarcely less pleasure than that evoked by Harry's visit when, the door opening, a quiet, self-contained Englishman of about thirty entered and took her outstretched hand in an undemonstrative grasp. He was a shade less tall than Harry, on whom he now bestowed a casual, disinterested greeting. His figure was muscular and closely-knit, and though he had an air of breeding he possessed neither the good looks of the younger man nor the latter's genial, effortless charm of manner. His clothes, too, suffered by comparison with Harry's. The ancient tweeds he wore were no more than presentable, and yet, in common with his features and voice, they were unmistakably those of a gentleman. These things Sarah noted, at the same time observing an unstressed but definite restraint of expression—guardedness, even—about the square, sunburned face; it just escaped sternness, though at the moment, under the glow of Miss Venables' friendly welcome, it had relaxed to something softer, but still hesitant. It occurred to her that if his hostess had been alone he might have managed a heartier greeting, but Miss Venables herself seemed not to notice anything lacking, so perhaps he was habitually inclined to keep a tight check-rein over his emotions. Arrogant or shy? Sarah could not have said which, but she did decide, instantly, that Dr. Gilcrest was a man to be won only after hard effort.

"How good of you to come, when you must have so much to do before getting off!" exclaimed the spinster gratefully. "I do appreciate it. As you see, I have acted on your advice. Let me present you to my companion, Miss Sarah MacNeil."

The smile on the young physician's face made a slow retreat. He bowed to Sarah across the intervening space of carpet, his manner again slightly stiff, and his eyes surveying her with keen and sober appraisal. They were blue eyes, but very different from Harry's, their colour the deep, grey-blue of slate, vivid against his exposure-tanned skin, arresting the attention, but repelling advances. They seemed to the girl to look far below the surface and to sum up at a glance her worst shortcomings. When they withdrew their discriminating gaze, she was left feeling humbled, as though she had been judged of small account and passed over. He made no remark, at once turning to Miss Venables, who had begun to make inquiries regarding friends in Ste. Brigitte, and Sarah, left on the outskirts of the conversation, listened with vague curiosity, hoping to learn something about the life she was soon to lead.

"The de Bellesnaves?" repeated the doctor. "I think you had most of my news the other day, though I've had one letter from the Baron since then. He is still playing about with his experiments, you know. Just now he's trying to find a serum for the bulldog's asthma." Once more a smile, this time of amusement, crossed the speaker's face. "I'm much afraid it's a hopeless job."

"Poor old, wheezing Polly!" Miss Venables murmured pityingly. "Still her master's shadow, I suppose? How I long to see them all again, especially the Baroness, whose last letter sounded rather low-spirited. She had just lost her little Pomeranian. Pets mean so much in that household, don't they. I was hoping Maddalena could get away for a bit, just to cheer her up."

"Actually she's in Paris now." The doctor made this statement diffidently, one might have said with studious detachment "I heard from her this morning."

"Really?" cried Miss Venables, eagerly surprised. "But that is news! Harry, dear, did you know the Baroness was in Paris?"

"Me?" demanded the nephew, again with the mirthful appeal to Sarah which in this case was obscure. "You surely don't imagine the Baroness keeps me posted as to her movements? Gilcrest, now, is a horse of another colour. A dark one, let me tell you, so keep an eye on him! You'll be seeing her, Gilcrest? Own up, aren't you taking her out to dine this very evening?"

Gilcrest vouchsafed no response, but Sarah fancied a shade of scornful annoyance contracted his features. Harry, from the glint of merriment in his eye, evidently perceived it, for, nothing abashed, he abandoned the topic and asked point-blank—with latent anxiety, Sarah suspected— what the doctor thought of his aunt's appearance.

"Can't you produce something new and with a long name that will put a bit of flesh on her? I warn you, Gilcrest, you'll take a fearful plunge in her estimation if you come here without ordering her some sort of medicine."

The slate-coloured eyes swept slowly over Miss Venables' thin figure. Without change of expression their owner replied shortly, "It's not medicine she wants. It's the right surroundings—and sun."

"Pay no attention to this tiresome boy of mine, doctor," said Miss Venables quickly. "You and Maddalena de Bellesnaves are both right. It is sun I want, and I daresay I shall soon pick up enough to satisfy even Harry. Seriously, though, while we are waiting for my sister-in-law, I should like your opinion of Miss MacNeil's wrist. Will you just take a look at it, and tell me how we can strengthen the muscles?"

She repeated what Sarah had told her about the accident, and the girl was slightly chagrined to find herself the object of what might have been unwilling attention. Dr. Gilcrest eyed her again, now with an interest purely professional, motioned her to the window, and taking her ineffectual fingers in his strong ones worked them back and forth one after the other. There was a moment of complete absorption, during which she grew embarrassed for no good reason. Then he spoke, and for the first time she was struck by a trace of accent which she instinctively dubbed "Oxford." It carried with it a faint suggestion of aloofness, superiority.

"Am I hurting you?" he asked.

"Oh, no! It's only that I can't use my hand properly, that's all."

"H'm . . . these affairs are slow. Massage may help, but the muscles will want re-educating. Effort's what counts. You must keep trying."

His manner of saying this seemed to imply that she was very spineless. It roused her ire.

"I do try, all the time," she retorted, with a laugh to soften what might sound snappish. "You don't suppose I enjoy being helpless, do you?"

He did not reply. He was looking down at her well-shaped nails, which throughout all her hardships she had never neglected to manicure and anoint with pale rose-coloured varnish. It had been a necessary part of keeping up her morale; but was she being judged as an idle and frivolous person? Something told her she was. The dark blue gaze met hers for one second, searchingly, with a question in it she could not decipher. Then her hand was dropped, and the doctor moved away—not, however, before a small detail had registered itself on her vision. Such a trivial thing, yet destined to influence her enormously. Shirt cuffs—freshly laundered, frayed at the edges. . . .

"Oh, there you are, Gracie!"

It was Miss Venables who uttered this exclamation. All eyes turned to see the stumpy figure of the sister-in-law sidle with a defiant air into the room. The predatory, beringed fingers still clutched the bursting shopping-bag, the leathery face had a look of physical suffering, overlaid by soured joviality. Later on Sarah recalled this. The woman was obviously ill.

"Oh, I'm here, like a bad penny," jerked Mrs. Venables with a sniff. "Pretty wonky on my pins, but thought I might as well let this young man of yours look me over and spin the usual rigmarole about my inside. Wish some of 'em had it, then they'd know!" Her pale eyes lighted on Harry. "Oh, so you've turned up too, have you?" she threw at him with a twist of malevolence. "Stock Exchange taking a holiday, I suppose?"

Sarah marvelled that under this ill-natured thrust Harry Venables could remain so placidly unruffled. She noticed too the businesslike tact with which Miss Venables marshalled her trying relative into the bedroom, and whispered to the doctor that the consultation was to be put down to her own account. A generous woman, it seemed; and there was further proof of this when, during the next few minutes, the question of Sarah's salary was discussed, and a figure named which exceeded the girl's wildest hopes. This was not all. Sarah would be needing clothes for the warmer climate, and anything of the sort Miss Venables proposed to supply.

"Oh, no!" protested Sarah, overcome.

"Yes, indeed. That is understood. And now I am going to write you a cheque. I shan't require you till we set off on Monday, but we'll consider your week starts to-day."

The couple from the other room reappeared, Mrs. Venables positively chirpy, the doctor still impassive. The latter was folding a sheet of hotel note-paper on which he had scrawled a prescription.

"More pills!" announced the new patient, tucking in a wisp of stringy hair. "Not that he'll be on hand to see what they do to me. Like the rest of you lucky people, he's off to France."

"But you could go, Gracie. Why don't you?" was Miss Venables' mild reminder.

The sister-in-law gave a snort. "Much you know about it, you with all your money to throw about on pleasure! Some of us have got responsibilities. Spring cleaning's mine, and John Venables' grave to put in order. Harry!" She turned pouncingly on her stepson who stood absently tapping a fresh cigarette against his gold case. "Since you've nothing better to occupy you, p'raps for once you'll make yourself useful. Get this prescription filled—and mind, don't you go carrying it round all day in your pocket! I know your tricks, my lad."

"No one better, Gracie!"

With an air ludicrously chastened, though his eyes still twinkling, Harry took the bit of paper, picked up his hat and gloves, and waited for the doctor to finish the explanation he was making in an undertone to Miss Venables. Some of the whispered exchange reached Sarah's ears. She gathered that it was impossible in so cursory an examination to discover the entire extent of Mrs. Venables' disorder, but that no time must be lost in getting the afflicted woman to a stomach-specialist.

"Meyhew's the man. I've written it down. All I've given her is the same mild palliative which has benefited you. It will relieve the symptoms, but she mustn't depend on it."

So saying Dr. Gilcrest made his adieux, including all but his own patient in a collective bow. On Sarah, however, his eyes rested in what seemed to her a grave and speculative fashion, suggesting that for all his apparent indifference he did not regard her as quite a negligible quantity. Just what did that glance mean? Was he wondering if Miss Venables' choice of a companion had been a wise one, or was there some other idea in his mind? Fleeting though the impression was, it was destined to recur to the girl at frequent intervals during the ensuing period, forming one of the puzzles—indeed, an integral one—of the adventure on which she had embarked.

When the door had closed Miss Venables remarked musingly that Dr. Gilcrest looked tired and worried. He had many cares, and she feared his holiday had not rested him.

"Humph!" grunted the other woman, who had been scrutinising her tongue in the mirror. "Conceit's his trouble. Young know-it-all, trying to impress. That's my judgment of him, Christine, and you may take it for what it's worth." The spinster shut her lips in exasperation. Plainly she had much to put up with from this quarter. It was only when she noticed the two young people about to take their departure that her expression lightened. Why, she suggested, should they not come back that evening to dine and go to a theatre?

"You, too, Gracie. All four of us will go. Wouldn't it be fun?"

"Not for me, with this grinding pain in my tummy. I shall get straight into my bed, but don't let me stop you."

"Well, then, we will go, if Miss MacNeil is free. I must say I feel inclined for a little celebration."

When Sarah quitted the room, she heard behind her an outraged gasp: "Chrissie Venables! Do you mean to tell me you've actually engaged this strange girl, and that now you're taking her out—with Harry? Well, you are a fool!"

Had Harry also heard? Her cheeks burned as he followed her to the lift, but he gave no sign of embarrassment, and again, on the descent, she felt pleasantly conscious of the sense of well-being his presence inspired. He did not speak until, in the lobby below, his long, loose stride had fallen in with her step. She saw, then, that his good-looking face had taken on a shade of unwonted gravity.

"By the way," he ventured, stopping in an open space and glancing cautiously round. "Did—did my aunt tell you her—her exact reason for wanting you with her?"

Glad that he had brought up the subject, Sarah remembered just in time her promise to say nothing about the detective's visit.

"In a general way," she answered guardedly. "No details. I was rather wanting to ask you what you thought of it all. This danger she speaks of—do you consider it serious?" Hesitant, disturbed, he balanced back and forth on his well-shod feet. His brow was corrugated into a frown betraying anxiety.

"I—I don't know," he admitted with reluctance. "In the beginning I thought some lunatic was having a game with her; and then . . . well, it's jolly difficult to decide anything. The way she puts it . . . you see, down there in the south rather a queer thing did happen. It concerned the death of a friend. She was frightfully upset, and I don't wonder at it. Accident, I suppose, but what with one thing and another she's . . ." He broke off, forcibly ridding himself of an oppressive burden. "See here," he continued uncertainly. "I'd better not spill any more. She'll tell you—but I will say just this: The great thing is not to let her brood. That's where you come in, and I'm jolly glad you're going to be with her. I can see you're absolutely right for the job."

His smile was like sunshine breaking through a cloud. She felt warmly drawn to him, with a sentiment partly comradeship, partly—but no, not so fast! Say that what she experienced was the effect of frank, virile magnetism plus the admiration for which she had long been hungering. One step at a time. . . .

"I say, can I give you a lift somewhere?"

Passing through the revolving doors they had halted beside a red Fiat car, new, smartly appointed. Conscientiously she declined.

"No, you must get to your work and I—" She did not like to say that her immediate objective was a restaurant in which to squander her remaining cash on the first square meal of many weeks; but as she saw him pause, carefree and easy as though time mattered nothing, she had an impulse to remind him of a duty he might perhaps neglect to perform. "Don't forget your stepmother's prescription," she said suddenly. "There's a chemist just over there, on the corner."

He would never have remembered. His guilty expression as he slapped his pocket assured her she had read him aright. His eyes, the eyes of a school-boy, met hers understandingly.

"By Jove, that was a near shave! Thanks no end for saving me. Over there? I see it. Well, pip pip till this evening."

He swung his long legs into the driver's seat, waved goodbye and left her to savour, with infinite thanksgiving, her amazing good fortune.

That night, back in the cold dinginess of her Bloomsbury bedroom, Sarah MacNeil would not have changed places with any creature on God's earth. Blessed security wrapped her like a warm cloak, memories of oysters, spring duckling and Burgundy mingled in her mind with brilliant lights, gay music, and agreeable company, while the flushed cheeks and sparkling eyes reflected in the glass seemed to belong to a totally different girl from the one who, only fourteen hours before, had punched a new hole in her belt and fought down fears which threatened to swamp her. Thanks to the impulsive kindliness of the woman to whom she had sworn allegiance she had slipped back into a world where want was unknown.

Not a single cloud darkened her horizon. As she slid out of the little figured chiffon frock, remnant of former smartness, she assured herself that not even the curious tale she had listened to that morning carried any weight.

"Naturally she's frightened," she argued confidently. "But whatever the truth about these letters, no one is in the least likely to harm a woman in her position. Besides, the mere fact that it's gone on so long without coming to anything proves there's nothing in it."

A smile played about her lips as she thought of Harry Venables. Yes, he was definitely attractive, with a buoyance of nature sufficient to make up for any lack of mental depth. She did not intend to fall in love with him—oh, not that!—but what fun it would be to have him to play about with, how soothing to bask in the glow of his serene good spirits!

"How different he is from his two women relatives! I suppose that's because, though all of them are just plain, solid north-country people, he's had the advantages of Rugby and Oxford. Still, Miss Venables, bless her!—is of an entirely different stripe from that appalling sister-in-law of hers. Her Albert Memorial hair may look a bit quaint, but she's travelled, broadened out, and then her genuine goodness of heart would win anyone's admiration . . . Goodness! What's that?"

The sleepy voice of a slavey called through the door to say that she was wanted on the telephone.

"What, me? Are you sure?"

"Yes, miss, you. They're 'olding the line."

Clutching her coat about her, Sarah sped down the dark, linoleum-covered stairs to the bamboo table where stood the telephone. Still thinking there must be some mistake she grasped the receiver and spoke a wondering "Hello." It was her new employer who answered. The tones were low-pitched, tense with suppressed agitation which sent a quiver along the listener's nerves.

"Miss MacNeil? I can't explain. You'll think me quite mad, but—will you take a taxi and come to the hotel at once? I want you to sleep here, Oh, please be quick!"

CHAPTER FOUR

BENEATH the wild conjectures filling Sarah's brain during her dash to Northumberland Avenue lay a stubborn belief that the midnight summons from a woman safe in the fortress of her hotel, with a relation within call, could arise from nothing worse than a neurotic whim. This, she told herself, was the sort of thing she must be prepared to expect in a future which might not, after all, prove entirely beer and skittles. Only when she flung open the sitting-room door and out of breath confronted Miss Venables did her opinion subtly alter.

The spinster, stiff-backed and self-controlled, still in her prim brown satin afternoon gown she had worn to the theatre, was superintending the making up of a broad divan into a bed. Save that her lips seemed drawn she showed no sign of disturbance, her brown eyes bright and intent as they greeted Sarah across the housemaid's stooping back.

"Thank you, my dear," she murmured with quiet gratitude, and Sarah decided then and there that one who could behave with such composure was hardly calculated to be swayed by chimerical delusions. The crisis which had arisen must be real, possibly grave. Setting down the bag containing her night-things and lending a hand with the smooth linen sheets she remarked that it was almost foggy outside.

"Is it so bad? Then you may not think it very dreadful if we don't open the windows. Don't imagine, though, that I usually sleep in a close room."

The stout housemaid took a pillow in her teeth, shook it into a snowy case, and having patted it into position slipped from the room. Instantly Miss Venables grasped Sarah's hand and led her into the bedroom, her flat chest rising and falling rapidly as she spoke with tense emotion.

"I appreciate you acceding to my extraordinary request without asking any questions. The fact is, I have had a shock. My sister-in-law is completely ignorant of all this trouble, and I don't intend to enlighten her. She would make far too great a hub-bub—and besides she is two floors below us. If Harry had not left me at the door—but I had sent him home before the night clerk handed me this."

She was pointing with a rigid forefinger to a sheet of paper laid face upward on the dressing table.

"Don't touch it. I must avoid getting unnecessary fingermarks on the paper so as not to confuse the detective. Read, though, and see for yourself the sort of outrage I have been subjected to."

The paper was common and ordinary, torn from a tablet. On it in irregular block script was written this message:

"March 17th. Lady, we laugh to see you trying to escape. Go on, we have given ourselves yet another month to accomplish our purpose, and we have shown you not only what we can do, but how hopeless it is for you to keep your whereabouts concealed from us. Maybe when you read these lines you will be spied on by someone who is only waiting his chance, someone so clever as never to be caught. All the same, we offer you a free word of advice. Go to France if you like, but once there, keep away from water."

Sarah's first impulse was to laugh. Only the suspended breathing and taut muscles of the woman at her side convinced her that the recipient of this farrago of nonsense saw in it genuine evil import. Then one salient detail struck her. How, she asked, did the writer know about Miss Venables' plan to return to France?

"I've been inquiring about reservations. I've been followed, that's evident."

Taking another look Sarah remarked that the communication was expressed in good English, but that the seven of the date was crossed.

"That doesn't suggest an English person, does it?"

"Whoever wrote this is not English," muttered the spinster with conviction.

"Then you do know that much?" exclaimed the girl in surprise.

"As well as I can know anything."

The tone was evasive, the speaker glancing over her shoulder so apprehensively that Sarah looked too to make sure they were quite alone.

"The other letters have all come from France, though widely separated localities," continued Miss Venables in a whisper. "Only this,"—she indicated a smudged envelope propped against a tortoise-shell box—"was posted not only in London, but here, close at hand, in the Charing Cross district. At noon today. In short, the writer may be under this very roof. In the adjoining room, perhaps."

"The district's nothing to go by," rejoined Sarah sensibly. "And anyhow you're safe with me here. What can this advice about keeping away from water mean? Do you often go bathing or sailing?"

"Seldom if ever," replied the other with a tortured sigh. "It has no meaning for me. I simply have not an idea what fate is in store for me. There's no earthly use cudgelling our brains over it. All I can do is to hand this over to Parsons—that's the detective—and see if it will help him. I never dreamed anyone knew I was in this hotel, but it has been the same wherever I have gone. Will you give me an envelope and pen from the writing-table?"

Sarah watched her companion draw on a pair of loose gloves, seal the villainous message up, and direct the new envelope to a detective agency in Lincoln's Inn.

"I wish," declared the precise accents, "this had come before Dr. Gilcrest left London. He might have advised me."

"Dr. Gilcrest knows about the previous threats?"

"He and Harry know. I have confided in no one else, except you."

"And you don't feel nervous about going back to Ste. Brigitte?"

"I am nervous anywhere, but as Harry and Parsons both point out I shall be as safe there, perhaps safer, than in a large city. You see, the local police have been informed and have promised to keep a sharp eye out for—for certain persons. At least I shall be among friends, not drifting from pillar to post in this unsettled fashion which is so bad for my health. You cannot run away from a danger like this. Far better rest quietly in a spot of your own choosing."

Sarah reconnoitered. "Listen, Miss Venables," she said earnestly. "Let me tell you about a case I know of which is rather similar to yours. It was in Geneva, and happened to a girl who was the daughter of a rich chocolate manufacturer. She began receiving anonymous love-letters— that is at first they were that, but suddenly, when her engagement was announced, they became violently threatening. No one could make out how her unknown admirer had such a close knowledge of her habits and movements. He seemed often to have been at her very elbow, and when he declared his fixed attention of shooting both her and her fiancé at the altar she and her parents were naturally terrified. The police were called in, the wedding-day arrived with plain-clothes men stationed throughout the church. Everyone who knew was petrified with fright."

"And then—?" whispered Miss Venables, her attention reluctantly chained.

"Well, nothing happened. The ceremony went off without a hitch. Nothing ever would have been found out only a few days later a waiter at the chief hotel ran amok and ended by stabbing himself with a carving knife. His room was searched, and in it were discovered a mass of insane scribblings, poems to the girl, unfinished letters, together with a lot of pathetic souvenirs stolen while the poor creature had been serving the object of his passion in the restaurant—a powder puff, a withered orchid, a frill torn from her dress."

Sarah paused, squeezed Miss Venables' cold hand, and added persuasively. "Now, mayn't this turn out to be something of the same kind? Don't you think the writer of these warnings may be a person outwardly sane but the victim of delusions, someone in the position to find out from friends of yours all your various addresses?"

"I should like to think it," replied Miss Venables regretfully, "but I'm afraid it won't apply in my case."

She shut her lips tightly. Sarah divined that she was held fast in the grip of some preconception, moreover that solid ramparts of reserve would have to be broken down before she divulged what that preconception was.

"Well!" sighed the unhappy woman at last. "It is late, and we are both tired. Let's leave discussion till another time, particularly as nothing can come of it. Would you mind bolting your corridor door and examining your window-catches? Mine have been seen to. I shall keep my reading lamp on, but there is no need for you to do the same."

Ensconced in the first downy bed for many months, Sarah sought to relax, but found her brain teeming with questions. Why was Miss Venables so sure the writer of these letters was not English? What was meant by, "We have shown you what we can do?" How sinister that sounded! Perhaps it was because Miss Venables knew what they could do that she was kept paralysed by fear. Why the warning about water? Or rather why any warning at all? It seemed so stupid to warn a person you proposed to murder. Had the threatener pursued his victim from France to England, and if not actually here at this moment, had he been here at noon to-day?

A sudden odd notion struck her. A letter stamped 12 P. M. must have been posted during the previous hour. Dr. Gilcrest had quitted the hotel at just that time—Dr. Gilcrest, one of the two people cognizant of these communications, and presumably well able to ascertain his patient's movements. No doubt he and she had kept in touch with one another all along. Sarah found herself asking if he had really caught the boat-train, or if . . .

"How idiotic I am!" she muttered irritably. "Whether or not I like the man, I've no excuse for connecting him with this. What would be his reason for frightening her? I might just as well think it of Harry. He left here directly afterwards. No I must collect more information before I begin weaving theories. Meanwhile, what can happen with the bolts shot, four stories up and lights in the street outside?"

All the same something did happen. She had just turned the corner of sleep, with the vision of frayed shirt-cuffs floating before her eyes, when her own name was called in an urgent whisper. Half dazed she sprang up.

"Yes, what is it?"

"Someone's knocking. Don't open. Find out who it is."

With pounding heart Sarah crept close to the farther door.

"Who's there? What do you want?" she demanded.

CHAPTER FIVE

A MAN's voice answered. "Sorry, miss, but the lady on the second floor—the one who's with you—sent me to fetch you. She's been taken very bad."

Sarah unlocked the door. Outside stood a brown-coated attendant whom she recognized, but who seemed taken aback at sight of her. His eyes, however, strayed past her to Miss Venables, just appearing with a dark red dressing-gown thrown round her and her hair in a long wispy tail. It was she who addressed him in puzzled alarm.

"You say Mrs. Venables is ill?"

"Yes, miss, very sudden like. I was told to fetch the hotel doctor, but to let you know about it first. She's too bad to get out of bed."

Every personal fear seemed banished. The spinster became full of electric energy.

"Quick! We must get on something warm and go to her. Poor Gracie! It is probably her appendix. I was afraid of this, though last evening she seemed fairly cheerful. Are you ready? Then come."

Sarah, less concerned over Mrs. Mark Venables' illness than was her companion, felt a haunting suspicion that here was some ruse to entice the latter out. Why hadn't the sister-in-law telephoned up? As they made their way down to the lower floor she glanced warily about, but the corridors were empty, every door closed. Their guide fitted his key into the lock of a door and the three of them entered a bedroom where, under the glare of electric light, they beheld a pitiable spectacle. Amidst the tumbled disorder of quilt and sheets the resident of Huddersfield quivered, far gone in the agony of an attack. Her leathery face was drawn and bedewed with sweat, she was barely conscious, unable to speak. There was now no mystery about her failure to telephone. The instrument, which she must have tried to use, had been knocked from the table to the floor where it lay beyond reach in a tangle of cord.

"Grace! What's wrong with you? Where is the pain?"

Bending over her Miss Venables felt for her pulse, but as the sole response to her question took the form of a gasping groan she transferred her look of frightened inquiry to the attendant.

"Was she like this when you found her?" she demanded.

"Well—she managed to ring, miss, and she could talk, though it sounded a bit thick. Shall I go now for the doctor?"

"As fast as you can . . . this looks serious. Oh, why couldn't she get properly overhauled before this happened? I wonder what we can do for her by way of relief? Brandy! She's got some, I think . . . but it may be the wrong thing . . . Gracie! When did this come on? Can you understand what I'm saying?"

The pale blurred eyes rolled towards the speaker with a faint glimmer of intelligence. One stumpy hand sought to loosen the thick flannelette nightgown as though to relieve the pressure over the abdomen while the other gestured in an appeal which even now was not wholly free from ill temper.

"Sudden—woke me up," mumbled the scarcely articulate voice. "Tried to take brandy—only worse. Now—"

A fresh spasm seized the victim. She writhed helplessly, and her head with its array of metal curlers fell back exhausted. A little saliva appeared at the corners of the mouth.

Sarah who had never once looked upon mortal affliction yet felt with overwhelming certainty that here was a woman near her end. More, she knew that her employer shared her conviction.

Endless minutes, in reality not more than five, elapsed, and then to their desperate relief a hastily clad figure joined them. The resident physician, a heavy, prematurely-bald young man with solemn spectacles, took a swift survey of the sufferer, swept aside the covers, and without a word began systematically prodding the distended body with a firm, exploring touch. Now and again the patient winced, though for the main part she bore his touch with indifference. Presently he straightened up and singling out Miss Venables put a low-voiced question.

"I hate to suggest this, but do you consider it possible for her to have taken anything? You know. Anything—well, poisonous."

Miss Venables recoiled in horrified dissent.

"That? Oh, never! My sister-in-law is the last person to . . . she's had other attacks, you know, less severe, of course. No bad ones for some time, I believe, though—"

"H'm! Well, there's only one course open to us. We must rush her as quickly as possible on to an operating table. I can give her morphia, but it won't help now. Her condition may be very grave, and we must be thankful Charing Cross Hospital is practically at our door. I will ring up while you ladies, if you like to come along with us, get on some clothing."

Even as he spoke his hand reached for the fallen telephone instrument. Miss Venables gave a troubled glance at Sarah, who nodded, and together they were hurrying away when Sarah saw the doctor, waiting for his connection, pick up a small phial of capsules and having examined the label extend his scrutiny to a chemist's envelope in which Dr. Gilcrest's prescription was contained. He glanced at the sheet of hotel paper attentively, laid it aside, and uttered an abrupt, "Hello!" into the mouthpiece. The woman on the bed did not stir.

What followed was like some cold and awful dream. Sarah retained afterwards a confused impression of long bare corridors, white-coated men and uniformed nurses gliding to and fro, the smell of ether, the ticking of a clock, and of herself and her anxious companion sitting bolt upright together, waiting for news. Miss Venables appeared slightly stunned, her brow furrowed, her dark eyes full of worry entirely unrelated to herself. Once she murmured, "Poor Gracie! I always knew she would leave things till too late. She does so hate spending money."

Finally the hotel doctor came into the waiting-room shaking a dubious head. It was impossible, he declared, to determine anything till the patient was opened up.

"May be an appendix, gall-stones—oh, a number of things! Pity we don't know her complete history." He paused, ruminating. "She's been taking some capsules," he remarked suddenly. "Do you happen to know if this Dr. Gilcrest is a London man?"

Miss Venables explained the circumstances, adding Dr. Gilcrest's urgent advice about seeing a specialist. The young physician nodded a little absently.

"I was thinking he might be the Gilcrest I used to be with at Bart's. Is his name Brian by chance? It is? H'm. I fancied so. He left here quite suddenly, didn't he, about three years ago?"

"It was just three years ago he took over a run-down practise in the south of France. He's highly thought of there amongst both the English colony and the natives."

"That's lucky for him."

"Oh, it's not luck at all! It's merit."

Sarah noticed the doctor glance once or twice at Miss Venables from behind his big spectacles, but he said no more and presently left them.

"I was thinking," mused the spinster, "that perhaps I ought to telephone my nephew; but after all, why disturb his rest when there's nothing he can do? It's not as though Grace, poor woman, meant a great deal to him. I'm afraid she's to blame for that."

Sarah asked if Mrs. Venables had any children of her own.

"None, so it's the more strange that when she could have had a real son in Harry, one to be proud of, she has always pushed him off in a rather unfeeling manner. She even resents his attachment to me, though she must realise the poor boy's had to turn somewhere for affection. Gracie was my brother's housekeeper," she explained, conscientiously discreet. "A most worthy woman in many respects, but with a jealous disposition and an unfortunate tendency to fancy slights where none are intended."

"From what you say I don't suppose your nephew spends much time in Huddersfield," remarked Sarah, making conversation.

"He has not been there for several years until this past Christmas when, in order to be with me, he most unselfishly ran up for a few days. No, his work is here, and he has his own cosy little flat in the St. James' district, where he's always inviting me to stay. I'm very pleased with the way he's forging steadily ahead. He seems to have inherited his father's excellent head for finance, in spite of which he finds time for healthy, out-door pleasures. But you can see what he is like, can't you? Just to be in the same room with him acts on one like a tonic."

"That's quite true. It's how I felt about him."

The old maid's fond smile faded slowly. Her hand went to her forehead.

"That horrid ether! Will this never end?"

It did end, unexpectedly soon. At this very moment a trio composed of the house-surgeon, a night-sister, and the hotel physician entered with grave faces to inform them that Mrs. Venables had died under the anaesthetic. Trembling and pale the spinster rose to her feet, but Sarah, putting out a hand to steady her, perceived that the shock had rendered her surprisingly calm.

"Dead! Might there have been a chance, if she'd been brought here sooner?" she faltered. .

"I hardly imagine so," answered the surgeon gently. "Though to be candid we don't yet know the precise cause of her attack. It was her heart that gave way, in view of which we shall be obliged to perform a post mortem. You understand, of course, that the law compels it?"

"A post mortem?" echoed Miss Venables, looking horrified. "But surely you can't suppose—"

"Any unnatural circumstances? Oh, no, nothing whatever to suggest such a thing. At least, I've not seen . . ." He hesitated, then went on reassuringly, "A purely formal affair, you know, just to enable us to sign a death certificate. It's a wise precaution, but there's no need to distress yourself over it."

"No, I see what you mean—and anyhow it can't be helped . . ." Sarah could not decide whether it was her own sharpened imagination which construed into the surgeon's manner a sub-current of dissatisfaction. The man struck her as vaguely puzzled—why, it was difficult to say, for if he had had any doubts as to the victim's illness he might easily have expressed them. Miss Venables did not press him further, and after a few hushed remarks began putting on her fur coat. She could do nothing by remaining here, so, escorted by the young physician, she and Sarah walked slowly out into the silent Strand and round the corner to their hotel.

Whiskies and sodas, fetched by the doctor, warmed and revived them. It was now three o'clock, but Miss Venables astonished her companion by the alert energy with which she was already coping with every practical detail involved by her sister-in-law's death, from the postponement of her own journey south to the various telegrams to be sent to Huddersfield. Only when ready for bed did she seem to recall her private problem. Making a dive under the pillow she drew forth the envelope secreted there, and held it up with a look half relieved, half ashamed.

"And to think a little while ago I was all taken up over my own stupid concerns!" she murmured, conscience stricken. "It makes me feel unutterably petty."

Sarah, wearily stretched between her smooth sheets, sank into instant slumber; but fleetingly, just at the last, there hovered in her brain a hazy speculation as to why the bald-headed doctor had referred to his colleague's sudden departure from London, and why, having heard Miss Venables' remarks, he had lapsed into so pointed a silence.

It was a matter destined to trouble her for some time to come.

CHAPTER SIX

THE Riviera Express roared through the night. Above the noise of it Miss Venables' voice was barely audible, but the tension in the tones whipped to life Sarah's lulled anxiety.

"Did you say you wanted me to see who is standing in the corridor?" repeated the girl, puzzled by the request.

"Just tell me what the man is like, that is all."

Sliding back the door of the wagon-lit compartment, Sarah took a careless survey of the short, bulky figure now blocking the window alongside and puffing cigar-smoke into the spark-filled darkness. Aware of her scrutiny, the fellow-traveller turned, removed the cigar, and favoured her with a bold, personal stare. She closed the door quietly and resumed her seat.

"Oh, it's only that swarthy, Turkish-looking man with the astrakhan collar on his coat who's got the compartment next ours," she explained. "Why? Was he bothering you?"

The brown eyes were watching her with a shade of fear in them.

"So, it is that man!" sighed Miss Venables with a sort of fatalistic despair. "I knew it! On the boat, when we were queuing up to get our passports stamped he kept his eye on us—on me, that is—all the time. That's why we stayed in our cabin the rest of the crossing. Again, in Calais—" She glanced apprehensively at the door. "When that is locked," she asked with quivering lips, "do you think anyone could break in?"

"Not possibly," Sarah assured her after testing the lock.

She added that by way of extra safeguard she would presently stack all their bags against the door; but as she uttered these soothing words she was thinking with amusement that if her employer only knew it was herself this beetle-browed Lothario was concerned with. She had seen him long ago casting admiring smirks at her ankles. Still, she was reminded of something, not comprehended at the time, which had occurred on the train-journey to Huddersfield. A man also Eastern in type had entered their carriage, and at once Miss Venables, who had been talking animatedly to Harry, had shrunk back into her corner to remain with white face and frightened mien until the intruder withdrew. Evidently men of this general stamp were connected in her mind with the threats which dogged her harmless footsteps—threats which even now, after a week, Sarah understood no better than at the beginning.

"Sure he was watching you?" she inquired casually.

A tormented breath escaped the compressed lips. "Am I sure of anything? No! How can I be? It's only my stupidity if I'm regretting, just a little, that I refused to let Harry come with us. Knowing how he enjoys that drive down I hadn't the heart to deprive him of it. Poor boy, he does want cheering up after this depressing time."

Sarah, too, was sorry Harry was not with them, but for a different reason. Although as yet she had been scarcely two minutes alone in his society, she felt that he and she were friends; moreover the mere thought of his broad shoulders and careless smile brought a comforting warmth about her heart. How bored he had been with Huddersfield! The dead Gracie's mid-Victorian mansion with its monumental brass fenders and hideous knick-knacks was not his milieu. She had seen from his dutifully-solemn face and restless manner how he detested the long-visaged mourners, the cowed maid servants still suffering from their late mistress' nagging sway, the snuffy family solicitor with whom he and his aunt had spent hours of tedious conference. It seemed a shame he had benefited so very little by his stepmother's decease, most of the widow's property having passed, by unbreakable entail, into Christine Venables' uneager hands.

"I don't need it, I don't want it," Miss Venables had explained. "But there it is, my brother's own provision in order to compel his son to stand on his own feet. He left Harry just sufficient to keep him—sensible, in a way, for now, instead of having been tempted to squander more than is good for him, Harry earns a decent living, and thoroughly understands the value of money. He'll have it all when I die—and meanwhile I'm pleased to say he never, on any occasion, comes to me for a single penny. If I choose now and then to make him a little present, why, that is my affair."

From the contemplation of Harry's staunch qualities and Miss Venables' kindly complacence, Sarah's thoughts reverted to the post mortem examination of Mrs. Venables' body. Any vague doubts she might once have harboured had been so summarily routed by the verdict that she was mortified to think they had ever troubled her mind. The woman had been in a bad way, a variety of ailments contributing to bring about a bleeding perforation of the stomach sufficient in itself to cause death, though the actual collapse had come from a weak heart. Those who knew her best showed little astonishment. Gracie would gorge, particularly when someone else was paying the bills, and if on her last day she had dieted rather strictly it was then too late to repair damage already done. She was gone, singularly unlamented, and if one or two queer impressions persisted in Sarah's memory, it was only because they related to a man whom for some reason it was hard to recall without contradictory emotions. Did she like her employer's physician, or didn't she? Better still, did she want him to like her? She could not decide, but it was certain she thought of him a great deal.

Miss Venables, winding her wrist-watch, suggested bed.

"But go on with your book while I undress. There's not space enough for the two of us."

Finally they were both tucked up, opposite each other, with spark-reddened smoke flying past the crack in the curtains, and the twin reading-lamps shining like glow-worms in their burnished metal holders. About to extinguish hers, Sarah noticed her friend's brown eyes fixed on her with a tentative expression.

"I'm not sleepy," she declared. "Were you wanting to talk?"

"Yes. I—I thought that now would be an excellent time to acquaint you with—my story. I have meant to tell you before we reached Ste. Brigitte, so you could in some degree appreciate my seemingly foolish fears. Shall I do it now?"

Sarah felt her skin prickle. She had longed for this moment. Outwardly nonchalant, she nodded, squashed her pillow behind her back, and propped herself up to listen.

"Mind if I smoke?" She lit a cigarette and took a few comforting puffs, mainly to put her companion at ease. "I'm dying to hear the whole thing. Harry told me one tiny bit. Hadn't it some connection, in the beginning, with the death of one of your friends?"

"Major Frampton. Yes. But oh, my dear!" whispered the spinster, clasping her thin hands together convulsively. "Nothing can persuade me his death was accidental. Major Frampton was murdered—by the same hand that is trying to murder me!"

CHAPTER SEVEN

THE passionate conviction of these words jarred through the girl like an electric shock. Tense with interest she drank in the forthcoming narrative, seeing each character it involved take a clear-cut vividness.

First, Major Ian Frampton, retired Indian officer, sixty odd, unmarried, and for eight winters Miss Venables' fellow guest at Ste. Brigitte-la-Mer. No detailed description of him was needed. Sarah had known hundreds of his type, stiff-backed, hard as a nut, with lean, unimaginative features, and close clipped moustache; watched them methodically performing the daily ritual which began with *The Times*, moved on to the round of golf, and ended with evening bridge. That nothing of a romantic nature had existed between this man and her employer she was quite ready to believe. Christine Venables had loved but once, a fiancé who succumbed to typhus fever in Natal many years ago. No, the Major had been a friend, no more, but as such highly valued.

Next Sarah caught a name she had frequently heard mentioned, always with warm regard—de Bellesnaves it was, the Baron and Baronne Henri de Bellesnaves, who though in greatly reduced circumstances were the chief personages of the neighbourhood, and occupied a villa about a mile out of the town. The Baron was a genial, uncomplaining semi-invalid, his wife, much younger than he, a woman of remarkable beauty and charm. Both were fond of contract bridge, which they played extremely well.

"I mention this," said Miss Venables, "because on the evening it happened Harry, who sometimes takes a hand with them, and Major Frampton were both their guests for dinner and bridge. Till ten o'clock when the game broke up on account of the Major's getting one of his bad sick headaches all four were together, so that we have the word of three witnesses for the Major's being undisturbed in his mind right up till the moment he left. He insisted on walking to benefit by the air, setting off alone. One can be sure, therefore, that the thing which upset him took place either on the dark stretch of coast road leading back to the village, or else"—her voice grew husky—"inside the dingy little Café des Anglais near the harbour, where he stopped for a drink."

The date was April 17th, nearly a year ago. Earlier in the evening Harry had driven his aunt to friends with whom she was dining in the direction of St. Raphael. It was Miss Venables' intention to return by taxi, but just after ten Mme. de Bellesnaves telephoned to say that as Harry was now free he was getting off to fetch her.

"I thought it very sweet of him to take that trouble for his old maiden aunt," remarked the spinster parenthetically. "Especially as I had told him not to bother; but Harry is always very considerate and thoughtful."

Aunt and nephew had driven back with the sea breeze in their faces and a young April moon overhead dodging between watery clouds. It was still only eleven-thirty when they reached the hotel and after garaging the car went straight in through the side entrance. As it was a Friday, one of the regular dancing nights, they were rather surprised to see no one about. The card-room and lounge were quite empty, even the musicians having gone and taken away their instruments. Where was everyone? It was really most peculiar.

"And then, turning into the lobby, we saw almost all the guests, M. Lefranc the manager, and the entire staff of waiters and chambermaids collected in a strained and silent group. At once we knew something had happened. They stared at us, but no one spoke. I caught hold of Colonel Bulstrode's arm and demanded what was wrong. Never shall I forget his expression—angry, red as a turkey-cock, with a queer look in his eyes. Pulling at his white moustache he blurted out, 'Frampton's fallen down the lift-shaft and broken his neck. That's what's wrong.' Then he turned and stalked away."

"Fallen down the lift-shaft? How could he?"

"My very question; but even as I gasped the words it came over me in a flash what everyone was thinking, and why the Colonel was so furious. You see, that lift was an old-fashioned model, about which there had been numerous complaints. The doors at each floor instead of automatically locking when the cage was not there had a way of springing apart, so that unless one was noticing one might easily step into the empty shaft supposing the lift itself was waiting to receive one. Only the week before Colonel Bulstrode had snatched his wife back barely in time to save her from death. Owing to the row he raised the manager had promised faithfully to have the defect put right, but of course nothing had been done, and now one of us had lost his life through pure negligence on the management's part—or so it now seemed. That the Major had left his glasses in his room and was very short-sighted without them offered no excuse. The entire hotel was up in arms."

"But I don't quite see—"

"Wait a bit. While I was trying to swallow the brandy Harry rushed off to fetch, Mrs. Bulstrode and a Devonshire girl called Beryl Tomlins drew me aside to whisper something to me. It appears they had been playing bridge when they saw the Major come in along the same side passage Henry and I had just used. Beryl, who was dummy and seated facing the door, called out to him in her joking way to know if he'd abandoned his game with the de Bellesnaves because he was losing. There was always a deal of good-natured banter going on between her and Major Frampton, who as a rule gave her back as good as she sent. Imagine, then, her astonishment when, not even turning his head, he muttered something brusque which she couldn't catch, and strode straight through to the lobby, to ask the clerk if I had come home. The music had stopped at the moment, so all four players heard his words quite plainly. The clerk himself added that on learning I was not yet returned the Major scribbled a few lines of jerky writing on a sheet of paper, sealed it up, and slid the envelope into the pocket of his dinner-coat. He then entered the lift, working it himself; and no more was seen of him till, some five minutes later, his body came hurtling down the shaft to arrive bruised and broken on the machinery in the basement."

Miss Venables' voice shook with emotion. During the painful pause Sarah asked if the note written by the Major was found on his body.

"One moment. The so-called accident occurred at ten-thirty-five, that is to say thirty-five minutes from the time he quitted the de Belle-snaves', and six or seven after reaching the hotel. Ordinarily he would not have taken half an hour to walk a bare mile, but as I have said we later learned about his stopping at the Café bar to toss off a double *fine*. Double, mind, and he took the drink standing—two facts which made me ready to assume he had by then already received the shock he wished to tell me about, and while requiring something to steady him, was too agitated to sit down at a table. Yes, that part of it is fairly convincing to me, acquainted as I was with his habits. . . ."

She showed signs of arguing the matter out afresh for her own satisfaction. Pulling herself together she took up the thread.

"Now for the note. Seeing me quite overcome, Harry begged me to let him see me up to my room. He unlocked my door for me—I'd taken to locking it because of some trouble over a light-fingered chambermaid—and there on the floor just inside lay an envelope addressed to me in the Major's handwriting. Very shaky writing it was. Evidently the poor man had slipped the note under the door in order that I should get it directly I came in. I tore it open, and Harry read it while I was fumbling for my lorgnette. Here word for word was what it said:

"It is my urgent duty to warn you at once, that your life is in imminent danger—probably mine as well.—Speak to no one about the matter, but tap on my door as soon as you get this chit. What I have to tell you must be in the strictest privacy. Yours, Ian Frampton."

"Hold on," interrupted Sarah. "Had you any idea of the sort of danger he referred to?"

"A very good idea, as it happened; but I shall come to that presently. I may say, though, that even if I had not been able to guess what it was, a warning like that, coming from a man now dead and that man never in the least given to stupid fears, would have made a deep impression on me. Harry must have thought as I did, for he offered a suggestion which I resented.

"'Harry,' I said, 'not once, in all the years I have known Major Frampton, have I seen him under the influence of drink!' Poor boy, his sole purpose had been to spare me alarm by pretending the note was written when the Major was not himself. However, many other people took the same view, and for less worthy reasons. The manager's insistence on it was understandable. It saved his face, making him seem the less to blame. But all that is a side-issue. I come now to a piece of evidence which to my mind entirely exploded the accident theory.

"The room next the Major's was occupied by an aged gentleman named Vansittart, who, notoriously inquisitive, often sat with his door open. That evening he saw his neighbour enter his own quarters, and then, soon afterwards, saw one of the waiters pass to knock on the adjacent door, mumble a message, and walk quickly away towards the lift. Two seconds later the Major came out and also hurried towards the lift. Mr. Vansittart naturally assumed that owing to the message just received the Major had gone downstairs again.

"This story caused a considerable stir. All the staff were questioned, but not one would admit approaching the Major's room, or even being on the fifth floor at all, so the upshot was that Mr. Vansittart was entirely discredited. He was eighty-two, his sight and hearing exceedingly poor. He had been mistaken, or dozing, that was all. Incidentally, the old man was so outraged over not being believed that he left in a dudgeon, swearing never to set foot in Ste. Brigitte again. Nor did he, for six weeks later he died of a stroke. I, though, had talked with him, and knew just how positive he was. He declared he had not recognised the waiter, noticing only that it was someone taller than the general run of our staff. As the only tall waiter was a youth called Gaston who, having the evening off, had stayed till one o'clock at a *fiançailles* celebration in Hyères, this item got no further. Personally I concluded that unless Mr. Vansittart had unconsciously exaggerated the man's height, the person seen by him was not a waiter at all but an assassin masquerading as such—a creature who deliberately lay in wait to assault his victim and push him down the shaft."

"Did you mention your view to anyone?" asked Sarah keenly.

"Very foolishly for me, I did. Driven by a strong conviction that my friend had been lured to his death, I went to the police and made a statement. As the result, what might have been a purely formal inquest became a sensational affair. Not that any good came of it. Mr. Vansittart and I were coldly treated, all we had to say branded as stuff and nonsense. In the end the Major's short-sightedness plus his tendency to imbibe a little was deemed sufficient to account for his expecting to find the lift where he had recently left it. There was no more to be said. The jury returned a verdict of Death by Misadventure."

"By the way, where was the lift?"

"Ah, there's another queer point! It had been run up to the top—two floors higher up—and to this day no one knows by whom. You see?" cried Miss Venables in triumph. "That alone shows . . . but would the jury admit it? Not they. They accepted the coroner's opinion that the guest or servant who last used the lift was simply too cowardly to come forward with the truth. No, my dear, the whole trouble was this: I was English, the manager was French, and the wretched man, helped by those above him, had that coroner in his pocket. At all cost no scandal must touch the hotel. Oh, you've no idea what forces are ranged against one in a foreign country! Lefranc, till then urbanity itself, behaved so insultingly to me that I had no choice but to pack up and go—not, however, before I had received absolute proof that I was in the right. Yes, immediately after the inquest, there arrived by post the first of the letters which have kept me on the rack from then till now."

Sarah felt a tingling sensation along her spine. "What did it say?" she whispered. "You have it here?"

"You shall see it; but in order for you to understand completely I must tell you of another thing which happened shortly before these events. Laugh if you like, for it turned entirely on artificial pearls. Yes, pearls! Isn't that absurd?"

"I don't know. Is it?"

"I'll explain. Coming back from the golf-links late one afternoon, the Major and I happened to meet two of those Oriental vendors who simply infest the Riviera with their rugs, tortoise-shell beads and so on. These fellows, wearing turbans, were strung all over with ropes of pearls, only, contrary to the usual habit of their kind, they did not pester us to buy but strode past as though in a hurry. Seeing the pearls reminded me that I was wanting a longish strand to wear with a black lace gown I had, so I called to the men to show me what sort they were selling. After some hesitation one of them came back, but the string he offered me was of so inferior a grade that I refused to look at them. We strolled on again, turning a deaf ear to the man's whining insistence, and presently the other peddler overtook us holding out a really beautiful strand, which after some bargaining I bought for thirty francs. I may add that it was growing dark, which possibly explains the error that was made.

"Still, I might never have known anything was wrong if I had not that same evening had the ill luck to catch the pearls on a door-knob and break the string. I crushed one of the beads under foot, and there on the floor lay a little heap of snow-white powder. My dear, it was cocaine!"

"Cocaine!" echoed Sarah, beginning to understand.

"Yes, the Major suspected it, got the doctor's opinion, and then, rather against my inclinations, reported the matter to the police. The two drug-sellers, never dreaming they had inadvertently sold me a strand not meant for ordinary trade, were arrested, and at their trial the Major and I were called on to give evidence against them. Being old offenders, both received long sentences; and as they were being led out of court the second one, a villainous brute, fixed his black eyes on us and muttered something in Arabic which the Major understood. It was a threat declaring that sooner or later we should pay with our lives for the mischief we had wrought.

"To me these seemed idle words, and I was rather puzzled that, by his disinclination to discuss the matter, Major Frampton seemed to attach more importance to the threat than I did. Having lived in the East he may have known something of these scoundrels' vindictive nature; but be that as it may, I recalled his attitude the moment I set eyes on his extraordinary message, very naturally concluding that, on his way home that night, he had got wind of a definite plot to exterminate us both. What else could I think? There was but one source of danger common to him and me. Even Harry, much against his will, was forced to agree when I pointed it out to him, although then and always he has tried his best to make light of my idea. Now, hand me my dressing-bag. I will show you the communication I received, and the others as well."

A folded sheet of common paper similar to what Sarah had seen in London was put into her hand. Rudely printed on it were the following words:

"Lady, we got your friend, now we go after you. It may take time, but no matter, we shall contrive another accident. We give ourselves one year. Make the most of it."

For the first time Sarah began to believe. One by one she read the entire series of letters—twelve in all—and, having pondered their monotonous contents turned her attention to the postmarks on the envelopes. These covered a wide range, Nice to Bordeaux, Vichy to Deauville, only this latest bearing the London stamp. All were dated the seventeenth of the month, the sevens crossed.

"You see?" murmured Miss Venables, watching her closely. "These itinerant vendors move about continually. Oh, I have never supposed the letters to be written by the prisoners themselves! That, I am assured, is an impossibility ; but if the culprits have friends in league with them it comes to the same thing. There are no finger-prints. The detective you saw supplied that information—and their spy-system must be highly perfected, considering that all my addresses are correct, even to the one in Oberammergau, where I spent only three days. It was there I got the bad attack of food-poisoning. In Ravenna I was nearly run down by a car with closed curtains—and those two incidents are not the only escapes I could mention, accidental though they may have been."

Her face had taken on a greyish tinge. She moistened her dry lips and reached for the letters.

"You have seen all you want of the horrid things? Then let us lock them away and close the subject. I shall sleep the better for having poured out my tale."

Sarah could now understand why one place was considered as safe as another, but she did not think to inquire if the Ste. Brigitte police were promising any sort of protection.

"They have their instructions from the Sûreté Générale of Paris." Was there a faint accent of pride in the reply? "And obviously in so small a town it is much easier to keep tab on dubious strangers than it would be in a large city; but my main comfort will be to settle down quietly again and be among friends, particularly the de Bellesnaves, of whom I am so fond. It is true they know nothing of all this, so be very careful not to mention it to them; but you can't think how reassured I shall be by the sight of their kind faces. Dr. Gilcrest's too." She sank back, her face gaunt but peaceful in the little pool of golden light. "No one stirring outside, I hope?"

"All quiet on the corridor front," declared Sarah with a smile.

She gave an answering smile, sighed and lay still. Sarah switched off the two lamps, and got into bed, her mind strangely torn between pity and an odd dissatisfaction.

CHAPTER EIGHT

IN DAZZLING sunshine the two women alighted at Hyères, from which terminus a car was to take them the remaining ten miles to Ste. Brigitte. A warm breeze soothed and thrilled them with its burden of alien scents. The terrible Turk had quietly vanished at Toulon, leaving Miss Venables' thoughts free to roam happily on the old friends she was soon to join.

As they drew into the station, lorgnette raised, she was peering along the platform. Now she gave a glad cry of recognition.

"Is it? Yes, to be sure, it's Jacques, the same chauffeur who always drives me. Really, this is like old times."

The black-browed Provençal grinned, jerked two dirty fingers towards his beret, and at once began shouldering their bags. About to step into the big rattle-trap Daimler awaiting them they perceived a two-seater, shabby and white with dust, just chugging in their direction. Again the lorgnette did service, and again the spinster exclaimed in pleased astonishment.

"Doctor! And you, Baron! To think you came all the way to meet us! How good of you both!"

The two men got out to greet them. Dr. Gilcrest, looking much improved by a deeper sunburn, nodded to Sarah with the same reserved indifference which had so annoyed her before. Somehow, for the preservation of her own conceit, she had hoped he would show her some attention; but the strange, gnome-like figure beside him comforted her wounded vanity by his gentle, smiling courtesy. So this was the Baron de Bellesnaves, this shrunken, gnarled little man in the piecrust coloured homespun suit far too loose for his wizened frame! She saw a face crisscrossed with wrinkles and yellowed to the same unwholesome tint of its owner's clothing, thin hair less grey than faded, and a pair of washed-out blue eyes in which world-weary sophistication mingled oddly with a childish and whimsical good-will. Prematurely aged by suffering, yet imperishably young—that was her first impression. Her second informed her that the Baron, serene in misfortune, belonged not to the upstart nobility but to the old regime well-rooted in the past. She was glad of this, having feared something different.

Glowing with pleasure, Miss Venables was saying, "Two friends—but where is the third? I don't see Polly."

"You think she would desert me? *La voilà!*"

The cumbersome, singularly repulsive white bulldog just disentangling its bulk from the steering-gear was, like so many pure specimens of its breed, a misery to itself and all beholders. It wheezed and snuffled through an ill-fitting jaw, its bowed legs seemed pathetically inadequate for its weight, its tail, twisted and withered, suggested the stem of a rotten orange—one good pull required to bring it away. It lumbered towards the group, bleared eyes upcast. Sarah patted it and moved hastily aside to save her stockings from its slobbering jaw.

The Baron chuckled. "Ah, *mon ange*, no one loves you but me! Gilcrest can show no greater proof of friendship than by allowing you in his car. *C'est vrai, mon vieux?*"

Sarah saw a smile of affectionate understanding pass between the two men. For an instant a veil dropped from the doctor's slate-blue eyes, revealing something likeable beneath; but the veil fell again as the Baroness' name was mentioned, a fact which recalled to Sarah Harry Venables' teasing innuendo.

"I hear Maddalena is in Paris. Indeed, she wrote me a day or so ago. How is she? As lovely as ever?"

"Unchanged, always the same." The Baron's genial smile remained, though his gaze now followed the bulldog's peregrinations round a lamppost. "But why not? At an age when the blood is like new, strong wine . . . ah, Brian, you are looking at your watch, which means we must be off."

"Rushed as usual, I suppose? I hear there's been a great deal of flu about. But won't you both dine with us this evening? Baron, as you're alone, perhaps just this once—" The little man gave a smiling refusal on the plea of a strict diet. Gilcrest hesitated and asked if he might leave it open.

"But certainly! Come if you can, just as you are. You got my letter?" Miss Venables asked in a lowered tone. "You were right about my poor sister-in-law, it seems. I had made the appointment, but that very night a crisis arose, and her heart gave way. It was sudden and shocking. I will tell you about it when we have an opportunity to talk." Sarah saw the doctor's sombre gaze just graze hers and drift quickly away. As on a former occasion she read in it what was either a question or troubled uncertainty whose nature she could not determine. The bare nod he gave made her feel the subject of Mrs. Venables' death was one he had little wish to discuss. Did he fear some criticism of his professional judgment?

She was still vaguely wondering about him when, from the departing Daimler, she looked back to see him, preoccupied and absent of face, wiping off the dusty windscreen of the two-seater. The Baron waved to them, and stooped with tender solicitude to hoist his unwieldy pet into the car.

"How devoted the poor man is to that unfortunate animal!" murmured Miss Venables with a compassionate shake of the head. "It is his child, his baby. As his wife says, one daren't think what will become of him when it's gone, and it can't last for ever, no matter how he pampers it. Old, spoiled thing!"

They emerged from the town upon a shore road on one side bordered by vivid blue sea, on the other by vineyards and occasional stretches of sand in which here and there a ragged palm tree stood sentinel. Nearing Ste. Brigitte the road swerved inland to encircle a large estate. This, Miss Venables told Sarah, was the de Bellesnaves' property.

"Look, there's the house, in amongst the eucalyptus trees. Rather dilapidated it is, and the Baron unfortunately has no money to do it up. It's called the Casa Giallo. Giallo means yellow, doesn't it? And you can just see that it was once yellow, though the paint is nearly gone."

Sarah looked at the long, rambling building visible for a moment as they flashed past. It had shuttered windows giving on a terrace, scaly iron balconies, and a mass of untidy creeper, mostly wistaria just coming into bloom, hanging from its dingy walls.

"Dear me, that's bad!" Miss Venables clicked her tongue over a hiatus of smashed palings in the side fence. "That's where the char-à-banc went astray. The Baroness wrote me they were haggling over damages. The grounds are very extensive, you see, going all the way down to the water, where they have a little private beach and an old sailing yacht. Harry, when he comes, will be wanting to take you out."

"Shan't you go too?" asked Sarah.

"I—I don't think so," replied her companion with a subtle alteration of tone. "I'm a bad sailor, and the squalls which come up so suddenly make me rather nervous."

The girl said nothing, but she knew Miss Venables was thinking of those sinister words, *Keep away from water*. Poor woman! Probably at no time was she free from apprehension. . . .

Two English women came with brisk strides along the sheltered lane. At sight of them Miss Venables sprang up radiant with smiles and waved a frantic greeting.

"Look, look! Two of my friends, Madge Whittaker and Beryl Tomlins! Madge, Beryl! Are you coming back for lunch?"

The couple nodded and gesticulated in high glee. Both wore knitted jumpers and flopping shower-proof coats, each carried a gay raffia bag. The gaunt, tall one had short, curly grey hair, a florid face and immense, protruding teeth; the short, stout woman was dark and sallow, with a decidedly jaunty air.

"Now, why aren't they golfing?" speculated the spinster, happily subsiding into her seat. "I expect Beryl's inside is queer again—or no, I've just remembered. It's Wednesday, the day she prepares her book-list for Mudie's. She's our librarian you know. Looks after the books, in part exchange for—ah, here's the village!"

They had plunged abruptly into narrow streets, half picturesque, half crassly modern. Over the tiled red roofs could be seen brown and white sails of fishing craft.

"Here's the Café des Anglais. Not nearly so nice as the British Tea-rooms, where you can get real homemade scones. Run by two Norfolk ladies. See those youngsters romping in the school yard, even quite big boys in those absurd black aprons! The doctor's house is just there, to the left—and in through that passage beside it you'll come on the market-place, all sorts of amusing oddments on stalls, but not so very cheap any longer. These natives are learning how to exploit us. The Roman Church . . . rather gloomy and smelly inside, but up in the hills we've our own delightful little English Church . . . yes, one of those quaint stone pools, where the townswomen bring their washing . . . the Casino. Smart, isn't it, with those bright red trimmings? This street facing us has the best shops. It leads straight up to—but look—just ahead. There!"

They had debouched upon a cobbled square fronting which loomed a snow-white building, seven stories high and U-shaped to enclose a court in which lopped plane-trees sheltered orange tables. Behind, like a painted backdrop, spread a peach orchard and low, bluish mountains against a turquoise sky; to the fore, plump, well-fed pigeons strolled confidently about, preening their plum-coloured breasts. The big building, as a span of newly gilded lettering informed the world, was the Grand Hotel du Golf and de la Plage. Clean and spacious, it lorded it over the semi-squalor of the town, looking the very last place in creation where anything untoward could happen. Indeed, as the car swept round the drive and halted at the wide portals, Sarah came near deciding that Major Frampton's fall down the lift shaft had been accident, no more.

But in that case, whence came the letters? One must search for some entirely different explanation to account for them. An unsuspected lunatic among the guests? Someone here or elsewhere in the town who through jealousy or spite bore Miss Venables and her elderly friend a grudge?

"It must be that," reflected the girl. "I must keep my eyes open."

During the lunch hour she did so, but saw nothing to confirm her idea. As she had foreseen, the Grand Hotel du Golf et de la Plage was a little corner of England transplanted to foreign soil but unchanged by the process. Could she suspect any one of these tweed-clad men, none under fifty, whose immaculate grooming and honest scrubbed rosiness made the undersized waiters seem a race of inferior beings? Or the women, also uncertain as to age, mostly widows and spinsters, with a strong repugnance to make-up and a tendency to woven kid sandals? From one to another she looked and said, No. Cranks there might be—all crocks, Harry had declared; but in all her life she had never encountered a more wholly conventional set of people. Moreover, there was no mistaking the universal glow of welcome evoked by the wanderer's return to the fold. At the end of the excellent meal the old residents gathered round to chat and gossip, and amidst the flattering reception accorded her Miss Venables, in her element at last, basked happily and drank in all the precious items of news.

It was nearly three o'clock before they went up to their rooms. Shut in the lift of ill-repute, Miss Venables whispered to Sarah, "You saw them all looking at you rather curiously? Remember, don't let them guess you are anything but a friend who's happened to come with me. The doctor urges me to give this affair of mine as little publicity as possible. I'm sure that's the wise course."

"This lift," remarked Sarah, trying the doors when they had emerged. "Seems all right now, doesn't it?"

"Oh, it's been seen to—now." The spinster's tone was grim. "And le Franc, the former manager, has been replaced by a very different sort of man, else I should have hesitated to come back."

They turned into the two large, light rooms reserved for them. Someone had brought a pot of rose-coloured tulips and placed them on Miss Venables' mantel. The parquet shone like glass, the casement windows opened on a panorama of mountains and the peach orchard, pink with bloom. Miss Venables insisted on doing her unpacking unaided, and after twenty minutes Sarah, looking in, beheld a dazzling transformation. Cushions, tea-things and books had been produced and distributed. A gorgeous Spanish shawl covered the sofa, and all the familiar belongings, including Harry's photograph in its silver frame, were ranged on the bedside table.

"But how nice you've made it!"

"More home-like, anyhow," agreed the owner with satisfaction. "We'll run out now and buy some fruit for that big majolica dish Beryl has kindly kept for me. Beryl . . ." Her brown eyes grew grave. "I don't believe she's very fit. Yes, she's the stout, dark one, in the red crocheted jumper. I didn't like those liverish patches."

"She seemed most lively, though."

"She always is, that's the wonderful part of her, for she hasn't good health. A lesson to all of us, I say, when one thinks she's not only delicate but almost penniless as well. I've known her for fifteen years, and I've hardly ever heard her complain. High spirits, jolly, friends with everyone. You may hear her called a gossip, but it's never in an ill-natured way. A really good sort, and—are you ready? Then let's explore a little before tea."

Sarah recalled the information about Miss Tomlins when, at seven thirty that evening, they met the lady in question sallying forth from the library with her raffia bag, crammed with knitting hung on her plump arm. She would not see fifty again. Her skin was muddy, her eyes like dregs of coffee, and her much mended dark green lace too tight for her matronly person; but complacence and jauntiness shone from her, skilfully camouflaging what Sarah divined as a grim determination to discover the truth about herself. Miss Venables was scanning the letter rack. The librarian fastened on Sarah and began operations.

"American, aren't you?" she demanded, friendly and pouncing. "I knew it. Madge Whittaker said no, I said yes. Can always spot 'em. Staying long?"

On guard Sarah replied that she would probably be here till the weather got too hot. "And you?" she inquired carelessly.

"Oh, I'm a fixture. Can't afford to live anywhere else, except when my friends invite me somewhere. Bit lucky in that way. Matter of fact, I'm starting off in a day or two for Nice." Miss Tomlins, still jovial, returned to the attack. "New pal of Chrissie's? Must he, or else . . . oh, you met her in London! I see. Then, if it's not a rude answer, you must know Harry. Met him, too?"

"Yes," admitted Sarah, slightly self-conscious under the shrewd eyes.

"Ah, you would, of course! Nice lad, Harry. Shan't be sorry to see him round here again. Nice, clean boy, charming manners." She smiled and patted the ill-dyed, shingled hair which swept from her forehead in a plastered mane. "She thinks something of him, I can tell you. I don't wonder at it, do you? Thinks a lot of our doctor, too. There's another nice man for you. Bit reserved, don't tell all he knows, but—he went to meet you, didn't he? Saw him, with the Baron de Bellesnaves. Great pals, those two. Baron's charming as well, or so they say, though he and his wife don't bother much about us English except for Chrissie."

A tinge of jealousy underlay the off-hand tone. Sarah detected it, and felt a secret amusement. It vanished, though, as, with a quick glance at Miss Venables' back, the librarian came closer and mumbled between rigid lips, "Heard about the big rumpus we had here last year? Oh! Shocking time it was. Major Frampton and she—devoted friends, you know. Suppose she's told you . . ."

She checked herself, her roving eye catching sight of Miss Venables at her side, and with a swift change of manner asked if it were true that Dr. Gilcrest was expected to dine.

"I invited him," answered Miss Venables with a smile, "but how on earth did you know?"

"Oh, little bird! Feather in your cap, eh? None of us can entice him round—but don't get too puffed up about it. He may let you down, you know."

Again, in spite of the airy gesture and the broad wink, Sarah scented jealousy, the reason being understood when, presently, she was told that Dr. Gilcrest stood high in Miss Tomlins' favour. Now, singling her out very pointedly, the plump Beryl declared that they must get together one of these days for a real, good pow-wow.

"When I come back, you know. Have tea with me in what a gossip-writer once called my 'wee, roof-top flatlet.' Ha, ha! Not bad, eh? I hate gush, don't you?"

Blithely she sailed away, leaving Miss Venables to remark somewhat dubiously that while Sarah must certainly accept Beryl's invitation it would be wise to be very, very cautious what she revealed.

"Trust me," whispered the girl reassuringly. "I can see what she's up to, but she shan't get it, never fear."

"Yet she can't suspect anything," mused the older woman. "It's not possible. How could she know?"

That, thought Sarah, was what she, without betraying anything, would make it her business to find out. Already she had formed the opinion that Miss Tomlins was probably better acquainted with what had happened last year than any other resident of the hotel. It would be interesting, perhaps useful, to get her angle on the harrowing event, and see if her version differed from Miss Venables'. A pity she was going away. . . .

Eight o'clock, and still their guest had not appeared. Sarah was disappointed. Without quite knowing why, she wanted to study this man. More, she wanted to compel him to notice her, and with that object in view had put on her most becoming frock and taken especial pains over her hair. She was not used to being ignored, and it irked her more than she cared to admit that in both encounters with the young physician her employer so highly esteemed she had been treated as a thing of no account. Gilcrest might not attract her as Harry Venables did. She even resented him a little; but that made her all the more eager to win his approval. Could it be done?

Miss Venables was reading in the lounge. Wandering into the lobby, Sarah paused before a show-case of enticing trifles to examine herself in the glass at the back. How well her frock looked, and what a joy to have some decent clothes at last! Green always suited her, and this little fluttering shoulder-cape. . . . She touched her lips with her lipstick, coaxed behind her small ears the lustrous tendrils of nut-brown hair, and then, becoming aware of someone close at hand looking at her, flushed scarlet and wheeled to see who was there.

Dr. Gilcrest had arrived. He had seen her complacence with herself. But why should those impervious, slate-coloured eyes of his seek to evade her own embarrassed glance? She was the one to be confused.

"Oh—good-evening!"

Her greeting sounded a trifle flat.

CHAPTER NINE

He looked down at the hand she had extended, lifting the fingers separately. His air of diffidence puzzled her, for she was sure in the ordinary way he was not lacking in self-confidence.

"Muscles getting any stronger?" he asked awkwardly.

"No," she returned, meeting his eyes with a smile. "But I'm still making that effort. I can just manage to feed myself," she added flippantly, hoping to stir some answering lightness.

"You're better in yourself, though," he stated impersonally. "More flesh, more colour."

Must he always be professional?

"That's the feeding." This time she laughed irrepressibly. "Nothing like three square meals a day, is there? Soon I'll have to begin banting."

As they went into the dining room, Sarah could not help noticing that the doctor's presence created a pleasant stir. Not the least doubt that he was well-liked in the hotel, but she felt that with the possible exception of Miss Venables there was no one here whom he regarded in anything but a professional light. She sensed that in an unexpressive, rather oblique way he was interested in her employer. Perhaps, under cover of his reserve, he had a slightly warmer feeling for her. At any rate his manner towards this one patient seemed softer, less impersonal, and at moments full of gratified appreciation, as when he found his favourite wine had been ordered. He thanked her with his eyes, from which, as had happened that morning with the Baron, a veil had fallen, and just in time he remembered to include Sarah in the silent toast he was drinking. With his second glass he had become much more human, and bit by bit, as what seemed a heavy load of preoccupation slipped from his shoulders, he even showed gleams of enthusiasm, notably in response to an inquiry about his private research work.

"Oh, I'm accomplishing a few stray bits," he answered. "Though I've only the evenings free—some of them, that is—and sometimes I'm too dead-beat to do much. I'm testing out a serum. If it turns out as I hope, I'll tell you about it." He paused, crumbled his bread, and continued slowly, "Henri's invaluable to me. I don't know how I'd get on without his assistance. He has the true scientific brain. It's one of the rotten tricks of Fate that his career was ruined by ill health."

"The Baron was badly wounded and gassed in the war," Miss Venables explained to Sarah. "Now, unfortunately, it's too late for him to accomplish much."

"Henri's only forty-nine, although he looks so much older—and he is, these last few months, in better shape. I still cherish hopes of building him a sounder constitution. If I succeed, it will be all the recompense I ask for—this." Gilcrest glanced with slight bitterness at the surrounding company.

"Never grow disheartened," counselled Miss Venables gently. "Even if you fail to restore the Baron's health, at least you've given him a new interest in life."

"Which is considerably less than he's done for me."

These remarks were comprehensible to Sarah, who now knew that Gilcrest had obtained the run-down practice in Ste. Brigitte through M. de Bellesnaves' influence. The Baron had known Gilcrest's father, and when owing to financial reverses the young man had been forced to abandon his projected career of biochemical research for that of a grubbing practitioner he had come to the rescue with the offer of this locum on very easy terms. In all this there ought to have been no element of mystery, and yet from a tinge of reticence on Miss Venables' part, Sarah had felt the existence of something withheld. She knew that whatever it was could not be considered discreditable either by her informant or by the young English dispenser she had met that afternoon when they called in at the doctor's dispensary. The girl, whom she had liked, showed every evidence of adoring regard for the man she served. . . .

"And does the Baroness still show that rather amusing interest in your experiments?" pursued Miss Venables with an indulgent smile.

Sarah could have sworn the faint red risen to the brown cheeks did not come from the wine.

"All over," Gilcrest declared shortly. "Mme. de Bellesnaves' enthusiasms are short-lived—just something to fill up her time." As though realising his brusqueness, he went on, more tolerantly, "she has little enough to occupy her, you know."

"True," sighed the spinster. "What a pity she has no children! To be sure, she makes the Baron her child, but for anyone with such tons of energy that's hardly enough, is it? Brave, clever little thing! I hate to see all her talents going to waste. I wonder how she managed to scrape together money enough for this little blow in Paris? I'm very pleased that she did."

There was one thing glaringly apparent: the doctor had no intention of discussing his friend's wife. A little later, when Sarah had tactfully left her two companions together over their coffee, a possible reason for this was given her by Miss Tomlins, who, on her way to the card-room, stopped to ask for a match.

"Dull for him now a certain person's away," confided the librarian with meaning nods in Gilcrest's direction. "That's why he turned up. Of course, he must have seen her in Paris. Notice how both of 'em managed to get off at the same time? Oh, yes! And once she's back, he'll have plenty to occupy him. You'll see."

"But he works at his experiments in the evenings, doesn't he?"

Miss Tomlins shrugged with massive scorn. "Experiments! Call 'em that if you like, but all the same she's generally hanging round. I tell you, my child, those two are thick as thieves. Not that I see any harm in it. I'm not nasty-tongued like some I could mention, and when two people are young and one of 'em has a husband that's just a crawling corpse, why, let 'em have a good time, I say. There's not much to amuse a woman like her round these parts. Wait till you see her, that's all! But not a word to Chrissie, bless her pure heart! She might misunderstand and be shocked to the core. Do you play contract?"

"Very badly. I haven't played for so long."

"Well, we'll get up a scratch game for you one evening. Heavens!" About to bounce off to the card-room, Miss Tomlins made a gesture of recalling something. "Fancy not taking my medicine, and with him here, too, to remind me! Must dash back for a glass of water."

She disappeared into the dining-room, leaving Sarah to reflect, with some distaste, on the sugar-coated morsel of gossip just retailed to her. Why she should resent the young doctor's attachment to a woman she had not yet set eyes on presented a puzzle, yet she did resent it, almost as bitterly as the stout old maid who, for all her pose of tolerance, could not conceal the rancour beneath her off-hand tone. Since she could not seriously want this man for herself—unthinkable on such scant acquaintance, and considering his impervious behaviour towards her—her feeling must arise from a dog-in-the-manger attitude which, in principle, she despised. It was particularly idiotic when she remembered the half-formulated suspicions she had nurtured only a week ago—or no, perhaps it wasn't. In her anxiety to atone for her gross error, she had allowed herself to like him too much, and to angle all through dinner for a response which never came. There was the rub—she had tried to attract him, and failed.

"I know your complaint," she told herself sharply. "It's just the complete dearth of full-blooded males in your immediate vicinity that makes you fasten on to the one masculine creature with brains and muscle. Well, you'll have to put up with doddering old colonels—at least till Harry gets here. There's nothing else in sight."

The clerk had crossed the lounge and was handing Miss Venables a telegram. Sarah saw the nearsighted brown eyes dilate with sudden alarm as the thin hands groped tremblingly for the lorgnette. She hurried to her employer's side.

"Is anything wrong?" she asked quickly.

"No, no!" Miss Venables laughed with mingled apology and relief. "It's just Harry, who says he's had a slight accident to his car, and won't be here till Sunday evening. I'm very stupid to get so flustered." She pressed her still palpitating heart. "I really must take myself in hand."

"You must, indeed."

It was Gilcrest who said this, his tone soberly firm. He was looking at his hostess, probingly, so Sarah thought. Miss Venables excused herself with a deprecatory laugh.

"I know, I know! And I have overcome a great deal of my nervousness. Miss MacNeil will tell you I'm trying hard to be sensible. Sarah, my dear, sit down. This is not a secret conference. I have just been telling the doctor about that latest warning." She had lowered her voice so that those about them could not hear. "He thinks—but repeat, doctor, what you've just been saying to me."

He stared down at the cheap Maryland cigarette he was smoking.

"Oh, my opinion's of no real importance," he muttered, slightly confused.

Sarah believed it was herself he did not consider important enough to bring into the discussion. Again his attitude galled her a little. Miss Venables did not press him, but by her own troubled return to the subject made clear what had been said.

"I've never supposed the letters to have been written by the actual culprits," she argued. "Indeed, that idea seems impossible; but even if there's no close fellowship between these drug-peddlers, could not a member of the original threatener's family—a son, a brother, perhaps— be following up a scheme of revenge? If not, then who can it be? And what object could the writer have in pretending a—a reason other than he expresses?"

"I don't know," replied the young man bluntly, yet with an odd embarrassment apparent to Sarah's eyes. "All I can say is that it doesn't somehow seem reasonable to me for anyone not actually the sufferer to take so much trouble. Besides, if he means business, why in the devil's name does he put you on your guard?"

"He does that, I think," whispered the spinster between drawn lips, "merely to torture me. A cat playing with a mouse. I can quite believe the warnings are deliberately contrived for that purpose."

Gilcrest ground out his cigarette almost impatiently.

"That's exactly why I can't accept your theory. After all,"—persuasively—"what proof is there that Major Frampton's death was not accidental? I know of none."

"His note was not accidental," returned Miss Venables with a shake of the head. "That is my proof. But there, we can't hope to settle anything, can we? Let's speak of pleasanter things. The Baroness—when will she be home? If I had her Paris address, I could wire Harry to look her up. Do you know it?"

"She's left Paris for Lyons, so Henri tells me." Gilcrest made this statement detachedly—too detachedly, so Sarah considered. "I imagine we'll be seeing her any day now."

"Lyons! Of course, she is spending a little while with that poor bedridden mother of hers; and you, I expect, are doing your best to keep her husband from being too lonely in her absence. I hope, though, you will come on Friday evening to dance with Sarah? I'm sure she loves dancing."

Sarah did, but could not well show enthusiasm while Gilcrest was murmuring doubts as to his being able to turn up. She felt certain he had no notion of coming, and now, meeting one of his reluctant glances, she elevated her chin and steered the talk in another direction.

About one thing she was right. On Friday the doctor failed to appear, and indeed for three whole days she and Miss Venables saw no one except the denizens of the hotel. Sunday arrived, a sparkling day, with late breakfast, an excursion to the English church, and at noon the return, in massed formation of all those who, according to unbreakable habit, had donned spick-and-span attire to do homage to divine service. Boredly amused, Sarah watched their companions troop into the lobby to consult the barometer, order apéritifs, and wait impatiently for lunch. Colonel Bulstrode, superb in the male-plumage of top-hat, morning coat and spats, boomed a bitter complaint about the non-delivery of his *Times*; his wife, a demure hen-pheasant in speckled silk and pince nez, agreed with Madge Whittaker that the canticle had been very nicely sung, but that the new vicar was a little too high for all tastes. An ancient baronet, Sir Claud Ames-Gower, flanked by his two daughters—one acidly-coy, the other stolid and four-square with Eton crop and horn-rimmed spectacles—hoped that the beef would not be messed up with one of those *cordon bleu* sauces; and a vast dowager, lobster-red visage glaring forth implacably from beneath a roof-garden of pansies, was just adding her criticism of foreign food when Miss Venables, who had been peering through her lorgnette into the lounge, uttered a glad cry.

"Maddalena! Is it really you? Dear me, but this is a welcome surprise!"

Following at a little distance, Sarah saw a small, slenderly smart figure surge forward with outstretched hands to rise on tiptoe and imprint a feathery kiss on each of the spinster's cheeks. A wave of subtle scent reached her together with a rippling contralto laugh, and at the same moment the sunlight pouring down through the glass dome overhead showed her a face of exquisite contour and colouring. Oval, olive-tinted, it was a Madonna's face, but for the scarlet thread of the curved lips, and the sparkle of animation. The features she had hardly noticed, all else being eclipsed and submerged in the magnificence of the eyes—dark liquid, effulgent, with heavy, black-fringed lids, eyes to haunt one, eyes to dream about, eyes to charm and conquer. Never, thought the girl, had she beheld anything to equal them for sheer, stupefying beauty. A woman with eyes like these could win whatever she wanted.

"How delightful! What a long time it has been! You are looking radiantly well—but then you are never anything else. What a lot we shall have to talk over, shan't we? It will take hours. Oh, I'm forgetting! Let me introduce to you my Miss MacNeil. She has been such a treasure to me, and I know you will be as fond of her as I am."

The Baroness detached herself inquiringly from her friend's embrace, straightened the tiny hat which perched rakishly over her left eyebrow, and let her dark gaze rest on Sarah. For an instant she was formal. Then a dimple appeared at the corner of her mouth and she smiled, frankly, charmingly, showing lovely even teeth, and took Sarah's hand in her cool, strong little fingers.

"So this is she! I have heard about her from Henri." The voice uttering these words matched the eyes in warmth and depth, and like them, one felt, could be caressing, merry or dramatic. Oddly enough, at the moment it combined all three. "I am so glad, so very glad, that she is with you. She and I will soon be friends, I am very sure! Yes,"—turning again to Miss Venables, "I arrived last night, but so tired, so dirty from the train, that all I could think of was a bath and my bed. That day-journey from Lyons—ugh! But you? Better, I hope? No more of the trouble—here?"

The speaker touched her own slim waist and searched her friend's expression with anxious concern. Her English was nearly perfect, only a trace of accent hard to define.

"Much better, I think, or I shall soon be, now I am under my own doctor again. I am thankful that you and he between you have overcome the shrinking I had for this place. Rather absurd, wasn't it?"

"Perhaps; but then it was so beastly for you last year. I boil over when I think of it." The Baroness glanced hesitatingly at Sarah and quickly changed the subject. "Mees—MacNeil, is it?—you like our little dull town, yes? You do not find it too quiet?"

"It's lovely here. I'm enjoying it thoroughly," Sarah said with an answering smile, and added, "I've looked forward to meeting you."

"Ah, then I know we shall get on together! I cannot stop now, indeed I must fly this instant, but what I came for was to ask you two to dine with us this evening. *En famille*, you know, only ourselves, and perhaps the doctor. You will come, yes?" She looked earnestly from one face to the other. "Please come!"

"It would be delightful," replied Miss Venables, "only we're expecting Harry, you see, some time this evening. I don't quite know—"

"Monsieur 'Arree?" The eyes ran over with indulgent amusement. "But bring him along too, of course! If he arrives late, he can follow. I had not realised that big, so agreeable nephew of yours was coming, but we shall rejoice to see him once more. He is always welcome. How is he these days?" Mme. de Bellesnaves inquired with an interest more polite than genuine. "He is busy making his fortune?"

"Well, he has been working hard, and needs a holiday, particularly as a rather sad thing has just happened. I wrote you about it, didn't I?"

"Ah, you mean his—how do you say it?—yes, stepmother. I remember. *Ma foi!*" She consulted with horror a minute diamond wrist-watch. "And the good Brian is waiting for me! Forgive me if I rush."

"What a pretty watch. New, isn't it?"

"Yes, but—" and here the Baroness bent forward with a gesture of mock secrecy to whisper, "not real diamonds! Don't give me away, will you?"

Wafting a kiss she sped lightly away towards the side entrance, through which her companions, following, saw her settling herself gayly into the front seat of the doctor's shabby two-seater.

"They can't afford a car now, so Dr. Gilcrest often gives them a lift," explained Miss Venables, raptly smiling. "He's lunching with them, I expect. How enchanting she looks in that smart little coat and hat! I shouldn't wonder if she made them both herself. She's extremely clever, like so many Frenchwomen."

"She must be, if she made that coat," said Sarah sincerely. "And she is simply lovely. Didn't you say she was half Italian?"

"On her mother's side, yes. The Italian blood gives her those amazingly beautiful eyes. They are marvellous, aren't they?"

Sarah was not attending. She had just caught sight of the doctor's face, bent over a refractory self-starter. It was tight-lipped, black as a thunder-cloud. He did not look up, but Sarah felt he was aware of being watched, and was displeased over the circumstances. If her reading were correct, then this provocative enchantress at his side, chattering animatedly with her hand resting on his sleeve, did mean to him more than he wished his patient to guess. A queer little stab of emotion darted through the girl's interior. She refused to analyse it, lest she should find it to be jealousy.

CHAPTER TEN

WHATEVER the emotion was, Sarah promptly forgot it on Harry's arrival. Harry was here at last, handsome, light-hearted, and so glad to see her that whatever feeling of inferiority she might have had vanished into air. In this quarter, at least, she was appreciated. Now there would be no more dullness.

It was nearly seven o'clock when the high-powered red Fiat swept up to the door and the dusty, long-limbed figure alighted. Seeing the pathetic flutter of female hearts caused by his appearance, and the pains a dozen maidens of doubtful age had gone to over water-waves and the donning of newly-pressed frocks, it seemed sheer cruelty to snatch him away again at once. However, in the brief interval before changing into dinner clothes he managed to scatter enough pleasantries to tide the disappointed ones over till the morrow and leave them in high good humour. Undoubtedly Harry had a way of managing these things.

"Naturally there's nothing outside yourself to attract him here," confided Miss Venables as Sarah hooked up her black lace gown for her. "The only youngish girl is Gladys Ames-Gower, and she's so hopelessly plain and stodgy. I saw him looking at you, my dear. I'm sure he thought how smart you were beside these others. That figured green frock is so charming on you."

"I've you to thank for that," answered Sarah, fastening snaps.

"No, it's your own nice figure. Slim, yet not thin. A regular mannequin form. I thought the Baroness, too, was full of approval."

These compliments from one who said only what she meant put Sarah in a glow of elation when, at a quarter to eight, she set off with Harry, stalwart and easy of stride, between her and his aunt, holding each of them by an arm. Miss Venables had suggested walking, because after so long a drive Harry must want to stretch his legs, and Harry did not object. The night, cool but not sharp, was sweet with the fragrance of budding shrubs. It must, thought Sarah, be very like that other April night when the two returning to the hotel had made their startling discovery; but she hoped her employer was not thinking of that. From her gay serenity she seemed to be for once wholly at peace.

The long lane which wound past the de Bellesnaves' estate lay white in the moonlight, with sparse poplars on one side and a high fence on the other. They pushed open a rickety iron gate, and there before them loomed the Casa Giallo, eerie under the shadowing eucalyptus trees, a terrace dotted with pale blue hydrangeas running the full length of the front, and more terraces falling away in diminishing orderliness to merge at last in a tangle of rank growth. The house itself, with its long row of shuttered French windows and the paint flaking from its walls, had a look of forlorn desolation. Even the bare patches of denuded trunk on the big trees grouped at the sides suggested poverty and neglect.

"And to think," whispered Miss Venables sadly, "that of three fine properties this poor ruin is all they have left. It wrings one's heart to imagine the subterfuges they must be put to in order to preserve a decent existence."

"Oh, I don't know," Harry said vaguely. "I daresay they're not in such desperate straits as you're so fond of saying. You worry your precious head too much over other people's troubles."

"They're selling their pictures," declared his aunt in the same guarded tone. "All the best have gone."

A shabby Italian man-servant admitted them to a hall so dimly lit that all Sarah could see were glimpses of bare parquet and a carved fifteenth century chest over which hung a splendid, dark painting. From a door on the right the Baron hobbled forth, his wrinkled features wreathed in welcoming smiles.

"You find us in semi-obscurity," he announced. "Our electric-plant has gone wrong, and we are reduced to candles. Come in, come in! We are delighted to have you with us again."

In the spacious salon, the groups of tall candles made one think of a field of lilies stamened with golden fire. Their charitable light hid the threadbare patches in the upholstery and curtains, showing only the exquisite shapes of the period furniture. A log fire flickered under a marble chimney-piece, the burning wood giving out an aromatic fragrance. In a dusky corner lit by one lone candle was a table laden with bottles, and over these Gilcrest was bending. Mme. de Bellesnaves was at his side, but as the guests entered she turned, let a crimson shawl slip from her shoulders to fall in a heap upon the faded Aubusson carpet, and with a rippling laugh and the alert, decisive movements characteristic of her swept forward to greet them.

The severely plain black taffeta she wore achieved a naive picturesqueness with its tight bodice moulding the almost childish contours of her body and its fringed flounces billowing to the floor. Her barbaric necklace and ear-rings of wrought silver, a heavy burden for her slightness, enhanced her delicate fragility; her inky hair, sleekly banded from a central parting clean as a moonbeam, framed in the pure of her face, and gave full value to eyes which, with the candlelight reflected in their depths, shone like pools of liquid fire.

Vivid, exotic, intensely charged with vitality, she chained and fascinated the attention. While she was in the room, Sarah thought, one would not find it easy to look at anything else.

"Ah!" The sound cooed in her throat. "Here we all are once more! It is like old times, is it not?"

The warm brilliance of her smile enveloped Sarah, somehow missing Harry, for her entire interest had centred itself on the removal of Miss Venables' sable-collared cloak, and the freeing of the stiff frizzed coiffure from the lace scarf twined round it. As with the swift, darting movements of a humming-bird her small brown hands busied themselves over their task, she prattled on, now laughing, now ironic.

"Old times! And all the old inconveniences. Again no lights, and this time no central-heating. Yes, that idiot of a Sebastiano put green wood on the furnace, so that we were forced to quench it, or be suffocated by smoke. You do not find it too cold in here, no?" She made a funny little grimace, coaxed into place the diamond brooch pulled awry in her zeal, and bestowed a final pat on her friend's shoulder. "Ah, well, ill-trained servants are perhaps better than none, though there are times when. . . . Well, Angela, what is wrong now?"

She had broken off to hurl this annoyed demand at an old Neapolitan crone, skinny and toothless, with kerchiefed head and gold ear-hoops, who from the gloom of the hallway was beckoning in dramatic fashion. As she flounced out to attend to the summons, the Baron shrugged and raised his left eyebrow whimsically.

"The old story," he remarked in a philosophical tone, "Angela has at the last moment discovered there is no Kirsch for the compote, or no paprika for the sauce. Never mind, all who frequent this house are used to makeshifts. At least, I can promise you some excellent *jambon de Parme*, for I chose it myself; and Gilcrest here, will mix us a fortifying cocktail. Draw near the fire. The evenings are still sharp."

The doctor, after shaking hands with the three, had returned to his task. Miss Venables was talking to the Baron, and Harry and Sarah, left together at one end of the hearth, were absorbed in each other when their hostess returned from her conference with the cook. Something had ruffled her, as the red spots burning in her cheeks plainly showed; but now, catching sight of Harry, who had just inquired about Sarah's wrist and had taken hold of it to examine the scar, she gave a shrill cry of compunction and broke into smiles.

"Monsieur 'Arree!" she exclaimed with light mockery just tinged with patronage. "What must you think of my bad manners? I have not spoken to you at all, you who are the complete stranger these days! *Comment ça va?* But no, I can see that you are well, and I do believe you have grown bigger than ever! I should ask, How have you been amusing yourself? Games, as usual. All you Englishmen are so keen on *le sport*, it is all you think about. I hear, though, you stopped over in Paris. An accident to your car, was it? *Alors c'est ça.*" She laughed wickedly, with a side-glance at Sarah. "So that is your story, *hein*? Well—perhaps."

All three laughed, but the Baroness did not stop for Harry's rejoinder. Swooping down upon the doctor, she linked her bare arm through his and demanded a taste of his concoction.

"Ugh!" Again she made the little grimace. "But what have you done to make it so insipid? I know, it lacks gin. Do open the other bottle, stupid! If Angela, through her imbecile forgetfulness, has spoiled the food, we have all the more need of a good drink. Here, give me the shaker." Unobtrusively Gilcrest had withdrawn his arm. Sarah noticed it, and saw, too, that the little Baron was regarding the couple with a quiet smile. Harry's blue eye telegraphed her a message to which she tried not to respond, even though it was pleasant to have him taking her into private communion with himself in this intimate way. He passed her a cocktail, clicked his glass to hers, and watched her as she drank. Her colour mounted. She knew that she was looking her best, and an occasional shrewd glance from Mme. de Bellesnaves confirmed her comforting conviction.

The meal, which was supper rather than dinner, was served in the warm glow of silver candelabra on a dark, waxed table. Delicious in every detail, it was for the most part Italian, since the Baroness remembered that Miss Venables had a fondness for Italian cooking; and there was something more she recalled. When a huge mound of spaghetti mingled with green herbs and garlic made its appearance, Miss Venables was given a little separate dish minus garlic. "But how kind of you!" exclaimed the spinster, pleased at the attention. "Really, Maddalena, you spoil me."

What a moment of all others for Sarah to think of what she had well-nigh forgotten—her potential capacity of food-taster! She was half-ashamed of the furtive, darting thought which made her look across at the innocent dish responsible for the remark, then at the gratified face of her employer. The latter reassured her. Christine Venables, knowing herself in the midst of friends, was happily serene. The Baron was filling her delicate old wine-glass with Chianti. Harry, at Sarah's side, was falling to with vigour. He had noticed nothing. The girl breathed an inaudible sigh. It was as though for one mad instant she had experienced a trick of eyesight, only to realize at once her foolish mistake.

No, it was not here, at the Casa Giallo, that one needed to be on guard; and yet as the meal proceeded Sarah became aware of obscure cross-currents in the atmosphere, influences at first wholly puzzling to define or to trace to their source.

She glanced curiously at the little wizened invalid, between whom and herself a kinship of spirit was fast growing up.

He had a brilliant mind, rare wit, and a shrugging, gentle tolerance which blunted the barb of his keenest quips. Perfect as a host, invariably mindful of his guests' requirements, he yet seemed to her more completely detached from his surroundings than any human creature she had ever known. He lived, she thought, in a realm apart, a condition particularly shown by his attitude towards his wife. Always chivalrous, he seldom looked directly at her, and if by chance their eyes met he made an instantaneous retreat behind the curtain of his pale lashes— no pointed withdrawal, but none the less effective. Of one thing Sarah felt sure: husband and wife moved, without clash, in separate orbits. A community of interests they might have, but of real contact, none.

Before long she formed a second opinion, namely, that Mme. de Bellesnaves, for all her singular beauty and charm, belonged to a sphere distinctly inferior to that of the man whose name she bore. Miss Venables did not guess this, nor was that fact remarkable, it being notably difficult to "place" individuals of a race different from one's own; but Sarah, who in her twenty-three years of nomad existence had developed a nice sense of such distinctions, never doubted her surmise was correct, even though it was nearly impossible to put her finger on any betraying item.

All this, however, was beside the point. What she wanted to discover was the origin of the peculiar unrest seething above and around her, and so, discreetly, she began to study the three people to whom she attributed it. Naturally the Baroness came first. A feast for the eye, she dominated by sheer magnetic attraction, bubbling over with gaiety, irresistibly captivating not only the repressed spinster's admiration but that of every other person as well, with one exception—Gilcrest; and yet was not his very refusal to respond a proof that he more than the rest was ensnared by her and afraid in the present company to show it?

She extended her investigation to him, and again and again saw the same thing happen. He would be speaking. Suddenly he would find his hostess' dark, provocative eyes fixed raptly on his face, drinking in his words, and instantly he would turn and address his remarks elsewhere. Once or twice he became silent, and bent an embarrassed gaze on his plate. Here, perhaps, was the clue she sought. These two were, as Miss Tomlins had broadly hinted, in love, or falling in love. The woman did not trouble to hide her feeling, the man, probably genuinely distressed over the temptation to betray his friend, was worried out of his wits lest the secret come out.

"But the Baron does know," she pondered. "Unless I'm hopelessly wrong about him, there's nothing he doesn't know, only understanding all he doesn't condemn. He's like that, I think. I suppose it's the open parade of the situation which the doctor wants to avoid, realising it would humiliate and hurt the man he's fond of. And then there's Miss Venables. I'm forgetting her. She's his patient—a rich one, too."

Ah, there was the crucial point! Miss Venables would not understand. If she were to discover a guilty liaison between her two favourites, her maiden prejudices would be stabbed to the quick. Kind though she was, she would grow bitter, alienated—and Gilcrest fully appreciated the danger. That was why, super-sensitive of injurious appearances, he had worn so black a look that morning when the Baroness, all transparent possessiveness, had tripped out to his car; that was why now he was trying so hard to seem impervious. Sarah decided she had solved the mystery; but it must be recorded that the explanation was not to her liking, nor did she fed pleased when she began to note that Harry, glancing back and forth across the table, broke into an occasional amused smile as though he too had drawn similar conclusions.

Polly, the bulldog, waddled persistently from one to another, questing tid-bits and making a nuisance of itself. Gilcrest pushed it firmly away. Miss Venables more than once had to hide her repugnance, and finally when it laid a slobbering jaw on Mme. de Bellesnaves's lap its misplaced affection met with so violent a recoil that the Baron rose, gathered the clumsy beast in his arms, and crooning softly to it carted it from the room. To Sarah the episode was somehow pathetic, and the same could be said of another incident which followed soon after.

They had returned to the salon for coffee, and Miss Venables, producing a tissue-paper parcel she had all along been guarding in her lap, unwrapped the small gifts she had brought from London—a bottle of scent for the Baroness, from a much-favoured shop in Jermyn Street, and a round, flat box of chocolates at sight of which the Baron's features lit with childish delight.

"For me?" he cried. "My own particular weakness—and you remembered it! My dear Miss Venables, I am overcome!"

It was when the chocolates had been handed round that Sarah saw the little by-play not intended for the general eye. The Baron, holding the box in his hands, gazed longingly at its contents, then up at Gilcrest with a whimsical pleading. The doctor whispered, "Well—just one, but no more," whereupon the Baron made a careful selection, and crunched his prize with deep enjoyment. As he did so the candlelight flickering on him showed up the unhealthily livid tint of his wrinkled face and it came over Sarah with absolute conviction that he was suffering from some grave internal complaint, perhaps unrealised by anyone save his medical adviser and friend. Evidently chocolate was forbidden, yet he was far too considerate to allow his guest to suspect it. Her heart warmed towards him, and again, before the evening was over, she was to feel the same sympathetic emotion, though for a different reason.

Eleven had struck. The Baron rose, and whistled to the dog, which was slumbering stertorously on the Louis Quinze canape.

"*Viens, mon ange!*" he called gently. "*Couche-toi!*"

The bull-dog cocked a bleared eye at him and lumbered obediently to the floor. Its master turned to Sarah, who was watching, and asked if she would care to assist at the coming ritual.

"You mean see you put her to bed? Yes, immensely."

"Then come with me."

Lifting a two-branched candlestick, he led the way through the hall to a red-tiled passage at the back, where stood a huge wooden cage. He let the beast out into a dark kitchen-garden to prowl and sniff amongst gooseberry bushes, and during its absence washed and refilled an earthenware drinking-vessel, afterwards plumping up a pile of cushions covered in faded red rep and shaking out an old grey army blanket. Presently the dog ambled in to dispose her ungainly bulk on the bed made ready for her. The Baron tucked her up so that only her great, ugly muzzle protruded like a snail's head from its shell. Sarah supposed the performance was over, but it had only just begun. Polly's dull eyes bulged at her master with eager expectancy. They were watching him search with slow absentmindedness through all his various pockets.

"Now, where can I have put the stuff?" muttered the Baron vexedly. "Is it possible I have none left?"

The bulldog's anxiety increased. The eyes watered painfully. At last with a cry of triumph the Baron fished up a small phial, unscrewed the cap, and let a single white tabloid trickle into his palm. He bent down, holding it out.

"Well, just one, but no more," he murmured in so exact an imitation of Gilcrest's manner that Sarah burst out laughing.

"What on earth are you giving her?" she demanded, seeing the loose jaws champ down on the coveted tabloid with intense satisfaction. "It looks like aspirin."

"It is aspirin." The faded eyes twinkled. "You find it ridiculous? Well—so it is. I pamper her, you see; but she is old, she is rheumatic, and she will not sleep comfortably unless she has her nightly dose. I, as it happens, have known what it was to wish for aspirin and not get it."

Sarah's amusement was checked. She noticed the sudden twist of pain about the little Frenchman's mouth as he straightened his bent back, and the absorbed devotion with which he stood regarding his loathsome pet compose herself for slumber. When he spoke again it was with a change of manner, to ask if Sarah liked paintings.

"I saw you looking at the Daumier in the hall. Come, I will hold the candles up to it so you can have a better view."

"So it is a Daumier! I thought so. I recognised the Don Quixote. What a lot of those he painted, and all beautiful! And during dinner I couldn't keep my eyes off the portrait opposite me. Is it an Ingres?"

"Yes, a portrait of my great-grandmother—one of the few good things left in my possession; but if it will not bore you, let us make a small tour of the others. Here, in the library, are some drawings you might care to see."

The library, with leather-bound books mounting to the ceiling, contained various treasures over which Sarah exclaimed in delight. The Baron must have divined her unspoken thought, for with a slight shrug he remarked that sooner or later they would have to go.

"Just possibly not in my time," he added, a smile like watery sunshine breaking through the gravity of his face.

It was while he was holding aloft the silver candlestick to illume a group of miniatures hung against the brown striped damask of the wall that Sarah received her first shock of the evening. In the cavern of gloom behind her a gruff voice spoke so unexpectedly that she jumped and looked round. In the doorway lurked a rough-clad man, squat, burly, with an inky, low-growing thatch of hair and cunning, almond-shaped slits of eyes set far apart in an oily dark face. She had thought they were alone, but that was not the only reason for the quick, odd beating of her heart as she took in the strange, uncouth details of the apparition thus accosting them. It was the fixity with which this brutish lout was looking not at her companion, whom he had addressed, but at herself. Half-bold, half-furtive, his glance sized her up, inquisitive, yet assured; self-contained. It reminded her unpleasantly of something similar in the near past, though at the moment she could not think what. Her skin began to prickle ominously.

"Well, Demo?" replied the Baron in French, kindly, as though to some blundering child. "If your work is done, what are you hanging about for? Go home to your wife."

There was a stubborn mumble in a thick patois incomprehensible to the girl's ears. With a tolerant shrug the Baron whispered that this was the gardener, who had been helping Angela in the kitchen, and that what he really wanted was a drink.

"I suppose I must give him one. You will excuse me? But first let me light you back to the salon."

"No, no, I can easily find my way."

As they passed the ill-smelling suppliant in the doorway Sarah was aware of shiny, crescent eyes following her with the same look of shrewd speculation; and now she knew why it was she had been so stupidly perturbed. Or was her agitation stupid? Certainly this appendage of the de Bellesnaves' household bore a striking resemblance to the swarthy traveller who had so excited Miss Venables' alarm, nor was that all. His features, his oily utterance, his mock-cringing manner as he had saluted her were definitely Oriental. Stick a fez or a turban on his head, and he could have passed for one of the itinerant vendors so inextricably associated in her employer's mind with threats of death.

CHAPTER ELEVEN

THE four guests, leaving together, took a short cut through the grounds in the direction of the beach, whence a path led direct to the harbour-end of the village. From the bottom terrace they turned to wave a last goodbye to the figures framed in wavering yellow light to watch their departure. Gay voices cried to them. For a moment the Baroness' sleek, raven head and glowing eyes were visible, her slender arm seen to link through that of her husband, whose wrinkled features, clearly fatigued, still shone with genial humour. Then the radiance blacked out, and the descending path became a pitch-black labyrinth.

Harry strode confidently ahead with his aunt clinging trustfully to his arm. Sarah and Gilcrest followed more slowly, in a silence which neither seemed able to break. Now, thought Sarah, was her opportunity to get better acquainted with this man whose stubborn diffidence continued to pique her curiosity; but how start a conversation with one who simply made no advances? That he possessed a more expansive side she had seen from his contacts with Miss Venables and still better the Baron, and she was growing steadily more annoyed that he declined to reveal it to herself. Either he had taken an unreasoning dislike to her, or some hidden influence put a ban on any freedom of speech where she was concerned. If he really were slavishly subjugated by Maddalena de Belle-snaves' fascination it might arm him against every other woman who ventured near; but was this the case? She felt a burning desire to find out.

An overhanging branch stung her face. She stopped, put up her hand to her bare head, and cried with laughing irritation, "Damn! My cursed hair's caught on a twig."

"Absalom," he remarked briefly. "Wait, I'll untangle you."

She was forced to submit while he set about the task as methodically as the dense darkness would allow. Patiently he loosened strand after strand of her curling locks. His fingers touched her forehead, and she was more than ever annoyed that she did not find this unpleasant. She was just thinking how differently many men would have behaved in a like situation and how little chance there was of his taking advantage of it when a heavy step passed them and the oily voice she recognised as the gardener's muttered an oddly impudent good-night. She wrenched free the final shred of her hair, and straining her eyes after the slouching form asked the question which had been in her mind for the past half-hour.

"That servant—he's not French, I know. What is he?"

"Greek, or supposed to be. His name's Demosthenes."

"Greek! He looks Turkish to me. Do you happen to know if Miss Venables has ever seen him?"

"Of course she has, scores of times. What's your idea? Oh—I see!"

His tone, faintly contemptuous, roused her ire.

"I don't like his manner," she said bluntly. "Oh, I know I've been inclined to agree with you about this dope-peddler business, but when this so-called Greek came into the library just now something made me think—that is I suddenly began to wonder—"

"See here, Miss MacNeil," he interrupted with ill-concealed impatience, "I do sincerely hope you're not going to introduce any new alarm into that poor woman's head. The worst possible course is to play up to these fears of hers. What we want to do is to ignore them."

"You really suppose I'd speak to her on the subject?" demanded Sarah incredulously. "Why, what do you take me for? I'm not that kind of an idiot!"

He was silent for a moment, obviously still brooding on some preconception of his own.

"The whole point is this," he explained presently. "And I give it to you because it's possible you don't understand certain difficulties of her case. It appears that each time she gets a nervous shock of any kind she has a relapse of her gastric trouble. I'm trying to cure her, you see, and I can't overestimate the importance of keeping her calm."

"I do understand, perfectly," Sarah retorted with some coldness. "I repeat, I'm not altogether a fool."

"Medicine's virtually useless," he went on, disregarding her words. "What can I do, when thanks to this damnable obsession she's lost two stone in a year? It's nerves, I tell you. If one fine day she gets a really bad attack the chances are she'll go under. I wish to God I knew. . . ." He broke off, slashing savagely at a bough of oleander which barred the path. Sarah detected in him a slight confusion. "Whatever the real source of these threats," he continued quickly, as though to cover up an admission, "your job and mine is to make as light of them as we can. You can do more than anyone else. You appreciate that, perhaps—or don't you?" She was now thoroughly angered by his brusqueness. "Certainly I appreciate all you're saying. If you'd bothered to inquire, I'd have told you that I'm doing my utmost to minimise her danger and keep her in a cheerful frame of mind. Why do you assume anything else? You know nothing whatever about me."

He was striding along, now and then stopping to hold back a branch for her to pass. His eyes narrowed now, in astonishment and through the gloom she saw a charily-apologetic smile.

"Sorry," he jerked. "I'm afraid I've offended you. I didn't mean to, you know. I confess it occurred to me that out of a mistaken idea of kindness you might have been a trifle too sympathetic. It doesn't do—and while on the subject,"—lowering his voice—"let me warn you against discussing any phase of this affair with the people at the Golf. That hotel is a seething hotbed of gossip."

Sarah laughed aloud. "As if I couldn't spot that at a glance! Why, I've spent half my life in just such hotels! I've never once mentioned anything connected with Miss Venables, nor do I intend doing so."

"Good. I'm glad you're so sensible. If the thing gets noised out, it can only do harm."

He was a tiny bit too relieved for her liking. After all, why should he so desperately object to the affair becoming known?

"At the same time," she hazarded, glancing askance at him, "what was the truth about Major Frampton? It's quite evident he was frightened over something. He had been here to dine, hadn't he? And for all we know he walked home along this very path. I confess when I saw that gardener staring hard at me I thought—but we'll pass over that. You examined the body, I'm told. I don't suppose there were any marks of violence on it, but there needn't have been if someone from behind pushed the poor man through into the shaft. How do we know that didn't happen?"

Again he said nothing for so long that her curiosity grew to uneasy proportions. When he did speak his manner had regained its former stiffness.

"I can see you've been theorising," he said. "Well, I can't stop you, but I can tell you this much: the old dodderer whose word helped to start the murder story had a cataract forming on both eyes. And Frampton, who was a decent soul, did drink rather heavily. He was my patient, so I know. It's quite on the cards he was fuddled that evening, which would account not only for getting a garbled idea of something innocent but for the accident as well."

Sarah forbore to argue, but having seen a deal of the seasoned topers the British army can produce she still had doubts about the effect of drink on a man whom she definitely classed as unimaginative.

"You may be right," she conceded. "And as I said before I don't wholly subscribe to Miss Venables' belief; but just supposing it wasn't an accident, surely one is permitted to speculate as to what's behind those letters she keeps receiving?"

"Oh, of course." He sounded ironical. "And if you're romantic by nature you may hit on something more picturesque than I can suggest."

"I fail to see anything romantic in the fact that every letter has been correctly addressed," she retorted. "That in itself is significant to me. How many people, for instance, knew that Miss Venables was staying at the Metropolitan Hotel in London? Yet a communication reached her there, posted in the district, at just about the time you left to catch your train."

She hardly knew what devil prompted her to bring in this coincidence. Having shot her bolt, she waited rather breathlessly to note the result. Apparently there was none.

"So I have heard," he answered indifferently. "But I don't know that I would make too much capital out of that occurrence. Undoubtedly Frampton's message started the ball rolling. As to the rest . . . well, if I were you I'd let the matter drop, and concentrate on the tactics we've been discussing. If we can get Miss Venables into a normal state, the whole thing may simmer down."

The oblique reply mystified her. It seemed to her that he was purposely withholding his private view, but as to what that view might be she was totally in the dark. At any rate, he abruptly closed the topic, and as they were now within sight of the sea and earshot of their companions she did not re-open it.

They skirted a sandy knoll on which an aged boat-house sheltered beneath straggling pines. Under the little structure, on the sea side, lay a dinghy side by side with a shabby motor-boat, and some thirty yards from the shore a small yacht with furled sails was anchored. At the far end of a narrow landing-stage Harry and Miss Venables were standing. The latter's lace scarf fluttered in the breeze and her front hair, usually so tidy, had been whipped from its encasing net. Sarah's own curls, after the bough episode, were a wreck. As she shook back the disordered mass from her face the vision of the Baroness' smooth, glistening coiffure rose before her, and in total absent-mindedness she uttered aloud her thought.

"She really is lovely. Quite wonderful, I think."

"Who?" Gilcrest came out of his own reverie to ask in surprise.

"Who? Oh, I was thinking of Mme. de Bellesnaves. I didn't realise I hadn't mentioned her name. She's one of the most beautiful women I've ever seen."

"Oh!" He drew in his breath and paused imperceptibly. "Bimi . . . yes,"—with slow detachment—"I suppose she is."

His response grated on her. She felt he was adopting this pose on purpose to hide from her his real enthusiasm, again crediting her with little perspicacity.

"There can't be much question about it, can there?" She said this dryly, and then, with a puzzled look at him, inquired, "But what was the name you called her? Did you say Bimi?"

"Her nickname. I imagined you knew it." He paused again, presently adding, "Bertrand's Bimi, you know. A story by Kipling."

Sarah stared. "I know the story you mean, but it's a horrid idea! Bertram's Bimi was an ape, surely? An ape that got jealous of a man's wife and—"

"Exactly. One day you'll see her do a very clever imitation of a monkey. It's a stunt of hers. Then you'll understand better how she got the name."

Sarah was already beginning to understand. Yes, it was that quaint grimace, in a flash transforming the Madonna-like beauty into something infantine and elfish—that and the restless fingering of things, quick hands seldom still—monkeying hands. . . .

"Yes, I see, but all the same I don't like it, nor should I think she would. Why, I couldn't sleep after I read that detestable tale! I hate to think of it even now."

"I can see you've a sensitive imagination. Don't let it run away with you—for various reasons."

"You needn't worry," she retorted under her breath. "I shan't."

Treading cautiously, Miss Venables returned in the shelter of her nephew's arm.

"Oh, there you are! We wondered what had become of you. Now, doctor, you and I will stroll along together and let these young people do the racing. They can wait for us at your house."

Harry took Sarah's arm and soon the other couple were left far behind. Sarah fancied him a little bored during the evening, but now he was in high feather, singing, whistling, and infecting her with his own high spirits. Like two children they sped along the rough beach and into the path beside the high fence of the Casa Giallo estate, chattering nonsense and laughing at every trifle.

"I say," Harry burst out suddenly, "I'm running up to Monte one of these days to try out a new system I've learned. Wish I could take you with me, but I suppose there's no chance. Chrissie hates Monte like poison, so she won't go. In fact, she's down on gambling generally, bless her! Ten bob on the Irish Sweep's her limit. Ever see her play bridge?

You've something to live for! I'm forever ragging her about her game. Not that she minds. If you ask me, the more I rag her the better she likes it."

"You're right there. The moment you arrived to-night she became a different woman. She seems years younger."

"She can do with bucking up," he agreed easily. "Someone's got to counteract all those dead-alives at the hotel and—but this is strictly between ourselves—that blighter back there. She's nuts on him, of course, but I can't think he's altogether good for her, a fellow that's always fidgetting about people's innards. Morbid, I call it."

"Oh, I don't think Dr. Gilcrest's at all morbid! Besides, it's his job to look after people's innards."

"Well, in his case it seems to've made him too damned self-important to unbend. How'd you get on with him, by the way?" He did not stop for her answer, but broke into a rapturous chuckle. "Bimi—Mme. de Bellesnaves, that is—she's got his combination. She takes him off in the most priceless burlesque you ever saw—Oxford manner, touch-me-not superiority, all the rest of it. Nice jolt it'd give him, hopelessly gone on her as he is—my hat!"

"You mean last year she did the take-off," suggested Sarah, shrewdly thinking that a year could change many things, and that Harry had not yet noticed what was too plain to her observation. "But it must have been last year, because—"

"What's that?" He sounded absent, still enjoying his recollection. "Oh, certainly! Not seen her since. A year back he was just beginning to fall for her. Now anyone can see it—except Chrissie, who's notoriously blind to such things."

Chucking away his cigarette he ran on casually, "Thundering good bridge-players, the de Bellesnaves. That's how I know 'em, though Chrissie and the Baroness are hand in glove with each other. Brought together by Gilcrest, I believe. Good-hearted little thing, Bimi. Look how she takes care of that hypochondriac of a husband! Even to humouring his filthy brute of a dog, which by rights ought to be chloroformed. Will be, too, one fine day, if it goes on poking its slobbering jaw round Gilcrest's place. I warned her in a joking way this evening. My word, the look I got!"

They had reached the doctor's modest dwelling, at the dingy front of which Harry cast a contemptuous glance.

"Tell me," he remarked, "that a bloke with a thriving medical practice can't run to a coat of paint for his door, or buy himself a new suit of clothes. Take it from me, all this talk about his refusing hospitality because he can't return it is sheer rot. Tight-fisted, that's what it is. Wonder if he's Scotch?"

Sarah's own impecunious state was still too raw in her memory for her to allow this criticism to pass unchallenged.

"We don't know what his finances are like," she protested. "Maybe he doesn't earn very much."

"Well, anyhow I can see he's got another champion," said Harry, laughing at her warmth. "Don't know how he does it, but he's got every woman in the place eating out of his hand. Have a gasper?"

She accepted a cigarette from the thin gold case, and they sat down upon the doorstep to wait. Overhead a mimosa, pale in the moonlight, shook out its downy, fragrant plumes. Cool and salt the breeze from the harbour blew in upon them, and in the night-hush the strains of a tango, played by the little Casino orchestra, fell upon their ears with a seductive sound. Sarah leant back, sensuously contented, watching the thin trail of smoke float from her lips into the air. After a moment she felt Harry looking at her. His gaze began thoughtfully with her slim, silk-clad ankles outstretched in front, ran slowly along her frock and came to rest on her face. Something pleasantly akin to a thrill awoke at his glance.

"Well," she prompted with a smile.

"Sarah," he said hesitatingly. "You don't mind me calling you that, do you? I was just thinking how glad I am you're here."

"So am I," she answered, and wondered, though not too eagerly, what was coming next.

With a gesture so affectionately harmless that she could not repulse it he laid his big, warm hand on her arm and let it slide along till it rested on her fingers.

"Even if you do happen to be pretty closely tied over this job of yours," he went on boyishly. "I don't see any reason why you and I can't—"

He broke off, for at this instant their two companions appeared at the gate. There was no undue haste in his manner when he removed his hand from hers, and she noticed that Gilcrest let his glance travel swiftly from one to the other of them, darkening as it did so. How absurd of him! Did he really suppose she and Harry were beginning a flirtation? A bit premature—and surely no business of his to object, if such were the case. . . .

Miss Venables drew Harry into the back garden to look at a view of the sea she had recently discovered, and thus for the second time that evening Sarah was left alone with the man who in some indefinable way had stirred her to mingled liking and antagonism. Again she saw that curious awkwardness descend upon him, and yet she knew that he was meditating another attempt to guide her, by his will.

"To return to what we were saying," he remarked in an undertone, staring down at the broken flags underfoot. "Take my advice about steering clear of those hotel-gossips. You won't accomplish anything by raking up the Frampton affair. I can promise you that."

"That seems to worry you," she returned lightly. "Well, I shan't so much as mention it just at present. Not, in fact, till Miss Tomlins gets back. She's the woman I've my eye on—and she's gone away."

"Miss Tomlins!" he muttered shortly and with evident annoyance. "So you're planning to tackle the most inveterate scandal-monger of the lot!"

"Why not?"—mischievously. "I'm told she's better informed than anyone else—and she's shown herself ready to discuss that particular business with me. I'm rather looking forward to it."

"She has a dangerous tongue. She may mean no harm, but her sole interest in life is manufacturing sensations. If I were you, I'd avoid her like the plague."

"But after all," argued Sarah, piqued by his opposition, "why should it matter to you what she says?"

"Me!" he retorted with scorn. "It's not anything to do with me. I'm merely warning you that if you begin talking to her you may easily give away more than you intend about this other affair. She's on the *qui vive* to find out what you can tell her about Miss Venables. Don't you realise that?"

"Well, she won't get any change out of me. Oh, I know you despise me for wanting to nose this thing out; but really, if there's any possibility of stopping these letters, I mean to do it. You can't blame me for wanting to, can you?" He gave her a curious, almost angry glance, shrugged, and turned from her. A pity! She did so want him to like her; now, by her obstinacy, war between them was declared.

CHAPTER TWELVE

NOT once had Sarah questioned her own safety. Never had it occurred to her that in her position of watch-dog she was likely to be molested; and yet within the week she met with an experience so terrifying as to lay her open to the most serious conjectures. That her life for a few ghastly seconds should hang by a thread might have been the result of accident. Devoutly she hoped it was, but at moments she saw in it a calculated attempt to remove her vigilance in a manner horribly cruel. Neither the one thing nor the other could she prove. All she could do was to keep her secret doubts to herself, and appear to accept the theory propounded by others.

She had passed tranquil days in the company of the two Venables, taking long drives, watching them play golf, or dawdling about the boule-table at the Casino. It had been pleasantly amusing to note the significant glances which followed Harry and herself, and not disappointing to know that the devotion causing invidious comment in the hotel was of a lighter nature than the onlookers imagined. Why she had not even expected to fall in love with Harry puzzled herself. Perhaps, for all his physical charm and buoyant resourcefulness, he had shown less mental depth than her personal requirements demanded; but at any rate, realizing her immunity, she did not quarrel with it. Intuitively she knew that with slight effort on her part she could have started a mild flirtation with Harry. That she would have had to do so under his aunt's eye may have deterred her, or just possibly another factor, not openly faced, was at work. Brian Gilcrest, seldom seen, still unapproachable, had begun to take an important place in her thoughts—slightly too important for her peace of mind, for what, she asked herself impatiently, was this elusive man to her?

But for the one Friday dance he had consented to attend she would not have had to consider him in this connection at all. However, he had danced with her three times—surprisingly well, as it happened—and the memory of some potency neutralising—or was anaesthetising the better word for it?—the antagonism between his will and hers lingered in her breast, a source of bitter-sweet irritation. Though they had talked but little, though he had never seemed to notice how nice she was looking in her prettiest evening frock, she was still conscious of the spell exerted over her—a spell too strong at the time to allow her complete enjoyment. Even though she had wanted the music to go on playing and never stop, with every step she had been forced to repeat to herself, "None of this counts. It's that woman he's infatuated with—and she with him."

It was the Sunday following the dance. Gilcrest and their own party were gathered for tea in the long *serre* which jutted out from the left wing of the Casa Giallo and, nearly denuded of plants, was used for meals when the sun was too hot or the wind on the terrace too boisterous for comfort. It was a pleasant retreat, filled with shabby deck-chairs, and backed by fig-trees the coarse green leaves of which thrust themselves in through the open windows and screened the occupants from the after-noon glare. Tea finished, the hostess, a charming figure in her white linen frock and gypsy-like scarf, had led Miss Venables away to inspect a new rose-arbour in the lower reaches of the garden. The Baron and Gilcrest had retired into the house, and Harry and Sarah were left alone.

"Whew! It's warm," declared Harry with a lazy stretch. "Four sets of tennis on a day like this doesn't leave me wanting to go looking at crimson ramblers. I'm going to help myself to a whiskey and soda. Shall I fetch you one too?"

"No, thanks—but you can give me a cigarette."

He did so, tendering her his Dunhill for a light, and sauntered through the inner door in quest of his drink. When he turned the bulldog ambled with him and straightway began nosing clumsily about Sarah's ankles.

"What are you after, Polly? A bone? Oh, I see, your drinking vessel's under my chair. Good thing I didn't upset it."

The beast lapped noisily, snuffled, and made for Harry, who propelled it into the house with a good-natured slap.

"Can't stick that foul-smelling brute round here, can you?" The young man yawned, stretched his long legs luxuriously on a battered settee, and let his gaze rest on his companion with sleepy appreciation. "That's a very posh get-up you're wearing," he commented. "Have I seen it before?"

"Do you really like it?" Sarah glanced down at the pleated ruffles of diaphanous stuff dangling from her wrists and rippling on the red-tiled floor at her feet. "I bought it yesterday, from that little shop opposite the Casino. The devil tempted me and I fell."

"Good work! Funny thing, but your eyes change colour, don't they? They've been green before, but now they're violet, like your dress. Every blasted rag you put on suits you, though. I was saying so just now to the Baroness, and she agreed with me."

"No—did she? How sweet of her!"

Sarah felt gratified at the compliment coming as it did from one who had a real genius for clothes; and she thought, too, that the Baroness was a charmingly tactful hostess not to insist on dragging her guests about when they preferred to remain in peace. A moment ago she had smiled a little shrewdly at the two she had left behind. Her assumption might be mistaken, but the feeling prompting it was genuinely kind. Yes, she was a delightful little thing—gay, volatile, but never anything but considerate. If she could not wholly conceal her passion for Gilcrest, more apparent than ever this afternoon, why, one must not blame her for that. At least Miss Venables continued serenely unaware of anything amiss. . . .

"Harry, my dear!" It was Miss Venables' voice, calling in the distance. "Do come, there's a good boy, and help us fasten up a climber that's come loose. It wants someone tall."

"Oh, hell!" Harry hoisted himself with a wry face to obey the summons. "Just as I was settling down comfortably. You coming?"

"No, I'm feeling comatose. I believe I could go to sleep."

As she spoke, she reached out to extinguish her cigarette in the dregs of her teacup. It was true, the warmth had made her deliciously drowsy, the sticky fig-leaves brushing her cheek gave forth a sweetish odour almost narcotic, while the complete solitude coupled with the knowledge that her charge was in good hands soothed her senses to a dreamy contentment. Nothing to worry about—in spite of all forebodings, everything going well. With this thought in her mind she relaxed at full length in her reclining deck-chair, and to the accompaniment of gently rustling foliage and the distant hum of bees drifted into a semi-doze.

Suddenly she jumped and sat up, clutching her forearm. Her first idea was that one of the bees had roamed in the open window and stung her. She saw nothing to account for the hot, sharp stab which had jarred her to consciousness, but as she stared about she became aware of an intense glowing heat mounting from beneath. Wide awake she sprang to her feet, and looking down found to her horror that pale orange flames were licking at her filmy skirts and attacking the frills on her sleeves. Good Heavens, she was on fire. Her entire frock was a sheet of leaping flame!

With misguided instinct she rushed for the door, the movement fanning the blaze till she saw herself a human torch. Here, this would not do! Had she not always been told that in a case of this kind she must lie down, roll up in a rug or a blanket? There was no rug in sight, only Harry's flannel blazer in a heap on the floor. She clutched it about her frantically, finding it of little use. Beating at the flames in futile desperation she uttered one piercing scream. . . .

"Sarah! My God, what's up?"

Across the dry lawn Harry came sprinting in great strides. He panted into the greenhouse and with lightning speed enveloped her in his arms, crushing, swearing, stifling the fire which threatened to demolish her. Before she could take in the marvel of her rescue, she was shivering and smarting in the ruin of her new frock, blackened remnants of chiffon smoking on the tiles, and in the corner behind her a canvas chair blazing harmlessly to extinction.

Harry turned on her a face as dismayed as her own.

"I say, are you much burned? Let's see. My word, but that was a close shave!"

She shook her head, wanting to tell him that thanks to him she had been saved from serious injury, but for the moment utterly voiceless. Dully she saw great blisters beginning to form along her arms. Her legs, too, stung furiously. All she had worn was torn away to the knees, her stockings a wreck.

"I can't imagine what happened," she managed to articulate. "It's most mysterious. . . ."

"I'd better get you a drink."

He did not immediately move. His arm still lay about her shoulders, and as she looked up at him she caught the quickening of his breath and saw his blue eyes contract with an expression not hard to interpret. In another moment he would have kissed her. She knew it, and at the same time realised she would have been powerless to resist. Even in her dazed state her pulses automatically throbbed.

Too late. Here, running towards them, were the Baroness and Miss Venables, while through the other door appeared the Baron and Gilcrest closely followed by the two servants. Everyone, it seemed, had heard the scream. In a trice Sarah was surrounded by clamorous sympathy, tinged with horror. "Scissors, quick! These sleeves must be cut away."

The doctor muttered this, angrily, so she thought, and issuing swift orders for oil and gauze at once set about ministering to her burns. Miss Venables, ashen-faced, assisted him, while the Baroness, kneeling at her side, moaned brokenly in Italian. The Baron hobbled away to fetch what was needed, and in ten minutes Sarah's arms and her left leg were encased in bandages. Most fortunately the blisters, though painful, would not leave scars, so she was assured; but now arose the question, what had started the fire? Had she set herself alight from a cigarette or an unextinguished match? It was the only possible theory to account for the accident, and Angela, poking amidst the debris in the corner, swooped triumphantly upon a fragment of charred stub.

"*Ecco! Mesdames, messieurs, le voici!*"

"Of course, that did it," Harry declared. "You were smoking. Don't you remember?"

Sarah knit her brow, thought a moment, and pointed to the sodden remains of the other stub reposing in the teacup.

"I—I'm positive that was my last cigarette," she faltered huskily. "And I didn't use a match, but Harry's lighter." No one argued with her, but from the nods and soothing replies she saw her story was discredited.

She had forgotten, that was all. The Baron, solicitous and perturbed, went on examining the sun-baked tiles, Gilcrest, glancing briefly at the damaged chair put an end to the discussion by ordering the victim home and to bed.

"I'd better dress those places tomorrow," he said tersely. "Meanwhile, she's had a bad shock. Venables has his car, I suppose?"

The Baroness, with the utmost kindliness, begged her to stay the night. Her husband seconded the invitation, and Miss Venables herself urged Sarah to accept, but the girl firmly refused, laughing at the fuss being made.

"I'm not an invalid," she protested. "These blisters are nothing."

"Nothing!" Miss Venables clasped her thin hands together, still upset by the thought of what might have been. "Half a minute more, and you would have been burned to death. No one's fault, to be sure, but all the same. . . ."

No one's fault? While a cloak belonging to the Baroness was tenderly folded round her, Sarah stared once more at the spot where calamity had befallen her. Without fully realising it she was registering details to think over in private; but as she measured the inches between the burnt chair and the open window she descried just beyond the clustering fig-trees, not ten feet away, a poised figure which caused her a queer feeling of renewed panic. It was the Greek gardener in a listening attitude, curious and watchful. Through the interlaced greenery she saw his glistening black eyes fixed on her face with a look which to her excited imagination was both lowering and malevolent. Catching her glance he moved away.

It was possible the fellow had that moment come up, but could she be sure this was so? She dared not make known her suspicion, which returned that night when, unable to rest comfortably, she fell to making a careful survey of her impressions.

"It was my last cigarette I put out in the cup," she reflected with conviction. "And there was no one but me in the greenhouse for quite a quarter of an hour afterwards. Fire doesn't start itself."

It came over her overpoweringly that while she dozed someone from outside had crept stealthily to the window and had thrown down a lighted match on the folds of her dress. Only by the luckiest chance had Harry reached her in time. If he had not been there to fight the flames . . . she shuddered, remembering that it required but one-fifth of the body to be burned in order to cause death. Even if she had survived, she would have been badly injured, hopelessly disfigured. Certainly she would have had to give up her work. Perhaps that was the idea. . . .

"But this is madness!" She made a determined effort to pull up the fancies racing helter-skelter through her brain. "I should never dream of such a thing if I hadn't got obsessed with this persecution notion. Why should anyone take the trouble to get me out of the way? I'm not important enough."

Mechanically she continued to tabulate her knowledge. The two women had been a hundred yards away at the rose-arbour. The men, but for Harry, were indoors—or so she supposed. In any case, it was unthinkable to attribute such a villainous act to either of them; yet try as she would she could not dismiss the belief that no random shot had been answerable for the mischief. The fig-trees would have intercepted any object cast from a distance. The match—if it was a match—must have been deliberately deposited, at close range.

"I wish," she mused, "I could find out more about that brute of a gardener. If he really is connected with those dope-peddlers everything would be explained. As it is, I can be sure of only this: there was a clear space all round me when I dropped off. Nothing under my chair but bare tiles. Nothing, that is except Polly's drinking vessel, with water in it." It was water, for the dog had drunk thirstily, otherwise she would have been tempted to believe the dish had contained some inflammable liquid. But— water! Why did the word strike a disagreeable chord? Of course—that sentence in the last letter to her employer. *Keep away from water. . . .*

Well, here anyhow was an absurdity to cause laughter. She did laugh, becoming so hysterical indeed that she deliberately switched her thoughts on to the other, minor crisis which for an instant had stared her in the face. If Harry had kissed her, would she have been glad or sorry?

"I'd have liked it. I can't deny that; but on the whole what a good thing he didn't! I expect he's realising that too. Harry's sweet, but I don't care deeply for him, and I never shall. All the same, I'll have to look sharp it doesn't happen again—chiefly on Miss Venables' account. She's such a dear, and she's been so wonderful to me, I wouldn't distress her for the world. If she once thought I had designs on this darling boy of hers it might create a rift between us."

As for the fire, she resolved to keep her haunting conviction strictly to herself and let her friends go on thinking it an accident due to her own carelessness. Perhaps it was accident. She would simply never know; and if for a day or so the idea of her personal danger preyed a little on her mind all thought of this was routed by the event, totally unforeseen, which almost at once was to affect her profoundly.

CHAPTER THIRTEEN

ON THE tiny deck of the de Bellesnaves' sailing-yacht, Sarah, her arms still bandaged but no longer painful, basked in sunshine. Silhouetted against deep blue sky Harry, in white flannels, and open-necked shirt, steered the small craft over the glinting waves, while in the lee of the mainsail the Baroness lay curled on a heap of striped cushions. Miss Venables, safe in the company of the Bulstrodes, was playing a round of golf. It was she who had insisted that Sarah accept the invitation, thinking a good blow would do her companion good.

The Baroness seemed asleep, but faint furrows round the corners of her scarlet mouth bore evidence of her recent displeasure. Whether she had been put out by the doctor's firm refusal to join the party or by the discovery of Demosthenes hanging about Berthe, Gilcrest's slovenly *bonne à tout faire*, Sarah did not know; but at any rate half an hour before she had flown into a hot Italian fury very funny to witness, stamping her sandal-shod foot, and calling the delinquent gardener a string of abusive names. Demo, it appeared, was a notorious Don Juan, forever neglecting work to dance attendance on the village sirens, and here the brute was, at ten o'clock, loitering in the doctor's kitchen, when he ought to have been cleaning the yacht and unfurling the sails. He was a *sale bête*, a tom-cat, and not only the Baron but his wife as well should hear of his goings-on.

By daylight Demosthenes looked common-place enough in his filthy blue blouse and baggy corduroy trousers. Sarah was ready to shrug with scorn over her recent suspicions when, coming close to the car and smirking familiarly into their faces he delivered himself of a question in halting English which by its wording sent a cold shiver along her nerves.

"Old lady not come?" He wet his lips and stared hard at Sarah's swathed arms. "Lady wait at beach?"

"No!" Intent on reddening her lips with the aid of a vanity mirror Mme. de Bellesnaves snapped at him over her shoulder. "Get along to the boat. And we shan't want you to sail us, either, only row us out in the dinghy."

Lady! That was how Miss Venables was addressed in the letters. The coincidence caused Sarah to dart a side-glance at Harry, who, however, seemed unimpressed by anything peculiar. The Greek was interested in them, though, for his covert gaze followed them till the car vanished from sight, and later Sarah could not help noticing the unconscionable time he took fiddling about what to her inexperienced eye looked a most unseaworthy shell of a boat. She could have sworn he was disappointed when told Miss Venables was not coming. For a second the sloe-black eyes had glowered with smouldering annoyance, and he had shown obvious reluctance, when the anchor was hauled aboard, to lower himself back into the dinghy.

"He's a lazy, drunken beast," the Baroness fumed. "I'd send him packing tomorrow, but Henri is too soft-hearted."

In spite of this manifest loathing Sarah still fancied her hostess' ill-temper had another cause, and that now, as she lay slim and childish in her white pique frock and coquettish scarlet sandals it was of the adamant Gilcrest she was thinking. Sarah likewise regretted his absence, though her brief glimpse of him just now had shown her a man so harassed with work that she had felt a moment's elation to note how little the Baroness' pleadings seemed to move him. She began to hope that after all the attraction was more one-sided than she had supposed, her spirits rising accordingly.

A light yawn, a stir, and pungent fragrance reached her nostrils as her companion raised herself on her elbow to survey the scene with dreamily-glowing eyes. First she gazed speculatively at Harry, who, his chestnut curls ruffled by the breeze and a pipe-stem bitten between his lips, was staring absently out to sea; then, wriggling closer to Sarah and playing aimlessly with the buttons on the latter's green cardigan she put a pensive query.

"Do you happen to know if dear Chreessie still clings to her belief about the poor major's death last spring? She has spoken to you of it, I feel sure, has she not? I have not heard her mention it again, so I have been wondering if at last she has put the thing down to—well, shall we call it indisposition?"

Sarah looked at Harry. As he gave no sign of interest, she made a discreet rejoinder.

"I think she continues to be a little mystified over certain features, but she hasn't said much. I've been wondering about it, too. That evening, before he left your house, did he give you the impression of being upset over anything?"

"I did not notice it." The Baroness shook her head slowly. "Nor did Henri. And you, 'Arree? Did you think the Major was worried?"

"Not he." Harry turned a moment in their direction and blew a cloud of smoke into the clear air. "He was winning, wasn't he? Which always put him in a good humour. It was at the end of the second rubber his headache came on, if I remember rightly. He had a bottle of aspirin in his pocket and took two with a stiff whiskey and soda, but it did no good, and presently he gave up."

"What did he have to drink before the whiskey and soda?" asked Sarah casually.

"Ah!" Mme. de Bellesnaves monosyllable was significant.

"Several cocktails and Bordeaux all through dinner, with a liqueur to follow. The point is, what did he take before he came to us? Because I had an idea he was a little—how shall I say?—exalted when he arrived."

"Old Frampton?" Harry smiled reminiscently. "Oh, I can tell you that part of it. When he came in from golf he always took a couple of stiff ones. That was his rule; and that night I picked him up in the bar getting outside a strong gin-and-bitters." He hesitated, apologetically. "I've had to keep mum on the subject, you know, but—well, you saw for yourself, didn't you? He was unsteady on his pins when he insisted on footing it back to the hotel. That's why I called out to him to wait and let me give him a lift."

And even after this the double brandy at the café! Sarah had been picturing the Major in the gloom of his homeward walk coming suddenly on a pair of whispering conspirators—Demosthenes and a confederate?— and catching just enough of a plot against Miss Venables and himself to send him terror-stricken to the safety of the bar before hurrying on with his dire news. Now her theory was shaken. With such an assort- ment of drink aboard the man must have been befuddled to the point of distorting whatever he saw. . . .

"So simple-minded, so amiable he was!" the Baroness mused aloud. "Henri and I were thankful that at the inquest—a horrid affair!—we were not pressed to make known his little weakness, and that the truth, since it had to come out, came from other witnesses. Poor Chreessie suffered abominably. She is too loyal to listen to one word against her friend. I have been thinking, though, that by now she may be feeling more toler- ant about the verdict of accidental death. At least, one may assume she is—*n'est-ce pas?*—since nothing has happened to bear out the Major's message to her."

The last statement sounded so much like an inquiry that Sarah realised the Baroness was eager to have it confirmed or denied. Fortun- ately at this juncture Harry shouted, "Heads!" and when the boom had swung over and the two women had re-established themselves he created another diversion by diving into the small, stuffy cabin to bring forth gin, vermouth and a basket of peaches. Sarah wondered if his manoeuvres were intentional. If so, he was more adroit than she would have expected of him. Managing the tiller with one hand he skilfully restoked his pipe with the other, meanwhile begging the Baroness to give them one of her famous imitations.

"Bertram's Bimi's the stuff. Show Sarah how you got your name. Remember Chrissie's face the first time she saw you turn yourself into a monkey?" He chuckled delightedly. "Go on, let's have the whole bag of tricks. I don't know who in hell Bertram was or Bimi either for that matter, but it always throws me into fits."

The Baroness hung back, protesting. Never had Sarah seen the exquisite face more Madonna-like, though she had a faint suspicion the look of exaggerated purity was assumed by way of jest. Then, like a flash, the transformation came and took away her breath. Gone was every vestige of beauty, in its place the lineaments of a gibbering ape, bestial, perverse. The contracted eyes became soulless and cunning. The gestures, the contortions, the senseless chatter, all incredibly resembling those of the beast portrayed, filled her with fascinated repulsion. She gasped and laughed, but to her the thing was not funny. For the moment she had the curious feeling that two beings dwelt in the woman's body, one of them a changeling like a *poltergeist* always ready to leap forth and wreak mischief. Even the red-tipped nails seemed to her an animal's claws dripping with blood. To the accompaniment of a shrill shriek they lunged at her face so that she shrank back with an uncontrollable shudder of disgust. . . .

Harry's rapturous shout broke the spell. Instantly the actress was herself again, and shrugging in mock disdain demanded a cigarette.

"*Les enfants s'amusent,*" she murmured, leaning forward for a light. "There! Are you satisfied? Then leave me in peace. I have a book to read which Brian has lent me—and Sarah, if I'm not mistaken—" her eyes lit with a mischievous smile—"must recover from a shock."

Although Sarah knew she was being teased, she later admitted to Harry that the sight of the vivid caricature had for a second been disconcerting.

"Perhaps it was too life-like. Anyhow, I don't want to see her do it again. It was a sort of nightmare."

Harry laughed. "You're imaginative, aren't you? But you're level-headed, too. I noticed how cagey you were when she got on the subject of Chrissie. Good girl!" He patted her bandaged hand.

"I remembered she wasn't supposed to know what has been happening. But, Harry," Sarah continued earnestly, "you and I have never really discussed those letters. Have you any theory about them?"

He shook his head, but she fancied his sunburned face turned a ruddier hue. Seeing him reluctant to commit himself she resumed: "Has it ever occurred to you that someone in this town bears your aunt a grudge and is taking advantage of what came out during the inquest to lead her off on a false scent? It might be a blind, you see, to protect the writer in case another accident took place and there was an inquiry."

"There won't be another accident," he answered confidently. "And I should wonder if the threats had come to an end, too. Somehow I feel the whole bally thing has petered out—though I can't give any reason except that it's nearly two months now since the last scare."

It was less than four weeks since the March letter arrived, but on the point of setting him right Sarah recalled that Miss Venables had not informed him of that particular letter lest he oppose her journey south. He still was in ignorance, herself repeatedly enjoined not to enlighten him, therefore she said no more, but the slight evasiveness of his manner convinced her he did hold an opinion, only that it was one he was unwilling to voice. In a curious way he made her feel the anonymous letters were a delicate subject, and this, oddly enough, was much the same impression the doctor had given her during their memorable passage at arms. The attitude of the two men was strikingly similar, though she knew they did not exactly like each other and had probably never compared notes. Both discounted the Major's warning, both made light of the danger-element, and neither wanted to delve into the origin of the threats. Were they aware of some hidden factor unguessed by herself?

Miss Venables met them in the lounge with the news that Beryl Tomlins had returned from Nice only to take to her bed.

"Isn't it a shame? Too much rich food, and by rights she ought to diet very carefully. I sent her up some flowers, and I hear from Madge Whittaker that she's going to keep to orange-juice and water for a day or so till she pulls round."

Thus it was that the heart-to-heart talk with the librarian was again postponed; but two days later it materialised, most unexpectedly. Sarah was left on her own, Harry having driven his aunt to their friends in St. Raphael, and since it was a Wednesday when the doctor's errand-boy took a half-holiday she volunteered to call for the prescription Miss Venables was in the habit of taking. Arrived at the side door opening into the dispensary she heard two feminine voices raised in argument. The soft, stubborn one belonged to Dr. Gilcrest's dispenser, Marjory Barrows; the heartier, rougher tones she recognized as Miss Tomlins' own. From the little she caught she could guess what was happening. The returned wanderer was doing her utmost to retail an item of choice gossip which Miss Barrows, a conscientious, reticent soul, was bent on discouraging.

"But you ought to know!" urged Miss Tomlins impressively. "When I tell you the man I met gave me a minute description and it tallied perfectly—"

"I'm not interested," interrupted the other, flippant but implacable. "What I do want to know is, if you've been seedy, why haven't you sent for him?"

"Oh, that! My good girl, why ask? I know what to do on these occasions, in consideration of which do you suppose I'm going to bother an over-worked man each time I get a pain in my tummy, especially when he simply won't hand in any bill?"

"He'll be cross when he hears."

"Tut tut! And who's to tell him if you don't? I'm well again now, or nearly so—but this other matter's important. You see, it was in—"

Sarah knocked a second time and walked in. Miss Tomlins checked her disclosures and her plump, sallow face, dark under the eyes from recent illness, broke into a jovial smile, while the dispenser's eager welcome showed her relief over not being forced to hear more.

"Oh, come in, Miss MacNeil! How nice to see you! Did you come for Miss Venables' capsules? They're ready, but do sit down and chat for a bit."

Miss Barrows was a slender, immaculate young woman with a nervous smile, a fine-grained skin which flushed easily, and clear brown eyes as devoted as a spaniel's. She beamed on Sarah, thrusting her slim, capable hands into the pockets of her snowy overall, and with an apprehensive glance at her other visitor rushed headlong into conversation. There was no need for alarm on her part. Beryl Tomlins bore the spoiling of her story with the utmost cheerfulness, inquired in detail about Sarah's accident—she already knew the main facts—and after a shrewd, doubting glance to make sure the victim was not withholding some vital matter, veered off to the subject of the doctor's skill.

"I hear he's on a baby case since noon," she remarked. "French couple, did you say?"

"Oh, we've a lot of French patients now," declared Marjory with pride. "And a surprising number of them are having babies."

"Don't notice her having any," said Miss Tomlins with a significant grunt. "Not in her line, is it?"

The dispenser glanced again at Sarah, seemed reassured, and smiled with toleration.

"The Baroness, you mean? Oh, but she oughtn't to, do you think, with that poor wreck of a husband? It wouldn't be right."

"Wouldn't be possible, anyhow. Don't believe poor old Henry could manage it, not even with the help of—but no, I mustn't be naughty."

Marjory leant forward with gloating expectancy.

"Oh, do go on, Miss Tomlins. What were you going to say?"

"Well, if you will have it, I was going to say, not even with the doctor's help. There! Are you horrified?"

Miss Barrows, painfully scarlet, laughed so convulsively that a vein stood out on her delicate temple.

"Oh, Miss Tomlins, how wicked of you. What will Miss MacNeil think?"

"Of me? My reputation's sound enough. Too sound, worse luck."

Having got her mirth under control the dispenser turned mildly defiant.

"His is, too," she declared earnestly. "I tell you there's nothing at all in this talk that seems to be going round. I honestly think it annoys him to have her popping in at all hours the way she does, coaxing him to go sailing and so on, only he daren't offend her, don't you see that, when her husband's his best friend? There's no harm in her, either—she just hasn't enough to do, and she wants amusement."

"So you say—but you'd stick up for Jezebel."

"No, really, she's sweet in her way." It was plain that Marjory Barrows was endeavoring to be impartial. "She's been in three times hoping to catch him to try on the pullover she's knitting for his birthday. She was here only a moment ago, but of course he was out."

"Pullover!" Miss Tomlins snorted like an angry bull. "So she's making him one too, is she? Well, that settles it. Mine goes to my sister's boy in Cheltenham. Pity—such a nice grey-blue. Chose it especially to match his eyes." She fulminated darkly for a moment, muttering under her breath, "Beauty and the Beast—that's my name for 'em. Beauty and the Beast . . ."

"Who's the beast?" demanded Marjory, on the defence. "Not the Baron, certainly, and as for my doctor—"

Miss Tomlins' little muddy eyes twinkled sardonically. "Maybe I meant the bulldog," she said. "You'll not deny it's a beast?"

"Oh, Polly! She is a horrid pest and no mistake, always tracking in mud on my clean floors and smelling to Heaven. I daren't say a word, though. She's the Baron's dear delight, and that ends it."

"You've a cupboard full of good stuff that would end it," remarked Beryl with a sly glance at the rows of bottles behind glass on the wall alongside. "Ever tempted to drop a little strychnine in its food? I would, if I had the run of this place."

"You will have your joke," replied the dispenser calmly. "Oh, must you go? Then here's your little lot of capsules—sorry not to have sent them round, but our fresh supplies were late in arriving, and I worked till eleven last night getting my prescriptions cleared up. Yours, too, Miss MacNeil." She handed Sarah a small parcel done up in white paper and sealed with red wax. "And I say, you two—don't mention to him that I was working here after hours, will you? He'd give me what for. I'm supposed to leave off sharp at six."

Miss Tomlins broke the seal of her packet, unscrewed the cap from the small bottle inside, and washed down one of her capsules with water drawn from the tap. Sarah, who had taken no part in the conversation, hoped she would suggest a stroll together, and this, after an approving comment on the primroses blooming in the neat window-boxes, was exactly what came about. She was on her own? Good. Then how about a prowl in the sunshine and tea in the Annex digs the librarian was eager to display?

"Ready? Come, we'll toddle along."

Miss Barrows beamed after them and returned to her tasks.

"Nice girl," murmured Beryl. "But innocent as Chrissie Venables—which is saying a good deal—and a regular mule over some things. Tried to tell her. If only she'd listen ... but I'd best hold my tongue."

Sarah was disappointed to find that what Miss Tomlins had sought to pour into the dispenser's ears was not going to be granted to her; but never mind, about the matter of main importance there would be no such restrictions. Her chance had come, nor was her elation diminished by an encounter, five minutes later, with the doctor himself in his dusty Citroen. She had not forgotten how sternly she had been warned against commerce with her present companion, and to be able to flaunt her defiance in Brian Gilcrest's face gave her a thrill of mischievous triumph. His bow was curt, his stare as he passed was hard with displeasure—but what of that? Once and for all let him accept the futility of ordering her movements. If she could not charm him, at least she could show him how little influence his ridiculous bans had over her.

So, her eyes green and sparkling beneath the rakish set of her beret, arm-in-arm with the woman she proposed to drain dry of information regarding the Frampton affair, she sailed blithely forward into the teeth of disaster.

CHAPTER FOURTEEN

"Hasn't our walk rather done you up? Suppose you sit down and rest and let me make the tea."

Miss Tomlins, panting after the climb up four flights of stairs, did look fagged. Her greasily pallid skin had a greenish tinge, but her spirit remained staunch.

"It's nothing, my dear girl—a bit winded, that's all. You can't knock off food for three days and remain in the pink, yet the starvation always puts me right, so I have to do it."

"Have you been really bad?"

Beryl shrugged nonchalantly as she threw her raffia-bag on the Indian bedspread and stooped to light a gas-ring.

"Usual thing. Beastly tropical germ I caught the year I was keeping house for my brother in Ceylon. Doesn't often lay me up now that Dr. Gilcrest has taken hold of me, but once in a while if I've been feeding unwisely as I did in Nice . . . nothing to make a song about. I just go on orange-juice for a bit, then I'm fit again. These capsules do me worlds of good. Take 'em steadily. Matter of fact, I'd run out, so when my friends dropped me on Monday the first thing I did was to pop along and order more. Like my Brittany cups? Present from Madge Whittaker. Good old Madge, she's been minding the books for me, and a nice muddle there'll be. What do you think of this nest? Not bad, is it?"

The low-ceiled room—it was really an attic—was gay and cosy with its couch-bed, Syrian patchwork covering discoloured spots on the wallpaper, daffodils in brass jars, and countless gewgaws and photographs. It had a homelike air, and Sarah, admiring the skill with which ingenuity had triumphed over straitened means, wondered ruefully if at Miss Tomlins' age and still unmarried she would make half so brave a show, or be so gloriously contented. One fact stood out. The boisterous Beryl might have ill-dyed hair, indifferent health and twopence to live upon, but she possessed plenty of good friends out of whose concerns she was able to extract enjoyment.

"Like a squint at my snapshots while the water boils? I've several nice views of the man we've been discussing. See if you can pick him out."

Sarah reached for the album while her hostess set a fresh jam sandwich on a plate, eyed it wistfully, and murmured, "No, Beryl, not for you!" As yet they had touched but casually on Major Frampton's story, Miss Tomlins being a trifle far-away in her manner from lassitude or an absorbing burden on her mind, it was not easy to tell which. She would have to be led on with tact, but on one subject she had wanted no coaxing. Already, though confined to bed till this afternoon, she had managed to glean all the tittle-tattle of the hotel, and directly she was alone with Sarah had started in to discover just how matters stood between the latter and Christine Venables' nephew.

"Heart of gold that boy's got," she had declared adroitly. "Lucky girl that gets him, that's what I say. Why he hasn't been snapped up before this is a marvel to me. Too many after him, I expect. All the same, he'll be wise to pick a wife Chrissie approves of. He couldn't run too many luxuries without her help—now could he?"

"Really, I don't know. Does she help him? She never said so."

"My good girl. Do you honestly suppose Harry Venables bought this brand-new model of a Fiat on his own salary? I haven't a doubt she slips him a nice, fat cheque fairly often. And why not? I'd do the same, if I'd plenty of money and only that one splendid young lad in the whole world to care about. These long holidays, too—he comes here to please her, so naturally she foots the bills. Stands to reason. The only question is, is his matrimonial choice going to suit her book?"

Sarah had endured some embarrassment under the forthcoming attempts to pry into her emotions. She had felt Miss Tomlins would have been sceptical if she had denied any especial interest in so obvious a prize, so she had refrained from mentioning how far she was from the designs attributed to her. Now, with the album open on her lap, coming at once to a group in which Harry and the doctor figured, she looked regretfully at the two men so unequal in looks and intelligence, and experienced the wish that she could have combined the more desirable qualities of each into one person. If Gilcrest could have appreciated her as Harry did, or if Henry had possessed a keener brain, a harder purpose, a will of iron strength, yes even though that will were violently opposed to her own. . . .

She turned the page quickly and beheld a stiff, elderly man in well-tailored plus fours, just taking careful aim with a putter.

"There!" she exclaimed. "Is this Major Frampton?"

Peering over her shoulder Miss Tomlins nodded. "Clever girl, aren't you? And that's Chrissie's skirt sticking out from the edge of the green. Devoted pals, those two. Chrissie was fearfully knocked up, you know. So was I—and I was as wild as she was when people tried to make out he was tight at the time."

"Then in your opinion he was perfectly sober?" asked Sarah, keeping her tone as casual as she could.

"Not a doubt of it. I say, who's been stuffing you up with the other tale?" For a second the muddy dark eyes searched her face, then a shrewd gleam came into them. With a noncommittal grunt their owner shut her lips together, gave another swift nod, and sinking into the sagging basket chair on the opposite side of the hearth prepared to become weightily instructive. "Listen to me, for I know. The Major never was tight—no, not even after our New Year's celebrations, when the Colonel himself had to be helped to bed. On that particular evening I saw him and spoke to him, so you may be sure if there'd been anything of the kind—but wait, let me give you the whole thing just as it happened."

She outlined a diagram on her rough red homespun skirt.

"Here's the card-room, two doors, this one open on to the side passage, the other open on the lobby. Here am I, dummy, and facing both doors. The Major comes by, I can see him as clearly as I see you. It's early, so I'm surprised, more so when he doesn't look in on our game, but stalks by without turning his head. I call out, ragging him, you know, and fully expecting a come-back in the same line. Do I get it? No."

So dramatic had the terse delivery become that Sarah, with rising excitement, visualized the entire scene.

"Did he speak at all?" she demanded.

"Only a mumble, impatient, even rude. So unlike him! It will prove to you what a shock it was, coming from a man invariably courteous, when I say that Mrs. Bulstrode trumped her husband's spade, which was the best one out, and lost the game by it. 'What's wrong with Ian?' she whispered. 'Something's upset him badly. Look at him now. He's trembling.' We looked. There he was at the desk, jerking out a question to know if Christine had got home. The clerk told him no, he swore under his breath, hesitated, and pulled a sheet of paper from the rack on the desk. You see? That inquiry he made shows the trouble, whatever it was, concerned Chrissie. Can't get round it, can you?"

"No," Sarah answered, speaking to herself. "You can't—"

"He blotted the first sheet," pursued Miss Tomlins. "Didn't know that, perhaps? Well, he did—and the clerk told us afterwards it was because his hand was shaking so he could hardly hold the pen. And what did he do? Drop the paper in the wastebasket? Not at all. He wadded it up and stuck it in the side-pocket of his dinner-coat. It was found there later. Now, isn't that proof that he didn't mean anyone but Chrissie to see what he'd written."

"It looks like it," answered Sarah doubtingly. She was thinking that the two de Bellesnaves and Harry could not have been wholly misled as to the Major's condition, and trying to reconcile their beliefs with the contrary but equally convincing account she was now hearing. Frampton already bordering on intoxication when he quitted the villa would not have been sobered after a double *fine* swallowed *en route* . . . "I was only wondering—"

"If I'm mistaken instead of the management and jury?" Miss Tomlins shrugged. "I can't say I looked in his eyes or smelt his breath; but I do say this: that Lefranc, a slippery scoundrel by the way, had every reason for seizing on an explanation which would shift responsibility from him. Here's something. The Major took himself up in the lift, and made sure his message would fall into no hands but Chrissie's by sliding it under her door. Do actions like those point to drunkenness?"

"That wasn't quite what I meant to say. I was wondering if he ever suffered from—well, mental lapses. Brain-storm. Was he at all inclined to imagine things and get worked up over them?"

"Ian Frampton? As level-headed, yes, and as literal a man as I hope to see. Why, he'd no imagination! I can't recall anything upsetting him except talk about home-rule for India, Bolshevism, that sort of thing. Not a coward, either. Got the D.S.O. three times during the War. No, take it from me, if he was in a state that night—and I'll stick to it he was—it was because he was frightened over some imminent danger to Chrissie and himself, just as he said in his note. Dope-peddlers? Maybe. And he may have been entirely wrong. That is, the danger he believed in may have evaporated. Does Chrissie say anything different?"

The question was eagerly put, and for the second time within three days Sarah felt obliged to parry it. Pretending not to hear she asked a random one of her own, little guessing what fact she was to elicit.

"You say he operated the lift by himself? And did he send it down again?"

"No, because just a minute later the doctor came in to pay a call on old Granny Pendleton, who was laid up with rheumatism. I saw him ring twice, wait a bit, and then go up the stairs."

Sarah's heart gave a violent thump. The doctor had followed the Major up with only a brief interval between. She had not known this. All at once it occurred to her that here might be the reason Gilcrest had not wished her to . . .

"On which floor was the old lady's room? I ask because I was wondering whether the doctor saw Major Frampton upstairs."

"He didn't. Granny was on the same floor as the Major—the fifth— but round the other side. Nor did he see anything of the lift, for he told us that afterwards. And why didn't he? I suppose you realise we never found out who'd run it up to the top. Someone lied. Point is, who?"

Who, indeed? Sarah sat very rigid, digesting the disagreeable fact that there was only Gilcrest's own word for the two statements just repeated.

"And Mrs. Pendleton—what's become of her?" she asked, carefully controlling her voice.

"Pegged out during the summer, poor old dear. She was eighty-two. And old Mr. Vansittart died before she did, swearing to the last that the waiter he saw going to the Major's room was taller than any of our staff. Get the possible meaning of that? Tallish man in a waiter's coat. Dinner-jacket it may have been. They'd look the same in a dim light and to bad eyesight. Horrid to think it might have been a guest, or a stranger who'd sneaked in on purpose to polish the Major off?"

As the librarian poured the hissing water into the teapot a grim secret-iveness settled over her features. Sarah, seated on a hassock opposite her, had listened to these last remarks with a sensation akin to physical sickness. Not enough that Miss Tomlins quite obviously had never connected the unidentified man with the doctor she so reverenced. The inference which escaped her blind trust found Sarah a writhing victim. Gilcrest there, directly afterwards, on the fifth floor, unseen by anyone—and the patient who might have provided him with an alibi dead! Was it that Mrs. Pendleton could not have declared exactly when he paid his professional call? Mr. Vansittart, too, silenced forever . . . and yet—Brian Gilcrest, whom she liked too well to want to think ill of him!

Occupied by dreadful conflict, she heard her hostess give out the answer to her unspoken question—stating it as something irrelevant, without any stress. Muriel Ames-Gower, having a girl staying with her, had implored the doctor to come and dance—and Gilcrest, for a wonder, had accepted, meaning to turn up earlier, but prevented by unforeseen calls.

"That's why we didn't have to send for him. He was here, you see, in Granny Pendleton's room, when the accident occurred, and actually climbed down the shaft before anyone else."

He had been in evening dress—or more probably a dinner-coat, since the dances were informal affairs . . . so great a hurry to reach the body . . . to make certain the victim was dead?

"One lump or two?"

"One, please . . . Miss Tomlins, do you yourself believe it was an accident?"

Beryl, her face suddenly cryptic, sipped the hot tea and set her cup on the hearth to cool.

"A week ago I'd have told you I had an open mind about it," she muttered with a troubled frown. "And even now a year's a long time, with everything sealed up as it was then." She seemed in a painful quandary. "Miss MacNeil," she blurted out with worried explosiveness, "perhaps you've noticed I'd something bothering me? The fact is I'm in a most difficult position and can't decide what to do for the best. Christine's been my friend for fifteen years. I'd die sooner than cause her needless pain, yet I'm asking myself if it mayn't be my solemn duty to make her aware of—a certain matter that's come to me. If I were to put it to you in confidence and ask your advice, could I depend on you to keep quiet till I'd decided whether or not to mention it?"

"Of course I'll say nothing. What is it you've found out?" whispered Sarah with a suffocating sensation. "Something that makes it—murder?"

"Um-um-um—might start a new investigation, with awful results. It's a terrible strain to feel it rests with me. Can't consult the doctor, as it happens. Twice I've tried to tell Marjory, but no good so far. On Monday he interrupted us, and this afternoon you came in. Now, dare I tell you, or isn't it wise?"

Gilcrest might have caught a revealing hint. To be sure, he had objected to Sarah's talking with Miss Tomlins before the latter's return from Nice—

"You must do as you think best. I can promise you not to let it go further. What sort of thing have you learned?"

To hide her tense expectancy, Sarah cut herself a slice of the jam sandwich and pretended to nibble it. The room was now in dusk, with a single ray of setting sun falling across the painted floor and gilding the little brass kettle. A cheap Dutch clock ticked loudly. The stout figure in the basket chair remained completely silent. Why didn't she go on?

All at once it happened. The wicker chair creaked, the cup and saucer crashed to the floor deluging its owner with hot tea. With tortured groans Miss Tomlins was on her feet, bent double, hands clutching at her stomach. Her face had gone livid.

"Good Heavens, what's wrong?" cried Sarah in dismay, springing up and capsizing her own cup. "Can I do anything for you?"

A protesting smile twisted into a grimace. Sweat had broken out.

"Tummy again. Come on like—like a thunder-clap. Never felt such pain. Can't conceive . . . ugh! It's boring into me, red-hot . . ."

There was a choking gasp, and the stricken woman toppled heavily to the floor.

CHAPTER FIFTEEN

Sarah dashed at full speed down the annex stairs and into the main lobby, to find the younger Ames-Gower girl and Madge Whittaker just in from golf. For all their phlegmatic composure they exchanged perturbed glances over her communication, and Madge, business-like and alert, took the situation in hand.

"The whole trouble, I expect. Oughtn't to have gone out in this uncertain weather and got over-tired. Here, Gladys, you ring up the doctor, and get him to come at once. I'll just fetch my brandy and run back to do what I can."

Slightly reassured, Sarah made haste to return, Madge overtaking her with long strides as she reached the attic room, and murmuring that a little stimulant would soon pull Beryl round.

"I've seen her taken like this before, though not for years, I'll admit. Sudden, was it? Yes, sometimes it . . . oh dear!"

A scant five minutes had elapsed since Sarah had managed to haul the stout form on to the bed and cover it with a quilt. She expected to be met by the same heart-rending groans which still rang in her ears, instead of which the low-ceiled room held an ominous silence. Miss Tomlins, her knees drawn up, lay huddled face downward without a flicker of movement. The quilt had slid in a heap to the floor.

Soothingly Madge bent over her, patting the plump arm in its tight, red knitted sleeve.

"Beryl, old girl, where's the pain? Tummy as usual? Easier, is it? Look at me, there's a dear."

No answer. They righted her gently and beheld a face drained of all colour, eyes nearly closed and filled with a dreadful blankness. The mane of stiff, dyed hair was dank with cold sweat.

A wild thought darted through Sarah. Once before she had seen an attack suspiciously like this—less precipitate, perhaps, but—

"Unconscious," faltered Madge, her own brickish ruddiness faded to mottled patches. "Oh, dear, what's to be done? Shall we try giving her brandy?"

The attempt was made, but the brown liquid trickled from the corners of the closed mouth and ran down on the bed. They loosened the red tweed skirt and the stays beneath, but still could discern no sign of returning animation. Madge felt the heart, drew in a hissing breath, and compressed her lips.

"I don't understand." Her voice shook with fear. "Never before ... and at noon she was quite bright! What if Dr. Gilcrest is out? Maybe we'd better telephone the old French doctor, Thiers. She mustn't be left, that's certain. Do you think you could—oh!" she broke off in sudden relief, "I do believe he's come!"

A rapid step mounted the stairs, Gilcrest strode into the room, and not stopping to ask a single question came straight to the bed. The two women made way for him, heard him mutter angrily and click his tongue, and in response to his peremptory demand for more light ran, the one to the second wall-switch, the other to the bedside lamp. The examination went on. Three, four minutes passed, and no word was spoken. Then the stooping figure straightened, faced round and met the two pairs of anxious eyes, his own strangely stern. He hesitated, his expression defying analysis. Was it that of a man stunned, mortified, and battling to cover his emotions? Possibly—but Sarah was not sure, and her first reaction of sympathy wavered in the clutch of something quite different.

"She's gone," he said drily. "She's been dead several minutes."

Madge uttered a whimpering sob. "Dead! Oh, doctor, it's not possible! In this short time? Is there nothing you can do? Oh, dear, how frightful! I can't take it in at all. ..."

Nor could Sarah. Miss Tomlins dead—and less than ten minutes ago she had been drinking tea, gossiping away, there in that basket-chair! It was as though some invisible hand had dealt her a sledge-hammer blow.

"Why in God's name wasn't I called sooner?" the doctor was demanding in an accusing undertone. "What was everybody about to let her get into this condition and say nothing? When did it come on? Was she alone? I now find she's been ill three days, but not a word was said."

They explained. He gave close attention, and at the first pause turned on Sarah.

"You say you spent the last two hours with her. What did she eat or drink? Any of those villainous liqueurs at the Anglais?"

She flinched, resenting his tone. "We didn't go there. She took one cup of tea, without milk or sugar, here, in this room. The moment she'd drunk it she gave a scream and collapsed on the floor. All she said was something about a terrible pain inside, like something red-hot. Those were her actual words—'red hot, boring into me.' When Miss Whittaker and I got back, a few minutes later, we found her unconscious."

As she spoke another recollection flashed on her. Her eyes on Gilcrest's, her breath suspended with an odd tension, she added, "Before we left your dispensary, she took one capsule out of the new bottle she'd come to fetch. I can swear that's all she touched, except the tea."

He seemed scarcely to hear. She had been about to tell him that in case he wished to examine the capsules they were still in the dead woman's knitting bag; but now, noting his apparent lack of interest, she said no more. Perhaps in truth he had been as unprepared for this catastrophe as herself. From the bottom of her soul she longed to believe it. If only she had not seen that other case. . . .

Miss Whittaker was mopping her reddened lids.

"What was wrong?" she whispered between her prominent teeth. "Why did she go like this, or can't you say just at once?"

Gilcrest did not immediately reply. He had returned to the bed, and was gazing down at the large, darkly-pallid features. He lifted one of the plump, inert hands and let it fall before saying, over his shoulder, "Mesenteric thrombosis. It's invariably sudden—instantaneous, in fact. I must take a little more time over my examination, but that's the answer right enough."

Was it? The medical term meant nothing to Sarah, but the hesitation meant a great deal. Instinctively she felt the speaker was either less certain than he wished to appear, or else that he was bent on giving them a false explanation calculated to satisfy. Doctors were all alike, she reflected. For their own self-preservation they must not admit doubt—and, oh, how easy for them to "put it over" on the ignorant layman!

Alone in her own room, Sarah found she was trembling like an aspen. The past half-hour had so completely unnerved her that all she could do was to repeat, like a stupid refrain, "Just now she was alive—talking to me. Now she's dead. Why?" Presently she lashed herself energetically. What excuse had she for connecting Dr. Gilcrest with this happening? Was there any reason at all for the horrible idea hovering in the back of her brain?

Only this: Gilcrest had strongly objected to her discussing a certain affair with Miss Tomlins—and Miss Tomlins, on the point of death, had been about to make a definite disclosure. Was this all? No, not quite. The woman had taken one of the doctor's capsules—from a brand-new bottle, just received.

"It might have taken two hours for the outer coating to melt. I don't know how long it would be—but why wasn't he interested when I mentioned it? Then, too, he couldn't have foretold when she'd take the first dose, or even that we were going to run into each other this afternoon . . . no, that doesn't help, does it? He might well have expected us not to meet quite so soon, as I'm generally with Miss Venables. He declares he's only just learned she was ill these last few days. Is that true? Mayn't he have known?"

Capsules . . . she gave a violent start as she recalled that Mrs. Mark Venables, also, had been given capsules. No getting round it, these two attacks bore a striking similarity. And yet—

"That, at least, is simply coincidence," she argued, annoyed with herself. "The other capsules came straight from a chemist—and besides, haven't we absolute proof that Mrs. Venables died a natural death?"

Like sunlight dispelling foul fog the actual verdict from the Charing Cross Hospital flashed before her eyes. She had seen it in black and white—and without the smallest doubt Beryl Tomlins' death was equally natural. Why not? The one extraordinary circumstance was that she, Sarah MacNeil, should have been present on both occasions.

Tears of relief ran down her cheeks. She wiped them away, and slipping on a coat hurried downstairs and out into the darkening square, thinking to wait for Miss Venables' return. She was now able to take a normal view of Miss Tomlins' interrupted confidence. Why bother about what would probably have been pure balderdash? In any case, it did not concern the doctor whom the woman so patently worshipped, while the mere fact that Miss Tomlins shrank from acquainting either him or Miss Venables with her "discovery" was a fairly sure indication of its worthlessness. Poor creature, she must have battened on sensations, mostly manufactured. . . .

Headlights dazzled her as the big Fiat swooped out of the narrow street opposite. Harry had spied her, and as she ran after the slowing car, Miss Venables leant out, forestalling her painful announcement with distressed words of her own.

"Sarah, such a dreadful thing's happened! So sudden, so—"

"You've heard?" cried Sarah, astounded. "But how?"

"Why, at the villa, of course. Poor thing, dead, quite inexplicably, too. The Baron—"

"The Baron!" Sarah perceived they were talking at cross-purposes. "Who do you mean is dead?" she demanded curiously.

"Polly—the bulldog. From your manner I supposed you were going to tell us about it."

"Bulldog!" The girl's laugh broke hysterically. "No, my news is much worse. Beryl Tomlins is dead, too. I was with her."

"What's that?"

It was Harry who gave the cry, blank, incredulous. His aunt, who had recoiled with the shock, was gazing at Sarah with utter dismay.

"Beryl?" she echoed, stupefied. "Was she so ill then? I never dreamed . . . what happened?"

The Fiat, just missing a lamppost, crept into the garage as Sarah, with one omission, told her story. Miss Venables was overcome with grief and pity. Poor, plucky Beryl—how like her to make light of her illness, even going to fetch her medicine when a dozen people would have gone for her!

It was chillier today. She must have caught cold in her inside. . . .

"No," said Sarah, "It can't have been that. Why, she was dead within five minutes! And her sufferings at first, all of a sudden—like your sister-in-law, I thought. She'd eaten nothing, either, unless you count the capsule she took about two hours before, at the dispensary."

Both faces held looks of intense concern. Harry's blue eyes were tinged with awe as he fumbled for a cigarette and lit it.

"Whew!" he ejaculated under his breath. "Makes you squirm, doesn't it? Five minutes—but you say she'd been seedy before. What about Gilcrest? Isn't he feeling a bit cheap?"

Miss Venables caught him up sharply.

"Really, Harry, what a word to use! I don't understand you."

"Sorry," murmured her nephew, chastened and abashed. "I only meant he might feel it a reflection on his ability and whatnot to have a patient he was supposed to be looking after popping off in double-quick time right under his nose. Maybe not."

"I hope," said Miss Venables with dignified reproof, "You don't imagine this death was due to either incompetence or neglect on Dr. Gilcrest's part. No physician can work miracles, and if poor Beryl got herself into this state without letting him know you can't hold him responsible. One may be sure it's not the first case of the kind. Do be careful not to make thoughtless remarks, won't you dear? And I think you ought to get Sarah some brandy. She's looking very white."

Reason is one thing, blind instinct another, and as they passed the empty card-room Sarah felt a slight shudder. What if Miss Tomlins had learned some new fact which would have reversed all conclusions regarding the Major's death? Unbeknown to herself that fact might have implicated Gilcrest. Oh, if only she had spoken sooner! Sarah, alive but ignorant, dared not open her lips on the subject, no, not to anyone— except, possibly, to Harry. What about telling him?

Over the stiff drink he brought her she watched him toss off another equally strong. Should she confide in him? No—for what good would come of it? Harry was not particularly clever, and besides he seemed unreasonably prejudiced against Gilcrest, a condition of mind which would make him less discreet than herself. What she must do was to keep silent and meanwhile take careful note of the doctor's manner towards herself. If there were guilt on the man's soul, he would be on the rack now to find out what she had heard.

"I must watch him, that's all."

Yet even as she formed this determination the pain in her breast seemed more than she could bear.

CHAPTER SIXTEEN

THE feminine population was gathered in the lounge, morbidly discussing the recent event. Sarah had been wrung dry, and now, to her relief, attention centred on Madge Whittaker, who, as Beryl's chief friend, was regarded as a superior authority.

"Did Harry go out?" whispered Miss Venables, peering round. "If so I don't blame him, poor boy. Only, I rather wonder where he's gone? I'm sure it's not to the de Bellesnaves. The Baron, as you may guess, is simply devastated by what happened, and Harry is always so affected by suffering."

With an effort Sarah switched her mind to the minor tragedy.

"What was wrong with Polly?" she inquired.

"No one has any idea. When the Baron took his usual nap in the boat-house, the dog was with him, but when he woke it had disappeared. The servants were out, so was Maddalena, who came home to find her husband whistling and calling. She became instantly alarmed, thinking how her own little dog vanished barely two months back; but she said nothing, only helped in the search. By mere chance they looked into the kennel—and there the poor beast lay, stone dead. It had vomited blood."

"Poisoned?" suggested Sarah, recalling Miss Tomlins' grim joke.

"Apparently not. The doctor came and examined the body, and according to him there's no evidence of poison. Some sudden illness, I suppose. The dog was fairly old, you know."

Miss Whittaker was speaking. They ceased talking to attend.

"Yes, the married sister has been wired. She's a Mrs. Cripps, of Cheltenham. I should think she'll be here the day after tomorrow, and naturally no arrangements can be made till she comes. Still, cremation's terribly expensive, isn't it? I imagine Beryl's wish will be carried out, and that she'll be buried right here, in our own little English graveyard. She'd chosen the spot."

Sighing heavily Madge held up a grey-blue pullover which Sarah realised must be the one Miss Tomlins had been knitting for Dr. Gilcrest. Only the casting-off remained, and this Madge was now doing. Touched as Sarah was by this last act of friendship, she could not help wondering if the raffia-bag on the worker's lap still contained the bottle of capsules, and if the latter would ever be questioned.

The pause was broken by a damsel with a high, polished forehead and an argumentative manner. She was a Miss Lowther, a newcomer no one particularly liked.

"Well!" she began, her air that of conscious rectitude. "I daresay I shall make myself most unpopular by saying this, but I must admit I find it rather astonishing that a doctor in good repute shouldn't have foreseen a danger like this. Perhaps he was not to blame, but I know how I'd feel if it was my sister who'd died. I'm not at all certain I shouldn't want it looked into rather closely."

There was a strained and hostile silence. Only one woman gave a quick, approving nod, the others compressed their lips and waited for Miss Whittaker to annihilate the heretic, which, after mute communion with Miss Venables, she proceeded, very politely, to do.

"This is your first season here, isn't it? And so, Miss Lowther, you can hardly be expected to grasp the situation. Perhaps I'd better explain that Beryl Tomlins for years past had had a tropical germ in her intestinal tract and suffered a great deal in consequence. These germs are extremely difficult to get rid of. A rich woman would have tried all sorts of expensive cures, but Beryl was not rich. She did, however, improve—oh, vastly!—under Dr. Gilcrest's treatment. For long periods she has been almost perfectly fit, and then as she took reasonable care about food and didn't fag herself out she got on splendidly. The trouble was—"

"I don't question that," interrupted Miss Lowther with stubborn persistence. "What I'm saying is—"

"If you don't mind, I'd like to finish. The trouble was, she wasn't always careful. She would overdo, and when she went visiting she would eat wrong things. This time she was undoubtedly far iller than she imagined. With a condition like hers an internal chill—"

"Chill!" grunted the monumental dowager on the left, examining her lace work and nodding vehemently. "Don't talk to me about chills. There's my own cousin, Lady Chetworth—wife of the general, you know—who caught a germ in Tutankhamen's tomb just after it was opened up to the public. To this day, if there's an east wind, or a sudden drop in temperature . . . to be sure, her step-daughter, Millicent, will have it there was a curse put upon her, but then she's—"

"To prove how much better Beryl was," continued Miss Whittaker, cutting across the stream of mysticism, "she no longer required any medicine except some disinfectant capsules, and lately, if she felt under the weather, she simply took a day in bed and dieted herself, without sending for the doctor. I admit I wanted him called yesterday, but she was quite positive there was no need."

"Excuse me, Madge," interrupted the elder Miss Ames-Gower, always a timid stickler for accuracy. "But are you sure that was her reason for not calling him? This time, I mean. I went up to take her some flowers, and from something she said I got the impression she didn't quite want to see him for a bit. She was a little odd—"

"Muriel!"

The stocky sister hissed this warningly, spectacled eyes owlish with reproof. Muriel turned an unbecoming red all down her thin neck, and bridled defensively.

"You needn't glare at me, Gladys," she muttered. "I'm sure I wasn't going to say what I shouldn't."

An electric tension made itself felt throughout the group. Most of the ladies were too well-bred to pry into the mystery, but an aged widow, adjusting her ear-trumpet, gratified everyone by inquiring with elaborate casualness if dear Beryl had expressed any discontent with Dr. Gilcrest's treatment.

"Oh, not at all!" denied Muriel, beating a headlong retreat. "All I meant was—no Gladys, it's all right—she gave me to understand she had a private reason for . . . but there, I've said enough."

She had said too much. Curiosity was rampant, and Madge's terse declaration that Beryl had probably felt guilty over her dietary indiscretions met with little satisfaction. Madge saw this, and later, when the conclave had dissolved, she came close to Sarah in the lobby to vent her annoyance.

"Those stupid girls!" she muttered. "Kitty Lowther, a stranger in our midst, making insinuations against the doctor's competence, and Muriel, who ought to know better, considering how sentimental she's been over him all this long time, giving Heaven knows what impression! When I think of all he did for poor Beryl—and between ourselves never charging her a penny—it makes me quite wild."

No, the doctor had not charged Beryl for his services. It was generous of him, unless, by chance, he had an unseen motive.

Her hand still on Sarah's arm, Miss Whittaker gave a start as the manager's private door opened, and Gilcrest came out. Now was the opportunity to observe him, but Sarah, watching narrowly, got little for her pains. He looked harassed and worn with fatigue, but though she detected in his air the same hidden perplexity she had noticed several hours before she could not see that her presence caused him any discomfort. Indeed, as he lingered talking to the manager, his eyes rested on her and her companion without the least awareness of them, and the parley concluded he was hurrying through the swing-doors when Madge strode forward and pressed a small parcel into his hands.

"Beryl was knitting this for you," she murmured. "I took the liberty of finishing it off. She'd have wanted you to have it."

Now Sarah sensed a definite avoidance of her eyes. He seemed amazed, embarrassed, pained, all at once, stood staring down at the gift in a nonplussed manner, and ended by muttering thanks and thrusting the parcel deep into his Burberry pocket. He had gone.

Why did the very sight of this man affect her so profoundly? Had she fallen in love with him that she longed thus eagerly to wipe from her mind every vestige of distrust? Surely she could not be so foolish; and yet she knew that her anxiety to settle her doubts came only in a secondary degree from her desire to protect her employer. It was the doctor himself who mattered to her. To think evil of him was torment.

Miss Venables, looking weary, came up. Sarah pressed the lift-button, but as frequently was the case someone above had not closed the doors, so the cage refused to descend.

"Never mind, I'll fetch it down."

Hating herself for the action, Sarah timed her walk up to the fifth floor, where the lift chanced to be. Two minutes—and needless to say the ascent by lift would consume but a few seconds. Did it mean that the interval between the two ascents would have left the Major ample time to reach his room before the man who walked up arrived on the same floor? Obviously it did—so obviously that it was stupid to make the test, but now she had made it she noticed something which gave her a bad jar—a housemaid's cupboard, close beside the shaft. What an excellent hiding-place if one wanted to spring forth and push an unsuspecting victim into the void!

Yes, Gilcrest could have run the lift to the top, walked down, and having delivered his message through the Major's closed door hurried back to this cupboard to lie in wait. He was much taller than any of the present lot of waiters, he spoke admirable French, and on the given occasion had worn a black coat. The entire episode need have taken but a few minutes, after which he could have gone to his patient's room and remained there till summoned. Had he done these things, and if so how did it fit with what Beryl Tomlins had wanted to tell her?

Hours later, too wretched to sleep, Sarah recalled that she had not put out her walking shoes to be cleaned. When she opened her door, Harry was tiptoeing past, and seeing her stopped.

"Chrissie calmed down?" he whispered.

"She's dropped off, I think. I wish I could, but I can't get that poor woman out of my mind. Oh, Harry, it was dreadful!"

"I can well believe you," he returned sympathetically, but eyeing her with a sort of reluctant fascination. "Rotten time you've had—but all the same, don't let it get on your nerves, will you? After all, what was she to you? And bad as it was, it was soon over, I take it?"

"I suppose it was rather worse because it's the second thing of the kind I've seen."

"Gracie, you mean? That's so, I was forgetting you'd happened in on her as well. It's a dashed shame, really it is—but with this affair, why not look at it in a sensible light? Here's a woman getting old, no money, soon going to be a burden on her relatives, a thing old Tomlins would have hated. She didn't suffer long, and maybe in a way it's a blessing in disguise. Don't you think I'm right?"

Harry's moralizing faintly amused her. It was good of him to take her distress so to heart, even though she suspected it was his own sensitive shrinking from the unpleasant which prompted his arguments. He had laid his big, warm hand on her bare arm. It was comforting, but reminded of her scanty attire she drew back into the doorway, only to see that he was thinking of something quite other than thin silk pyjamas.

"I say, that was a bad brick I dropped about Gilcrest, wasn't it? Silly ass I was! I could have kicked myself blue. For all I know, he's a marvel of efficiency, only—well, with Chrissie believing in him up to the hilt and—and absolutely in his hands, if you get me, I should jolly well like to feel sure . . . understand what I'm driving at?"

His concern for his aunt elevated him in her esteem, but made her wonder uneasily if the doubt she was trying to stifle had entered his mind as well as hers. He was looking a little worried as he continued uncertainly, "Everybody's satisfied, I suppose, that it's no fault of his?"

"Everybody who counts," she assured him. "The general opinion seems to be that it was just one of those unfortunate cases where nothing could be done."

His brow cleared with such evident relief that she smiled, maternally indulgent.

"Where did you go?" she asked idly. "To the Casino?"

"Me?" He reddened, as if the question disconcerted him. "No—oh, no! The—the fact is," he blurted out boyishly, "there's an English girl over in Hyères. I'd asked her here for the next dance, but then I thought there wouldn't be any dance, do you see? So I just popped over to put her off. To be perfectly honest, I couldn't stick the concentrated gloom of this place. I suppose I'm a coward about some things . . . my word, I could do with a drink! How about you? I've got the makings in my room. Like to slip along?"

She declined, reminding him of how little it took to start tongues wagging, and giving his hand a sisterly squeeze retreated, to stand for long moments reflecting on what he had just said.

"He's right about one thing," she thought. "Miss Venables is absolutely in Brian Gilcrest's hands . . . and yet, how dare I breathe one word to her until I know more than I do now?"

Sleep at last, but with it a ghastly vision of a figure she knew creeping along dim-lit corridors. She woke, shaken from head to foot, and burst into silent sobs.

CHAPTER SEVENTEEN

MORNING light has a magical power for restoring sanity. Drinking her coffee, with birds twittering outside and sunshine streaming in gold bars across her bed, Sarah suddenly beheld the fundamental flaw in her arguments—entire absence of motive.

Eagerly she reasoned it out. Since Gilcrest stood to gain not a penny from any of the deaths under consideration, she had been assuming that each victim represented a menace to his safety. Logically this led her back to Miss Venables—for was it not she the Major had sought to warn, and she alone who possessed money enough to warrant cupidious designs? If Gilcrest had planned—was still planning—to profit by his rich patient's decease, his need to remove those who were able to ruin his scheme would be wholly comprehensible; but could he profit? No! Miss

Venables had plainly stated her inability to will her fortune as she liked. Bound by an unbreakable entail, it passed entire into Harry's hands.

"That squashes it! Oh, if I'd had the wit to remember it sooner! The utter fool I've been!"

She was light-headed with joy. No foul deed had been done, or certainly not in the cases of Miss Tomlins and the poor woman back in London. Major Frampton's end still puzzled her, but at any rate she could not reasonably lay it at Gilcrest's door. When it came down to it, she had never reconciled Miss Tomlins' utter confidence in the doctor's good character with the rest of her jerry-built theory. She had also lost sight of the anonymous letters, surely an important factor in the Frampton-Venables affair.

"I still long to know what sort of thing Miss Tomlins was going to tell me. Unless that dispenser girl has some idea, I suppose it's gone forever. Too bad!"

Looking into the other bedroom, she found her employer already dressed, and alert with energy over an unselfish project—that of consulting at once with several of the more prosperous guests to see if they would band together for the purchase of a gravestone.

"If not, I mean to do it myself; but I think Beryl's other old friends would dislike being left out. You see, the Cripps family in Cheltenham are badly off, and a funeral is such an expense!"

"As usual, all your thought is of other people," said Sarah, "Well one person at least thinks of you—Harry. I saw him last night, and he stopped to ask if you were asleep. He was worried about you after what happened, you know."

"Dear boy!" Miss Venables flushed with pleasure. "And did he say where he'd been?"

"To Hyères, to call on an English girl."

"Really! Now who can that be?" mused the aunt, her brown eyes bright with interest. "I hope," she continued in her precise accents, "I'm not becoming a tiresome busybody, but I confess to a rather keen curiosity when I find Harry paying attention to the opposite sex. At one time he was so very impressionable, and I used to be afraid he'd tie himself up with some not very desirable person. That phase has passed, and now I sometimes wish he'd show a little more interest in matrimony. You can never tell, though, can you? Perhaps he is in love, and with this new girl, only hesitating to tell me. I must—"

A light tap interrupted the weaving of romance, and sent Sarah back to finish her dressing. Through the crack of the door she heard the delighted, "Maddalena! Is it you?" followed by the Baroness' apologies for the early call.

"I felt I simply must express my sympathy over the death of your poor friend. Miss Tomlins—she was a good creature, was she not?—and though I scarcely knew her, it is unbelievable to think she is dead. Why, it seems but yesterday I passed her in the town, and she looked so stout and well!"

"It was indeed a sad shock to us all, and especially for Sarah, who was with her when it happened. But who—"

"Ah, you wonder how I know? I persuaded my poor, distracted Henri to go to the laboratory this morning, hoping to get his thoughts off the unfortunate dog. I went with him, and so, naturally, Brian told us. He spoke of your Sarah's truly marvellous presence of mind. How I admire her cool head, I, who invariably go to pieces at the sight of pain!"

In the adjoining room Sarah caught her breath. The doctor had praised her? Incredible—and coals of fire heaped on her head. Her colour rose, and when Miss Venables called her in no one could have guessed her nerve-racked night. Mme. de Bellesnaves, on the contrary, looked haggard and wan, her encircled eyes filled with anxiety. She cast a swift glance at Sarah's trim figure, inquired solicitously about the burns, and sank back with a weary sigh into the corner of the sofa.

"So you, as well as we, have been through a distressing time! Ah, it sounds stupid enough to make such a fuss over a dog, but I can assure you ours is no ordinary case . . . however, you, and just recovered from that other experience! You were having tea with her, *n'est-ce pas*? When, how, did the illness begin?"

Whether out of compliment to Miss Venables and herself or from morbid curiosity the Baroness showed a surprising concern over the gruesome details. She drew Sarah out, her dark eyes vivid with interest, once even filling with tears.

"Mon Dieu!" With a fatalistic sigh and a faint gesture of crossing herself she relaxed, shaking her head. *"Comme c'est incroyable!* So very seldom does such a crisis arise, and when it does—phut!—one can do nothing."

"Then the doctor has explained to you the exact reason for her death?" asked Miss Venables with interest. "What did he say?"

"He gave it a long name quite impossible to remember. It meant a blood-clot forming suddenly and causing a hemorrhage. I gathered that even if he had been on the spot at the time she was first taken ill the result would have been the same. There is no remedy."

Miss Venables glanced at Sarah with quiet satisfaction.

"I was sure of it. I shall repeat what you say to one of our guests who was trying to hint the case might have been mismanaged."

The Baroness' eyes flashed with anger. She was like a tigress defending its young.

"Someone suggested that? Who?"

"A young woman, no one who matters. I, too, was up in arms. So ignorant of her!"

"He is a man of genius," declared Mme. de Bellesnaves sharply. "Henri, who knows, tells me it is deplorable for him to be buried in a place like this, with his exceptional knowledge of the chemistry of the human body."

It was dreadful to think what the final phrase would have meant to Sarah only a few hours ago. Even as it was, the words, "chemistry of the human body," stuck fast in her brain. . . .

"Who knows?" Miss Venables was saying hopefully. "He is still quite young. His chance may yet come."

How inquisitive the Baroness was! Momentarily the monkey peeped forth as with narrowed gaze she searched the speaker's calm face. At once, however, she lapsed into abstraction, and began picking up one by one the various objects on the little bed-table at her side. It was a familiar trick of hers, and usually, so Sarah had noticed, meant she was thinking of widely different things. She appeared not to see what she fingered, but all at once, with a return of attention, she held up the last article seized upon. It chanced to be the new bottle of capsules fetched the day before.

"I see you still take the same prescription," she remarked carelessly. "You find it helps you?"

"Oh, immensely! I'm giving it up, though, when this lot is finished. The doctor thinks I can do without it."

"Ah, I am glad! That shows you are really better." Laying down the bottle, the Baroness passed to Harry's photograph. "Here is your medicine," she said with a teasing laugh. "The moment this big boy arrives you need no other—is it not so? I agree. He is a nerve tonic, this youth. It would pain you to lose him, would it not? And yet, one day, I suppose you will have to give him up."

"To a wife, you mean? I should be only too pleased, provided it was the right one. Funnily enough, we were discussing that only a moment ago, apropos of some new girl he is interested in."

An odd thing happened. The Baroness' smile froze, her whole slim body stiffened as on steel wires as with a brusque swiftness she echoed,

"Girl? What girl? When? Where?" Was it possible she was jealous, of Harry, to whom at times she was hardly civil? Sarah felt she could not be wrong in believing that Harry bored her—and yet. . . .

"Dear Maddalena!" exclaimed Miss Venables, mildly diverted. "You think I am in danger of being deserted? Don't worry, Harry will always be devoted to me. Besides, we know nothing, except that he went last evening to call on some friends in Hyères. I was merely speculating about her, that's all."

The Baroness stared, and burst into silvery laughter. For some reason the explanation seemed to amuse her highly.

"Hyères!" she repeated, with a side-glance to include Sarah in a joke impossible to elucidate. "So he has found romance in that dull spot! Who would have thought it? It is as bad as here."

"It is good to hear you laugh," rejoined the spinster, smiling if vaguely mystified. "Before that you were looking so mournful."

"Was I?" Hilarity vanished, and a cloud descended over the mobile features. "It is true," the Baroness said in a lower tone, "I am much, much concerned over Henri. As you know, I always feared for him when this situation arose; but a grief so dumb, so hopeless as this is a thing I cannot deal with at all. What am I to do? I speak, he does not hear. All night long he is walking about his room. He will not eat. Think, for thirteen years he and the dog have been inseparable. Now it is as though a spring had snapped. I. . . . I am frightened . . ."

"There, there, it can't be so serious! It had to come, didn't it? And your husband is too sensible a man to remain overpowered for long. Perhaps another pet . . . He won't hear of it? Well, later on he'll feel differently. You'll see."

Mme. de Bellesnaves rose, dug to her comforter for a moment, and, her great eyes swimming in tears, went quickly from the room. Miss Venables gazed after her with a troubled sigh.

"I did my best," she murmured, "But really, when I consider the poor man's state of health and so on I myself can't help feeling slightly worried. It is terribly distressing for her, though it is a good thing she appreciates his condition. Sometimes I think she has a sixth sense about any danger threatening him. It comes, I suppose, of the very spiritual bond existing between them—that, after all, is what counts in marriage, isn't it?"

Sarah agreed—in words. She was picturing the Baron, physically less than half a man, charming to her by reason of qualities which could scarcely recommend him as a husband. She did not question Mme. de

Bellesnaves' anxiety on the Baron's account, but spiritual bond! Mentally she shrugged.

Why had Bimi shown that sudden wrath when the English girl was mentioned? And was the subsequent laughter designed to cover up the lapse? Probably. Twice she had been annoyed, the first time over hearing the doctor's ability criticised. That was understandable, but Harry's affairs were another matter. The woman could hardly be in love with two men. Most certainly she was indifferent to Harry, a fact which might call for some explanation, but which Sarah saw no reason to doubt. Perhaps, like most strongly possessive members of her sex, she wanted to attach every male in her vicinity, primitively resenting encroachments on her claims.

"I couldn't blame her for that," Sarah reflected with another shrug. "I'm faintly tarred with the same brush."

They had come up from lunch. Miss Venables, according to her neat habit, was tucking in the sofa-cover left baggy by the last occupant when she gave a little cry and dangled aloft an object which sparkled. It was the Baroness' wrist-watch.

"Deep down in the crack," she declared. "How lucky I found it instead of the maid. I saw her fiddling with the catch. What a pretty thing it is! Amazingly good for imitation. She'll be disturbed over losing it, only how shall we get it to her? Harry's gone again to Hyères. Did you notice how red he turned when I asked where he was off to? I'm sure there's something . . . I shall be busy in the town with Mrs. Bulstrode till quite five o'clock. Couldn't you run up and return this?"

"Of course. I'll go now."

If Miss Venables had used her lorgnette she might have been even more impressed by the excellence of the imitation. These brilliants not real? Sarah knew diamonds when she saw them—and some of the stones, set in a new design round the tiny, lozenge-shaped face, were quite large.

"So here's another puzzle," she thought, as, slipping the watch into her purse, she set off on her errand.

CHAPTER EIGHTEEN

SARAH concluded that the Baroness' pretence about the diamonds could have but one explanation. The watch was a gift, its owner dared not say from whom.

"Pretty expensive gift! Come to think of it, what about some of the clothes she wears? They cost money, too, whatever Miss Venables may choose to believe. Who gives her all this?"

It puzzled her slightly that Mme. de Bellesnaves on discovering her loss had not rung up to make inquiries; but at this point, reluctant to become like her petty-minded companions of the hotel, she desisted from further speculation. Really it did not matter to her.

Abreast of the doctor's gate her heart gave a fluttering bound to see Gilcrest himself just getting into his car. Their eyes met. Hesitating, he approached, not immediately speaking, merely looking down at her with an expression which, though preoccupied, was softer than any she had seen him wear. Tongue-tied she waited while one of the obscure battles seemed to go on inside him.

"That was a bad time for you yesterday." His voice was low, dry, uncertain. "Wish it could have been avoided. If I was a bit rough—"

"You weren't," she lied, eager to put him at his ease. "You had to ask me things, naturally. I quite understand—and you were upset."

"I'm glad you saw that. I was." His eyes fell from hers to rest on the thin sleeves of her frock. "Your arms—are they comfortable?"

"Not hurting at all. See, I've taken off the bandages."

"Stay in the shade. That skin's tender and will blister again."

"Yes, I'm keeping it covered."

She hoped he was going to continue the talk. She even believed he was tempted to do so, but with a touch of the old chariness he gave a quick nod and without looking at her again slid into his seat and drove away. Through a warm mist she watched the disappearing car, infinitely thankful she no longer suspected him of wrong-doing, and deeply stirred by his changed attitude towards her. For it was changed, and brief though the encounter had been it filled her with wistful hope. For the first and only time since they had met he had shown sympathy in a non-professional way. His eyes, slate-blue, still guarded, had not been cold. . . .

"Miss MacNeil! Oh, do stop for a minute! I've so longed for someone to talk to!"

The voice was that of the dispenser, framed in the doorway. Her brown spaniel's eyes were clouded with anxiety, her hands smoothed down her snowy overall in a nervous manner. Glad to speak to her, Sarah went into the dispensary, and at once Miss Barrows fell to lamenting Beryl Tomlin's fate.

"Only to think she was in this very room yesterday afternoon, making jokes in that gruff way of hers! About the dog—remember? And now she's gone, and the dog, too. How awful it all is! I can't get used to the idea—nor can he, though he says so little, I can see how bitterly he's reproaching himself—quite without cause—for not foreseeing such a condition would arise. I'm sure he's wrong. No human being could have guessed; but still, I daresay I shouldn't want him to feel differently."

The girl spoke as though moved, and bent her face quickly over a piece of mending she had taken out of a cupboard. Sarah, in a glow over the foregoing remarks, glanced at the worn fabric.

"His," Marjory informed her with an apologetic laugh, holding up a masculine undervest. "And I have to keep it hidden when he's about and pretend it's Berthe who darns for him. Oh, I'm not gone on him, don't think it! Got someone of my own, back in Eastbourne—but when a man's as decent to me as he is I simply love looking after him. I could tell you of places very different from this. My last job—but we'll not talk of that. He's straight, through and through, which is why I defended him yesterday when poor Beryl kept getting in her little digs. I could have said more. The Baroness does run after him, hard. Places him in an awkward position, with the husband his friend and all. He can't well refuse to drive her about in his spare time, but that doesn't mean he likes being seen with her so much."

It really might be so. . . .

"Then you do think she's in love with him?"

"Anyone with eyes can see she is—head over heels! Her behaviour alone is enough to start this silly town gossiping. I hate saying so now, but Beryl was the worst of the lot. I suppose in a hero-worshipping way she was in love with him too, which would explain her treating his affair with the Baroness as an established thing. Bravado, you know. She was afraid I'd suspect her of personal motives in trying to open his eyes, as he called it."

"Was she trying to do that?"

"Oh, decidedly! Especially since she got back from this visit. She didn't dare do it directly, and had made up her mind I was to take on the dirty work. I saw her only twice, and each time she started in to stuff me with some rigmarole she'd heard in Nice, hoping I'd pass it on. As though I should! Why, he despises anything of that sort even more than I do!"

Sarah felt her muscles grow tense. "You mean she'd heard something against the Baroness? What, I wonder?"

"I've no notion, for I choked her off. I wasn't interested."

"But the doctor—could he have caught a bit of it? The first time she began. Was he here?"

"Could he have done? I hardly think so, though he did come in, and that shut her up like a trap. No, I'm pretty certain he didn't guess. Anyhow, knowing, her, poor soul, I shouldn't have attached any importance to it, whatever it was, nor would he, even if it had made him angry. Her stories were never very trustworthy."

Probably true—but oh, to think that Marjory had been on the verge of learning what was now forever lost, and from her own scruples or the dread of her employer's displeasure had thrown away the chance! Much as Sarah liked the honest-eyed girl she could have wished her a little less conscientious.

"I suppose," Marjory continued, her smooth brow puckered in thought, "The Baroness hangs on to him largely because he gives her so little encouragement. Some women are like that, wanting only what's difficult to get. Potiphar's wife, you know. Sometimes when I've seen her tempting him as she does even before me I marvel she doesn't yet seem to have succeed—"

She had broken off to stare hard at the laboratory door, her attitude that of strained listening.

"What's wrong?" asked Sarah, following her eyes.

"So silly of me!" The dispenser gave a shame-faced laugh. "Do you know, I keep fancying I can hear that old dog snuffling in there? Just habit—and nerves." She sewed busily for a moment, only to lay down her work with a despairing sigh. "No use," she muttered. "I can't help feeling how almost uncanny it was, those two dying on the same day, both without warning, and both in horrible pain. Had you thought of it, too?"

"Not especially." A sudden wild notion made Sarah add with knit brow, "See here, Miss Barrows, you can't mean to suggest that the bulldog died from the same cause as Miss Tomlins?"

"Oh, no, not that!" denied Marjory, hastily. "And the dog wasn't poisoned, either—at least it couldn't have been one of the well-known poisons, or he'd have recognised the symptoms at once, while the strange poisons are so hard to get we can safely rule them out." She seemed to be arguing with herself, not for the first time. All at once, a vein trembling in her transparent temple, she leant forward to whisper agitatedly, "Miss MacNeil, don't breathe a word of what I'm going to say! It would ruin me—but here it is: I've a feeling that beast was deliberately got rid of, somehow, for some purpose. What's more, I'm positive the Baron thinks so, too."

Her tense conviction startled Sarah. There was something behind this. . . .

"Why do you say that?"

"I don't know. That's the trouble, I've no good reason. Now and then I get these strong feelings. They're seldom wrong."

"Still," insisted Sarah, bent on probing the mystery. "Something must have given you the idea. Was there anything odd about the dog's death?"

"Yes—in a way." Marjory glanced fearfully round. "The boat-house door, for instance. When the Baron fell asleep, it was propped open with a stone, and Polly, as usual, was snoring on the floor. When he woke, Polly was gone, and the door shut fast."

"The wind blew it to."

"Yesterday? Not enough wind to dislodge that big stone. I've seen it a hundred times. No, it looks to me as though Polly was lured outside and the door closed so the Baron couldn't know what was happening in time to do anything about it. Lured to the house, maybe, since she was found in her kennel. Greedy old thing, she'd go anywhere for a meal! Then the drinking-vessel—bone-dry, although it had been filled after lunch. Makes one think the dog had eaten food that made her terribly thirsty, or else that the water itself had been tampered with. The stuff must have been tasteless, because Polly was very pernickety."

"Did the Baron tell you these things?"

"No, Angela. He's said nothing at all. Too little, in fact."

"But mightn't one of the servants—"

"I'd never suspect either Angela or Sebastiano. They're too fond of their master to injure his dog. Demo I would suspect. He's an under-handed brute, and cruel to animals. Once I saw him give Polly a savage kick, and I've always thought he may have done away with the little Pom that disappeared—killed it or sold it. It used to snap at him. However, he's out of the question in this case. He was in Toulon, on business for the Baron. Yes," musingly, "they've lost both dogs in two months. That's odd, too. . . ."

Again Sarah sensed the withholding of important matter. "But why do you think the Baron agrees with you if he hasn't said anything?"

"Don't you understand, he wouldn't speak if he realised there was no proving what he thought? It's the look in his eyes that tells me. Stunned misery—and questioning. You can see him asking himself over and over who could have done this vile thing to him and why? For it was vile! The surest, most wantonly calculating way of dealing him a crushing blow. Only a fiend could have conceived it."

Ashamed of her unwonted violence, Marjory reddened and took a calmer tone.

"I've no right to talk like this. All I mean is, assuming it was deliberately done, the effect on a sensitive invalid might be very serious. It might actually loosen the poor man's hold on life, make him do something desperate."

"I see," Sarah spoke slowly. "Then the Baroness may not be exaggerating after all."

Marjory fixed mutinous eyes on her face.

"Oh, so she's been running on about it, has she? Stupid woman, just revelling, I daresay, in the chance to show off her emotional temperament! Why can't she hold her tongue, and why can't she leave that husband of hers in peace? It's all he asks—just to be let alone, not treated like a lunatic that can't be trusted out of sight. She's letting him see exactly what's in her mind. If it wasn't so like all she does, I'd be prepared to say . . ."

"What?" prompted Sarah, consumed with curiosity.

"Oh, I'm talking rubbish! Don't pay any attention to my maunderings, will you? I expect you've noticed the Baroness loves dramatising a situation. Maybe she is a bit of a child, just fond of working up sympathy and so on. We'll leave it at that."

Hurriedly she folded the undervest, rose, and asked if Sarah would like a peep at the doctor's room.

"I tidy it when he's out, but it never stays tidy. All the same it's rather homey, don't you think?"

She had led the way to a fair-sized bedroom looking out on the small back garden, and furnished with a divan-bed covered in brown linen, a Louis Philippe commode, a couple of worn basket chairs, and a table littered with medical journals. Sarah's discerning eye took in two reproductions of Blake drawings, a pot of blue hyacinths—Marjory's contribution, no doubt—and a row of crowded bookshelves whose contents had overflowed into stacks on the floor. There was a pleasant odour of tobacco in the air.

"A real man's room," commented Marjory, laying the mended garment in a drawer and joining Sarah in her inspection of the photographs ranged along the top ledge of the bookcase. "He keeps his pipes clean, I'll say that . . . doesn't she look like him about the eyes? His mother. And the boy in rowing-kit's his young brother, just gone up to Oxford on a scholarship. These are hospital friends, and farther along . . . oh, I see, you're looking at her. Well,"—in a tone hardened, apprehensive. "And what do you think of it?"

The dispenser must have guessed that the large and expensive photograph confronting them stood forth as a glaring refutation of her theories.

Some likenesses are non-committal, meaning nothing. This one bore an intimate message there was no misunderstanding—or so Sarah, coming down to hard earth with a bang, felt wretchedly convinced. It was not alone the modestly veiled seduction of the pose, the too-stressed withdrawal into the shadowy background, nor even the glint in the heavy-lidded eyes so paradoxical a contrast with the Madonna setting. No, it went beyond these, unanalysable but compelling in its suggestion, pervading the whole picture and extending to the scrawled *Bimi* in the corner.

Marjory muttered uncomfortably, "Suppose he felt obliged to put it up since it was given to him, framed and all. I'm glad it's in here, though, where his patients don't come. I never let Beryl see it. She'd enough wrong notions as it was."

Wrong? The girl's ardent defence was but dust to blind her own eyes. Gilcrest was no fleeing Joseph, whatever for policy's sake he might choose to pretend. Sarah's original belief swept back on her, to the accompaniment of aching pain.

On the path to the private beach, the thought of the photograph tended to eclipse the really important revelation culled from her interview. She knew that if she had displayed the wrist-watch Marjory would have hotly denied that Gilcrest could be the donor—and indeed it did seem fantastic that he could have squandered eight or ten thousand francs at a go on a bauble of this kind; but would these arguments have touched the main issue? Bimi might have a rich lover in Paris, with the doctor here as her *amant de coeur*.

Gradually this unpleasant field of conjecture gave place to what mattered more—the fact that Beryl Tomlins' intended announcement concerned the Baroness. Impossible to imagine any connecting link between Major Frampton's 'accident' and the Baroness, nor was it easy to pick flaws in the story vouched for by three people, of whom the Baron and Harry were two, even though this version failed in one respect to coincide with Beryl's. For that matter, those at the villa had a better chance to judge the Major's inebriety than the woman who had merely seen him at a distance. No, as Marjory averred, the thing must have been a mare's nest. Beryl in her absurd jealousy had snatched at some far-fetched nonsense to use as a weapon against one she disliked. Very rash of her, if true; but Gilcrest had declared she possessed a dangerous tongue. He was probably right.

But what about Marjory's evasive hints regarding the bulldog? Another mystery in the offing? Hating herself for it, Sarah longed to tear from her memory Harry's light-hearted jokes about the doctor's aversion to the beast, as well as the look of loathing seen on the Baroness' face when the creature came near her. Worse still did she deplore ever having heard that telling phrase, "the chemistry of the body." Few would dream of cutting up a dog's body to discover what killed it, and something told her that the Baron would be the last to take such a step if he suspected his wife and his close friend of a cruel complicity.

"Whatever put such a horrid notion in my mind? It isn't Marjory's at all! Why, in the same breath she was protesting against any intrigue between those two, and declaring what a vile act it would be to inflict suffering on—"

Her musings were arrested by a pathetic sight. She had come upon the boat-house, through the gaping door of which she beheld the Baron de Bellesnaves, a hunched and dejected figure prone on a dilapidated cane settee. Asleep—but the twitching lips, the sparse lashes moving against the withered cheeks spoke of unhappy dreams, while the hand groping blindly towards the floor at his side seemed to be mechanically feeling for the departed comrade. A lump rose in Sarah's throat.

Wedged against the door was the big stone Marjory had mentioned. No, it would take a strong gale to displace that. The thing did look queer.

She tiptoed past and entering the choked path soon lost herself in semi-tropical growth into which the sun scarcely penetrated. All about her were budding oleander, feathery tamarisk and festooned creepers starred with crimson blooms; the air was close and fragrant as a hothouse. Here and there, almost buried in foliage, was a leaden cherub or a dusty bench. Once she came on a small fountain, a stone dolphin in the centre spouting water into a basin green-glazed with frog's spawn. An enchanting wilderness in which to loiter and explore if the mind were free to enjoy it, and even as it was Sarah made frequent halts to sniff the honeyed scents or gaze back at the sapphire patches of sea through gaps in the trees.

Suddenly she stopped, her heart in her mouth. What was this—a child's grave? Half in horror she stared at the mound of freshly turned earth neatly encircled with plants, then broke into uncertain laughter. Polly's, of course! Old, snuffling eyesore of a Polly laid to rest beneath primroses and violets! Ridiculous—and sad. Here, in the mould, she saw the imprint of the master's shoe, and beside it a smaller depression of a toe and heel, showing that the Baroness had helped with the task.

A rustle of leaves drew her eyes to a path ahead. There, just emerged from the thicket of rhododendrons, stood a swart figure in a workman's blouse so drenched with sweat as to reveal the powerful chest-muscles to which it clung. Demosthenes—familiar, malignant, watchful—and he was completely barring the way by which she had to go. In his hand was a sharp pruning-knife.

The villa was yet far distant. She was alone with the creature—at his mercy, if he really wished to harm her. The new skin on her arms smarted with the heat, but she needed no reminder of the ideas she had been harbouring about this Greek. The moist cigarette pendant from his smiling lips recalled the charred stump Angela had found beneath the chair. Who but he could have set fire to her? And having failed once he would seek another opportunity. . . .

"Lady look for house? See! Up there."

He pointed with a blackened forefinger, but did not move an inch.

"Thanks, I know the way."

As she pressed against the reeking body to get past panic seized her lest the knife be driven into her back; but no, she was safe, and though she could feel him looking after her as she almost fled towards the terraces he made no attempt to follow. Now she reviled herself for her absurd cowardice. It must be the two successive shocks this week had contained which had left her so unstable; all the same fright had reduced her to so quivering a state that she knew she would not again venture about these grounds unaccompanied.

The blue hydrangeas looked wilted, the long facade of the villa lay blistering in the glare. No one answered her ring, and she was frowning up at the shuttered windows and wondering what to do when from the left wing of the building she caught the low rumble of a man's voice, indistinct, as though a pipe were held between the teeth, and hard upon it a peal of silvery laughter. The Baroness was entertaining a caller in the *serre* of evil associations—and with the vision of the photograph clearly outlined before her eyes Sarah had little doubt who the caller was. Perhaps—detestable thought!—he chose the siesta hour, well knowing the Baron would be dozing in the boat-house, and the servants, according to habit, roaming at large. Her cheek, burned as she tried to stamp out her fatuous delusion, telling herself that even while she was reading tender meanings into Gilcrest's glance his one preoccupation had been to keep his clandestine appointment here.

Should she turn back? No, it would be too difficult to explain matters to Miss Venables. Still, as she rounded the corner of the terrace, she paused, unable to go on, and it was this momentary halt which gave her the chance to witness, unobserved, a bizarre little scene taking place within the greenhouse. Past the row of windows Mme. de Bellesnaves was parading with strides long and ungainly yet curiously mincing.

Perched on her head was her husband's battered old Panama hat, a raffia bag dangled from her arm, and her free hand, stiffly upright, supported some object evidently intended to represent a lorgnette through which she nearsightedly squinted.

It was but a glimpse, for a rapturous guffaw brought the performance to a close. The actress, soft and supple, again, swept off her grotesque head-piece, stretched her bare, brown arms with a cat-like grace, and turned her vivid, laughing face in the watcher's direction. She gave a start. For one instant the scarlet lips rounded in transfixed astonishment, then uttered a cry of welcome slightly too shrill to sound genuinely pleased. There was a little rush, and Sarah's arms were seized with an impetuosity which caused their owner to wince.

"Mon ange! C'est vous—et toute seule?" A quick glance round. "But why did you not at once join us? You have but this moment come? Ah, I see! You rang and got no reply. Psh, those execrable servants, sliding like eels into the mud when one's back is turned! No matter, you have found me, basking in the sun, and entertaining—but look, see who is here."

Her voice tinkled like ice in a glass. For all the fireworks' display of hospitality there was no pleasure in it, but Sarah, half led, half pushed into the *serre*, had no choice but to enter. Out of the green blur spread before her sun-dazzled eyes she made out a table with bottles and a siphon, and behind it a long, lithe figure just risen from the depths of a canvas chair, and wiping the warm moisture from his sunburned face.

She stared at him, nonplussed, then immeasurably relieved.

"Why Harry! It's you!"

CHAPTER NINETEEN

"AND whom, pray, did you expect to find?" retorted Mme. de Bellesnaves, bantering but a trifle snappish. "I can assure you there are few men who would dare invade my privacy at this hour!"

Harry looked sheepish.

"I apologise," he said humbly. "You see,"—turning to Sarah—"when I got to Hyères everybody was out, and that left me at a loose end. I knew Chrissie wouldn't want me while she was inspecting tombstones, so I took a chance and barged in here."

The Baroness made a moue at him. It was a bit puzzling to reconcile the recent hilarity with her present very real irritation—and had that late scene meant what to one person's horrified eyes it had seemed to mean? Harry, at least, could have put no such interpretation on it, but then he was not exactly quick-witted. Whatever the case, the atmosphere of the *serre* was uncomfortably strained. Sensing it, Sarah hastened to get her errand over and depart.

"Your watch," she said, laying the jewelled band on her hostess's lap. "Weren't you worried about it? We found it stuck down in the sofa."

The dark eyes opened wide, but with dislike, as though it were a toad they rested upon.

"That!" cried the owner in contempt, almost annoyance. "But do you mean to say you've given yourself this long walk in the sun to bring it back to me? You are exceedingly good, but really you should not have troubled."

As she toyed viciously with the clasp, Sarah got the impression that instead of rendering a service she had committed a faux pas. Why, she could not think, for surely the Baroness must be glad to recover anything so valuable. Perhaps she guessed the pretence about the diamonds had been detected, or she might be simply out of temper over the second visitor's arrival. Harry, however, appeared to be included in the ban, and to be dimly conscious of the fact.

"What," he ventured mildly, "would you have done if you hadn't got it back?"

"Called on the town crier, of course. You must know by now that we still have that custom in this benighted community. Not that he's of much use. He had no luck at all when my little Fifi was lost, though we offered a reward larger than the price of the poor angel. Fate, I suppose, does not mean us to have any pets."

She sighed bitterly, but more in anger than in grief, so Sarah thought. It was the first and only time she had shown this lack of cordiality. She seemed to be brooding over something, and impatient not to be alone. Sarah, for her part, was feeling all at once critical, aloof, even suspicious— though what she suspected was not quite clear. A long silence ensued, which no one appeared able to break. Sarah rose, and was not surprised to find Harry following her example. The Baroness' protests sounded insincere. What, so soon, and without refreshment? Her manner softened.

"Do forgive me," she begged, "if I am a little distrait. It is my husband, you understand. I am so disturbed over him that I scarcely know what I am doing. I can make myself gay for a moment, but—" She shrugged. "It does not last long, *comprenez*?"

She addressed this to Sarah, searching her face a little anxiously. Content with what she found, she turned to Harry and with forced heartiness said, "Good luck with your gambling. You are off to-night, is that so? Personally I detest Monte Carlo, but all the same I hope you will break the bank."

So Harry was going at once to Monte Carlo! Sarah had not heard it mentioned. As they set off towards the gate she was about to inquire when he had made this decision, but at that moment the Baroness called him back to fetch his tobacco-pouch, and she was left standing on the terrace. A bent figure hobbled out of the shrubbery. It was Henri de Bellesnaves—and how shrunken and yellow he looked! A living corpse was what Sarah thought of as with bared head and pale eyes dazzled by the sun he stopped and held out his hand.

"I'm so terribly sorry," she murmured awkwardly. "About Polly, you know. I've wanted to tell you."

He pressed her fingers in silent appreciation, smiled at her in his usual whimsical fashion but with an indescribable pathos, and let his gaze wander over the landscape. His shoulders moved upward with a gesture of quiet stoicism.

"It had to be," he said at last. "It had to be,"—and turning he limped away towards the front door.

What patience, what philosophy there had been in those age-old, incurable infantile eyes! Eyes that seemed to see everything that existed . . . and what exactly had he meant by those words, "It had to be?" They troubled her strangely. She began to feel that perhaps, after all, the Baroness had cause for alarm.

Harry came up, stowing his pouch in his pocket.

"Yes," he remarked as they got into the car, "I thought with this cursed funeral coming off I might as well clear out. It was Chrissie's idea. She mentioned it when I plunked her down with Mrs. Bulstrode at the undertaker's place. Wish you were coming with me."

"So do I," said Sarah absently. "Harry—do you think there's any danger of the Baron's—well, doing anything rash?"

"You mean on account of losing that foul pest of a dog?" He looked at her with a slight frown. "Oh, I should hardly think so. She's got that notion on the brain, anyone can see she has; but I told her just now it was all flaming nonsense. He'll pull around all right. A crock like that always does. If I'd realised how worried she was, I wouldn't have dropped in, but I did do my bit to liven her up. She can't miss a chance to rag, can she? She got on to me over this girl—the one in Hyères, you know." He chuckled with enjoyment. "You should have seen the imitation she did. Her idea of the English. It was a scream."

"Oh, so that's what she was doing!"

Sarah was feeling comfortable again—or nearly so—and for no good reason was taking solace from the fact that it was Harry who had been here and not Gilcrest. What if the main situation remained as before? At least she had seen nothing, and that left her some slight hope.

In the lobby they came upon Miss Venables and Mrs. Bulstrode, just returned. Harry vanished to pack his bag, and the spinster, eager with interest, gave Sarah the result of her expedition.

"I believe Mrs. Cripps will approve our choice—just a simple marble tablet, with a flat wreath carved in front. Beryl would have hated anything fussy. We're going to plant primroses and violets on the grave, with wall-flowers and forget-me-nots to follow."

It would look exactly like Polly's grave, in fact—but as Sarah was struck by this perverse thought, another, equally unbidden, sprang into her mind. Her eye was caught and held, fascinated, by Miss Venables' hat, large, wobbly and misshapen, and by the clumsy shopping-bag pendant from her arm. The gesticulating lorgnette as well . . . it was as though an adder just crushed had reared its ugly head to hiss in her face. Harry might believe the impish Bimi had been portraying a general type of Englishwoman, but the thing had been like, far too cruelly like, to please her. Her doubt returned in full force. She would have given a good deal not to have seen that entertainment.

Soon after this they saw Harry off, and so did a bevy of dejected maidens. Carefree, unable to hide his relief, he was like a school-boy suddenly let off exams. When he was seated in the car Miss Venables, bidding him good-bye, surreptitiously pressed a folder bit of paper into his hand. He blushed under his tan and tried not to take it.

"Oh, I say! I shan't be wanting this. Here! Hold on!"

"I daresay it will come in useful," said his aunt, smiling fondly at him. "But if it doesn't, then just tuck it away to your account. No high stakes, remember. I have your address, I think? Oh, yes, dear, don't worry about me. With Sarah here, I shall be quite happy—that is, as happy as one can be just at present," she corrected herself, recalling the funeral of her friend. "Have a good time."

Sarah, a tiny bit wistful, gazed after the disappearing red streak. Then she remembered her meeting with Gilcrest, and things brightened directly. What did it matter if for a time he had been captured by another enchantress? She was tempted to think that attraction was on the wane, and that if she played her own cards well enough. . . .

Miss Venables was standing by the letter-rack, her attitude ominously tense. The last delivery was just in, and she was clutching a square, cheap grey envelope which looked familiar. Coming quickly to her side Sarah saw a rudely-printed superscription and at once knew the reason for the trembling hand, the suddenly-dry lips.

"Not here," whispered the poor woman between chattering teeth. "We'll look upstairs. But I'll tell you this much: it was posted to-day, here, in this town."

CHAPTER TWENTY

IT WAS still daylight when Miss Venables and Sarah hurried across the gravelled square fronting the squat, stone building occupied by the Commissaire de Police.

"I can't bear reviving all that tiresome talk of last year," muttered the former, casting furtive glances to left and right. "That's why I refuse to have any of these officials come to the hotel. I would not see the Chef at all if I didn't feel it my duty. You do think it's the right thing?"

"But you must tell him about this!" declared Sarah warmly. "It's his duty to protect you."

Posted in the town . . . when Sarah recalled what had followed hard on the last letter, posted at Charing Cross, her heart stood still with terror. Strange that even now she could not wholly dispel her doubts concerning the sister-in-law's death! Indeed, an explanation had just occurred to her : suppose that somehow, between the chemist-shop and the Metropolitan Hotel, the medicine ordered by Gilcrest had been tampered with? Some undiscoverable substance inserted, with the idea that it would be taken by Miss Venables, not the other woman? It might have been done. All she felt confident of was that Gilcrest could have had nothing to do with it.

Through the bare, dingy entrance-hall Miss Venables led the way to an anteroom from which, after a tedious wait, a sleepy subordinate admitted them to the presence of the Chef. The latter, a brown-bearded Provençal, sat laboriously writing in a ledger. He raised shrewd eyes to the older woman's face, extended an incurious regard to Sarah, and waving his visitors to seats prepared to listen. When, in her careful French, Miss Venables had stated her case, she laid the offending missive face-upward on the blotter. In a voice kept low to restrain its trembling she added a few words.

"In Ste. Brigitte I fancied I should be quite safe. I do not blame the police for this, for naturally no one can prevent a letter being sent by post; but still, after the assurances I have had, I thought it impossible for the writer of these threats to be actually on the spot. I realise the prisoners themselves are still powerless to harm me. This person, evidently a confederate, has been detailed to follow me wherever I go, and at the first opportunity bring about my death. As you will see, I am given one more day to live. Is there the slightest use applying to you for protection?"

The Chef, playing negligently with his pen, darted her a glance in which cool arrogance was mingled with Gallic sophistication. He then inspected the document, which was a curious affair. The paper contained a rough chart, something like a calendar, with thirteen squares each occupied by a date, beginning with April 17th of the previous year and ending with the same date in the present year. The first dozen seventeens were crossed off. Beside the thirteenth was an interrogation-mark followed by the single sentence, "If you escape this time the chase is ended—but to do so you must remember our last advice."

The Chef looked up. "I do not read English," he said. "Will you favour me with a translation?"

When Sarah had given him the French rendering he sat in sceptical silence, pinching his full lower lip between a not over-clean finger and thumb.

"And what was the final word of advice?" he inquired unemotionally.

"I was told to keep away from water," the spinster replied.

"Ah! And have you done so?"

"Yes—after crossing the Channel; but how is one to know just what is meant?"

A shrug was the only answer to this, but presently, leaning back in his chair, and weighing his sentences with scrupulous deliberation, the Chef delivered the following pronouncement:

"Mademoiselle, every itinerant vendor of the sort you suspect, as well as all Orientals of whatever description, have been subjected to close observation with entirely negative results. The police have concluded that the threats you have received—empty ones, thus far, as you yourself will admit—cannot emanate from the alleged source. We must therefore continue to regard them as a species of hoax, the purpose of which I do not venture to postulate. That is, unless your own knowledge can suggest an alternative theory?"

"I have given you my explanation. I know of no other."

He shrugged again, raised resigned brows, and tapped the paper with unveiled contempt.

"If you choose to leave this with us, we can test it for fingerprints. Is that your desire?"

Miss Venables, who had winced and grown a shade more rigid, gave an indifferent consent.

"There was nothing but my own finger-prints on the other letters. I imagine this will be the same."

"Precisely. That is the answer I anticipated," retorted the official with an irony which conveyed a covert insult.

"Then—" She flushed dully. "You can do nothing for me?"

"I fear not, mademoiselle; but pray let me impress upon you, there is nothing to dread; the danger is not real. The very wording of the present message allows you a loophole, does it not? Well, rest assured that after to-morrow—that is the seventeenth of April—you can abandon your morbid apprehension and write *finis* to the whole episode."

Was this sarcasm? Sarah, torn between sympathy for the woman so singularly defenceless against cold-blooded officialdom and curiosity to know what this singular consolation had meant detected a lurking smile on the bearded face. That smile seemed to indicate some private assumption on the speaker's part, some hidden conviction which nothing could shake, but what it could be she was at a total loss to imagine.

"You see how it is?" Miss Venables burst out as soon as they had quitted the building. "I must be murdered before the law can make a move. Well!" Her lips tightened in stoical restraint. "Come what may, I shall not set foot inside that building again. At least let me cling on to some shreds of self-respect."

That she had suffered deep mortification Sarah did not doubt. What she could not guess was whether the impression gleaned from the interview coincided with her own.

"Why," she hazarded delicately, "did he behave as though it were the height of folly to take these threats seriously?"

"But surely you understand! To me it is clear as day. If he admits danger it is tantamount to saying Major Frampton was murdered—a thing in no circumstances to be conceded. I expected as much. In fact," with a tortured sigh—"I was fully prepared for it."

Sarah was not wholly satisfied, but linking her arm through her employer's and keeping pace with the long, nervous strides she took another tack. Had Miss Venables been worried as before without betraying her state of mind? For if so neither Harry nor herself had seen any sign of it.

"I am in constant apprehension," was the unwilling reply, whispered lest some passer-by should hear. "Yes, even though I've had both of you with me, as the seventeenth draws near I watch every post. I have tried hard to conquer my fears by repeating just what that man has pointed out—but the series of false alarms may mean only luck on my part. Death in an apparently accidental manner cannot be very easy to contrive."

"Not easy at all! I should say it was so difficult we needn't lose any sleep over it. All the same, if it would make you more comfortable to have Harry back, why not let me ring him up the moment he reaches Monte and tell him what's happened?"

"On no account!" the spinster exclaimed with surprising energy. "Egotistical I may be, but I draw the line at frightening the poor boy and spoiling his pleasure when his presence here can guarantee no protection. Don't say a word to him. You give me your solemn promise?"

Sarah agreed, howbeit reluctantly, comforting herself by reflecting that though Harry would wish to be told future crises might arise when he was beyond call, while she was being paid to assume complete guardianship. Actually the visit to the Commissaire, for all it had angered and mystified her, had removed the worst of her fears. Already she could foresee this time passing by as harmlessly as the others had done.

"We will speak to no one of this," Miss Venables was saying with great earnestness. "No one, mind—not even the doctor. I don't mean to suggest that he has been at all unsympathetic—far from it!—but merely that I have grown highly sensitive about—well, making a fool of myself before those whose opinions I value. If I go on crying 'Wolf!' each time these excitements occur, I shall soon turn into an intolerable nuisance."

"Never!" cried Sarah loyally. "You couldn't be that."

"Oh, but I could! And now that another, and possibly the final test has come, I intend to take a firm line. Witness what I am going to say; until the seventeenth is past I shall take reasonable precautions, but after that, if I still live, none at all. I am tired of cringing. Once this period is past, I shall throw caution to the winds and never refer to this wretched persecution again. Have I made myself clear?"

"I think you are splendid!" murmured Sarah, squeezing her arm. "And do you know? I've a feeling this will be your last fright. Something tells me our precious lunatic—for it is a lunatic, can't be anything else—is weary of the game and wants to quit."

"I am quitting, which is more to the point," returned the good woman grimly. "And if I keep you on—which I should much like to do—it will be in a different capacity from that of private nurse. We get on well together, don't we? I—" She had stopped in the middle of the pavement, and was staring straight ahead. "S'sh! There is Dr. Gilcrest, coming out of that house. Don't allow him to suspect . . ."

Sarah's pulses gave a bound as she saw the doctor glance with particular interest at herself. He approached, with slight diffidence, and explained that he had just dropped in at the local vet's to inspect a young wire-haired terrier he was proposing to buy for the Baron.

"Six months old, and a lively chap. A bit too lively, I'm afraid, but now we've met, perhaps you'd give me your advice? I've said I'd think it over."

Either Miss Venables welcomed the diversion, or else, as Sarah had noticed on former occasions, she was always ready to sink her personal worries in the concerns of others. Her drawn features became alert with eagerness, her one desire that of seeing the dog. They walked round to the kennels at the back, and soon she was exclaiming over the antics of a frolicsome terrier which tore at her gloves and leaped frantically to lick her cheek.

"But he is a darling! No, no, he not at all too lively. The Baron cannot help but take to a friendly little creature like this. Why do you hesitate?"

"He'll chew things. The Baroness may object."

To Sarah the explanation sounded cold. Was Marjory right?

"Maddalena object to what gives her husband pleasure? Never in this world! I suppose you don't want to consult either of them for fear they'll refuse. Is that it? Yes, much better just to present him to the Baron. I had the same idea. What is the vet asking? A thousand francs? Oh dear, I cannot permit you to do this! It must be my gift. See, I have my cheque-book in my bag."

"Keep it there," retorted Gilcrest, smiling but firm. "No, I won't lend you my pen. If you approve of the dog, then it's all settled, and I shall take him home with me. Miss Barrows will keep him a day or so just to see if his habits are respectable. Will you come and see him installed?"

To Sarah's joy the invitation was accepted, and soon the dispenser was exclaiming over the mass of affection strung on steel wires which made an exuberant onslaught on her orderly appointments.

"Oh, how adorable! What's his name? Max? A real bundle of mischief—no, I don't mind. We'll borrow one of your cushions, doctor, to make him a bed in the laboratory. He can't hurt anything in there. See, here's Polly's saucer, washed clean, and—but do look at his lordship, already rooting out those dreadful old slippers! Let him alone, Miss MacNeil, this will force the doctor to buy a new pair."

Before leaving Miss Venables asked permission to look through the doctor's books in search of something light to read. Sarah fancied that he hesitated slightly as he went ahead to switch on the lights, and when after a brief interval he invited both guests to help themselves to whatever books might please them, the reason for the delay became apparent. Sarah's first thought on entering the room was the Baroness's photograph, which her employer had probably not seen. She glanced swiftly towards the corner of the bookshelves and felt a blankness descend on her.

The picture was gone.

CHAPTER TWENTY-ONE

A QUALM of chilled doubt, then an excuse for the diplomatic manoeuvre suggested itself. Hiding the photograph need mean nothing more serious than the wise desire to prevent Miss Venables from forming wrong conclusions. At any rate this was the comforting view Sarah intended to embrace till confronted by contrary proof. During the past half hour Gilcrest had been entirely human and natural with her, making her every whit as eager as Marjory to absolve him of unworthy suspicion, and more anxious than ever to shine in his esteem. A pity to spoil things when they were going so well.

The three pored over the book-shelves while the spinster made her selection, but now the latter had returned to the dispensary, leaving Sarah still ostensibly absorbed in titles. Gilcrest, at her side, glanced after his patient with a questioning frown, then at herself. Twice he had done this, and now as before Sarah was sure he wanted to venture some private inquiry. However he shut his lips, and the idea that he had noticed something amiss lost itself in the onrush of emotion roused by his physical presence. Strange but true that even from the first, against her will as it were, he had exerted an attraction for her. The feeling, fed on obstacles, had grown till now, bodily and mentally, he drew her more than any other man had done in the whole course of her twenty-three years. She could not account for it, for he was not good-looking in an obvious sense, nor till this afternoon had he shown her anything but the most unflattering indifference varied by active antagonism. At times he had seemed to resent her—she could not think why. Still, there it was. She wanted him—and realising that moments like these were hard to capture she clutched at any excuse to prolong them.

"May I borrow something too?" She held out a volume bound in faded green silk which she had taken at random from the top of the case. "The novels in the hotel are all so piffling—and I've read them all."

"Take anything you like," he answered, looking at her in the hesitant manner which always made her feel the existence of a barrier between them. His eyes wrenched themselves away from her face to glance at her choice, then with change of expression, he exclaimed, "Flaubert— The *Trois Contes*. Think you'll care for that?"

She had hardly noticed what book it was.

"As a matter of fact, I've read this, too," she admitted with a laugh. "But it was years ago, and I loved it. I still remember this first tale. The style is something you can't forget, isn't it?"

"Flaubert! Yes, it's wonderful stuff. So you read French easily, do you?"

There was kindled interest in his tone, and the look he gave her sent the blood racing through her veins. Here was an unexpected bit of luck! She told him that she read French almost as freely as English; that, indeed, a good part of her intermittent schooling had been in France. He seemed surprised, though whether it was the information which held him she could not tell. Perhaps those level, attentive eyes were chained by the sudden brilliance in her own or by the curved length of her dark lashes. She knew that with so much pomegranate red risen to the pale olive of her cheeks she must be looking transfigured, but then she had mustered as many charms before and made no impression. Whatever the reason, he seemed prone to tarry, even willing to please.

"So you were at school over there—and in other countries as well? That accounts for it, I suppose."

"You mean for my smattering of an education?" she flung at him provocatively. All her boldness had returned, she was not afraid to be herself.

"For you." He waved the raillery aside, but not with his usual scorn. "Well, my French books are down below, on the bottom shelves. Want to look them over?"

"Please!" She slipped to the floor. "All my favourites, I see. Gautier— Stendhal—Verlaine—my father read Verlaine to me, and so beautifully."

Her lap overflowed with the volumes she had pulled out. After a brief indecision Gilcrest joined her, and together they explored the collection, dropping comments, exchanging understanding glances. From literature they passed to other, more personal topics. Were they friends at last, and would these easier relations lead to something better? Sarah wanted to think so. At one moment she did think so, and then at the very summit of her elation doubt gnawed at her heart. Although he had shown the first beginnings of curiosity concerning her own past life and surroundings, he was giving her almost nothing in return. Again and again, seeking to draw him out, she fell back before stone ramparts of reserve impossible to assault, had the feeling that he was shielding, guarding from her some part of himself that must not be permitted to come into the open. An inhibitive force—was it the other woman?—held his impulses in leash.

"Oh, Max! You're killing me!"

She had cried out as the terrier, rushing on her from the rear, fastened on her bare arm with playful violence. Gilcrest cuffed the dog away, swore under his breath, and taking her by the wrist bent to see the damage.

"Just where you were burned, too! God, that must hurt!"

"A little. His teeth are like needles."

He still held her arm, gently, and with a touch that thrilled. His head was so close that she could see the clean line where his cropped hair ended along the red sunburn of his neck; a faint masculine odour crept intoxicatingly to her nostrils. Self-consciousness overpowered her, but she was afraid to speak again lest the spell be broken. It was he who resumed, meditatively, and as though his real thoughts were elsewhere engaged.

"Extraordinary luck that Venables got to you in time the other day. If he hadn't—but we'll not think of that."

Taken by an impulse, she leant towards him. "I've been thinking of it, though," she confided, low-voiced so she would not be overheard. "I'm afraid to mention this, because you'll be annoyed with me again, but suppose—just suppose—someone had wanted to put me out of the way? If so, it came jolly near working—didn't it?"

His blue eyes darkened. Frowning, his tone as subdued as her own he demanded, "What do you mean, put you out of the way? You can't imagine you were set on fire deliberately?"

"It had occurred to me. I've kept quiet about it. There was no lighted cigarette near me, you know, whatever the rest might believe. But—I was very close to the window. After it was all over, I saw that Greek looking in on us. I told you before, didn't I, that—" She dared not finish, searching his face for the displeasure she expected.

"That's impossible nonsense," he assured her flatly. "There's no real harm in the fellow, beyond drinking and pilfering. The affairs mysterious, I admit, but no doubt there's a simple explanation if we could find it. I hope you've not let this notion prey on you?"

"Oh, no! Only, if I had got burned to death, there'd be no one to bother much except Miss Venables. I'm an orphan child," she laughed,

"No foot-hold, no visible connections—just a vagrant, and nobody cares what becomes of them, do they?"

"I didn't quite realise how—how unattached you were," he said soberly, his gaze on hers. "You don't look it, you know. When I first saw you, I supposed . . ."

"What?" she whispered, at the same time aware that from the other room her name was being called. "What did you suppose about me?"

His hand had tightened on hers. Now as though the contact stung him he dropped it, preparing to rise.

"Can't interest you. I'm talking pure rot. Shall we go back?"

A door had banged to in her face, but that did not distress her. Something had happened between the two of them, something which rendered her radiant and weak and frightened all at once. He might beat a retreat, but for a few seconds he had shown her a glimpse of what hid behind the stone barricade. If she were wise, if she played her cards with skill. . . .

"You've made one conquest," he informed her when, at the gate, he was obliged to tear the terrier from her skirts. "Young Max is yours, body and soul." He sounded defiant, grim.

"Max, indeed!" she flashed back with gay scorn. "Here, take your dog. I don't value conquests as easy as that."

He eyed her from the doorway, the dog struggling frantically in his arms. In his mordant, half-sarcastic gaze she read, "So, you're like the rest—not that it will do you any good." Or, wouldn't it? she thought. Well, one must see. As it was she had seen one thing which enchanted her. Gilcrest, the impervious, was afraid of what future tête à têtes might do. . . .

Miss Venables' voice brought her to earth with a jar. Did Sarah think the doctor or Marjory Barrows had noticed anything in her manner? She had tried to behave quite naturally.

"You succeeded. No, how could they guess?" asked Sarah, guiltily waking to how completely her employer's situation had vanished from her mind.

"Perhaps they didn't. I trust not. I only fancied the doctor glanced at me rather closely, that was all."

He would take care now to let a long time elapse before another meeting took place. Sarah recognised the signs, and knew the danger she would welcome was what Gilcrest would run miles to avoid. Yes, having seen the snare, he would walk more warily than before. It might be days, weeks . . . how would she support so long a period of doubt and inactivity?

She was mistaken in her surmise. That same evening Gilcrest called, though why she could not make out, since he took little notice of her and seemed in subtle ways to have fallen into his old attitude. Indeed, there were grounds for assuming his interest centred solely in his patient, though that did not supply a satisfactory answer either. In short, the visit remained a puzzle to both her employer and herself.

She had been up to fetch Miss Venables' knitting, and as she emerged from the lift there he was, with an air at once aimless and purposeful, just turning in through the main doors. Astonished at seeing him so soon, she inquired whether someone were ill.

"No." His eye wandered from the distant card-tables to the groups in the lounge, vague, restless, concealing something. "No, I had a free interval, and I thought . . ." His attention returned as he demanded with jerky abruptness, "Is Miss Venables all right? She struck me as a little tense."

What acute perceptions he must have! Dared she tell him about the letter? No, for that would be going directly counter to her instructions, much as she wanted to do so.

It might get her in trouble. Simulating surprise, she shook her head.

"No fresh upset? Miss Tomlins' death may explain it. I daresay it does. Is she sleeping well? Eating normally?"

Miss Venables' dinner had consisted of dry biscuits and a boiled egg, even the shell of which had been examined furtively to see if it were uncracked. Precautions had begun.

"This evening she was rather Spartan, but then she often has what she calls a day off. It's dull, of course, with Harry gone. She told you, I suppose, that he'd run over to Monte Carlo?"

His eyes narrowed as they searched hers. Muttering an affirmative he added tersely, "He'll be missed."

She had always realised he had small liking for Harry, but never had she conceived the wild notion that he might be jealous. Too preposterous! Yet how to account for his present tone?

Mischievously she replied, "Oh, very much so! In this community Harry's an important figure. Still, he'll be away only a few days, so we'll manage to survive."

"Humph! I see." Wheeling he showed signs of departure, only to halt in indeterminate fashion. "As I'm here, I may as well have a word with her. Is she in the lounge?" His eagerness to remain trying to hide itself under cover of duty excited her imagination, but promising as it looked she could not be wholly sure of his reason. Throughout the ensuing conversation he was absent and uncommunicative, giving laconic replies to the questions Miss Venables, in her anxiety to steer the talk away from herself, took pains to ask.

"Miss Barrows thinks that poor animal succumbed to some sort of gastric disorder. Was it that, or couldn't you tell?"

"Looked like it. Difficult to say."

Sarah, watching him through her lashes, was unable to decide whether he shrank from discussing the dog's ailment or took no deep interest in the subject. Anyhow, it was at this moment he leant forward, unobtrusively, to place his fingers on Miss Venables' wrist.

"My pulse?" The spinster eyed him with an uncertain smile. "I'm sure it's behaving quite well. I confess to being a bit over-tired this evening, but that's nothing."

"Make a quiet day of it to-morrow." He slipped his shirt-cuff into place over the watch-face he had been studying. "And,"—he paused—"keep on with your capsules. For the present, at any rate."

"I will. I've just begun on a new bottle."

"Good. I should turn in now, if I were you."

He rose, shook hands with both, and with a swift, undecipherable glance which seemed to graze Sarah's face and veer away before she could probe it, he had left them.

CHAPTER TWENTY-TWO

THE night passed safely, and if a dozen times Sarah woke with all her faculties alert the total silence coupled with the recollection that the windows and doors of both rooms were securely bolted set her mind at rest. Once she lay wondering as to why Brian Gilcrest had called, wanting to believe it was she who had drawn him, but vaguely dissatisfied as to his real motive. The book she had borrowed as yet unread, lay within reach. She caressed the cover, thrilling as she had done when the owner's strong fingers had lain on hers.

"Oh!" she breathed into her hot pillow, "if after this I should find he was actually entangled with that woman, how could I bear it? But he isn't! I'm positive the whole thing's a made-up tale."

Towards dawn, with startling suddenness, she recalled something which had happened on the way home from the doctor's. Stopping at a wine shop Miss Venables had bought and conveyed back by taxi a crate of Vichy water, now locked in her wardrobe. At the time there had seemed nothing strange about it, but now full-grown the question sprang into being, "Does she think it may be *drinking-water* which will kill her?"

Slipping out of bed Sarah had stolen into the next room. There on the bed-table was the tumbler half-filled with Vichy water which, on retiring, the spinster had used to wash down her nightly capsule. No one could have got in to meddle with the contents, but all the same Sarah rinsed the glass and replenished it. She was taking no chances.

She looked at the wan face, dimly visible in the dusk. Last night Miss Venables had admitted a slight discomfort in the gastric region, making light of it as an occurrence to be expected when her mind was disturbed, and declaring that after her usual dose she would have a comfortable night. Apparently she was right, for her breathing was calm. Reassured, Sarah crept back to bed, to wake no more till breakfast time.

The seventeenth of April was here. One year to the day since Major Frampton perished. . . .

Sarah suggested making the doctor's orders about keeping quiet an excuse for remaining in her room, but Miss Venables, obstinate in her sense of duty, held fast to her intention of meeting Beryl's sister in Hyères. The car was ordered and could be kept closed; the chauffeur would be the same who had driven her for ten years. Nothing untoward was likely to happen on the short drive to the station and back, and what would poor Mrs. Cripps think, coming all this distance and on so sad an errand, if no one met her?

"Mrs. Bulstrode or Miss Whittaker would be glad to go."

"They are strangers to her. No, as the one acquaintance she has in Ste. Brigitte, I really must do it. Once that is over, I can stay in retirement, which I shan't at all mind, for by the signs we are going to be in for a mistral."

Sarah saw the futility of argument, so gave in. After all, it was wiser not to dramatise the situation.

"Did you rest well?" she asked. "You were writing rather late, weren't you? I heard your pen scratching."

"I was." Miss Venables adjusted her hairnet, turned, and picked up a pile of sealed envelopes from the table. "This," she said, handing Sarah the top one, "is for you. No, don't open it. Perhaps you will not have to do so at all, for if by to-morrow I am unharmed I shall have it back again to destroy. If not—" She paused, then continued steadily, "Well, read it, and carry out the instructions I have given. The other letters—they are for Harry, Maddalena de Bellesnaves, and Dr. Gilcrest—are to be delivered at once, but only in the event of my death. I shall put them here, in this drawer, so you will have no trouble in finding them. No harm, is there, in being prepared for any emergency?"

"Of course not," agreed Sarah, treating the matter with more calmness than she felt. "But there won't be any emergency, so don't let's think about it."

Always practical, always provident, Christine Venables had, so to speak, put her house in order. Now, outwardly at least, she was surveying the future with tranquil resolution. What character she had!

Sarah's own envelope was oddly bulky. What was written on the many pages it enclosed? Probably they would never be read. . . .

They had returned from Hyères. Mrs. Cripps—a pale, freckled woman, very dowdy and dishevelled from her journey, and inarticulate from fatigue and a sort of helpless distraction—had just gone into the hotel, leaving her companions to follow, when from the shade of the lopped plane-trees Demosthenes slouched forward to lay a grimy paw on Miss Venables' sleeve. Sarah, all her vague fears revived, thrust herself between, but already her employer, at first startled, was giving an apologetic little laugh.

"Is it you, Demo?" she asked kindly. Evidently the Greek held no terrors for her. "And what is that you have—a note for me? Wait, then, till I see what it says."

She examined the note through her lorgnette and clicked her tongue in dismay.

"Dear me! This is very distressing. I had no idea—but then, it seems, neither had she . . . thank you, Demo, no answer is required."

The gardener pocketed the ten franc tip bestowed on him, sidled closer, and smirked boldly into her face.

"Fine weather," he announced, blandly disregarding the heavy dullness of the sky and the leaves twisting their pale undersides upward in ominous fashion. "Lady like sail? Monsieur say I take you and other lady this afternoon, tomorrow maybe, what time you want go. Two o'clock, maybe?"

He appeared to know that Harry was not here. Perhaps he had found it out from Berthe, the doctor's servant, who had come into the dispensary yesterday while Miss Venables had mentioned her nephew's absence; but what would Miss Venables make of his suave insistence? Nothing—or else her smiling refusal was very carefully managed. Demo was to thank his master, who was indeed thoughtful to have sent so kind a message, but just at present she had no fondness for boats. It did not seem to occur to her that the invitation might well have been issued without the Baron's knowledge, although when the messenger, sullen disappointment apparent beneath his oily grin, had swaggered off to the café across the square, she did remark on how surprising such courtesy seemed in view of Maddalena's communication. Her brow was deeply furrowed with anxiety on her friend's account, and as soon as they were again in the safe haven of their rooms she showed Sarah the note. It had been written the evening before, and announced the Baroness' immediate departure for Arles.

"But this is extremely sudden, isn't it? She said nothing about it yesterday."

"Something alarming occurred. I do hope she's doing the wise thing to get her husband into different surroundings. A lonely château seems hardly the best place, does it? Though I suppose there's small choice. How glad I'd be if only she'd accept help from me! It's no use suggesting it, though. I've tried before and came near offending her."

The château was the property of the Baron's cousin, Comte Hector de Lagniolles, an archaeologist who lived for the main part in Nice. Sarah had heard him mentioned, and as she was much attached to the Baron it was natural for the Baroness to seek his advice. On being telephoned about the difficulty he had at once placed the château at his relatives' disposal, merely saying that as the building was in a ramshackle state little fit for habitation Mme. de Bellesnaves had better inspect it before making the move. He had sent his car to take her to Arles. She must have been driving all night, having left Gilcrest in charge of her husband to see he came to no harm.

Again Sarah interrupted her reading. "The doctor didn't consider there was any danger, did he? Don't you recall how impatient he was when you asked him about the Baron?"

"Yes, but that was before he heard."

The last paragraph explained matters: ". . . I found Henri loading his old service revolver. It is hidden now where he can't find it again, but what good will that do if this frightful idea is firmly fixed in his mind? I am desperate about him. The one remedy I can think of is complete removal from anything which can remind him of the poor dog. Am I not right? You will visit us at the château. Dear Chrissie, I depend on you so! Hector's car is waiting. I am too shaken to write more, but I shall be back tomorrow evening at latest." Sarah herself felt shaken. The huge, ill-formed scrawl had every appearance of having been dashed off in great mental stress, understandable enough if the writer's statement was accurate. (Why the qualifying clause? Till yesterday it would have passed unquestioned.) These events must have taken place immediately after she and Harry left. She remembered the Baron's manner, and wondered if while he had stood talking to her this thing had been in his thoughts.

But the Baroness! Was she really as perturbed as she made out? The loss of her husband could not mean a heartbreaking disaster. Almost certainly the man was an encumbrance, freed of which she would seek a different life—marry again.

Marry whom? Against the distasteful possibility which leaped into Sarah's brain could be set one shrewdly definite idea: Bimi de Bellesnaves' very evident ambition, her longing to expand and shine. Flirtatious dalliance was one thing, alliance with a struggling country physician another. No, it did not seem likely she would fasten on Brian Gilcrest as a husband. His prospects were too poor. . . .

"Perhaps it will be as well to have our lunch served up here. Mrs. Cripps will be coming in for tea, but between times I'll rest."

So, in spite of the counter-irritation provided by worry over her friends, Miss Venables had not entirely forgotten her own situation. Within these walls the seventeenth of April could pass in safety. It was half gone now, and thus far there was nothing to distinguish it from other days. Sarah breathed a sigh, and rang for the waiter.

At two o'clock—the hour Demosthenes had proposed for the sail—the mistral burst in full fury, to continue for many hours. Soon every nerve was lacerated by the monotonous scream of the wind and by the incessant patter of sand beating on the closed window-panes. Fine, reddish sand it was—desert sand, driven all the way across the Mediterranean to sift through the tiniest cracks, lie in minute drifts along the parquet, render gritty every object one touched. Ever afterwards Sarah found it impossible to think of this trying afternoon without its twin irritations of shrieking sound and inescapable grit. To her a mistral was always to mean a herald of doom.

Mrs. Cripps arrived, battered and raw from an excursion to the graveyard, her red-rimmed eyes watering, little trickles of fawn-coloured particles dropping from her dowdy black coat and skirt. She was a vague, irresolute creature, utterly unlike her sister, but exasperating as Sarah found her she created a diversion—unwelcome though it turned out.

Something was wrong. It made itself felt from the furtive glances, half frightened, half conscientiously-determined, which sought first Miss Venables' face, then her own. Beryl's sister had a problem on her mind, and was afraid to speak of it.

"I'm glad you've spoken with the doctor," the spinster remarked, calmly pouring tea. "I'm sure you've a better understanding now of the reason for your sister's sudden collapse."

The gale whistled, always on the same high note. Mrs. Cripps blew her nose, swallowed nervously, and gave a gasping response.

"I never heard of it before. I—I wrote the name down." Fumbling in her bag, she fished up a bit of paper and recited haltingly, "Mesenteric thrombosis . . . that's what he called it. He said it meant the sudden formation of a blood-clot and—and a fatal hemorrhage. In the intestinal tract it was . . . or seems to have been," she added in a strained whisper, almost a mutter. "Is—is that what you heard?"

"Exactly. These cases are fortunately very rare. She couldn't have been saved. It all happens so quickly, you see."

"So he explained . . . but—" Another covert glance darted from under the pale lashes. "We—we've only the one man's word for it, you know. No time for a consultation. What I mean is, can we be quite sure she did die of this mes—mesenteric what's its name?"

Sarah eyed her attentively. Miss Venables, slightly stiffening, set down her cup.

"Dr. Gilcrest is too experienced to make mistakes," she declared in a polite but distant tone. "Have you any reason to feel dissatisfied with his diagnosis?"

"Not—not exactly. That is I do know quite well how highly he's thought of amongst you all. Beryl had perfect belief in him—and it's true, I suppose, that he did her a lot of good, before this?"

"A vast amount of good! She became a different creature. But you seem troubled about something. May one ask what it is?"

"I—I hardly like to mention it . . . but," with another gasp, "I feel I must . . . I—I—Miss Venables, perhaps you can tell me: do you think that my sister Beryl had any enemies in this town?"

"*Enemies?*" The word was repeated with an incredulous frown. "Your sister, Beryl Tomlins? No! Certainly not! Why do you ask?"

"She might have had," murmured Mrs. Cripps, looking stubborn. "She was very outspoken, wasn't she? You see, I shouldn't have thought of it but for a thing that happened lately in Cheltenham. It—it was a physician in very good standing—but I don't want you to imagine . . . it seems he had done something of an illegal nature, and one of his patients had been talking . . . she died. There was an inquest, and it all came out. The papers were full of it."

Sarah no less than Miss Venables was staring at the speaker in outraged indignation. Incredible to think that two short days ago ideas as foul as this were buzzing through her own head! Now she could have smitten Beryl's sister, shaken her where she sat till her stupid teeth rattled in her head. And then, it came over her that by "enemies" Mrs. Cripps might have reference not to Gilcrest but to someone else. Quite evidently dissentient spirits had got hold of this weak creature since her arrival. Was it significant that last evening Janet Lowther and Muriel Ames-Gower had been hobnobbing in a corner of the lounge, ceasing to whisper when Sarah passed? All she had caught was Mrs. Cripps' name and Muriel's doubtful, "Ought we to mention it?" Whatever the information was—and it must be the same so hastily suppressed two evenings ago—it had been mentioned, with alarming results.

"Oh, Miss Venables, don't misinterpret me!" The visitor twisted her damp handkerchief, backing water dismayedly. "I didn't in the least mean to accuse Dr. Gilcrest of anything, except, possibly, being mistaken as to the cause of death. What I had in mind was something quite different— altogether too trivial to repeat, even if I hadn't faithfully promised . . . please don't press me to tell you what it was. I daresay there's nothing at all in it—and you certainly can't imagine I *want* to believe my poor sister was—"

"Poisoned?" supplied Miss Venables, breathing in through tightened nostrils.

The close room held a terrifying silence as the antagonists' eyes met and clung. The only sound was the dry, hissing patter of the sand on the panes, and the shrill screech of the mistral. Sarah hung tensely on the coming answer. In the back of her brain floated the two death-scenes she had witnessed, curiously merged into one.

CHAPTER TWENTY-THREE

IT WAS Mrs. Cripps who wavered.

"It—it would have meant poison, I suppose; but oh, do let's say no more about it! I did wrong to speak of it at all." It seemed high time to take her firmly in hand. Miss Venables did so, her hauteur admirably held in check by patient if slightly elaborate courtesy.

"My dear Mrs. Cripps, I don't think you can have taken in all I told you this morning about your sister's case. You see, for three entire days prior to her death she lived on tea and orange juice, prepared by herself. No food at all—but wait till I've done! At the doctor's dispensary she took one dose of the medicine she had come to fetch. Miss MacNeil saw her do it, and can vouch for the occurrence. Now," in a tone of triumph, "can you appreciate the full weight of your suggestions?"

Mrs. Cripps, looking like a mesmerized rabbit, could not, so her instructress elucidated: "Since Beryl's own tea and oranges could scarcely have been tampered with, the one remaining source of poison must be the medicine. You would not care, I think, to cast suspicion on either Dr. Gilcrest or the very estimable young woman who puts up his prescriptions? No, I thought not; yet that, intentionally or not, is what you would be doing if allowed such prejudicial statements to become noised abroad. Injuring innocent persons is a grave affair. I don't like to mention the law of libel, but—there is one, you know."

The warning seemed to pass completely over Mrs. Cripps' head, but that the spinster's purpose was achieved was shown by the ecstatic relief transfiguring her freckled features.

"Tea! Orange juice!" she murmured. "No, I hadn't realised, and I quite see how it alters the case. How good of you to tell me all this! I can breathe easily now. I do trust I haven't upset you by my stupid remarks?"

Miss Venables was very seriously upset. No sooner was she alone with Sarah than her righteous anger burst into storm. Really! What next, pray? Not a doubt of it, some malicious person had been chattering. The Lowther girl, or Muriel—perhaps the two of them together. They were hand in glove now. No wonder Mrs. Cripps had ended by looking thoroughly ashamed of herself. As to what the silly story was, it was beneath one's dignity to inquire. Beryl Tomlins, hail-fellow-well-met with everyone, the very last creature on God's earth to have roused enmity! If it had been herself who had died a sudden and painful death, there might have been some excuse. . . .

"However, that's not the point." She pulled herself up hurriedly. "It is the doctor's I'm concerned about. He'd be the sufferer, if this tale got about. It might do him incalculable harm. Poor young man! As though he hadn't had enough obstacles to contend with, all along, from the very outset of his career!"

Obstacles? More than once these had been hinted at, never with definiteness. Christine Venables had deep reserves, but Sarah, secure in her trust, felt exultantly certain the facts withheld from her could only redound to Gilcrest's credit. She, too, was furious, but after her one spasm of nerves the conclusion drawn from Mrs. Cripps' suggestions was very different from her employer's. She could guess what person it was about whom Beryl Tomlins had dropped dark hints, also that it was the identity of this person which made both Muriel and Mrs. Cripps afraid in Miss Venables' presence to name names. The librarian's jealousy had warped her judgment. From the very nature of things Beryl's theory must be false.

Bedtime came at last. For nearly nine hours they had not set foot outside their own quarters, and now the dreaded day was all but ended. Was it true after all that the threats were a grim and pointless jest? Some idea of the sort must have occurred to the victim, for she had begun to wear an ashamed expression.

"There's no knowing, of course, what might have happened if we'd taken less care. A tile might have dropped on my head, I might have been run over by a car. As it is . . . well, it's a bit early to crow, but it does look as though I were out of the woods. One more night . . . with this horrid mistral still blowing, we should in any case have to keep the windows shut, shouldn't we?"

Once it had been a fog, now it was the mistral—both good excuses. Sarah nodded and examined the window-catches in business-like fashion. Then she opened a new bottle of Vichy water and filled the tumbler she had previously washed out, privately wondering why these danger periods appeared to centre round a definite date, and if the threatener had any deep-lying motive for directing attention to one short interval out of each month. It might, she thought, be a ruse to put his victim off guard for the remaining time, but on the surface there was something rather silly about it—as silly as the letters themselves. Miss Venables must realise these things, which was probably why she shrank from apprising her nephew and her doctor of the latest scare. Then again there was another possible explanation. It came to her as, turning from her task, she noticed how much older and thinner her employer seemed after the strain of the past thirty hours.

The spinster had removed her afternoon frock, and was standing in the full glare of the overhead light clad in her skimpy silk underslip. Great hollows on each side of the collar-bones—the lifted arms painfully attenuated, the drawn corners of the mouth, indicating physical as well as mental discomfort—all these signs pointed to the effect produced by fear. Yes, hardly had she recovered from one crisis before another pulled her down. Devilish, as though her enemy knew this, and had invented these regularly spaced shocks for the sole purpose of inflicting refined torture. Nor was this the only idea grazing the girl's mind. Resistance to illness was being steadily weakened. This frail body could be expected to put up but a poor fight against any sudden attack.

Would this prove the final fright? At any rate they were agreed to regard it as the finish. After to-night no more closed windows, an end to boiled eggs and biscuits out of a tin.

"There, I mustn't forget my medicine."

Miss Venables shook one capsule out of the little flat bottle, put it into her mouth and washed it down with a sip of Vichy water. Then she smiled good-night.

"You've been a great comfort to me, Sarah. Have a good rest, and let's both try to put all this behind us."

For half an hour the rattling casement in Sarah's room kept her awake. It was a worse irritation than the sand on her pillow, for that she had shaken off, though more kept sifting from her hair. At last she sat up exasperated, turned on her lamp, and searched about for something to wedge the loose-fitting frame. An edge of blue paper caught her eye, protruding from between the pages of *Trois Contes*, still unopened. A book-marker—but it would serve. She drew it forth, lovingly because it was Gilcrest's, and glanced close to make sure it was of no use.

It was a whole sheet of note-paper, with a familiar crest at the top, and covered all over with an equally familiar scrawl. Had the Baroness been reading this book, and was this a memorandum left in it? No—it was a note, exhaling a faint suggestion of the writer's scent. A note—to Gilcrest. Unimportant, or he would not have let it lie here for the first comer to read. The book had lain on top of the shelves, therefore the chances were that it had only recently been borrowed and returned—why with a note when the Baroness saw Gilcrest almost daily it was puzzling to imagine.

Too late to argue over rights and wrongs. The first words had registered on her brain, and now, avidly, she was devouring what followed, not missing the intimate *"tu,"* the use of *"ami,"* which could mean much more than "friend," and the big B at the end. This is what she read:

"One little word for your eyes alone, most dear friend, since I could not thank you properly for this so magnificent present while Henri was with us—could I? Poor darling, he must never guess what those delirious hours in Paris meant to us! Here I am in prison again—but I dream of that too-brief freedom, and count the days till it can be repeated. Ah, but how rash of you to commit this wild extravagance! For once it is you, not me, who must be reproved. Could you not have waited till fortune smiles, as it is sure to do before very long? And then—!"

Sickened through Sarah looked truth in the face and cursed herself for ever having seen it under a flattering guise. These two were lovers—had been for some time. Here they might be keeping up a show of discretion, but they had been together openly in Paris and were planning to meet again. Miss Tomlins had known, others guessed, only she through wilful blindness had refused to believe. Even Harry knew. She had seen it in his eyes yesterday when her astonishment at finding him at the villa betrayed her own expectations. That Miss Venables never suspected proved only the same innocent-minded loyalty which prompted Marjory Barrows' defence.

As for the "magnificent present," what could it be but the diamond-studded watch? No wonder the Baroness never wore it except when her sleeves were long. Sarah had noticed that. On the day when its owner came to invite them to supper she had just received her gift, and naturally enough, on its being observed, had been obliged to spin her little fiction. Her failure to ring up and inquire if she had lost it at the hotel was also accounted for. She had intended to search for the watch herself, and it was easy to see why she was annoyed when it was brought back by someone as keen-eyed as Miss Venables' companion.

Sarah had dropped the note as though it were a toad, but she picked it up again to re-read one puzzling passage. "*. . . till fortune smiles, as it is sure to do before very long!*" Evidently the writer confidently anticipated some speedy improvement in her lover's finances. For that matter Gilcrest would hardly have lavished thousands of francs on his mistress if he himself had not.

But this, at least, need not concern her. There could be nothing in the terrible idea just grazing her mind, for the total impossibility of the doctor's reaping any benefit from a certain occurrence vetoed it at once. In addition, the Baron, very much alive despite the professed fears for his safety, constituted a substantial barrier to matrimonial plans. The de Bellesnaves were Roman Catholics. The Church does not countenance divorce.

No, nothing in this except the complete demolition of some stupid day-dreams. Cut, slashed to ribbons—and a good thing, too or else she would have gone on for an indefinite period setting up a clay idol on a pedestal and making a god of it—more shame to her for being such a fool! Man-like, Brian Gilcrest was not above responding to a fresh attraction thrown at his head; his vanity had been titivated; but even while his hand had rested on hers he must have smiled scornfully to himself.

"Oh!" she raged, overpowered with self-disgust, "if only someone could kick me as I deserve to be kicked! I've brought all this on my own head—and the worst of it is I'll have to go on seeing him, knowing what he thinks!"

It was not the worst, and well she knew it. What hurt most was the knowledge of having parted irrevocably with a secret treasure which had turned the humdrum life of Ste. Brigitte into rapturous romance. Dullness stretched ahead, nothing to look forward to but barren, unexciting routine, no hopes, no thrills, yet she would have to put up with it. Day after day the same. . . .

Tears scalded her eyelids. She dashed them furiously away, and, in thick darkness again, lay listening to the banshee wail outside and to the strong, hard pounding of her cheated heart.

"*Sarah—Come!* Oh, quickly!"

Through a fog of sleep the agonised cry reached her ears. Stumbling up to grope confusedly for the light she hit her head a dizzying bang against the wall. Dazed though she was, she caught the sound of a groan so like other groans fresh in her memory that at the sound of it her blood froze.

"Yes, yes, I'm here. What is it?"

Into the other room she blundered, turning on the light as she went.

CHAPTER TWENTY-FOUR

THREE minutes later Sarah was pounding frantically on the Bulstrodes' door. An age before the Colonel, red and swollen with sleep, thrust out his tousled head, another age while Mrs. Bulstrode bundled a Burberry over his vast mauve pyjamas and propelled him on his errand. Even then, implored to be quick, he turned to stare queerly.

"Violently ill, you say? What, another one? Helen, I don't—"

"Hush, Ronald! Just telephone. I'll do what I can."

Sarah had already reached the stairs when Mrs. Bulstrode caught up with her to pant in comforting tones that she mustn't be alarmed. Christine had been taken with these bouts before, but painful though they were she had always rallied fairly soon.

"You say it came on quickly?"

"Frightfully so. It woke her up—and oh, Mrs. Bulstrode, when I think of Miss Tomlins—!"

"That's nonsense, dear. Christine's trouble is gastric, Beryl's was lower seated. Not at all the same."

However the sight which met their eyes upset even the older woman's calm. Miss Venables' highly flushed skin with sweat pouring from it, the terrifying paroxysms of pain succeeding each other with scarcely any intermission, bore evidence to something far worse than ordinary cramps. To Sarah it was but a nightmare repetition of the scene in the attic room. Paralysed by the same despairing helplessness, she gripped her companion's arm and demanded what was to be done.

"Bismuth," was the brisk murmur. "Has she any?"—and while the distracted girl rushed for the bottle of milky fluid kept for such emergencies she stooped to catch what the sufferer was striving to impart.

"Burning sensation—here. So it is the stomach," she whispered when Sarah returned with bottle and spoon. "Ptomaine, perhaps—or ulceration. This may give some relief till the doctor gets here."

At the word "burning," Sarah turned sick with fright. So Miss Tomlins had described her agony, and just as she had done when the brandy was administered this other poor victim fell back, prostrate and writhing with a fresh attack of pain. Soon she lay exhausted, with vaguely shifting pupils which told of ebbing consciousness. The pulse Mrs. Bulstrode felt was "thready," faint—but then, as though galvanised to new strength by a thought just come to her, she sat up, clutched Sarah with fingers of steel, and fixed on her a look of awful awakening.

"They've done it!" she gasped. *"It's poison!"*

"Oh, no! Oh, impossible!" Sarah soothed her, choked by sobs of abject terror. "How could it be that when you've eaten nothing? Dear Miss Venables, you'll be better very soon. Dr. Gilcrest is coming. Don't be frightened, it's all—"

"Delirious," muttered Mrs. Bulstrode, significantly, but the stricken woman shook a stubborn head.

"Poison!" she repeated. "I know it. Sarah—listen to me. Understand—full possession senses—read my letter. I look to you—"

A renewed spasm rent her speech. When it had passed thick, dark blood streaked with a brighter red welled from her mouth. At the very moment the Colonel knocked and entered to say that Gilcrest was away on another case, she had sunk into a semi-stupor.

"They're getting through to him," explained the Colonel. "He'll be here as soon as he can. A trifle easier, is she?"

Sarah pummelled his broad chest with her fists.

"Oh, don't stand here talking! Get the French doctor, get anyone, anyone with an ounce of medical knowledge! For God's sake do something, or she'll be gone!"

He lumbered off, and Sarah, on her knees beside the bed, wrung her hands and moaned, "It was my job to look after her, and I've fallen down on it! I've failed!"

"Hush, child! Don't carry on like this. Even a hemorrhage needn't be fatal, and she does seem quieter."

"It's a coma. It means the end."

She was right. Miss Venables did not regain consciousness, and in just under the hour her laboured breathing made a harsh rattle and ceased.

Sarah remained by the bed. Dishevelled figures crept in, crept out again, but still she did not stir. Finally someone took hold of her and led her to her own room. She became aware that Madge Whittaker was trying to make her drink brandy.

"Do take it, dear! Why, you're like ice!"

All Sarah said was, "When the doctor comes, I must see him."

"Yes, yes, of course! Poor man, what a fearful blow for him! Not to have been able to get here, and then coming so soon after Beryl! I still can't conceive how it happened. Was Christine ill yesterday?"

"No. She wasn't ill."

"Not—?" Miss Whittaker goggled at her. "No sort of warning?"

"Scarcely any. Much less than in Miss Tomlins' case."

"Why do you mention Beryl? Surely, there was no similarity—?"

"Miss Venables took longer to die—and she vomited blood. Their suffering was the same."

It was as though a mechanical voice had answered for her. She now noticed that Mrs. Bulstrode had joined them, and was signalling a quiet negative to Madge.

"Seemed the same," corrected the Colonel's wife, firmly. "You are over-wrought, my dear, and I don't wonder. Better lie down."

Sarah looked slowly from one face to the other. Kindly women, both, but neither of them could understand. In this entire hotel there was no one of whom to seek counsel, simply because not one individual appreciated the meaning of Miss Venables' dying words. There was Harry, of course. She had forgotten him. She stooped down and began to draw on her stockings.

"Why bother to dress, dear? There's nothing you can do."

"There is. I must telephone Harry Venables."

She was told it had already been done.

"Oh, that poor boy!" sighed Madge. "Like losing a mother, isn't it? And how sad for it to happen while he was away! Mrs. Bulstrode, the Colonel is beckoning to us. Shall we see what he wants?"

The Colonel craved only to give vent to the turbulent emotions seething within him.

"Blasted tuppenny-ha'penny hole!" Sarah heard him rumble savagely. "Drains bad, food abominable, slackness everywhere—and we put up with it! English subjects—backbone of the place, too, damn it!—dying like flies, and not a doctor who'll come when he's sent for! The Frenchman I can understand, but Gilcrest, too, seems to have caught the infection. Look at the time! What's keeping him?"

"Ronald, be reasonable! No doctor can be in two places at once, and even in London . . . yes, I understand how you feel, and so do I, but you'll admit there's such a thing as coincidence."

"Damn coincidence! Why didn't Gilcrest know what was wrong with these two women? His business to know. I tell you straight out, I've lost faith in him. I intend to speak my mind."

"You'll do nothing so foolish. S'sh! Here is Dr. Gilcrest now. Go, get yourself a whiskey and soda, you'll feel more like yourself then. Madge and I will see to this."

He was here. He had gone into the other room. In a moment she would be facing him and what was she to say? A new rigour drew her taut as she finished dressing, and opening the door softly took a silent survey of the death-chamber.

No one noticed her. Within the bathroom Mrs. Bulstrode and Miss Whittaker were conferring in sibilant whispers, while the doctor, bent over the bed, made his examination. She shuddered as a movement on his part revealed the still, ashen profile with a long, wispy tail of dark hair lying limp over one shoulder. With an effort she withdrew her gaze to let it wander past the pile of under-clothing neatly folded on a chair to the bed-table whereon nothing seemed to have been disturbed. She took stock of its appointments. There was the reading-lamp, fluted shade aslant; the little travelling-clock, a book, the biscuit-box, Harry's photograph, and, in full view, the bottle of capsules.

Her heart beat with sledge-hammer blows. She heard again the precisely-worded harangue with which her employer had silenced Mrs. Cripps' suspicions, and in the same flash recalled that three sudden deaths had followed the taking of capsules all prescribed by the one man. Was it chance that in the first instance there had been a post mortem, in the second disquieting rumours, while the third victim had sworn she was poisoned? That Miss Venables had certainly never dreamed of suspecting the medicine, still less of connecting her illness with that of

Miss Tomlins, did not weaken the argument. If Miss Tomlins had dieted strictly, so had Miss Venables. Facts were facts.

Yet Mrs. Mark Venables had died from natural causes, neither food nor medicine being called into question. Was the same true in these other cases? If so, the person who brought accusations would be landed in a situation too frightful to contemplate.

"I daren't risk it—I can't! I'll run away first. How can I, single-handed and a nobody, shoulder the responsibility?" Her knees shook, the scene before her swam in a black mist. No, to make any move was sheer impossibility. All she need do was to hold her tongue.

In the centre of her brain a voice spoke its gasping appeal: *"Sarah!"* it said. *"Read my letter. I look to you. . . ."*

That was so, the letter. Back in her room she took the thick envelope out of her dressing-table drawer and tore it open. No wonder it was bulky. Its written enclosure was folded round ten crisp English banknotes—a hundred pounds ready cash, drawn in anticipation of what might happen, and designed to keep want from the door till new employment had been secured. What forethought—what generosity! The iron band encircling Sarah's heart snapped asunder. With the money and letter crushed between her fingers she broke down and wept without restraint.

Through a blur of tears she saw that her hotel bill had been paid a week in advance so that her departure need not be hurried; and then, passing over the brief reminder about delivering the other letters she came to what was expected of her now. If Miss Venables' death in any way invited question, she, Sarah, was to make an immediate report to the police and command an inquiry. If the event took the form of illness imperfectly explained, a post mortem must be performed.

"I do this in the interest of justice. I should be failing in my duty to society if I allowed my murderers to escape unpunished."

"And I should be failing in my duty to you," whispered Sarah as though the dead woman could hear her, "if I neglected to carry out your wishes. Don't worry, darling Miss Venables! I shan't let you down."

Slightly steadied, she bathed her eyes, and was just stuffing the notes and message inside her jumper when the two Englishwomen slipped in again, their manner subdued but purposeful. She waited for them to speak.

"My dear," began Mrs. Bulstrode, quietly, "we wanted you to know that not even the greatest specialist would have saved Christine. She died of gastric ulcer—a very sudden development, and a rupture which caused instant hemorrhage. Occasionally, you know, these things come about with scarcely any warning symptoms. Even if Dr. Gilcrest had been here from the onset of the attack, it would have been impossible to operate soon enough. It is simply another of those unfortunate cases where no one is to blame."

Sarah looked at her, but said nothing. Both women, she thought, had an uncomfortable air.

"You may recall," added Mrs. Bulstrode, "that her sister-in-law died in much the same way. Strange, wasn't it? Not as though they were blood relations."

Strange, indeed—but still Sarah forbore to comment. Mrs. Bulstrode went on, very explicitly, to point out how little real parallel there could be between a stomach ulcer and the intestinal blood clot from which Beryl Tomlins had died. She had said, had she not, that Christine's chronic weakness was differently located from Beryl's?

"You see, Miss Whittaker and I had known them both for years, and had seen their improvement under Dr. Gilcrest's care. It is just because Dr. Gilcrest is so conscientious that we so deeply deplore this double calamity. It does seem as though Fate had played him a most cruel trick; and while he is not a man who makes a parade of his feelings, I can assure you this second loss has bowled him over very badly. He has all our commiseration."

"And sympathy," hissed Madge Whittaker between her teeth.

"And sympathy. So that, Miss MacNeil, brings me to my other point. I feel sure you, like myself, must have realised that our unhappy friend was not quite in her normal senses at the last? Therefore you will agree that it would be wantonly unkind to mention the odd statement she made to you just before she completely lost consciousness."

Receiving no answer to the implied question, Mrs. Bulstrode continued with still greater firmness, "We old friends know that an assertion so wildly improbable, so—well, manifestly absurd, could never have been made if Christine Venables had been herself. If repeated it would not only cause needless distress, but be positively unwise. I myself shall not speak of it even to my husband. If I confided in Madge, it was solely to get her opinion as to the proper course, and I find her in complete agreement with me. That is so, isn't it, Madge?"

"Oh, decidedly! Miss MacNeil may not realise as we do that dear Christine, whom we devotedly loved, and whom in no sense do we wish to criticise, did sometimes say rather excitable things. No doubt it was due to her loyal and impulsive nature, but in a case like this, where there can be no shadow of doubt as to the cause of her death, it would seem a pity to—"

"The greatest pity! Unthinking people—and how many there are!—might actually censure Dr. Gilcrest for not taking steps the sensible among us would wish to avoid. Indeed, if he is told what Christine said he may be made gravely uncomfortable, and naturally, in the circumstances, one can't wish to give him extra embarrassment. Christine herself, I may say, would want to spare him anything of the kind. Not a doubt of that, I think?"

The direct question forced a reply.

"No," Sarah answered musingly, "she would have been the last to cause the doctor any unnecessary pain."

The two listeners looked intensely relieved.

"Ah, well," breathed Mrs. Bulstrode, "then you do see matters in the same light as ourselves. I felt you would, and that you could be trusted to treat those unfortunate words as though they had not been uttered. We shall do the same . . . and now, Madge was going to suggest that as you might not care to remain in this room until the body is removed to the mortuary you might like to share her quarters? She has a wide divan you could sleep on."

"It's extremely kind of you both," replied Sarah. "But I'd rather stay here, I think."

"Very well, dear, if you are quite sure you don't mind. Try to get some sleep. You look altogether exhausted."

The visitors withdrew. They had spoken in all sincerity actuated by the deep repugnance for the sensational which lies at the heart of conventionally-bred people the world over; but would they have taken this attitude if acquainted with the facts? Perhaps even then they would—and it was certain that if they had guessed Sarah's intention they would have regarded her as an enemy in the camp. For this reason and to save her energy for the coming interview she had kept her own ideas hidden. Afterwards they must think what they chose.

Gilcrest was still beside the bed, looking down. Hearing her step, he turned, revealing to her a face leaden-grey in tint, set and drawn as by a stupendous effort of will, but negatively impassive. What emotion was he struggling to conceal? As on that other occasion, she could not tell. She paused three paces away, the strong overhead light shining on both of them. Her throat was dry, the voice which came from it seemed to belong to a stranger.

"Dr. Gilcrest," she said steadily, "before we go into this, I had better make one thing quite clear. One of us—and it should, I think, be you—will have to insist on a post mortem."

CHAPTER TWENTY-FIVE

SHE had not meant to use that tone. Capsules might haunt her, but she had no charge to bring against this man, besides which she hated to think her discovery of a purely personal intrigue could bias her against him. Something quite beyond her control had made her statement sound extraordinarily like an accusation.

"Post mortem?"

He frowned incredulously—yet was he as dumfounded as he was trying to convey? She met his gaze without flinching.

"Yes. She believed, you see, that she was poisoned. She told me so, and left definite instructions. How does one go about it?"

He was eyeing her strangely.

"See here," he said after a pause, "if you're not careful, you'll be going to bits. What about a little mild sedative?"

He had laid his hand on her arm. Trying to placate her, a voice whispered—as he had wanted to do yesterday. Perhaps he had been advised to take this course. She backed away from him.

"You think I'm hysterical? I'm not. Mrs. Bulstrode heard what she said, only she won't tell you, because she wants to believe it was delirium. It wasn't. She was as sane as you or I."

He was silent for another long moment. When he spoke his voice was low and expressionless. "And you?" he asked. "Do you think it was poison, too?"

"What I think doesn't matter, does it? But—it does seem to me possible." She looked him straight in the eyes. "Isn't there a chance that she was right?"

His glance gravitated towards the bed, dwelt there briefly, and returned.

"No!" he replied shortly. "Not the faintest chance. Didn't those women explain to you the reason for her death?"

"Oh, yes; but then you may be mistaken, mayn't you? We shall have to make certain, that's all."

Friends a few hours ago, and now—were they enemies? As they stood there facing each other it seemed to Sarah that Gilcrest was stupefied, nonplussed by the change in her, but dared not ask its meaning. Did he know she had the whip hand of him?

"Let me assure you," he said with an effort, simply, logically, as though expounding matters to a child, "there can be little doubt over what has happened, lamentable though it is. Several times, before Miss Venables came under my care, she narrowly escaped an operation for gastric ulcer. For two years she improved, but last spring she slipped back into her former condition. She was a highly nervous subject, you know. When I saw her after an interval of almost a year—she had come to London, knowing I would be there, in order to consult me about returning to this place—I was shocked by the alteration in her appearance."

"And you advised her to come here?" Sarah demanded.

"I did certainly. She had made up her mind in any case, and was sure to be happier in her old surroundings. I see, you are thinking about the persecution business. Whatever your opinions, common-sense will tell you she was as safe here as elsewhere, and in many ways better off."

As on former occasions she got the impression that he was not being entirely frank. She let him go on, reserving her comments.

"I may say this, that her case has been a difficult one, complicated by obscure issues. With a nervous system like hers there was always a danger of the gastric trouble recurring for which reason I've watched her closely, or tried to do. Not that I expected a sudden crisis like this, or that, having no previous knowledge of danger, I should be miles off in the mountains. Still, when an artery ruptures, the damage is done. Collapse is certain, and in this case very quick."

"It took, in all, a little over an hour. Is that unusual?"

"Not very, but it does happen. It depends on several things—general stamina, rapidity of development, exact location of the ulcer—but what is bothering you?" His voice, though abrupt, was kind. "Haven't I made matters sufficiently clear?"

She had begun to tremble.

"Quite clear," she said carefully, "why she ought to have died from gastric ulcer. Not at all clear that she did die from that cause. Aren't you trying to convince yourself as well as me?"

"Why in God's name do you say that?" he flashed back, turning a dull red. "I'm only doing my best to disabuse your mind of an utterly absurd idea. This isn't poison. There's not a single indication of it. Don't you suppose I should know? I don't say it's not a shocking, damnable occurrence. It is. Why, I saw her only last night! Was she feeling ill and keeping it dark?"

"Listen. I'd better tell you the whole story."

He gave attentive ear, and before she had finished cut her short with an annoyed exclamation. Was she imagining it, or did his indignation not ring quite true?

"So that's what happened! I'm understanding things. At least," he corrected himself, "according to her these gastric bouts always went hand in hand with the mental disturbances. Couldn't you have given me a hint? I felt something was wrong. If I'd had any inkling—"

She interrupted him coldly.

"You believe that fright brought on this attack? I'm sure it didn't. If she'd shown any sign of real illness, I'd have sent for you, but beyond a very slight discomfort the evening you were here there's been nothing, nothing."

"In most cases they faint at first, and the pain comes later," he remarked. "But you say she was asleep? Then we can't know what happened, can we?"

Was he speaking to her? She continued, "Isn't it natural that, waking up in violent pain she should jump to the one conclusion? What else was she to think, or—" she whispered it, "I, either?"

"No belief can alter facts," he muttered stubbornly.

"Perhaps you're mistaken about the facts," she retorted. "If I report this—as I must do, if you refuse—the Chef de Commissaire may insist on an investigation."

"You think so?"—dryly. "I'm afraid you've little knowledge of the official attitude in this country. The French authorities aren't likely to concern themselves over an alien's death unless direct pressure is brought by the next of kin. You may find that Venables is entirely satisfied with the death-certificate I, in all confidence, am prepared to sign."

"Harry be satisfied? I promise you he'll do everything in his power to carry out his aunt's wishes."

"You seem very certain," he observed caustically. "I should have said he was the sort of man who'd be only too willing to avoid unpleasantness of this sort."

Just though the criticism might be, it roused her ire. "You'll see," she said. "But I think you'd better read the note Miss Venables wrote me twenty-four hours before she was taken ill. It will show you exactly how she felt."

This, she fancied, would end his opposition. Easy enough to discount words spoken in the extremity of suffering, but when orders were set down in cold blood it was another matter. She watched him narrowly as he took the note and studied the dead woman's fine, sloping characters, saw his expression alter, but not quite as she had expected. He seemed to ponder before replying—playing for time, she thought.

"I see," he mused. "Well . . ." He drew a deep breath. "As you probably realise, a matter as important as this calls for more consideration than either you or I can give to it now. Suppose we postpone further discussion till to-morrow morning, after we've both had some sleep and a chance to think things over? I'll be with you at nine, and when Venables arrives we can tell him what's decided. You agree to that?"

"Certainly—though I shall feel exactly as I do now."

From his constrained and diffident manner she saw he was aware of the unfortunate impression he was making and wondering how to correct it. She did not mean to give him the chance; but there remained his own letter from Miss Venables, and this he must have at once. With a word of explanation she crossed to the bed-table and took it out of the drawer.

With the envelope in her hand she hesitated, and then, half ashamed of her action, did something she hoped he did not see. The still figure on the bed seemed to accuse her, but that could not be helped. Turning, she handed him his letter, which appeared to puzzle him.

"For me? Written at the same time?"

"You were to have it if she died. There's one for Harry, and another besides." She could not bring herself to mention the Baroness' name. "Good-night."

He slipped the envelope into his pocket and cast a doubtful glance at her set face.

"And now, what about you?" he suggested awkwardly. "Can't I give you something? You want looking after, you know."

She shook her head woodenly. "Thanks, I'm all right as I am."

She retreated to her room and closed the door.

Now she was alone, her false strength ebbed entirely, leaving her shattered. Why, oh, why had she locked those capsules in the drawer and taken the key? If he noticed they were gone he would jump to a far worse conclusion than she herself was prepared to admit. He had not seemed troubled about Miss Tomlins' capsules. These might not interest him either, though what would that prove, save that what remained in the bottle were harmless?

She pulled herself up sternly. What if his failure to fall in with her wishes did seem astonishing, even a little callous? The idea of an investigation horrified him, rather naturally. Never mind, he would come round. But would he? Instinct warned her it was not so. On the contrary, he meant to fight her every step of the way till she forced him to give in. She could force him, that she knew, by the simple means of going with Harry to the police; and she would do it, if he kept up this attitude, painful though it was. Perhaps it was as well she had seen that love-message of the Baroness'. With this silly romance of hers nipped in the bud and only the blackened remains of it to look upon, her coming task would be easier to perform.

When she woke, the mistral had ceased—when she did not know—and the maid was at the door with her coffee. Promptly at nine o'clock a waiter came to say that Dr. Gilcrest was waiting for her in the card-room. She picked up the copy of *Trois Contes* and walked steadily towards the lift.

CHAPTER TWENTY-SIX

BARS of mote-filled sunshine streamed into the lounge. No one was about save two waiters in striped aprons who eyed her curiously and went on with their cleaning. The card-room looked deserted, but no, Gilcrest was there, at the far end, staring out of the window. His greeting was perfunctory, accompanied by one searching glance. He seemed about to make some inquiry, thought better of it, and drawing out one of the little green armchairs from the farthermost table mutely waited for her to sit down.

She had steeled herself for the encounter, and imagined he was doing likewise. However, as she stole a covert look at him across the square of green baize she was struck by an alteration in his expression which she was at a loss to understand. His face still had the greyish pallor and lines of fatigue she had noticed the night before, and she guessed he had not slept, but what else was it? She could not make out if he were dazed, stricken, or dogged by fear. Certainly he was keyed up with some new emotion which, as always, he was making strenuous efforts to hide. Even the deadened matter-of-factness of his tone seemed a mask for acute distress.

"Well," he began evenly, "and what have you decided?"

"I told you I didn't need to reflect on this. We'll have to order the post mortem."

He flinched slightly and said in a low voice, "Because she wished it?"

"That's reason enough, surely."

After a moment's pause he remarked, "People in violent pain are apt to snatch at irrational explanations. She was especially prone to do so; but I gathered last night that you, also, considered the poison theory well-founded. May I ask why?"

"You insist on knowing?" Now she would have to speak. She had hoped to get out of it, well aware that her beliefs were largely a matter of instinct. "Let me think . . . well, first, there was the warning. It laid emphasis on the date. Yesterday, you know, was the anniversary of Major Frampton's death. Then the writer was present in the town. He—or she—might even be someone in this hotel."

He appeared unimpressed. "Yes. And then?"

"The food Miss Venables ate. From the time the letter arrived she had nothing whatever but boiled eggs, biscuits, and tea which we made in her room. She even drank Vichy water—her own."

"Wait! Do you realise that what you're saying now is argument not for but against poison?"

"But there's one thing I've not mentioned." Her heart beat suffocatingly though her gaze remained unwavering. "We're overlooking the capsules. One after each meal, one at night, just an hour before she was taken ill—"

"Capsules?" he echoed brusquely. "What on earth are you getting at?"

"Only that we've no right to leave the capsules out of our calculations. Let me finish, please! Miss Venables is not the only patient of yours who died soon after taking medicine you'd prescribed—and each time it was a capsule. Miss Tomlins, who'd been dieting even more rigidly, fell ill two hours after her dose. Both these women were dead inside of twenty minutes. Both suffered in much the same way. The two bottles of medicine were fetched at the same time."

His eyes, never quitting her face, smouldered ominously.

"You can't mean this seriously," he muttered. "Different complaints, different prescriptions . . . what made you connect the two cases?"

"What I saw—and heard. Remember, I was with them, you weren't. In trying to describe the pain they used almost the same words. They spoke of it as a terrible burning."

He continued to stare. Sweat had broken out on his forehead. He shook his head and brought his clenched fist down softly on the table.

"Utterly impossible! The composition of those two lots of capsules was totally dissimilar. If it interests you to know, Miss Venables was taking valerian, which acts as a mild nerve tonic, Miss Tomlins an intestinal disinfectant. You see how ridiculous it is?"

"Yes, if the capsules were all what they should have been. But mistakes do happen," she reasoned, unconsciously quoting Mrs. Cripps.

"Not in my dispensary," he retorted. "Not only were the ingredients taken from our usual stocks, but what about the capsules which didn't cause trouble?"

"Miss Tomlins had only one out of her bottle. I saw her break the seal."

"It can't affect the main issue." He made an impatient gesture. "The whole notion is insane."

Why did he make no reference to the remaining capsules? It would seem only natural to be curious about them, unless—petrifying thought!— he knew that nothing harmful was left behind. She was seized by a cruel longing to shake his confidence.

"Another thing," she said slowly, still watching his face. "Miss Venables' sister-in-law in London—she had capsules, too . . ."

He started, blood surging to his temples. "Kindly explain what you mean by that," he demanded in a stifled voice. "Let's get this quite clear. What's in your mind?"

She quailed but stuck to her guns.

"I realise," she said, "that her prescription came from a chemist shop, and that the post mortem examination brought a verdict of natural death; but is it one more coincidence that she was supposed to have died from the identical cause you give for Miss Venables?"

"Why not?" he flung back at her. "They both suffered from the same weakness. I knew the other woman was in a state where anything might happen. I frankly admit I had no such fears over either Miss Venables or Miss Tomlins, who, let me repeat, were subject to quite different complaints, as a number of symptoms showed. Appearances in these two cases were deceptive, besides which in one of them I should have been warned and wasn't. But seeing that a clear verdict was given over the London affair, just why do you bring it up in the present connection?"

"Only that all three of these women had been taking your capsules, and all three died painful and very sudden deaths." She had grown as stubborn as he. "Call it what you like. Surely you must think it extraordinary?"

He mopped his brow. "It's more than that—in a way," he burst out, evidently against his will. "It's—devilish! Yet it can be nothing but chance. Even assuming it isn't, what underlying cause could link up three individuals unrelated by blood, two of them not so much as acquainted? Whatever you may choose to imagine about the two Venables, Miss Tomlins is in a class by herself. For theoretical purposes she was a nonentity, above all so poverty-stricken as to be utterly removed from—"

"Oh, I quite see that! All the same, are you still perfectly satisfied as to what killed her?"

"Perfectly!" His jaw set hard on the word. "I'd stake my entire professional reputation on it. And on the other cases, too."

They had reached a deadlock, but Sarah had yet another card to play. She led up to it adroitly.

"Let me ask you this: can you positively deny that not one of these deaths could have been contrived in such a manner as to appear natural to you? You see, I'm not questioning your sincerity, only trying to find out what is possible."

From the way he hesitated she felt she had driven him into a difficult corner. She pressed her advantage boldly.

"I happen to know from Mrs. Cripps that there has already been talk. After last night there's bound to be much more, even though Mrs. Bulstrode and Miss Whittaker mean to hold their tongues. Once doubt has arisen, do you think it won't go on, spread like wild-fire? It will—and nothing can stop it but a medical investigation. You owe it to yourself to clear matters up. It seems to me you can't possibly afford not to make the necessary move."

To her dismay, he remained silent, examining his clenched knuckles. Her heart beat suffocatingly, and scarcely knowing what she said she began to stammer broken words of insistence.

"We must do this—we must! Whatever you may believe, I, for one, can never have a moment's peace if I've failed in my duty to her . . . after all her kindness to me—oh, don't you understand how I feel? I owe her so much. It's a point of honour, of common loyalty, not to disregard her dying wishes. How else can I prove my gratitude, my—"

"Gratitude!" His vehemence startled her. "Good God, as though I, too, hadn't cause to be grateful! Need you remind me of obligations, of honour? You must think me a swine. Here—look at this!"

It was the letter she had given him, dragged from his pocket and thrust in front of her. Taken aback, half-suspecting some new bid for sympathy, she let the paper lie where it was.

"Read it," he ordered in a choked voice. "Then, just possibly, you'll see how I'm placed."

After all, why not read it? If the dead woman had confided some secret relating to the present situation she ought to know about it. She picked up the letter, scanned the opening lines, and gasped.

Merciful Heavens! Was she dreaming? In defiance of every preconception, Christine Venables had bequeathed her beloved physician an income of a thousand a year!

CHAPTER TWENTY-SEVEN

THE firm rock was blown to atoms. No motive? Lo, here it was, stupendous, ugly, unvarnished—the motive of Gain. . . .

There was no mystery. Miss Venables had possessed a private fortune left her by her mother and independent of the one controlled by the entail. This she could bestow as she wished, and had first meant to leave it to a research institution. Latterly—in point of fact some fifteen months before—she had conceived the idea of relieving Brian Gilcrest of financial strain to enable him to engage in a wider work. She had not informed him of her intention, thinking that if she lived and the present danger ceased she would find means of settling the income upon him in such a way as to spare him the embarrassment of previous knowledge; but now, with a strong presentiment of death haunting her, she had wished to prepare him for the fortune soon to be his.

"From my own observation of your character and abilities," the letter wound up, "I feel confident the money will be wisely used. So easily could you have enlisted my sympathies by disclosing the events which interrupted your chosen career; but this you have never done, thus leaving me to learn the truth from one whose admiration for you equals my own. You may guess to whom I refer. That you may live long and find many ways of alleviating human suffering is the earnest wish of your grateful friend and patient, Christine Venables."

What unconscious irony was contained in this last sentence! Yet throughout the whole letter breathed dignified restraint—no emotional gush, nor any hint that Gilcrest was expected to act as an instrument of justice if suspicion over the writer's death arose. More than ever was Sarah convinced that certain terrible words would never have been uttered if Miss Venables could have foreseen whose honour would be involved. Still, having been uttered, they altered everything.

The man opposite waited with harassed impatience, his expression half challenge, half appeal.

"Well?" he prompted at last. "Now do you see—?"

She did see, far too much. Underneath a frozen exterior, her brain leaped feverishly from one significant point to another, grasping causes hitherto obscure, solving perplexities in hideous fashion. What she saw might yet prove conjecture. It would have to be substantiated, of course— but how wickedly plausible it was! She had never really known Gilcrest. Always the essence she had sought to capture had eluded her efforts. Now he was straining every nerve to win her over, counting, perhaps, on her ill-concealed preference for him. Matters lay in her hands. He knew it, and he was afraid. Well, he had reason to be. Her cheeks burned with slow fire as she drove herself to face his urgent gaze.

"Is it true you had no knowledge of this legacy?" she asked. He made a violent gesture of repudiation. "How could I have guessed? There was no indication of it—none. She was my patient. No more. I respected and liked her—who could help it?—but good and kind as she was it never once crossed my mind she meant to load me with benefits either during her lifetime or after her death. It's a bolt out of the blue." He drew his hand almost savagely across his forehead. "I tell you, I'm stunned by it. Bowled over."

It was inevitable for him to protest ignorance, thought the girl; and yet for a moment she found her sympathies wavering in his direction. What he said might be true. Mechanically she folded the letter and pushed it across the table.

"Well," she remarked evenly, "in view of this it seems to me still more imperative for the death to be investigated—and for you to make the report. You can hardly do otherwise. Isn't that so?"

He bit his lip to force back an angry retort. "But certainly it is imperative," he replied coldly. "It wasn't before, but it is now. Why else do you suppose I showed you the letter? In fact, I came here this morning for the express purpose of telling you the post mortem would have to be held."

Had he really meant to capitulate? Feeling suddenly weak and confused she had to remind herself that this change of front might well be unpremeditated, the result of her failure to compromise.

"But all along you've been behaving as though—"

"I wanted first of all to hear your precise grounds for suspicion," he returned stoically, "and to see if there was anything in them to shake my conviction. There wasn't—but that can't alter the very evident fact that rumours will get about, not only over this event, but over the other as well. My inheritance settles that. Yes, I shall have to see the thing through. Miss Tomlins' funeral was to have been held to-day. It will have to be postponed."

"Miss Tomlins too!" She reeled, her sensations much the same as on an occasion long ago when trying to reach the top-drawer of a tall-boy she had brought the whole chest down upon her. Startled and curious, she eyed him searchingly as she said under her breath, "Then you do admit her death was queer as well!"

"I admit nothing—except that if I've been unlucky enough to make one wrong diagnosis there's an equal chance of being wrong over the other. That's a bad enough admission for any doctor—but I shall have to make it."

She could not think that this was the attitude of a guilty man—and if he was not guilty she was slightly appalled by what she had done. She must not show it, though. Bowing her head she murmured that no doubt his decision was wise.

To her astonishment he winced. "Oh, so you think it's wise, do you?" he demanded in a voice bitter with resentment. "I see . . . in that case, you might advise our exhuming the Baron's dog to find out what caused its death. Had that notion occurred to you?"

The sarcastic suggestion took away her breath. If this was meant as a joke, it had come at a bad time. A tremor partly hysterical ran through her, but meeting his eyes she retorted with perfect seriousness, "Well, and why not? Now you've mentioned it, it strikes me as an excellent plan."

He glared back at her so thunderstruck that she found herself retreating from her firm stand. Was the second post mortem really necessary? She faltered. After all, Miss Tomlins had made no accusation, and if he was convinced that mesenteric embolism did bring about her death. . . .

He cut her short by an obstinate shake of his head. "If as you say there has been talk about her already, there'll be more now this other thing has happened and I am known to benefit by one of these deaths. What sort of talk I'm not interested to inquire, but I must put a stop to it by the only means at my disposal." He paused, adding pointedly, "Assuming of course, that a medical verdict will stop it. There may be others who, like you, are little impressed by post mortems."

It was a well-merited rebuke. Sarah reddened, about to protest, but at her sudden movement the copy of *Trois Contes* she had been carefully guarding slipped from her lap to the floor. In a flash she was reminded of the Baroness's note, full to the brim of suspicious implications, so that by the time Gilcrest had picked the book up to lay it in front of her she had experienced a sweeping revulsion. Had the sheet of note paper fallen out? No, she still saw the edge of it safe between the pages. She rose without looking at him.

"I wanted to return the book to you," she said in a hard tone. "I've finished with it—and now, I suppose, I can leave this entire matter in your hands. Do you want me to explain the situation to Harry?"

"If you like—but I had better have a talk with him, too."

Afraid of weakening again, she walked quickly away, holding herself erect and stiff, and aware that his gaze was following her. Yes, he hated her, as she had known he would do, but it was nothing to what he would feel when he came to discover the evidence his own carelessness had put into her grasp. It would have given her a cruel joy to witness his horror on reading the frank allusion to his coming good-fortune. That single sentence would show him how thin his profession of innocence must have sounded to her ears.

"He knew this money was coming to him. He must have known. The Baroness spun the story—false, of course—which influenced Miss Venables to make that will. She was in on the whole thing from the beginning, and kept him primed while he went on being impersonal and reserved in order to impress Miss Venables with his disinterestedness. But for finding that note I might have believed him just now. For a moment I did believe, and even now, with all this staring me in the face, I don't know . . . suppose poison is found, and he's not responsible? Can he prove he wasn't?"

It was a ghastly possibility, the trouble being that she could not see how anyone save Gilcrest could have meddled with the capsules—except, to be sure, the dispenser who made them up, and the idea that Marjory Barrows could be guilty was too far-fetched to consider even in passing. Marjory had nothing to gain by removing either a potential slanderer or one who stood between the man she served and a substantial legacy—nor could she be a criminal lunatic who killed without reason.

"But who else is there? The Baroness fingered the bottle the other morning, and she did inquire about Miss Venables' health; but I was watching her all the time, and I can swear she never touched the capsules inside the bottle. There's the gardener, of course . . . he's at the doctor's house often enough, so they say, but it's silly to imagine him putting poison into two bottles, one intended for a woman quite outside any scheme of revenge."

All at once it struck her that in all the recent discussion there had been no reference whatever to Miss Venables' own theory. Gilcrest, she was aware, had always behaved a little oddly on this subject, but it was extraordinary to have ignored the entire matter of drug-peddlers, seeing how closely the anonymous letters were interwoven with the dead women's fears. It was as she re-entered her room that a solution once considered and dismissed with scorn rushed back into her mind. *Suppose Gilcrest himself wrote those letters?* No one better than he understood the effect of constant terror on a hyper-sensitive nervous system; no one could more surely have reckoned on recurrent gastric attacks induced by alarm making a last, fatal attack seem so like what had gone before as to deceive even the victim herself. The dietary precautions provoked by each warning could have been expected to banish any logical suspicion of foul play. No poisonable food, no poison, so the argument would have run—only, by sheer mischance, Miss Venables had given utterance to an illogical suspicion. In the face of reason she had declared herself poisoned.

"Oh, God," Sarah groaned. "It may be true! His manner last night suggested he had come up against a difficulty quite unforeseen, one he wasn't at all prepared to meet. If it wasn't so, why did he fight tooth and nail against a post mortem? If he's given in now it is solely because he can't help himself. She made that statement before two witnesses. He simply has no choice but to go through with the investigation . . . and yet, how is it he seems so confident of the outcome? I can't somehow believe it's bravado. He's not just acting. He really is confident no poison will be found."

Hope rose for a moment, only to perish. In such wise a man would behave if by previous experience he knew there was nothing to fear. Since the Charing Cross Hospital affair had turned out successfully, why not a second and third? His first reluctance would come from an understandable shrinking from disagreeable publicity, to be avoided if possible. Now he saw himself forced to invite inquiry he could afford to put a bold face on it, well knowing the method he had hit upon would defy detection.

"The Baroness must know, too . . ."

Certainly she knew—and now one could see the reason for Major Frampton's death. Somehow, somewhere, the Major had got wind of the plot against Miss Venables' life, only a scant half-hour prior to the "Accident." Probably he had come upon a meeting between the two lovers, in the dark grounds of the villa, and had been seen but not caught. It had been necessary to prevent him from carrying his information to the victim, and the faulty lift had served the purpose admirably, though if this hasty plan had failed another expedient would have been tried. The doctor must have followed hard on his heels, given the message which enticed him from his room, and pushed him through the open shaft. Recently Miss Tomlins had learned some item implicating one of the plotters, and she had been suppressed as well. As for Mrs. Mark Venables, she might have proved a menace also.

"Or—wait! There may have been another reason for killing her. Suppose it was hoped that the additional income to be derived from the sister-in-law's death would make Miss Venables settle the thousand a year on Gilcrest during her life-time. She could have done it, only she didn't. So the first plan had to go forward."

As the various bits dovetailed together Sarah felt acutely sick. At the same time realising that none of her conclusions must be mentioned—least of all to Harry, who, already not liking the doctor, might be led to make a premature accusation. Truth to tell, this prejudice of Harry's argued the worst. She had believed it largely due to a small boy's jealousy of a rival in his aunt's affections, but now it hinted at a deeper origin. Harry might instinctively have guessed Gilcrest's designs, while Gilcrest's faintly apparent antagonism for the young man probably came from covert fear. Harry had always seen the doctor's infatuation for the Baroness. A word from him would have sufficed to alter Miss Venables' regard for both her favourites. If he had not spoken that word, it was only that he was too fond of his aunt to cause her distress. Trivial Harry might be, but he had a kind heart.

Feverishly Sarah began to long for his return, confident that he would unite with her in zeal to clear matters up. Knowing him she did not imagine that grief would for any long period stir the sunny shallows of his nature, but he would not fail in loyalty to the woman who had loved and mothered him, the woman whose death had made him a rich man.

"Funny," she mused, "that's an aspect I've only just thought of. I wonder how it will affect him? He can't ever have had any real money worries, but now—why, he'll have none at all! He won't even need to work. What will he do? Play about, make whoopee?"

No, that was a horrid idea! Harry might seem to her rather lazy, rather inclined to seek the line of least resistance, but he had good north-country blood in his veins, which would undoubtedly make him take his responsibilities seriously. There was no harm in him, none. A strong-willed girl might work wonders with such pleasantly malleable material. She herself . . . but why was it she continued to view this dazzling prize with such supine indifference? If she really wished to win Harry, the next seven days of intimate companionship and co-operation in a painful duty would present immense opportunities for conquest. She might actually bring it off. She knew she attracted him, that if nothing had yet come of their friendship it was mainly her fault. She had moreover just made a sickening mistake about another man. The moment was ripe to let her maternal feelings—for that best described her attitude towards Harry— develop into the necessary sentiment. Was it possible? It ought to be.

A heavy, rapid step outside set her trembling. Not already—? A knock, the door burst open, and the subject of her reflections poised on the threshold. He was haggard, dusty, unwontedly dishevelled. His red-rimmed eyes held a stricken expression, his breath came in gasps.

"Sarah!" he panted. "My God, is this true!"

Her first thought was that Harry was much more deeply moved than she had expected; her second that the question she had been asking herself was answered in the negative. She pitied this poor boy from the bottom of her heart, she must be very gentle with him—but love him she never would.

CHAPTER TWENTY-EIGHT

HE HAD heard just enough from the manager downstairs to send him headlong to her for the explanation, which now he was here he seemed too shocked and bemused to take in. Overwhelmed, he sat on the side of the bed frowning past her, now and then mopping his sweat-streaked forehead with a crumpled silk handkerchief, and shaking his head in a puzzled, helpless fashion.

"What an ass I was to go barging off!" he muttered, abject in his contrition. "I believed those foul letters had stopped coming. Why on earth didn't you tell me?"

Patiently she went over again the reasons for her silence. "She refused to let me send for you, Harry—and it couldn't have made the least difference if you'd been here all along. As for this other development—well, there was no foreseeing that, either. It's damnable, but as you see things have got beyond our control. You've had a long drive, haven't you? No sleep, and no food, I expect. I don't wonder you can't get your bearings. Drink up your brandy and soda. It will help pull you together."

Mechanically he whispered, "My God!" in the same tone employed already half-a-dozen times, reached unsteadily for the drink she had ordered for him, and gulped it down.

"Post mortem!" he murmured, mystified and blank. "I can't for the life of me see why . . . but you were with her. Was this attack any different from others she's had?"

She reminded him that she had never seen his aunt really ill before, adding that it did not seem possible for the illness to have arisen from anything to eat or drink. He looked towards her keenly.

"That's what I'm getting at. How could she have been poisoned? Stands to reason she wasn't. Gilcrest says not, and he ought to know. How is it, if he's completely satisfied—" He stopped, eyed her more closely, and spoke in a subtly altered tone. "I see, it's that inheritance that's bothering him. Afraid like hell of what people will say, what? Well,

I shouldn't be the one to talk. Maybe it is a thundering lot of money to leave a chap who's no sort of claim on you; maybe I am a bit knocked by the news, for I give you my solemn word this is the first I've known of it. Poor Chrissie was very quiet about her own affairs. . . . Still, with no proof that it wasn't all square and fair, what right have I to question his behaviour? I don't. So, as far as I'm concerned, his diagnosis can stand."

"I don't think you understand," Sarah said quietly. She knew that this was her cue to mention the capsules, but to do that meant bringing up much more about which she dared not speak. "Dr. Gilcrest insists on reporting this death for his own sake, not yours. You're forgetting she went to the police about this latest letter. In fact the police have all the letters on file. That in itself might lead to doubts which would keep cropping up unless there were a definite medical decision to silence them."

"Oh, the letters!" He waved her objection aside as of no account. "Did the Commissaire chap take any stock in these threats?"

"N-no," she admitted. "He didn't."

"Exactly! And I, for one, can't conceive of any connection between them and her falling ill and dying like this, sudden though it was. When I got the news late last night such an idea never entered my head. The more you say about it the surer I am there's nothing in it. Gilcrest himself is clearheaded enough to—" Again he broke off, stared confusedly into his empty glass, and grew obscurely embarrassed. "What I mean is, none of this would have come up but for his getting that money. Maybe,"—with a look of hope, "if I talk to him sensibly he'll drop the business."

"Do you want him to drop it?" she demanded, amazed. "Remember, she wanted it done."

He was staring with a sort of shrinking fascination at the door separating the two rooms.

"Hacking up her body for no purpose," he muttered painfully. "Beastly thing to do! Oh, it's not the sensation I'm thinking of. She can't have realised what it would mean . . ."

"She did realise, Harry. After all, your stepmother—"

"With Gracie it was different."

"I understand." Sarah's brow cleared, and she looked at him with softened eyes. "It seems to you a kind of desecration, doesn't it? Wait, I'm going to let you read the letter she left for me—and that reminds me, there's one for you too. Here they are."

She put the two envelopes into his hand. He stared dazedly at the familiar writing, slowly read both enclosures and gave her his own communication to examine. In slightly different language it reiterated what had been said to her.

"'In the event of peculiar circumstances,'" he quoted with knit brow. "Point is, were the circumstances peculiar? Gilcrest says not. What's your idea?"

"I've no knowledge of medical matters," she answered him evasively. "I do know, though, that the doctor feels obliged to take action simply to protect himself. There's Mrs. Bulstrode to be considered—and Miss Whittaker."

"But they don't regard things as peculiar, do they?"

"Not now, but they will as soon as your aunt's bequest is made known. Think what can be said, what will be said. A well-to-do woman dies. The only medicine she has been taking—" (There, in spite of all she had brought out the word "medicine!" Well, it was done now.) "—was prescribed by a doctor who benefits enormously by her will. Just before her death she announces that she has been poisoned. You see?"

In trepidation she waited for the expected comment, but to her relief it did not come. She continued, thankful that her hearer was too dulled by grief to catch her meaning. "Talk to Dr. Gilcrest, of course, get his own views; but unless you've some strong reason, I shouldn't advise your opposing him in this. Stupid as it sounds, you yourself might be harshly judged if you tried to hush matters up."

"Me?" He blinked at her in so startled a fashion that she had to stifle a hysterical desire to laugh. "My God! Would I be questioned, too?"

"That was a bad jolt, wasn't it? But you ought to face facts."

It was funny to be taking this school-mistress tone to a man five years older than herself and the heir to a large fortune, yet it seemed wholly natural. Harry would not have perceived this unaided, and if he was shocked the effect achieved was satisfactory. He drew a deep breath and nodded in sober agreement.

"Absolutely right," he murmured. "Hadn't looked at it in that light, but I quite see we're in for it. Yes, it'll have to be, and the sooner it's over the more comfortable for all concerned. Not that it'll come to anything. Simply couldn't. We can set our minds at rest about that part of it."

As confident as Gilcrest, she thought, surely with less reason, for the other had knowledge and experience at his command, while this attitude could be sponsored only by optimism and the sane outlook of one to whom crime at close range was unthinkable. Curiously, his belief shook her more than all Gilcrest's logical assertions. She was beginning to be alarmed at having stuck her oar into what so easily might have been left alone. What would come of it? And yet, quite aside from her duty to Miss Venables, it would have been wrong to hold her tongue. It was but fair to let the doctor see his position and not walk blindfold into ruinous criticism—while the same, in minor degree, applied to Harry. He, though absent at the time, might have been subjected to slight but disagreeable doubts. As affairs had turned out, even his manifest attachment to his relative might not have shielded him from obloquy, realising which she rejoiced to find him resigned to an inquiry he considered both painful and useless.

He sat hunched on the bed, looking wretchedly befogged and almost frightened by what his mental vision beheld. Like a lost child, she thought, her sympathy stirring anew. Suddenly he raised his bloodshot eyes to hers.

"You'll stay, I suppose? Till the thing's cleared up, I mean. You won't go running off, old thing, and leave me alone with these infernal old women?"

She told him the thoughtful provision his aunt had made, adding her intention to remain while she might be wanted. Probably, indeed, she would be expected to do so. His face smoothed, his hand straying absently towards his pocket only to withdraw with self-conscious compunction. She understood the abortive gesture and smiled.

"Smoke, if you like. What's the harm?"

"None, really." Gratefully he lit a cigarette, puffed at it jerkily, and relaxed. "Odd how things come about," he meditated aloud. "But for this blasted legacy no one would have dreamed of making a rumpus. There's no more sense in it than there would have been if old Tom—" He gave a violent start, his dismay verging on the comic, and once more ejaculated, "My God—!"

Sarah's nerves were badly jangled. It seemed to her that if he said this once more she would scream.

"Why, what's wrong?" she asked wearily.

"Nothing, except—did I hear you say Tomlin's body was being examined, too? Didn't take it in. It is so? Lord, what a mess! Has the fellow gone balmy? What's the idea? She wasn't murdered, whatever they may choose to say about poor Chrissie. No cash, no . . . here, give me a line on this. I'm all at sea."

She explained as best she could, advising him to get in touch with the doctor.

"But not till you've had a bath and something to eat. You're too worn out to discuss matters now. I told the waiter to bring coffee to your room. Go and drink it."

He rubbed his hand ruefully over his unshaven chin.

"Good old Sarah! Right as usual. I must look a sweep, but what with the mistral blowing like hell and wanting to get here in double quick time I never stopped the whole way. All the drive I kept thinking how I'd left her well and cheerful and was coming back to find—" His voice broke.

She put her hand on his arm. "Harry," she said gently, "if you'd care to see her once more . . . it's not at all dreadful, you know . . ."

He drew back, shrinking like a child. "Need I? That is, do you think I ought—?"

"There's no ought, about it, dear. Don't, if you'd rather remember her as she was. I was only thinking they'd be taking her away to the mortuary quite soon. Anyhow, the doors are locked, and the manager has the keys."

"I would rather hate it, you know. Anyone as close as that . . . get how I feel about it?"

"Of course I do. Now run along."

Ashamed of his relief, he blundered out. She stood for a moment gazing after him in puzzled thought, then made a movement to call him back.

"Harry—one second! I wanted to ask—"

His door had closed, she could hear the water running for his bath. Never mind, her question could wait, and besides it hardly mattered now what theory he held about the letters, the subject of which he had again treated as negligently, in a way, as Gilcrest or the insolent Chef de Commissaire. Nothing mattered now except the post mortem, all lesser considerations being swamped by the one great problem of how Christine Venables met her death—and if that death proved an unnatural one, neither Harry nor she could produce anything beyond a few surmises. As for herself, she was now aware of having committed an appalling blunder in giving the Baroness' note back into its owner's keeping. That message would never be seen again, while without it any hint of the intrigue it disclosed would sound mere spiteful malingering. Only those already prejudiced would believe her. As well might she bring forward an accusation against the gardener for setting her afire, or harp on her belief that on a given occasion the great lady of the neighbourhood had mimicked her most devoted friend.

"What do beliefs count for? Nothing—and yet I myself am certain what she was doing. Two-faced schemer! That one little touch gives her away."

Hypocrisy was bad enough, but to ridicule a victim one wished dead before that victim's unsuspecting next of kin was an act the cold perversity of which filled Sarah with shuddering horror. No wonder the woman capable of it had been nicknamed Bimi. The ape in Kipling's tale was not more wanton or cruel. Had she bewitched Gilcrest, or was he as vile and heartless as herself? It had never been possible to see one inch below his surface. If he really had planned and executed a whole series of murders. . . .

Turning back her cuffs she stared down at her arms. Once more she saw Gilcrest disappearing into the house behind his host; once more she sensed about her the drowsy stillness of the *serre*, felt the panic of fright as hot flames licked her skin. Gilcrest no less than the Greek could have stolen round to the window beside her. Why, though, should he have done it? Then and later she had liked him far too much to dream of connecting him with certain events. There was no reason at that time to suppose she would ever think differently. How carefully he had dressed her burns, but with a smouldering anger in his eyes she had not tried to comprehend! And the Baroness, devastated over the accident befalling a guest under her roof, had come next day to inquire, bringing a great armful of tulips . . . no, as before, the episode was an enigma. If Demosthenes had a hand in it, then there were two plots, separate and parallel. Again she gave it up in despair.

Several persons, their voices hushed, were entering the death-chamber. A pause, then someone tapped on her door. She called a nervous *"Entrez!"* and braced herself for the next dreaded encounter.

CHAPTER TWENTY-NINE

It was Marjory Barrows, come to tell her that the body was being removed and arrangements made to convey it to Nice, where the examination would be done.

"Don't go in, it will only distress you. He's there, and Jolivet, the manager, overseeing things. It will be over in a moment."

She clasped Sarah's cold hand in a tense grip till the heavy footsteps had creaked to silence and in the distance was heard the faint *ping* of the lift-doors. Then she turned a face flushed and tragic with sorrow and burst forth in a passionate lament.

"Oh, Miss MacNeil, why should this have happened? Two patients dying suddenly within a week, and now one of them—a darling, don't think I'm criticising her!—declaring she's poisoned! It means absolute ruin for him. He'll never, never live it down!"

Marjory could not yet have learned of the legacy. Sarah, however, writhed inwardly as she asked, low-voiced. "Has he told you it meant ruin?"

"He? Never! He wouldn't want me or anyone else to sympathise. I know, though. And to think the trouble he's taken over both these poor women! It's wicked—it's damnable!" She pushed her neat hat awry and blew her nose with violent protest against fate. "He, of all doctors, to have this come upon him!"

"I don't understand. Why, if he's proved right, should there be anything to live down?"

"Oh, my dear!"—with a despairing gesture. "Don't you see how it will be? Of course he's right. It's not that I'm worried about—but how will that fact help him? It's admitting doubt that's so fatal to a physician— and he's admitting it over two cases. Every patient he has will lose faith and boycott him—but that's not all."

Tears welling to her brown eyes, the dispenser continued, "You may not realise it, but people have a holy horror of the doctor who's once called in the police. They're terrified that same thing may happen to them if one of their relations dies, in which case they'd be placed in a hateful position. It's quite understandable. You can't blame them—and it's almost worse to find it isn't poison, for if it was he'd be patted on the back, while if nothing comes of it he'll be set down as an alarmist not to be trusted. Either way he's in the soup, a man at all costs to be avoided. In a big city it would cause talk enough. Here, where every human soul knows everyone else, it's the finish. There'll be nothing for it but to throw up the sponge and start all over again, right at the bottom, far away from Ste. Brigitte."

Faced by so blind and touching a loyalty Sarah experienced unreasoning pangs of conscience. She alone had forced this investigation. If she had done a terrible wrong, the consequences were on her head.

"Yet how could I have acted differently?" she murmured, hesitantly. "I had to tell him what Miss Venables said."

"You?" cried Marjory, astonished. "But of course you had! He doesn't blame you. Considering the sort of place this is there'd always have been doubt in some minds, and I suppose he couldn't well have asked for one inquest without making certain about the other woman, too. Miss Tomlins' family might have objected—though why, I don't know, for it seems Miss Venables' case was a thing apart, because of some fixed idea . . . tell me this: did she strike you as at all hysterical?"

Sarah pondered the question. "No," she replied, "she didn't."

"Yes she must have been, or else why ever should she have jumped to so idiotic a conclusion? Even the Baroness, who knew her better than anyone, declares she was—well, a bit queer."

Sarah gripped the arms of her chair.

"The Baroness! She's in Arles. How does she know?"

"Just now she rang up to inquire about her husband. When the doctor told her about this—he was bound to tell her, for I could hear her frantically demanding details—she went up in the air. Of course, she knows how it will affect him, though I imagine in his state of mind her expostulations were just the last straw. She was still sobbing when he cut off."

Bimi had rung up—obviously to assure herself an expected event had taken place during an absence no doubt carefully planned. Gilcrest had cut off because his dispenser was nearby, but not before the partner in his designs had been badly upset over an unanticipated piece of news. Long after Marjory had gone Sarah dwelt on these happenings, seeing in the deliberately curtailed conversation a single faint glimmering in a wall elsewhere solid. Sooner or later another conference would occur, and this, if overheard, might furnish the key to a plot locked and sealed from outer ken. She would never have the luck to listen in on it, but Marjory could manufacture opportunities. Ought she to have undeceived the girl, enlisted her aid?

"No," she whispered, "it's the one thing I couldn't do."

From now on Sarah passed from one trying interrogation to another, preserving so stony a silence that those who crept soft-footed and sympathetic to her room went away in chill displeasure. She felt sorry for Mrs. Cripps, who, chalk-faced and dithering, was the first to besiege her for an opinion, but the woman's spinelessness irritated her so that she hardened her heart against admissions. Was her refusal to commit herself an attempt to protect the man she argued must be guilty? She knew that it was, and that just as long as a chance of his innocence remained she must do him no injury. She was grateful to Harry for being so fair-minded. It was much to his credit. As for herself, it was one thing to fight an adversary face to face, another to aim blows at his back. Meanwhile, if these females, agog over the sensation, chose to think ill of her, she did not greatly care. They could hardly accuse her of murder.

Seven o'clock came, and with it the last, faltering knock. Laying down the comb she had been wretchedly drawing through her hair she opened the door only to draw back with every nerve in her body taut as a violin-string. There stood the Baroness—swollen-eyed, dressed in sober black, her lovely face working with a grief which seemed wholly real. The slight form hesitated, then cast itself upon Sarah, who felt nauseated with the engulfing scent. Her unresponsiveness must have been sensed, for after a convulsive pressure the clinging woman withdrew to gaze with dark, swimming eyes into the dry ones opposite. Sarah remained completely dumb.

"I have just reached home," the visitor began chokingly. "I've heard—and I am completely stupefied. Dead—Chreessie dead! I can understand nothing." Her hands fluttered distractedly. "I was so absorbed in Henri, I never noticed . . . why did she die? You called the doctor at once, yes? And before he came she said—she imagined—"

"That she had been poisoned."

The Baroness recoiled, covering her eyes with one hand while the other seemed warding off an attack. Against the black of her gown her nails showed blood-red.

"Ah, ah!" she moaned. "Are you sure she spoke those actual words? You did not misunderstand her?"

"There were two of us who heard."

The dark eyes stared hard at her. "Then it is true. I found it impossible to believe till now. Yet even so, I cannot . . . why should she think that? So incredible, so fantastic!" The Baroness mused, apparently thunderstruck, and shook her head helplessly. One would have said she was for the first time realising things of which she had no previous knowledge. "But," she resumed, searching Sarah's immovable features, "it is still more grotesque that Dr. Gilcrest, so sensible a man, should be taking her belief seriously enough to—to—"

She paused, evidently hoping that Sarah would help her out, but Sarah said nothing. She continued falteringly, "What can it mean? That not being present he has some slight doubt?"

"I think," said Sarah steadily, "that's a question you had better ask him."

"Ah, no!" cried the Baroness, confused. "Henri himself would not like doing that, and I would certainly not dare. If there has been some error in diagnosis, Dr. Gilcrest will be feeling most sensitive about it. Though I cannot think he has made a mistake," she added firmly but in so formal a tone that she might have been speaking of a mere acquaintance. "No, no, we shall see that this has been only an unhappy delusion. How could one suppose otherwise? What puzzles me is that I, close to her as I was, should never have guessed her capable of such ideas. It is all very strange."

She sank on to the edge of a chair, her eyes upturned to Sarah's as though she sought information but hesitated to pry into what did not concern her. It was natural, thought the girl, for her to try, subtly and plausible, to detach herself from the whole situation, most of all from Gilcrest. She no longer used his first name, and her manner regarding him had become almost prim. Recalling the intimate phrases of the note left in the book Sarah felt she could bear no more.

She opened the dressing-table drawer, took out the message from Miss Venables and with a brief explanation laid it in the Baroness' lap.

"For me. But why?" murmured Mme. de Bellesnaves, wonderingly.

"Because she thought she might die."

With another bewildered glance, the Baroness tore open the envelope, read what was inside, and crushing the paper between her fingers dissolved into a flood of tears.

"*C'est trop!*" she sobbed, great drops coursing unchecked down her olive cheeks and carrying with them little flecks of eyeblack. "Poor, poor darling! She has left me all her jewels. . . ."

Miss Venables' jewels, as Sarah well knew, comprised only a modest row of pearls, some old-fashioned diamonds seldom taken from their cases, a handful of antique ornaments also rarely worn, a dozen strings of amber, jade and the like. Clearly, if a murderous plot had been hatched with this woman as instigator, then Gilcrest's legacy must form the sole motive; but was there a plot? With a sudden revulsion of reason Sarah began to doubt it. All the evidence before her might read in two ways, besides which the Baron was alive, might go on living for another twenty years, in which case it was hard to see just how his wife could share in her lover's good fortune.

However, this was not all. Watching narrowly, Sarah could not detect the smallest sign of anxiety regarding the post mortem, or even any marked interest in its result. It seemed to her that the Baroness was shocked, that in an aloof way she disapproved what she considered an unprovoked and pointless procedure, but not personally concerned. Essentially she was indifferent, even more so than Harry, and definitely more than the doctor, although in one respect—the entire absence of fear—her attitude echoed theirs. Was Sarah the only one who scented wrong-doing? Perhaps she had over-valued the statement of a woman over-wrought by suffering and mental stress. She had not forgotten how Mrs. Bulstrode and Madge Whittaker had looked at her last night. They had thought her a person liable to run away with excitable ideas—as possibly she was.

Genuinely moved as the Baroness appeared to be, Sarah could not warm towards her—and yet, oh, the unutterable relief to feel that nothing actually evil had been done! Her eyes had been blinded by a noxious fog. All the atmosphere round her had breathed of poison gas. Let her sweep it away. . . .

"Sarah, old girl!"

Harry had burst in without troubling to knock, taken two quick strides, and laid his hand impulsively on her shoulder. All at once he perceived the Baroness. The affectionate familiarity of his manner dried up, he gulped in disconcerted embarrassment.

"I say—I didn't know . . . so it's you, Madame!" He was stammering awkwardly, his good-looking face fallen into depression. "You've come back then?"

Mme. de Bellesnaves had risen. Her tears had ceased, and she was struggling to command her voice. She did not immediately raise her eyes, but when she did their dark irises were filled with quiet, deep compassion. She had become very gentle, very maternal, but somehow far removed.

"Mon cher!" she murmured brokenly. "I did not think to see you. I—I—forgive me, I cannot say what I wish. It is too soon. I—perhaps I had better go."

She pressed his hand quickly, bade Sarah a wordless au revoir, and with the same new dignity which made her the more appealing slipped from the room. Harry wavered, seeking Sarah's advice.

"Think I ought to see her home? It's dark, you know."

Not waiting for a reply he followed, but in a minute or so came back to say that he was not wanted, as she had come in her cousin's car. He was subdued and thoughtful.

"She's no end cut up over this, isn't she? She was fond of my aunt, not a doubt of it. Expect it'll be duller than ever for her now." He ran his eye absently over Sarah's array of toilet articles, smoothed back his hair and frowned. "I asked her what she thought about this beastly business. Like the rest of us she thinks it's all bunkum, but she says we're doing right. If Chrissie wanted it, why, there's no more to be said."

"Harry," Sarah reminded him, "didn't you come in here to tell me something?"

"When?" He stared at her. "Oh, you mean a moment ago! Yes, I did. It seems you and I—and I suppose Mrs. Bulstrode—have got to be interrogated by the police. In fact, a whole flaming consignment of 'em are coming here to-morrow morning to put us through the mill. Jolly prospect, what? No way out of it, though. Just thought I'd prepare you. Think you'll mind?"

"No. I can only tell them the truth."

"Same here—and that's not a lot, is it? Still, I'll be thankful when it's over. My French isn't up to much."

Like the rest of his type, he had been long trained to show no emotion, and yet by the way in which he lit a cigarette, took a few jerky puffs and ground the remainder under his heel Sarah knew that he was far from unshaken.

CHAPTER THIRTY

AT ELEVEN next morning the local commissaire arrived, accompanied by a deputation from Nice technically termed *le parquet*, and consisting of the Juge d'Instruction, the Médecin Légiste, an inspector, and a secretary. These functionaries were ushered into Sarah's room by the manager, whose dour glance showed that he regarded Mademoiselle as solely responsible for the present débâcle. Who better than he knew the extent to which his precious English colony might be affected by any sensational proceedings? He might at one swoop lose half his guests. A scapegoat must be found, and Sarah suspected that it was she who had been singled out to fill the rôle.

Her turn had come last, and as the stodgy officials filed in, blotting out the sunshine with their thick, dark clothing, her heart failed her. She distrusted the precision with which they chose seats against the light so that she must face it. There was something ominous and inquisitorial about the sallow visaged judge as he adjusted black-rimmed pince nez and studied her through them. Even the drab secretary, spreading out an impressive portfolio on the table before him and dipping a fine nibbed pen into the ink bottle, made her nervous—and yet, until her first moment of hesitation, there was no real cause for alarm. It was then that the judge pounced on her, scenting evasion, and her pulse, subsided to normal, gave an apprehensive bound.

"You say that since your connection with this lady began, two anonymous letters arrived, but that in neither instance did you observe any physical disturbance. Let us take the first, received while at the London hotel. It did not precipitate an illness?"

"N-no," replied Sarah cautiously. "I can't say that it did. She might have been more disturbed, if—"

"We are not here to discuss what might have happened," interrupted the judge smoothly. "However, you may state whatever circumstances surrounded that event and allow us to decide if they are relevant."

She had not meant to speak of Mrs. Venables' death, but there seemed no avoiding it.

"Her sister-in-law became violently ill in the night. In fact, she died almost at once. Miss Venables' entire attention was taken up with that, which prevented her dwelling on her own anxiety. She was always like that," Sarah added her own comment.

She saw the commissaire glance with smug satisfaction at the judge, who nodded to himself.

"Let us hear all, Mademoiselle. You say this death was sudden?"

Ignorant of any especial significance attending his stepmother's decease, Harry could not have thought fit to mention what was now drawn, bit by bit, from the reluctant Sarah. Only that could explain the fact that her hearers had learned nothing about Mrs. Venables, or even known she existed. Five pairs of eyes dwelt keenly on the narrator's face, especially when Gilcrest's brief connection with the affair came to light, but for a moment there was no remark. The judge then reverted to the letter, inquiring the exact time of its delivery.

"Posted at noon, in the same district, you say . . . and the English doctor, when did he leave London? Also at noon . . . h'm! Well, in view of the autopsy, we need scarcely concern ourselves with the other lady's death. But, stay! Where was her medicine made up?"

"At a chemist near the hotel. I should think Mr. Venables could tell you what shop it was."

"Did anyone but the lady herself handle the medicine?"

"Before her death, I am sure no one did. I myself saw her take it from the clerk at the desk when we all came downstairs to lunch. At the table she broke the seal, took one dose, and put the bottle in her bag. Late that night I saw it lying on her bed-table. I imagine she had taken three doses, but I don't know for sure. The hotel doctor examined the label, and the prescription."

"The medicine was in what form? Liquid?"

Sarah tried not to waver. "No, capsules," she answered steadily.

"Capsules?"

The Médecin Légiste leant forward suddenly. The inspector also appeared to prick up his ears, but the judge and commissaire remained calm. The last named conferred in a whisper with his superior, who nodded and waved him aside. Clearing his throat, the judge began anew.

"Now, Mademoiselle! You tell me your employer always assumed these communications emanated from a very definite source. I suppose she made a romantic story of it, built up an atmosphere of intrigue, posed, in short, as an interesting martyr? She did, did she not?"

What was he getting at? His words as well as his tone roused Sarah's antagonism.

"Not in the least," she denied emphatically. "Miss Venables was one of the most simple and practical women I have ever met. She hated causing needless excitement. To prove that, I may say she confided in only three people outside the police."

"And those three were—?"

"Dr. Gilcrest, her nephew, and myself. Even her nephew never knew all that was going on. She didn't like to distress him."

"But she did show fear? She took elaborate precautions?"

"She might have taken more. For a woman who considered herself in constant danger, she behaved very normally." The judge stroked his pointed beard. "Yet for a day and a half previous to her attack she confined herself to an extremely limited diet. She appears to have been taking one of her physician's prescriptions. Did she continue with it?"

"Certainly. She felt a tiny bit bad—in a physical sense, I mean—and the medicine relieved her."

The Médecin Légiste—he was a dry, sharp-nosed man—interposed.

"Pardon! Just when did she take her last dose?"

"About eleven o'clock, on going to bed."

"Ah! And what has become of the bottle?"

At last!

"I locked it in the drawer of her table. If you like, I will give you the key—and Miss Tomlins' medicine is probably still in a raffia bag with her knitting. Either Miss Whittaker or her sister has it."

She had expected a sensation, but none occurred. Questions continued, and soon she began to feel that what had gone before was but preliminary patter leading up to something of real importance. The judge polished his glasses, set them back on his nose, and addressed her in a slightly more peremptory manner.

"Mademoiselle: has it ever entered your head that these warnings were in the nature of a myth, a deliberate hoax? In plain language, did you at no time suspect that your employer might be writing them to herself?"

Sarah gasped as though cold water had been dashed in her face.

"Did I suspect—? Never!" she cried indignantly. "Why, it's impossible! Preposterous!"

"Not at all," retorted the judge with irritating composure. "On the contrary, it is not only a most probable solution, but the one which from early days has occurred to every official concerned. Think it over. These letters, with two exceptions, went from France to addresses widely separated and in some cases known only to the lady herself, or to her immediate family. The exceptions were posted in the same town as the victim, so could easily have been managed in person. The others could have been dispatched by her in self-directed envelopes, under cover, to a hired accomplice in this country, who in turn reposted them, taking pains to wear gloves so as to leave no finger prints—as she herself would have done when she wrote them."

"I don't believe it!" burst out Sarah, then stopped short, flushing to the roots of her hair. She had remembered how Miss Venables, when handling the letter received in London, had put on gloves. "It can't be true," she went on, fighting down her confusion. "Why on earth should a woman as sensible as she was do such a thing?"

"It is a well-known device of hysterics," explained the judge with a tolerant shrug. "Designed to centre sympathetic attention on themselves. We of the legal professions, as well as medical men, are quite familiar with the ruse. Ego-maniacs whose vanity has suffered—"

"Miss Venables an ego-maniac! There you are entirely wrong. She was the least selfish woman alive."

"Mademoiselle's excellent qualities, which I make no attempt to deny, form no obstacle to the theory. Besides, it served her purpose to win your affection. No doubt she took pains to do so. Let us put the case in a dispassionate light." Eyes on ceiling, finger-tips fitted together, he pursued in the same coldly reasonable strain, "Mademoiselle Venables—who, by the way, was known to you for only a short time—was unmarried, of a critical age, and possessed of neurotic tendencies which, on one occasion at least, led her to make extravagant and unfounded assertions. I refer to the regrettable accident which befell her friend, the English major, last year. Publicly discredited, filled, let us say, with humiliation which grew to a rankling sense of personal injury, she quitted this town, at the same time, no doubt, casting about for some means of striking back at the law which had shown her up in a foolish light. Mind, I postulate nothing. I merely point out that persons in a similar position have acted in the manner I am going to describe. If justification was her aim, how better achieve it than by herself receiving threats presumably from the agents whom she declared had murdered her compatriot?

"In any case, just such threats began to arrive, and were forthwith handed to the police as clinching proof that she had been right and they wrong. That the police, after careful investigation, declined to accept her theory, disappointed and annoyed her, whereupon, to bolster up her pretence of evading a real pursuit, she spent her time wandering about Europe. Tiring of this and wishing to settle down again, she carried on the deception by engaging a companion-protectress. You did not see her physically affected by the letters? Nor did anyone else. That detail was invented, but she had, throughout, been troubled by an internal weakness likely to recur. It did, unexpectedly, recur, in an aggravated form, and taking advantage of it she made a dramatic declaration. Never supposing she was about to die, she told you she had been poisoned, and demanded an inquiry. It was a final gesture, perfectly in keeping with the whole. Do you not see how well it falls in with all her behaviour?"

Though every instinct revolted, Sarah had listened, appalled by the uncanny adroitness with which all her objections had been silenced. Now she was free to speak she sought vainly for one single argument to refute what still seemed to her a monstrous, insulting suggestion.

"Suppose it's true," she said in a dry voice, "surely it was odd to keep the thing so secret? I repeat, she didn't want it known. She didn't tell even her closest friend, the Baronne de Bellesnaves."

She saw the commissaire hide a smile.

"Since her chief object would have been to impress the police," returned the judge shrewdly, "it was natural she should try to offset her hysterical conduct of last spring by a dignified reticence. She was clever enough to know that to be ridiculed by her friends would only add to her mortification. However, let us consider whom she selected as her three confidants. First, her physician, for his own sake unwilling to endanger his position by opposing her; second her nephew, equally reluctant to offend one on whom he was dependant for certain luxuries; and third, yourself—a paid dependant most unlikely to dispute her statements, no matter how wild. Briefly, she imposed her fraud only on such individuals as, so to speak, she held in her hand."

About to blaze a furious retort, Sarah stopped again, blinded by the light suddenly flashed on her brain. Gilcrest—Harry . . . was she alone a credulous simpleton?

The cool voice went on, "Mademoiselle, your loyalty does credit to your heart, if not to your understanding. I will say no more, but if the coming post mortem reveals nothing abnormal, the reason for that circumstance will be clear."

It was over. The five sets of footsteps were receding towards the lift, and Sarah, the blood pounding in her temples, was making headlong for Harry's room. In the corridor she met Harry himself, and brusquely put her question.

"Harry! I've got to know. Did you think all along that she was responsible for those letters?"

He jumped, turned red, and whispered painfully, "My God! Have I got to answer?"

He had answered her. She grew very still.

"And I never guessed . . . you felt certain about it?"

"How could anyone be certain of anything?" he muttered reluctantly. "I felt a swine to imagine such a thing, even though it was a relief, in a way, to believe she wasn't in danger. I couldn't tell you. I was too fond of her—and besides, I couldn't prove it."

"What made you think she wrote the letters?"

He considered, evading her accusing eyes. "It was an inspector down here who first gave me the tip. I came near bashing his head in. Then, little by little, I began noticing things. My stepmother had always said—not that I'd go by Gracie's opinions—that she was a bit odd. She had a name among us for being—well, excitable. And she kept things to herself. We never quite knew . . . oh, I say, can't we drop it? She's dead, you know. What's the good?" In a sort of dumb agony he mopped his moist brow.

"So you thought the whole tale was made up. No, I'm not blaming you. And Major Frampton—?"

"Tumbled down the shaft because he was stewed. Wrote that rigmarole for the same reason. Been brooding over what those Turkish chaps had said, I suppose, and may have run into some dark-skinned scoundrel who reminded him of them. Anyhow, he was stewed—to the gills. I know, because I was with him just before it happened. Gilcrest knows, too. Ask him."

Suddenly, without any excuse, she hated Harry, almost as much as she had hated those impervious Frenchmen. With a rush of tears to her eyes she left him, closing her door in his face.

Truth—what was it? A purely relative quantity. On the one hand she was tormented by earnest brown eyes, beseeching her to keep faith; on the other she saw with equal clearness a self-invented fiction on account of which she had set fire to gunpowder calculated to blow an honest career to atoms. Fragments of thought rose to the surface of her mind, but like driftwood on a raging torrent slid away from her grasp. Christine Venables had, perhaps, never been in peril—yet she had died, terribly and without warning, much as two others had done. If she did not write the letters, who did? If it were Gilcrest, he would naturally find it convenient to pretend they were a hoax. Convenient—yes, for whatever the case he did benefit by her death. It was the one stark fact nothing could alter.

"Still, Harry benefits much more. Why don't I suspect him? Because he's not clever enough? Because he's—no, wait! I knew there was another reason. Beryl Tomlins, the woman I wasn't to talk to, the woman who nearly told me something against the Baroness—she died, too. Harry never cared how much I questioned her. He never thought of her at all. It was Gilcrest who bothered. Whatever he may be doing now, I can't wipe that out, nor can I wipe out his affair with—"

Every tap at the door startled her now. Were the police back again? But no, it was a waiter, bearing a huge bouquet of lilies-of-the-valley, hidden in which was a note from the Baroness. Shrinkingly she opened the message, which further confounded her. What! She was invited, nay, begged, to come as guest to the Casa Giallo? She could not believe it— and then she remembered that except on one small occasion, possibly due to some worthy excuse, Maddalena de Bellesnaves had treated her in the most charming fashion. At all events the latter could not guess what went on in her mind.

"We shall not be leaving for Arles just yet, as Henri refuses to desert his friend during this trying time. It is not gay *chez nous*, for Henri is still in a sad state, sadder than ever now this great loss has come to us; but I think perhaps it will be pleasanter for you to be with us than at the hotel. Christine would have wished it. Will you not come at once, and remain at the villa as long as you are in Ste. Brigitte? It will give me much pleasure, and it may supply a new distraction for my husband."

It sounded genuine. Quite possibly the invitation did spring from bona-fide kindness of heart, in which case . . .

"I like the Baron—and I know I shall be miserable every minute I'm forced to stay in this hotel. They're turning against me here, from Jolivet downward. I can see it. There's only Harry, and even he . . . after all, if the letters weren't real threats, then what is there left to go on?"

She picked up a sheet of paper and a pen. For several seconds she paused, wavering first in one direction then in the opposite, unable to decide. At last, pushed by nothing better than an unconquerable dislike which might mean only jealousy, she wrote thanks and—a refusal. She sat looking down at the somewhat wobbly characters which were the best her weak wrist could manage. Then she sealed the note up and put a stamp on it.

No more now, except to await the verdict from Nice. If a negative result was declared, then two delayed funerals would take place, and

Sarah MacNeil, a wrong-headed meddler, must pack her trunk and purchase a railway ticket back to obscurity.

CHAPTER THIRTY-ONE

"SARAH—the verdict's in!"

She looked up from the trunk she had been desultorily packing. Her face had gone white, the eyes that met the haunted blue ones opposite were wide with fear.

"What is it?" she whispered drily.

"Those cursed blighters haven't said. Want us to come down to the Commissariat and find out. Quick, jam on a hat!"

With shaking hands she obeyed, mentally execrating the youth who had come so utterly to depend on her moral support that he could not even go after the crucial information without her.

For three interminable days—the most harrowing period in her remembrance—she had had scarcely ten minutes free of Harry's society. Shunning the ready sympathy of the women about him, refusing to visit the de Bellesnaves, he had clung to her as a child to its nurse, following her when she went into the town, persistently taking her on aimless drives, and pestering her with attentions till she yearned to be alone with her own racked thoughts. Flattering? Yes, if she had cared to profit by the opportunities showered upon her, but somehow they meant still less than in the happier stages of the acquaintance. It galled her to see the significant glances directed at herself and her stalwart, subdued cavalier and to know she was being credited with a success she had not wanted to attain. Her nerves were frayed. She had grown sick of the anxious, slightly vapid face eternally imploring her for the reassurance she could not give—which was what Harry wished of her, to be comforted and made easy in his mind, though she believed it would be fairly easy to rouse in him other desires if she had chosen to try.

"They won't find anything, will they, old girl?" he had demanded twenty times a day. "What do you think?"

"I'd rather not think, Harry," she would reply sententiously. "After all, I don't know any more than you."

"It's only the ghastly unpleasantness, you know. I'd hate like sin to suppose Chrissie'd been . . . but it's nonsense to suppose it, what?"

So it had gone on, while the atmosphere round them, seething and fulminating, brought to birth a rapid change in the feeling towards the doctor. The fact of his inheritance had leaked out—how, Sarah did not know—and instantly the mercury dropped to zero. Two of the older guests fell ill and failed to send for him. A pompous, black-bearded physician with dirty nails—till now the butt of disparaging jests—appeared in the corridors, or was seen secretively hobnobbing with the manager. It was hinted that just as soon as the great question was settled a wholesale exodus would take place. Gilcrest and his dispenser were given a wide berth.

Sarah herself was fast becoming a social outcast, at sight of whom conversation pointedly ceased. Mrs. Cripps had the air of harbouring a deep grievance. Mrs. Bulstrode and Madge Whittaker, though studiously polite, veered away at her approach. Undoubtedly she was regarded as having taken undue powers upon herself, even by those who held darkest fears. She was the snake in an Eden soon to be desert waste—and yet, if murder was established in either of the cases under investigation, opinion would instantly alter and make her a heroine. Was this what she desired? A thousand times no! All she prayed for was proof, complete and incontrovertible, that Brian Gilcrest, who in no circumstances would ever be hers, was guiltless of a dastardly crime. The dread that he was not had robbed her of all peace and reduced her to quaking misery. Life would be insupportable if this suspense went on, but it would be ended now, within a few minutes. Ended in what way?

The tyres of the Fiat crunched over the gravelled square and stopped before the squat stone building. Harry got out, glanced appealingly towards her, and disappeared into the dim doorway to leave her counting the seconds till his return. She had reached five sixties when his steps echoed again. Here he was. She leant forward, searching his face.

"Yes, what does it say? Is it—?"

Jubilantly he beamed on her.

"Absolutely and totally okay. Not a sign of poison in either of 'em. Wasn't I right? All this hullabaloo for nothing! Whew, I'm thankful it's over!"

He slid his long legs into the seat beside her and wiped his streaming face with a brick-red silk handkerchief. His whole handsome being radiated relief.

Something whispered to Sarah that she had always known this would be so. She ought to be rejoicing much more than Harry, but instead all she experienced was a feeling half flatness, half doubt. Was it possible that out of all her suspicions not one was rooted in fact? She found it hard to believe.

"Did they give it to you in writing?" she asked. "Because I'd rather like to see exactly what it says."

He was straightening the mat under their feet and did not at first seem to catch what was said. She repeated it.

"Oh, certainly, I've got it all here, though I must confess it's a bit too technical for me to grasp. Take a squint if you like."

He threw a lengthy document in her lap. She scanned it closely, and looked up in a frown.

"But Harry," she said hesitatingly, "have you looked at this? That is to say, have you taken it all in?"

"Not in detail. The chap in there assured me both deaths were perfectly natural affairs, so I let it go at that. Why? Notice anything especial?"

"Well . . . it says that they found acute inflammation with perforations and hemorrhage *in both cases*. That's one odd thing."

"Is it? Why?"

"Only because I understood that mesenteric thrombosis didn't mean perforation, only a blood-clot. I may be wrong, of course. And then, look here: although it's admitted that the trouble in each instance occurred in the precise locality specified by the doctor, they mention that neither time was it quite typical in appearance. The ulcers don't seem to have been quite ordinary affairs. What do you make of that?"

"Only what it says. I'm pretty ignorant in these matters, but I daresay some ulcers may be a little bit unusual. Cases differ, you know." He paused to light a cigarette. "Matter of fact, I inquired into what you've mentioned. Seems a typical ulcer's got rather especial edges, whereas these looked just slightly like burns from some corrosive. Couldn't have been burns, though, for they applied every possible test, and besides if either of these two had swallowed any sort of corrosive there'd have been dark stains round the mouth and down the throat. Read on, you'll see that no kind of blame attaches to Gilcrest, in spite of that small error in calling Miss Tomlin's complaint mesenteric thingumbob. They say he'd a perfect right to diagnose it as he did."

Had he? Perhaps; but what Sarah was thinking was that a corrosive substance need not leave outer stains if encased in a gelatine covering.

"The great thing," resumed Harry, "is that there wasn't a trace of toxic or otherwise suspicious residue in either body. Toxic means poison, doesn't it? So that's that."

"Then you're satisfied, are you?"

"Hang it all, why not? You can't get behind a statement like this. These medical blokes declare it's all right. The Chief himself's had a pow-wow with the Nice fellow, and tells me there's not the foggiest chance of anything being wrong. What more do we want?"

"Did they analyse the two bottles of medicine?"

"Oh, Lord yes! They were okay."

Obviously. She had guessed as much; but could sufficient corrosive be compassed in a single capsule to cause arterial rupture, and if so what corrosive could it be which left behind no trace? Futile to mention such thoughts. They could only unsettle Harry, who could not be blamed for being content with the law's inability to class these deaths as unnatural. In any case nothing could be done, so perhaps it was as well he did not see the flaw so apparent to her . . . the flaw which left Gilcrest still under a cloud.

"The body'll be brought back here tomorrow. That means I can clear out of this blasted place in a couple of days at latest—maybe sooner. Thank God for that."

The funeral, Sarah knew, would be held in Huddersfield. Harry would convey the body there to be interred in the family vault.

"Where are we going?" she asked dully as the car rounded the waterfront and turned into a narrow street.

"Thought I might as well pop round to the undertaking establishment and tell them to get a hustle on. There's my reservation, too, and the arrangements about shipping the car. Your ticket, too. Shall I book a couple of wagon lits while I'm about it? We could travel as far as London together—if you're going there."

Sarah had not intended to go first class, but Harry routed her suggestion.

"Think I'm going to let you economize after all you've been through? Not a chance! The drinks are on me, so don't let's argue. The very least I can do."

She was too listless to demur, or to move her hand when his warm one rested upon it.

""Thanks, Harry. It is really most awfully good of you."

"Not good at all! I want your company, don't you know. Besides, rotten as this has been, I see now what a thundering sound idea it was to egg Gilcrest on in the first place to having these post mortems—or anyhow hers. That head of yours is pretty level, what? I expect you saw what a hole he'd have been landed in if things hadn't been cleared up. I'd always have blamed myself. Not much use tumbling into money if people are going to make a song about how it was come by . . . here we are. I won't be two ticks."

No, Harry did not see. To him all was serene and Gilcrest, whom he had never questioned, had come out of it squarely without a stain on his character. She must not undeceive him.

From the dingy shop-window wherein a ghastly marble angel posed between the hideous iron wreaths the French nation loves to inflict on its departed she averted her eyes to the brown sails showing above the low roofs. Behind them rosy clouds floated on a pale turquoise sky; the air was warm, with a tang of salt in it. Back in London it would be grey and showery, the streets devoid of colour, her boarding-house reeking of cabbage, yet as ardently as Harry she longed for the change. Ste. Brigitte she wanted to put behind her and never set foot in it again.

Someone was running towards her, crying her name in breathless sobs. It was Marjory Barrows, whom she had not seen since the morning after Miss Venables' death, Marjory hatless and distraught, heading for the harbour road. At the same instant Harry came out of the shop, and she fell upon him, gibbering in her panic.

"Mr. Venables! Take me with you! Drive, oh, as fast as you can, to the Casa Giallo boathouse. Yes, the boathouse, that's where he is. Angela's just been, but the doctor's gone to Nice and hasn't got back. Now she's tearing round the shops hunting for the Baroness. Oh, my God, to think he's done it, after all!"

She was in the back seat, poised in readiness to spring out. With the engine in motion Harry turned on her a blanched face.

"Who's done what? I say, you don't mean—"

"Yes, the Baron. Hurry! There may be a chance."

The sea, the high wall over spilling with rank growth, flashed past. They reached the anchored yacht, the bent pines, the strip of rocky beach. Only one sound broke the evening stillness. It was the shrill, nervous yapping of Max.

Marjory was racing up the slope to the boathouse, at the gaping doorway of which the others overtook her. Inside the hut was twilit gloom and a curious stench, faintly that of bitter almonds. Sebastiano in his shirtsleeves was hovering affrightedly over what looked like a heap of crumpled home-spun huddled on the cane settee. Marjory fell on her knees beside it and gave a despairing cry.

"Too late! He's been dead for hours. Look, smell! It's prussic acid."

She pointed to the two halves of a small pill-box, the lower of which retained a grey, viscous smear. So the Baron had come here prepared to end his life, choosing his interval of solitude so that no one might thwart him. It was suicide. It could only be that—but what did it matter? The being Sarah had recognized as an obstacle was now removed. Maddalena de Bellesnaves was free.

CHAPTER THIRTY-TWO

WHETHER from the actual sight of the lifeless body or from the sudden vision of a scheme rounded up and completed, Sarah turned faint. For a second all went black, but as she swayed Harry caught her.

"Steady on!" she heard his hoarse whisper. "Get you back to the car!"

She shook her head. Just aware that Harry's arm remained round her waist she had seen through the windows a sight which brought her dulled faculties to cool alertness. To the foot of the knoll an old rattle-trap Citroen had careened, and from it two figures had precipitated themselves. They were the Baroness, and the swart-bearded French physician now patronized by the hotel clientele.

The Baroness sobbed and panted as she tore up the slope, the damp, heavy mass of her black hair quivering loose on her neck, her small feet blundering in the sand. Sweeping past Sarah and Harry she cast herself on her husband's limp form.

"Henri!" It was a wild shriek. "Henri! *Qu'est-ce tu as?*"

Her starting eyes strained down into the sightless ones, then as her companion lumbered through the door she collapsed on the dusty floor. Pompously the doctor took charge. No, Madame had not lost consciousness, but this other—*sacré Dieu!* Clicking his tongue he bent over, lifting the flaccid arms, turning back the eyelids, sniffing the lips. The empty pill-box caught his eye. He examined it, nodded heavily. Cyanide of potassium—probably a colossal dose. Easy enough for an amateur chemist to obtain the stuff—and in paste form. Ugh! But what was this brownish trickle running from the mouth. Chocolate? Decidedly. One could smell chocolate. Now how was that?

Sebastiano indicated a round, flat box with a decorated top, open on the window-sill, and well within reach of the settee. Sarah recognized it as the box of chocolates Miss Venables had brought the Baron from London—chocolates especially chosen, all with coffee centres. But that was weeks ago! Were there still some left? There were—just two. Then she remembered how the Baron had asked Gilcrest's permission to eat even one.

Monsieur adored chocolate, Sebastiano explained. He kept this box here, but he indulged only now and again. For days at a time he never touched them.

"He was forbidden to touch chocolate. That's why," said Marjory.

The doctor turned toward her with tufted brows raised, and shrugged.

"A man intent on suicide does not trouble about restrictions," he commented tersely. "It is quite evident what happened, and one may say in full agreement with M. le Baron's character to remove a disagreeable taste with something pleasant. However, to make sure, let me smell." He sniffed each of the remaining chocolates and shook his head. "No, they are harmless. I daresay the authorities will wish to examine them, but—" Another shrug. "The thing explains itself."

He then inquired when and in what condition the body had been found. In broken French, deeply agitated, Sebastiano gave his account. At two o'clock, *comme d'habitude*, Monsieur had set off for his siesta, taking with him the young dog. Madame had already departed for the town, to fulfil a number of appointments. Six o'clock arrived before it was realised that the master had not turned up for his usual cup of tisane, and although no anxiety was felt the prolonged and excited barking of the terrier had sent Sebastiano to investigate. He had found the dog tugging at Monsieur's sleeve, at once sensing the presence of something wrong. The body was then clammy to the touch, the mouth gaping and the eyes glazed, all as one saw them now.

"H'm—ah! And what is it the woman, the cook, said about a written message Monsieur had left?"

"Here on the table, Monsieur. I saw it on the floor, crumpled, as though it had been clutched in his hand. Also there was his fountain-pen, uncapped, beside it and the pillbox."

Sarah watched the Frenchman pick up what appeared to be a large-sized single sheet of the Casa Giallo note-paper, at the top of which appeared one line of writing ending in an ink-blot.

"L'affaire se termine—inutile continuer," recited the hushed bass voice. "Ah! One sees . . . M. le Baron was an ill man. With his medical knowledge he was no doubt fully aware that his condition was hopeless. Cancer, perhaps? I should have said cancer of the liver. Be that as it may, he realised he had not long to live and would suffer much, in addition to which he has recently been plunged into deepest melancholy by the loss of his dog. He chose cyanide because the action is swift. One would say the whole thing was finished inside a quarter of an hour. Even as he

wrote this message the agony overcame him, hence the blot. He probably died early in the afternoon—exactly when it is impossible to say."

With solicitude tinged by clumsy gallantry he stooped over the huddled figure of the Baroness to show her the paper.

Mme. de Bellesnaves stared blankly at the scrawl, covered her eyes, and moaned.

"Me, I am to blame!" She beat her breasts with her small clenched hands. "Never, never should I have left him alone!"

"Madame, madame!" the doctor soothed her. "It is unthinkable that you should reproach yourself for something no one could help. Remember, if a man has this in his mind no power can stop him. And though you had planned to remove him to other surroundings, he had refused to stir from home, is it not so? That, too, may have its meaning. Who knows but that some shocking event—I must not put it more plainly— may have influenced his wavering decision? You tell me he learned this morning of a certain report which sent his friend, my English colleague, to Nice? Ah!"

The booming whisper carried. Sarah saw Marjory's face flame with sudden fury, and looked to see what effect this suggestion, which it was safe to say a large portion of Ste. Brigitte would be repeating before nightfall, had made on the Baroness. It was her lover who was being attacked. Surely she would say something in his defence? But no, sunk into herself she gave no sign of having heard.

Angela, mouthing and crossing herself, had slipped into the room. Behind her hovered Demosthenes, inky-browed, inscrutable. The small confined space teemed with humanity, the afternoon sun, now slanting in at the windows, made it so hot one could scarcely breathe. Sarah, backed into a corner, felt Harry's grip on her arm tighten like a vice. At the same moment there was the sound of a third car arriving, and before she could speculate as to what it meant the ghoulish servants were thrust aside and Gilcrest was in their midst. In two imperious strides he had reached the body. Once again absent at the time of the catastrophe, but on the spot when nothing could be done. . . .

He took not the slightest notice of those round him. Kneeling on the dusty boards he raised the gnarled figure in his arms to scrutinise the sightless eyeballs, the brown saliva now drying about the corners of the mouth. As he did so the sun sank behind a purple cloud-bank on the horizon, and the room became dark. Without turning he issued a peremptory order.

"Fetch a lamp—and telephone the police."

Sebastiano ran to do his bidding. Mme. de Bellesnaves, her black hair uncoiled and hanging over her hidden face, did not stir.

"Suicide, as you see," volunteered the Frenchman, loftily officious. "It was cyanide, two grains, possibly more, to judge by—"

"Of course it's cyanide!" jerked the younger man impatiently. "The point is, who saw him last? Why did he eat chocolate? Here!" He turned brusquely to Marjory. "You tell me what you know."

While the dispenser was supplying the details, Gilcrest as his predecessor had done, sniffed at the untouched chocolates, tightened his lips, and set down the box. The Baron's dying message was shown him. He pored over it long and tensely but with an expressionless face, then, the two portions of the fountain-pen held in his hands, grew very still, and remained for long moments without speaking. He seemed unaware of Sarah's or Harry's presence, and not once did he look towards the woman, hunched and shuddering on the floor. Good acting, thought Sarah, her heart so stunned within her that it might have ceased to beat; always in supreme command of himself. Another idea dragged itself laboriously through her brain. She reflected that while a thousand pounds a year was not a princely income, the total achieved by adding to it the proceeds from the sale of this estate and pictures and bibelots the owner had clung to so tenaciously would probably represent far more comfort and freedom than the Baroness had yet enjoyed.

Harry's hard breathing rasped in her ear. The Frenchman, while they waited for the light, kept up a prosy, half philosophic commentary which no one heeded. Somewhere in the distance the terrier continued to yap. Through the deepening dusk, against the whitish blur of Marjory's overall, Gilcrest's profile could be seen, turning slowly from the dead man's face to the medley of small objects on the table. A silence, then, taking out his old-fashioned watch, the French doctor opined that the inquest—in the circumstances a purely formal affair—would doubtless be held here, as soon as the police arrived.

In and out the choked paths a twinkling star threaded its downward course. Brighter it grew till, becoming a globed lamp balanced in a brown hand, it split the gloom into alternate segments of blackness and yellow light. The corpse's drawn features leaped to view. A hovering shadow from above made the left eyebrow appear to twitch. Sarah, stiffening convulsively, all but heard the Baron uttering the last words he had spoken to her: *"It had to be. . . ."*

Harry muttered, "Let's go!"

As they made the movement to slip quietly away, Gilcrest, his face starkly illumined by the lamp, wheeled in their direction. His eyes fell on the girl, but stern and terrible seemed to stare through her. What she saw in them made her head whirl. Stumbling in her dizziness she pressed blindly on till she brought up against the mud-guard of the Fiat within ten paces of the lapping water. She roused to hear Harry cursing under his breath as he fumbled with the starter.

"Get in! That's about done for me. A drink's what I want."

Perhaps a drink would do her good, too. Anyhow, she did not demur, even when two hours had passed and still they faced each other across a table covered with red oilcloth in the dirty little café where Major Frampton had taken his last brandy.

She wanted no dinner, nor did she trouble about her companion's shaken state. All that occupied her was the effort to comprehend.

If she was wrong in supposing this culminating act of drama had been contrived with deliberate intent, then she was wrong about the other acts as well—but right or wrong, she knew the police would accept Henri de Bellesnaves' death as suicide, which no doubt it was, though suicide forced on a man by cruelty and suggestion did in a moral sense amount to murder. Still, it might not have been, she supposed, only how could she learn the truth?

There was no way of learning it. Even if the future actions of two persons gave a likely answer, still it would not be proof.

"I'll never find out," she thought. "I'll live and die without knowing."

CHAPTER THIRTY-THREE

THE front door of the Casa Giallo opened, and before it closed again a man's shadow fell sharply across the paved terrace outside. Above, in a curtained room, the woman who was now free lay in her Italian bed with the tall twisted posts, her brain clouded with bromide, while in another chamber alongside a stiffening form reposed between flickering candles. Neither of those would know or care what was done out here—and the servants were safe for hours in their red-tiled kitchen, their heads together over Chianti and cheap spirits. Hyppolite Thiers, bungling old ass, had taken a smug departure. So had the police inspector and his sergeant, their note-books filled with completely satisfying statements. There could be no better time than now for a project which must not be seen by curious eyes.

Night silence brooded over the vast wilderness stretching between the terraces and the sea. Casting an upward glance at the shuttered windows, the man just emerged set out quietly and with grim purpose for the tool-shed abutting on the side wall, with the aid of the late Baron's electric torch found a pick and shovel and some old bits of sacking, then turned towards the shrubbery.

As he set foot in the first transverse path, he stopped and swore. That cursed pest of a terrier—loose again, and somewhere, off there in the wilds, making a row frantic enough to rouse the household. Two more minutes of this and Sebastiano would come to haul him indoors. Was it wiser to hide and wait for this to happen? No, best collar the dog at once and silence him. Calling softly, he plunged headlong in the direction of the barks.

His voice had an intonation which on one occasion had been called precious, but there was nothing precious in the stream of invective it uttered when, instead of ceasing, the yaps waxed shriller, more excited, bordering on the hysterical. Where was the terrier? The noise seemed to come from an uncut growth at the farthermost limits of the estate, seldom if ever penetrated, because of a species of salt bog now impeding the pursuer's progress. Squashing through mire, his face stung by the spines of long "feelers," the man ploughed on, bent only on quieting the ear-splitting clamour. Sweat rained from his body. He swore again, but kept going.

Now he caught sight of the dog, a dim, pale blur in the surrounding darkness. As he had expected, the little creature was digging furiously, throwing up a spray of damp earth from the hole he had made, and punctuating his efforts with piercing yelps. The old bulldog would never have dug like this. With its impaired sense of smell it would not even have guessed the hidden attraction of a dead mole or rabbit, but the terrier's keen nose had soon scented this out.

One last spurt, and the digger was pinioned, wriggling like an eel to get back to his job. The yaps, however, had subsided to a nervous whimper as, coat bristling, Max strained a sniffing muzzle into the hole, then turned to dart an inquiring tongue at his captor's cheek. The man stooped to look.

"Well, and what have you got?" he muttered. "It stinks, anyhow."

The stench of animal decay. Far down in the black cavern the torch sent its dazzling beam to play upon what? Thick layers of moist newspaper which parted at a prod and disclosed within something dark and once fluffy, now matted, crawling with maggots. Too long a coat for a rabbit. A cat? A Persian, then . . . but no, it was not a cat. Might as well see what it was. Two pries with the spade and it lay revealed—the decomposed carcase of a small dog with soft, black hair, the neck encircled by a rotting collar at one time red.

Terrier and man surveyed it—one gloatingly, the other with disgust, which, as he looked, turned to tense interest. He looked again, then glanced alertly over his shoulder. No question about these far-gone remains. What the live dog had unearthed was Bimi de Bellesnaves' lost Pomeranian. . . .

As the *mairie* clock struck twelve Gilcrest set the last of a row of test-tubes in the rack before him and drew a deep breath. The air of the little laboratory reeked with disinfectant, but the knives and forceps used for the loathsome task had been washed and put away, the mangled carcases—there were two of them—pushed under the table and covered over with sacking. The green-shaded light shone down on nothing more revealing than these innocent-looking tubes, and a pair of glass containers in which reposed certain portions of two canine stomachs.

Which showed? Merely eroded tissue, taken place on surfaces elsewhere normal. Nothing in either, nor in the test-tubes, to indicate the cause of death. That was the beauty of it. In other words, here were situations practically speaking identical with the ones disclosed by the human organs viewed that afternoon in Nice. Only this small difference: the dogs had eaten raw meat, as the undigested contents of the stomachs proved, while the human stomachs had been empty of food. It was true that one detail might have given rise to remark. The Pom's skull had been crushed in by a blow, administered after death, but unless the finder was already on the right track no further examination would have been undertaken. Still, it was just by chance Gilcrest and no other had come upon this. He had the new terrier to thank for that bit of luck.

"And I'd have hesitated to buy the dog if she hadn't advised it! There's irony for you. It might mean justice, if the thing led to discovery—but how in hell can it?"

As he washed his hands at the sink, he searched the shelves overhead as though looking for the answer. Nothing in any of these jars to give the show away, nor in the dispensary drug-cupboards. He had satisfied himself on that point days ago, but there was no harm in going over the lot again, just to leave no stone unturned. If he had made a slip, and the stuff was here all along, ready to leap to the first inquiring eye. . . .

Having examined all the drugs, harmless as well as poisonous, he replaced the jars in their former neat order, so that Miss Barrows might not guess anything had been disturbed. His frown deepened, the frown of a man caught inextricably in a trap which has no outlet. That, in spite of himself, he had been forced to invite these post mortems! As things had turned out, he could scarcely conceive of a worse calamity befalling him. He had run not his neck—oh, no!—but his whole reputation into a noose, though not until he had seen the Médecin Légiste had he imagined how hopelessly landed he would be. The fellow had said little, for there was no need of comment with those odd appearances staring up at them. He had looked—and in his cynical, almost admiring eyes narrowed with speculation Gilcrest had read legal security—and professional doom. Yes, the analyst, like himself, had seen how completely the affairs were sealed up. Not only unproved, they were unprovable. There lay the catch.

"But Henri's death—is that sealed up, too? It seems to be. Even if I ventured to point out what I noticed, is it likely these benighted police would pay attention?"

Not they! Every man jack of them was hypnotised by a pair of marvellous eyes which already had had their way with men infinitely more enlightened—and besides, while it was true his eyes had detected a flaw in evidence other observers had passed as perfect, that flaw could never be substantiated to any jury's satisfaction. The way had been paved for suicide, and as suicide the death was accepted. Here, as in the other cases, the real facts lay buried for all time—or so it seemed.

But the girl Sarah, so soon to fade out of his knowledge—what was she thinking of all this? She, with her conscientious meddling, her woman's "instinct" which, like the rest of her sex, she set high above reason? Another irony that she had been right. She did not know it, she could prove nothing, but that would not prevent her holding against him a judgment he was powerless to refute. She was too sharp not to see through that hellish verdict—and she might have seen into other things as well. Still, if he was not to face her again—and there was no chance of it after this—why indulge in the weak desire to justify himself in her opinion? It couldn't be done, so there was an end of it.

In spite of these reflections, he swept a gesture of savage revolt.

"Yet there must be a way out!" he muttered. "If brains invent a trap, brains can find a means out of it. I've got to . . . good God, who's this?"

A knock, of all places, on the laboratory door! He strode back into the carbolic-reeking cubby-hole, satisfied himself that no outward signs of his labours remained, and opening the door a crack peered distrustfully into the pitch-gloom of the back garden.

"Venables!" he exclaimed, not over-pleased.

The latecomer stepped inside, drawing a nervous hand over his roughened chestnut hair. He looked flushed, horror-haunted.

"Saw your light," he explained hesitantly. "And wanting to ask a few questions, I thought I'd drop in."

Saw the light? Gilcrest shot a quick glance at the window. The old blanket he had pinned across it had fallen to the floor. The brilliant patch would be noticeable, through the gap in the wall, to anyone taking the short cut to the street behind. Shrugging, his manner decidedly inhospitable, he said, "I see. Well, what is it?"

Not at once replying, Harry Venables sniffed the nauseous fumes and made a grimace of repugnance.

"Experimenting, what?" he inquired, looking aimlessly round. "God, the stink! I—it's this de Bellesnave's business. Ought to have hung on, I suppose, to offer my services and so on, only Miss MacNeil turned queer, and as I didn't seem to be needed . . . did they hold the inquest? How did it come out? It was suicide, of course?"

"So it appears," was the brief response. "Was that all you wanted to know?"

"Yes—oh, yes, that was all." The blue eyes, oddly small somehow as they blinked in the strong light, lost their strained expression. Their owner exhaled a long breath and fumbled for a cigarette. "Well, I must say I'm thankful to hear it's all settled. I mean, bad as it is, it would have been worse if it had strung out into one of these long sessions, wouldn't it? No end of a trial. I know something about it—and so do you, what? Which reminds me: congratulations and all the rest of it on the way these other affairs have come out. I may say I never had any real doubts, but all the same it's jolly comfortable to know for certain there was nothing in it. I daresay you're feeling pretty relieved too."

Gilcrest searched his visitor's features in contemptuous silence. Was it possible the man could be fool enough not to understand how far from comfortable matters were? If so, it would be waste of breath to contradict him. He, at least, would not have to suffer . . . but what was wrong? With a face suddenly blanched the young man was staring hard at the table. Why? Nothing about those test-tubes or containers to excite peculiar interest—and the sacking was well tucked round what lay under the table. No, it was the table itself. . . .

"Can you see your way?" Gilcrest asked, holding wide the door.

"What's that?" With an effort, Venables wrenched his gaze away, backed towards the darkness, but for an instant turned on his host a sickly smile. "Sorry! It's this vile stuff you've been using. Never could stick. . . . goodnight!"

He was gone, bolting like a hare. The side gate clanged to.

"Ass! What caught his eye?"

Running a keen survey over the work-table, Gilcrest himself descried what sent a chill along his spine. Fallen behind the test-tube rack, but protruding enough to be seen from an angle, were the two dog collars—one broad, steel-studded, the other a narrow band of morocco, red and stained with dark patches. No wonder the fellow had stared.

"Only why in God's name didn't he ask me about them? It's a damned good thing he didn't, but for the life of him I can't see. . . ."

The reflection remained suspended. Into Gilcrest's face had come a look of profound, almost stupefied, meditation, a look at once concentrated and blank. Like this he stood for several minutes, finally shaking his head and muttering to himself like a person asleep. His movements, too, were those of a sleepwalker as he removed the dog collars and locked them in a cupboard, switched off the light, and went slowly into his own room. Once there he seemed not to know why he had come.

"Either I'm hopelessly out," he mused, his brow deeply furrowed, "or else . . . but what difference would it make if I weren't? None. None . . . and the money! What good'll that do me if I'm to go through life with a stigma attached to my name? What's done must be done now—now—and what can be done?"

He went into the little kitchen, found the coffee made ready for his evening meal, and heated it. Then carrying the pot and a large cup he returned to his bedroom, mechanically stoked his pipe, and sank into one of the bagging wicker chairs. He was too tired to exert himself. Paper he must have for this job, but there was none within reach, only that bit sticking from between the pages of a book. That would do for a start, and the book itself . . .

The title registered on his brain. He winced and dropped the volume as though it had burnt him, as he did so seeing vividly Sarah MacNeil's grey-green eyes regarding him across a card-table with scorn and accusation in their depths. The paper, however, had dropped out. He picked it up, flattened it on his knee, and got out his pen meanwhile muttering doggedly to himself.

"H Cl plus x equals y . . . blithering fool! Can't work a simple equation with two unknowns. Must find some hypothetical substitute for one of 'em, just to test out . . ."

This writing! It was hers. But how did it come here?

He stared, his features distorted with livid rage. The note, the book in which it had lain hidden—now he knew why the girl had held that manner towards him, now he understood why she had insisted so stubbornly on the post mortem! She had read this, of course!

Every vestige of torpor fell from him. He leaped to his feet, jerked open a drawer with such violence that it crashed to the floor and with two movements ripped a photograph from its frame and tore it across. This, anyhow, should not be seen again—nor the note, either. A match spluttered, and in another moment or two he was stamping out a smouldering debris on the hearth to blackened powder. Even now, with these mute witnesses destroyed, he was too shaken to be fit for the labour of cold logic he had set himself. He plunged his face into water, poured a second cup of coffee, and gulped it down, his eyes, blood-shot and hunted, searching the room in a furious quest for other incriminating signs.

At two o'clock the carpet round his chair was littered with fragments of paper, all jotted over with what looked rather like hieroglyphics. The letter x abounded, and on the last scrap, still retained in his hand, x had been given a fixed value.

"It works—in theory—but how does it help? I'll still be in a cleft stick. Yes, the very perfection which has saved me from trial and probable death-sentence makes it totally impossible to vindicate myself. I saw it before, I'm convinced of it now. Too brilliant, by half. There's no chance left but one, and that will simply never . . . God! What now?"

The telephone at his elbow had sent forth a nerve-shattering peal. Someone was calling him. He had supposed no patient would summon him again, but it seemed he was mistaken. Too early yet, for him to be utterly dished. Might be a day or so before. . . .

"Allo!"

A woman's voice broke into excited speech, half French, half Italian, the tones cracked with fright. As he listened he grew stony and intent, but he asked no questions and at the first halt in the breathless volley he delivered himself of three words: *"Bien. Je viens."*

A minute more and he had locked the house door behind him and in the dark garage was climbing into his car.

CHAPTER THIRTY-FOUR

THE suicide presented a new sensation for the community to gloat over, but it was not the last. By the following noon there was a buzz of excitement over the sudden and violent illness with which, during the night, Madame le Baronne had been smitten. Yes, the beautiful widow, so young—not thirty, *croyez-vous?*—seized all at once with mysterious and racking pains; two doctors at the bedside, one the worthy if neglected Hyppolite Thiers, even a priest in readiness for the last offices. Touch and go it had been for fully four hours, and at one time all hope given up—but then, by a miracle, the sufferer had rallied, dragged as it seemed from the jaws of death!

As the nature of the attack was yet unknown, peculiar rumors sprang up, in the town, and in the Golf Hotel. One unauthenticated story had it that Mme. de Bellesnaves, more deranged by grief than might have been expected, had tried to end her own life. A second suggested that a new and medically baffling malady had barely failed to snaffle another victim in addition to the two unfortunate Englishwomen, and that soon the whole Riviera would be ravaged; but a third—whispered in small groups and with bated breath—took a more sinister turn. What, it was said, was one to think about these strange illnesses cropping up amongst people, all women, who in some way bore a connection to each other? The same doctor was in close contact with the three. Two had died, and their deaths had been declared the result of natural causes, but was it enough that no poison had been found? There might be other things beside poison which can kill. One heard that Dr. Gilcrest had intended to pursue the career of a bio-chemist. Without being quite certain what bio-chemistry meant, was one not safe in saying a profession of that kind indicated unusual knowledge of physical reactions? Obviously nothing could have been hinted if the man hadn't by one of these deaths got hold of a substantial fortune; but this being so, and Colonel Bulstrode having taken the trouble to obtain a copy of the post mortem verdicts—well, one could not help putting things together, could one?

To all this Sarah listened, appalled. She was not surprised to find the Baroness' name openly coupled with Gilcrest's, but one theory—it was sponsored by the grim Janet Lowther—left her stupefied. Could anyone believe that Gilcrest, fearing he was about to be forced into marriage, had attempted to rid himself of a blackmailing encumbrance? Whatever else might be true, that at least struck her as fantastic. The Lowther girl—so-called by courtesy, since she was thirty-seven if a day—had till lately been "crushed" on the doctor herself, and now had her knife into him. The same applied to Muriel Ames-Gower, who wavered weakly between upholding this view and turning so faint with revulsion that she was laid low with hysteria and hives. Her sister Gladys glared woodenly through her spectacles and pursued her solitary round of golf. Mrs. Bulstrode and Madge Whittaker shut stern lips and stuck closely together, but even those partisans looked shaken.

It was the report on Beryl's case which did the damage. On her return from Nice Beryl had dropped dark hints about a highly placed individual she could ruin if she chose, and though she had named no names it had been easy to conclude she had meant the Baroness. On her own admission she had approached Marjory Barrows on the subject—and who could doubt that the dispenser had informed Gilcrest?

"We mustn't forget that Beryl didn't die of this mesenteric thrombosis at all. No, it was a bad perforation—in a different place, but just like the one in Miss Venables' tummy. You see the inference? Poor Beryl! She would chatter—"

The sum total of it was that Brian Gilcrest was done for—and that Sarah's interference was to blame. Perfectly just, if he were guilty—but suppose the entire thing was a lamentable mistake? The official analyst had declared the diagnosis on Beryl amply justifiable in the circumstances. An error was made, but a natural one. Still, that statement did not counterbalance the further assertions, so that in Sarah's mind, as in others, doubt would always remain, eating in like a canker.

"If only I knew!" was her constant groan. "It wouldn't put matters right—in a case like this nothing could clear him—but I, at least, might be spared this absolute hell. I had to act as I did. I'd do the same all over again—but oh, to think I'll never know whether or not I've ruined an innocent man."

A man she had loved. Had? If he was not a murderer, she still loved him. Ah, there lay the sting.

Reason told her there could be one conceivable means of establishing the truth, and that she had held that means in her grasp and thrown it away. Why, oh why, had she declined the Baroness' invitation? At this moment she might have been housed under the Casa Giallo roof, scheming at any rate to overhear some scrap of clandestine conversation which would clinch matters once and for all—but it was too late now. Her reservation was taken, she was catching the evening train from Hyères and putting over a thousand miles between herself and the source of information. After that discovery of any kind would be hopeless. The unsolved would become the insoluble—and if one fine day news of a certain discreet marriage should reach her ears, would even that finality bring peace? No—for she still could not swear that these five deaths were not blameless affairs. At dead of night Gilcrest's face as she had last seen it would rise to haunt her with its eternal challenge. She would lie sleepless, tormented with doubt, no nearer certainty than before.

She was locking her steamer-trunk when the reprieve came. Incredible! Her presence at the villa was desired again—and this time the message took the form of a passionate supplication.

Old withered Angela, worn out with vigils, implored her, in the name of Madame's kind English friend, to take pity on the stricken household. Madame, still pitiably weak, was entirely alone, her mother, a bedridden paralytic in Lyons, unable to come to her aid, the Comte de Lagniolle, who had been here till now attending to the Baron's funeral arrangements, obliged to take his departure in order to make his sailing for the island of Crete. It was not much that was asked, only that Mademoiselle stay with the desolate widow until recovery was assured. Surely she had not the heart to refuse? Unless someone was there, Madame would get up too soon and bring on a dangerous relapse. She, Angela, knew it would happen, and with her own work to do she was powerless to prevent it.

"It is the loneliness, Mademoiselle. Picture to yourself what the poor lady has endured, both in body and mind. Only just saved from death, and Monsieur yet unburied! If you could see her white, tragic face, with the great tears rolling down it. There is no one but you she can call upon— and God will bless you for so noble an action. Mademoiselle will come?"

She had prayed for this. She would be a fool not to accept . . . only why was Maddalena de Bellesnaves so eager for her company? It was true the Baron's wife had never cultivated the local people—and yet, with the old peasant's hollow eyes searching her own, Sarah felt again the curious doubt she had from the first entertained over this sudden illness. With Harry she had gone yesterday to inquire, had listened to Angela's emotional account, inwardly querying it, as she must query whatever touched the Baroness' behaviour, and burned to know the real facts. Marjory might have enlightened her, but how screw up her courage to face Marjory now she had seen the latter's worst prophecies realised to the last letter? Besides, she might have run into the doctor. . . .

Out of the blue an explanation flashed on her. She was probably wanted up there as a species of chaperone, to safeguard the proprieties and allow the doctor to continue his visits without undue remark. The widow must know that disagreeable stories were circling about, more than ever since her husband was dead and her supposed lover fallen under a cloud. At present she would want to pretend she had no lover— and what better method than by securing someone like Sarah MacNeil to act as a shield between her and a censorious world?

"But of course! I see it all. According to her arguments she's being very clever. She can't guess what I'm thinking—"

Couldn't she? Sarah drew up. If Gilcrest had found the note concealed between the pages of *Trois Contes*, wouldn't he have warned his mistress that Miss Venables' companion knew too much? Evidently he had not found it. Well, it would simplify matters to have both of them in the dark as to her suspicions, regarding her as a harmless dupe who, when her purpose was served, would quietly vanish out of their lives. Even so they would try hard to pull the wool over her eyes. She would have to act the sneaking hypocrite, prowl, eavesdrop—oh, a loathsome business!—but since it was her only hope. . . .

"Can I manage it?" she mused aloud, carefully keeping the excitement from her voice. "You see, Mr. Venables and I were leaving tonight, but if Madame really wants me—"

"You will come? I may take the message to Madame?"

"Y-es—I think so. I'll get Mr. Venables to drop me on the way."

She had done it—and now to tell Harry, honest-eyed, impartial Harry, who alone had turned a deaf ear to all that was being said, at most reddening with a muttered, "Muck—every word of it! Can't a doctor be mistaken over a diagnosis without getting himself foully misjudged? Gilcrest's a decent chap—straight as a die. As for some of these harpies, I'd like to strangle 'em." Conscience-clear himself, unable to conceive of a cruel infamy being done—was it the earnest of a fair or merely of a stupid mind—a mind hard set against its tranquillity being disturbed? Alternately Sarah admired and grew irritated. A commendable attitude if only it did not spell sheer indifference . . . how, she wondered, would he take this decision of hers?

He was damped, crestfallen, vaguely perturbed.

"I say! Do you honestly think it a sound notion? Ill hostess, corpse in the house—won't it get on your nerves?"

So this was all Harry considered! She suppressed a smile as she answered that the Baron's funeral would take place tomorrow, and that Miss Venables would have wished her to go. There was her reservation, of course. Could it be altered?

"Oh, I can look after that! Must say it's jolly decent of you. She asked you before, didn't she? Well, you know best, I suppose. I'm ready to push off when you are. All the same—"

A word from her and his calm would be shattered. Dared she, at this late hour? Sorely tempted, she stifled the impulse. After all, Harry had not her excuse for caring, so why load him with a burden he could neither shift nor deal with? Let him return to England comfortably believing his full duty discharged—as, on the face of things, it was. Strangely enough, this had become her affair.

It was the dressing hour, consequently they were able to get away without encountering any of the persons whom by tacit agreement both wished to avoid. It was true that since the post mortems there had been slight signs of thawing where Sarah was concerned, but that did not wipe out what had gone before, and even now there were those who could never forgive her for the rumpus she had caused. One was Jolivet, the manager, who by black looks betrayed an implacable enmity. Another, whom she could not altogether blame, was Beryl Tomlins' sister.

Good Heavens, wasn't that Mrs. Cripps now, leaning from her window and making frantic signals? She had caught Harry's eye.

"Now what do you suppose she wants?" Harry demanded, tentatively slowing. "Think we ought to turn back and find out?"

"No!" snapped Sarah decisively. "She's a tiresome woman and can't want anything worth bothering about. Drive on, pretend we didn't see."

A whirr of pigeons, the car shot forward into the narrow street, and the Grand Hotel du Golf et de la Plage was shut from view. Sarah heaved a sigh of relief. Whatever else happened, she hoped she need never set foot within that smug white building again.

With a single halt at a flower-shop they made straight for the Casa Giallo, where Harry hesitated, wondering if he ought to stop long enough to say good-bye to the Baroness. It was plain that the prospect depressed and embarrassed him, and Sarah, anxious to give nothing away, could not help him out.

"I daresay I must—that is, if she feels equal to seeing me. Here, Angela—suppose you just trot up and inquire?"

The two servants were handling Sarah's luggage. Angela left her task to shuffle obediently upstairs, presently reappearing to beckon and lead the way to a large, spacious chamber overlooking the side garden. Here she paused to whisper that Monsieur must not stay more than a minute or two, since Madame was too weak to bear any excitement. She then opened the door and stood aside. Sarah and Harry went in, instantly exchanging dazzling sunshine for a gloom so sombre that for a moment few objects were distinguishable.

The thick damask curtains were closely drawn, shutting out every glimpse of the bright, spring day, the air stuffy and lifeless, overburdened with a cloying mixture of scents and medicaments. From a pair of tall vases white arum lilies soared like pallid flames; in a far corner one lone candle burned before a prie-dieu containing an ivory crucifix.

Near the door rose the twisted rosewood columns of the bed, wide and low, in the centre of which lay the Baroness. Her still body made a scarcely perceptible mound under the coverlet of faded pomegranate silk, her small, pinched face against the embroidered pillow might have been a death-mask of olive-tinted wax for all the animation it showed. There was something quite dreadful about this livid pallor and the deep wells of shadow surrounding the half-closed eyes. Even the dense black hair, falling heavily over the thin shoulders, seemed to have lost all lustre. Indeed, it needed but a glance to dispel one uncertainty lurking in Sarah's mind. Whatever the cause, Maddalena de Bellesnaves had been and was still extremely ill.

A barely audible murmur came from the pale lips. It was addressed to Sarah, for Harry, hanging back, had not been noticed.

"You have come. What an angel you are. I—it is impossible to express what I feel about your kindness to me."

The voice trembled to silence, the frail hand which stole forth to take hold on Sarah's had a convulsive strength somewhat startling. Only for an instant, however. Harry, subdued and awkward, had moved forward, depositing his load of yellow roses on the bed. At sight of him the sufferer relaxed her grip, turned languid eyes on her other visitor's face, and with a visible effort spoke again.

"Roses . . . how beautiful! But I have not yet thanked either of you for what you sent me yesterday. Was it yesterday? It seems so long . . ." Tears were slipping quietly along her wan cheeks. Commanding her emotion she continued with forced politeness. "So, you are leaving us. It means, I hope, that what was troubling you is now quite cleared up. The unfortunate affair . . . all settled?"

"Oh, absolutely. Just as we expected. But then it couldn't have been anything different, could it? It was just that my aunt—and Gilcrest, I suppose—"

Harry stopped, clearing his throat in evident embarrassment. The only response had been a faintly murmured "Of course," and a vague nod as though the listener through sheer exhaustion had grown inattentive. Sarah was prepared for this attitude, the beginnings of which she had observed days ago—total indifference towards what was regarded as a foregone conclusion, that was what the Baroness had shown when the post mortem was contemplated, and her present calm acceptance of the result was a logical sequence. One would have said that she had forgotten all about the Tomlins case, though she must surely be aware of the analyst's peculiar findings. If Sarah was on the right track, the woman must be a superb actress; but seeing the spent form lying there so unconcerned, so powerless to summon suitable interest, the girl experienced a decided qualm of doubt. It was clearly impossible for Harry to mention the suicide. Inarticulate, anxious to end the trying ordeal, he glanced at his watch, and then, fumbling at his gold-bound note-case, fished out one of his cards.

"I'd better just leave you my London address," he muttered. "If you're coming my way any time, you'll be sure to look me up—won't you?"

The ghost of a smile—was it sardonic?—flitted across the dark irises.

"Thank you, *mon cher*, but England is far away—too far, I think, for me to pay it a visit. Still—who knows?—we may, one day, see each other again. *Au revoir*, then—and a comfortable journey."

Angela, hovering in the shadows, shepherded Harry out, and Sarah followed to speed him on his way. As he paused before her, with the afternoon sun glinting on the crisp brown waves of his hair and lighting his warm, ruddy skin, she thought she had never seen any human creature more wholesome, more comfortingly sane. His shoulders were so broad, his blue eyes so stainlessly clear! Even his lack of perception, at moments intensely exasperating, seemed all at once the one thing needed to restore her balance. Often, lately, she had reminded herself that Harry Venables was of as little real use as one of those magnificent juiceless oranges which, the peel removed, prove wholly disappointing; but now she was losing him he appeared the sole normal being in a world gone mad and distorted. The chances were she was making an idiotic mistake. If so, it was not yet too late to repair it. She could still have her luggage carried back to the car. . . .

"Harry," she whispered, her hand on his arm. She got no further. At the same moment he had smiled down into her eyes, and that smile, bland and a little fatuous, threw cold water on her impulse. With no perceptible pause she heard herself saying composedly, "Well, good-bye, my dear. Thanks so much for everything."

"It's a hell of a little I've done, Sarah, old girl." He was looking uncomfortable again. "It's you who've been a brick, all through. I'll not forget it. The best of luck to you. Er—cheerio!"

With a hard squeeze of her hand he was gone, so precipitately that it was a second or two before she woke to the rather odd fact that he had said nothing about a future meeting. Not that she particularly cared to see him any more—indeed the idea bored her—but considering his devotion to her all this time . . . he was too chastened and confused by this gloomy atmosphere to collect his thoughts, that was all. He could always reach her through the American Express, and no doubt he regarded this parting as only a brief one.

From the lower floor she heard Sebastiano's fervent, *"Merci bien, Monsieur!"* and knew that a thumping tip had changed hands. Harry was very generous. The Fiat's engine whirred. She roused from her reverie, and tiptoed back into the darkened chamber, schooling herself to master a strong feeling of repugnance.

Something burning? She sniffed the close air, but noticed nothing to account for the acrid smell. The Baroness' eyelids were closed, nor did they stir when she leant over to gather up the roses. Suddenly she detected a tiny wraith of smoke trailing upward from the still-warm wick of a night-light placed on the table beside the bed. The flat disc of candle stood in a saucer of water, and round it floated a few tenuous wisps of blackened paper.

She glanced again at the supine figure, covered to the chin. No sign of movement—but all the same within the last two minutes or so this depleted woman had moved. She had sat up and exerted her feeble strength sufficiently to burn something—but what had she burned, and why?

CHAPTER THIRTY-FIVE

THE dark eyes were open now, and fixed with searching intensity on Sarah's face. Had they seen her glance towards these flecks of burnt paper? If so, they gave no sign.

"Tell me," the Baroness begged, "that I am not being a selfish beast to ask this of you. You would have preferred going with him. Is it not so?"

"With Harry? Oh, no! Why should you think that?"

"One never knows. You like 'Arree—yes?"

Puzzled by the sharp challenge of the tone—it was more accusation than question—Sarah hesitated before replying that of course she liked Harry. Who didn't? He was really very sweet. She saw at once that her rather inane answer gave annoyance.

"Sweet!" echoed the Baroness, mocking, petulant. "Ah, yes, you have well described him. He is sweet—and big, and very simple. Handsome, too. No doubt many are content with such things." She shrugged and lay silent.

An idea struck Sarah. This bitterness probably meant that the Baroness, besides despising Harry for his mental shortcomings, resented his failure to pay her the homage she expected of all males. She might have sensed his wariness of a ridicule at any moment likely to be directed against himself, and therefore grown nervous lest her monkeyish tricks had betrayed her real character. There had been no acting about the relief she had shown over his departure. Was it his card she had destroyed? She might have done that. It was like her.

But no, there the card lay, engraved side upward. It had been something else, then—and Sarah was still turning the small mystery over when Angela, coming in with a vase, furnished a clue. The doctor had paid one visit that day, and at Angela's earnest desire was returning at nightfall. He had jotted down a few directions, which Angela could not read. Perhaps Mademoiselle . . .

"I laid them here, on the table. Now, where have they gone?"

The notes had disappeared, and Madame, on being questioned, shook an indifferent head. Ah, well, it was no serious matter, as he was coming again presently; but Sarah thought she understood. The patient, on her guest's arrival, had got rid of what in reality had been a personal message, the inference being that thus far she and her physician had been granted no opportunity for private speech. Only a little could be scribbled under Angela's eye, therefore one might readily assume that at the approaching call Bimi had been instructed to send the watch-dog from the room. So much had happened since these two could have been alone together—Gilcrest's visit to Nice, whither he must have gone solely to learn the precise extent of his peril from the post mortems, the Baron's suicide and inquest, the alarming spread of gossip throughout the town—oh, there could be no doubt that vital matters clamoured for discussion. There was evidently no danger of a charge being bought, but there was a delicate situation to be met, one which demanded collaboration—and in addition to all this, Gilcrest was a badly infatuated man.

The chance might come soon, provided it was possible to overhear anything from the bathroom adjoining this chamber, for it was there Sarah had resolved to retire the moment the pair were shut in here alone. Perhaps, if she could contrive to open one of these windows . . . she made a move to do so, but stopped. The burning eyes were following her much too closely. She set the roses on the dressing-table, uncomfortably wondering if it was her acute consciousness of playing a dual rôle that made her feel she was being watched, and with a purpose. She did not see how or why the Baroness should suspect her motives, but if by a sixth sense her real object was divined, she might as well give up at once all hope of discovery.

A knock, and the Comte de Legniolles entered to make his adieux. Sarah would have slipped away, but no, she was detained and presented to the lean, brown Frenchman—he was perhaps sixty, and had a fine bearing and manner—who bowed with grave courtesy and approached the bed to explain about the forthcoming funeral-mass. He was formal, almost cold, as he remarked that naturally in the circumstances Madda-lena would not be expected to be present at the church. Sarah got the impression that he was not wholly at ease with his cousin's widow; but there was deep regret in his voice when he excused himself for not remaining for the ceremony and interment.

"The difficulty is that I am to preside at a most important meeting of my *confrères*, due to take place immediately on my arrival at Crete. A week ago I could have made arrangements, but now, unfortunately, it is too late. I am glad, though—" here he glanced politely at Sarah, "that I am not leaving you alone. You still do not wish for a nurse?"

"Ah, but there will be no necessity for one now! Mademoiselle—is she not a saint?—has kindly promised to stay with me up to the moment I quit this place and go to Lyons. Yes, as you know, I intend to join my mother as soon as I am well enough to attend to all the arrangements we have spoken about, but with Mademoiselle's assistance I believe every-thing may be done within six weeks."

Six weeks! And what was this about a promise? The listening girl had suddenly the feeling of being lured here under false pretences and trapped, held, against her will. Angered, inexplicably nervous, she kept silent while the Comte, eyes lowered, laid a small packet within reach of the invalid's hand. Here, he said, were the souvenirs of Henri's last moments on earth—the written message and the pen, neither of which was required by the authorities, who had handed them to him to bring back. The Baroness dissolved in tears, her convulsed face buried in the pillow. The Comte waited patiently till she had recovered, bent stiffly over her hand, and withdrew.

As the door closed, Sarah's fingers were again seized in a posses-sive grasp.

"Have I been very wicked?" the Baroness besought with pathetic eagerness. "Ah, say you are not cross with me for telling Hector that little lie! He has been so distressed about my having to be alone all these weeks in a house that is haunted with memories—do you also see what it would mean, long hours with no one to speak to, only the ceaseless torment of thoughts? If you desert me, I shall go mad—quite mad."

Every trace of lassitude had vanished. Words poured from her, and when Sarah tried gently to remove her hand it was forcibly retained and stroked with tremulous caresses.

"Henri—if only I had not left him. You see, from the moment I was told of Chreessie's death I had terrible migraine—oh, such an agony of pain, which only my little masseuse could rub away. At last Henri insisted that I seek relief. I believed him much more tranquil, though I now know that all he wanted was to be left in peace to carry out—" She broke off, shuddering, her sharp red nails digging into Sarah's skin. "It was my fault," she moaned. "I should have guessed, known what was in his mind. That night I prayed to die—but it seems I am not easy to kill. Only when someone is with me can I throw off the horror. Ah, you will be kind, you will stay till I go to my mother?"

Some portion of this might be true. There was yet no disproof of it— and yet the dark eyes now striving to compel consent were lit with a flame so fanatical that Sarah felt only a strong and hidden motive could actuate these entreaties. Point-blank refusal would do nothing but precipitate a tempest of weeping. Uneasily she resolved to temporize.

"Six weeks is rather a long time," she hedged. "I might stay until you found someone else, but—well, you understand I've got to get back to London to hunt a job."

"Only that! Then why hurry? One time or another will be the same. You will be saving expenses—and that, surely, is worth considering?" There was a different gleam in the eyes now, showing that their owner could be shrewdly practical. "Besides, you are pale, you too have suffered, and require a long rest, with good air and sunshine. Are you sure there is nothing else to draw you to London? No family? But I recall it, your people are in America. A man, perhaps. Ah, you are turning red! Who is it—a fiancé?"

Sarah could have laughed at the blunt question, which only a Latin would have thought of putting with such candour.

"No," she denied lightly. "There's no such person, worse luck."

As though dissatisfied with her reply, the Baroness scrutinised her ringless hands with a curious intensity.

"No? *Bien*—in that case—" She started, listening alertly. "Who is this at the door?"

Angela poked in her kerchiefed head to announce the doctor. He was waiting downstairs, and might she make her mistress ready to see him?

Sarah's heart beat fast. Gilcrest was come—and she must not run into him. Her moment of discovery might be at hand—and was it not significant that she was being allowed to depart at once, without opposition? Angela showed her to her room, which was a large front one facing the stairs. She threw off her hat, waited till all was quiet, then opening her door a mere crack stationed herself by it to watch.

She saw Gilcrest come up and conducted by Angela go into the Baroness' room. Momentarily expecting the old woman to emerge alone, she held her breath, but nothing happened. The minutes lengthened to five, and then the two made their exit together, the doctor taking determined strides, Angela tagging after him with anxious questions he seemed disinclined to answer. At the head of the staircase he halted.

"No," he said curtly. "As I told you at noon, your mistress can get on very well now without medical attention. Low diet and rest. That is all she requires. Her temperature continues normal."

The wrinkled face looking up at him seemed puzzled, inquisitive.

"Pardon, Monsieur—but does this mean that you are, in truth, about to leave Ste. Brigitte?"

Sarah saw the square shoulders stiffen. After a moment's pause she heard an expressionless voice say, "Who gave you that information?"

"It is being mentioned in the town, Monsieur. I was wondering what to do if Madame grew worse—and also about the little dog whose barking will drive Madame insane. Did you not say to her that you would take him away with you?"

"The dog! Yes, give him to me now . . . I repeat, Madame is not alarmingly ill, but you can call Dr. Thiers if you feel worried about her. I am very busy and shall not come again."

Not coming again? For a single instant Sarah was swept by exquisite joy. This was too good for belief—but then, as Gilcrest moved, she caught sight of his eyes, and her elation suffered total collapse. He was lying. She knew it—and the reason was not far to seek. He wanted to fool the servants, and through them the whole neighbourhood, into thinking that his connection with the Casa Giallo had ceased with its owner's death. Indeed, if he realised who was occupying this room—and he must be aware of it—then he was hoping to hoodwink her as well. In other words, not content with the Baroness' half-measures, he was taking his own, drastic method of outwitting scandal—a method which meant shipwreck of her plans.

To be used and at the same time cheated! Furious with rage and disappointment, she stood motionless, listening to the delighted yaps of

Max as he was borne away, and eyeing with loathing the pleasant, green-walled room which all at once represented simply a prison in which she was to be confined by an imperious will. Not a moment's liberty would be hers. She would be chained, on one pretext or another, to her hostess's side, made the recipient of false confidences, her sympathy demanded, every minute of the day—for six weeks? No? She would not submit, she would go, to-morrow—get hold of a car, and catch the early train from Hyères. She was a free agent, no one could hold her. Her things had been unpacked? Never mind, she would pack again tonight—and meanwhile, let her escape from this terrible house with its scheming mistress, who was probably not ill at all, and its stark corpse awaiting burial. Air! She must get out, or she would suffocate!

It was sunset when she fled, past the dark painting of Don Quixote, into the cool, fragrant grounds, to race, without stopping, to the sea. Through a labyrinth of bloom she pushed her way—for riotous rhododendron, waxen syringa, oleander, Japanese plum, all in a few days had burst into blossom which drooped over the paths and scattered a carpet of petals on the dry earth beneath. Wilderness into Paradise—and then, abruptly, it ended with the twisted pines, the landing casting a black bar of shadow far out into the rosy water, the lone yacht riding at anchor with sails tight-furled against the sky. Her feet sank in sand, and before her, dreadful reminder, lay the boat-house.

In the sun-baked gloom of the interior she could just make out the vacant settee, the pile of paper-covered books, and, on the dust of the window-ledge, a circle, clean-marked, where the chocolate box had stood. Out of every corner Death peered, whispering of sacrifice.

Few men, she thought, might be capable of removing themselves to make room for others, but for Henri de Bellesnaves to have done this thing seemed not at all strange. She believed that he had known why and by whom his dog had been slaughtered, that recognising every move in the cruel game he had bowed his head and quietly stood aside. Probably those weary eyes of his had seen the truth about the two victims at the hotel, and that realisation, as the old doctor had hinted, had given him the final push towards self-destruction. Gilcrest was astute enough to guess what had happened, and to know that the right conclusion was being drawn by many others. What wonder to find him retreating, shutting doors, exerting every nerve to stem the ruinous tide of gossip?

They would come together, away from here—that went without saying. The only point of argument was, would they wait till then to see each other without the presence of a third person? Such restraint would be scarcely human—and there could be small doubt that the declaration about not coming again had been merely a blind.

A blind! How stupid not to have seen at once that those words, that aloof manner, were designed to cover a totally different intention. If Gilcrest was planning to quit the locality—and he had not denied Angela's suggestion—there was good reason for supposing the rendezvous she had counted on would take place promptly, only it would be a safe time—late at night, most likely, and with infinite precautions against detection. The scrap of paper the Baroness had burned—what could it have been except a notification of an appointment? And as the woman could not very well go out to him, he would come to her. With the servants both sleeping in the distant wing over the kitchen, there was only the guest, herself, to consider.

"Max would have barked, of course. Was that why he took him away?"

Her heart began again to thump wildly. The canny removal of the terrier seemed to clinch matters. Oh, decidedly, it would be foolish to retire from the field just yet. A night or two—she would not have long to wait. Even so, it would be no easy task to follow and overhear the conspirators without being caught red-handed—but this difficulty she had always foreseen. Her job was to keep wide awake, be ready at a moment's notice to chance her luck.

Polly's grave? On her slow walk back she had come upon the mound, oddly sunken and trampled, the primroses flattened into the dirt. By the look of it one might almost have said . . . but where in all this did the Greek gardener figure? She had not seen him about, and only now did she realise how completely he had disappeared from her calculations. Assuredly she had nursed some silly ideas—and if the squashing of them left her devoid of a theory to explain her own "accident"—well, accident it was, and she had been half-witted to doubt it. Everything had fined down to one crucial question. If she could so much as see Gilcrest on these premises at a suspicious hour of night, she would know the answer.

"And he will come. I know it. I saw it in his eyes. He'll come, simply because he can't keep away."

The Baroness had been inquiring for her. Angela was carrying up her dinner on a tray, so that she might have it with Madame, who, in a little while, would take her bromide and perhaps get off to sleep. It would be less trying for the poor lady once Monsieur's body was gone from the library underneath, but at present her nerves were in a lamentable state.

"I have cooked a young pigeon for you, Mademoiselle, and an artichoke, freshly picked. You will eat now? Then perhaps, if you will be good enough to hold open the door . . . aie!"

The old woman had given a wild shriek and nearly dropped her burden. Sarah snatched the tray to set it down, and together they dashed to the spot where, before the prie-dieu, the Baroness lay in a crumpled heap, her upturned face so horribly blanched that for an instant a new idea threatened annihilation of all previous ones. If this were another suicide—

It was only collapse, from weakness. She had been praying, and her legs had given way. Her body was limp and feather-light as they bore it back to bed, and Sarah saw that one hand trailed a rosary, while the other let fall a sheet of note-paper easily recognisable as the Baron's last message. Angela scolded and wept, now soothing her mistress, now darkly muttering that the English had hearts of ice—a reference Sarah understood as a comment on the doctor's refusal to return, though the victim of this callousness gave no sign of having heard. She insisted that she was none the worse for the small mishap, and with great obstinacy protested against Angela's passing another night in her room. Angela was old, and after two broken nights badly in need of rest.

"If you fall ill, what will become of me? No, no, the bromide sends me into a deep sleep. I shall want nothing till morning, and if I did, Mademoiselle will be within call. You may give me the bromide now. I hope you did not forget to bring wine for Mademoiselle."

There was a flask of Chianti on the tray, but Sarah did not touch it, only her coffee, and that she made a feint of not drinking. Wine made her drowsy—and if the scene just witnessed had been a bit of theatrical display aimed at conquering her resistance and throwing her off guard, she would need to keep her faculties alert. She was acting now, ostentatiously concealing yawns and hoping her exhibitions of fatigue were noticed; but it was hard to tell if they were, for very soon the Baroness' own lids were drooping, and although a faint murmur begged her to stay on for a while her presence seemed almost forgotten.

Long minutes dragged by. The room had become unbearable with its burden of stale scents, and with insufficient light to read by there was nothing to do but sit idle in the deep-cushioned bergère, her head dully throbbing, her eyes wandering from the still mask on the pillow to the dim reflections in the mirrors, and thence to the spark of flame pulsing before the crucifix. At last her release came. The Baroness was breathing with heavy regularity—as she would do, if she had really taken a drug.

She was certainly sound asleep—which looked the reverse of promising. Not a muscle stirred, the black lashes rested flat in the pools of dusk beneath the eyes.

How lovely, even now! Not a line of guile—and beauty which did not rely on make-up. Who could say she was not just a spoiled, emotional woman, a little intriguing, a little inclined to play with fire, but nothing worse? Deception need mean no serious guilt—and was there anything to show that murder had been committed in a single one of these cases? No, nothing. At the same time—

Very softly she crossed to the window nearest the bath and unlatched the long casement. Peering through the curtains, she saw that two feet away was the end of a narrow iron balcony, the last window—that of the bath—opening on it. She viewed it with satisfaction, thinking that if the anticipated conversation took place in this room the corner of the balcony must be her chosen spot. If she stood close against the wall, the wistaria would hide her—a useful screen, in case one of the two looked out.

She lit the night-light, placed the ghostly lilies outside the door, and with a final look at the slumberer crept along the landing to her own room. Only a few hours of this strain, and she was as dead-beat as though every drop of vitality had been sucked from her veins! Her whole body cried for sleep, and she must not yield.

The bed was soft, the linen cool, lavender-scented. What a good thing she had drunk none of that Chianti! As it was she would have a hard fight to keep awake. She must flog her brain to prevent its clouding over. Think—that was it, think hard. Think of Harry, not half so comfortable in his wagon-lit, speeding rapidly towards Calais—think of the unknown thing Beryl Tomlins had tried to tell her, and of what could have caused those terrible lacerations which had made the fat librarian bleed to death in a few minutes' time—think once more, to as little purpose, of the anonymous letters.

By the way, what had become of them? Given back to Harry, she supposed—and Harry, because he regarded them as a shameful secret, would destroy and forget them. It would not occur to him to submit them to a handwriting expert, who might at least settle one doubt—not that knowledge on this point could affect the main issue. Keep away from water—ugh, another yawn!—would one never learn what was meant by that particular warning? Although, if the warnings were self-concocted, one need not look for meanings. It was a hateful thought that they might have been. No matter, the sight of Gilcrest here at dead of night would tell her what was vastly more important There was small chance of his coming tonight, all the same. That sleep was too real.

What was that?

How long she had dozed it was impossible to say, but she was awake now, her skin prickling ominously as she listened for a repetition of the sound which with lightning suddenness had roused her. There! She had heard it again—the crunch of a foot on the gravel bordering the terrace.

Slipping from bed, she flattened herself against the wall and scanned the outer gloom. Ten feet from the terrace she saw him. His felt hat was pulled low, but there was no mistaking the set of the head, the strong, closely-knit shoulders. He was watching this window—hers. He moved, and with excruciating pain she recognized the man she had so desperately prayed not to see.

CHAPTER THIRTY-SIX

SHE saw him hesitate, glancing this way and that, and then in a purposeful manner skirt the terrace in the direction of the library, immediately above which lay the Baroness's room. Gone—and with him vanished the last shred of hope to which she had clung.

For a brief space she was physically nauseated, but the feeling passed, and in its place came resolution hard as steel—the resolution to secure proof, if possible the sort of proof to convince juries. There were as likely as not window-catches which were broken. In another second or two Gilcrest would be inside the house and on his way up to his mistress' room. She must gauge the exact instant to seek her hiding-place, from which with an ounce of luck she might hear . . .

But what had happened to him? Ear pressed to her door she waited, so long that she lost count of time. Perhaps he was having trouble getting in, or else making a tour of the house to satisfy himself the servants were asleep. Still, the interminable delay mystified her, and she was just moving to the window again when a new sound, close at hand, sent her trembling again. The creak of a loose floor board—and she knew where it was situated, on the landing midway between the Baroness' room and hers. Swift as thought, warned by instinct only, she regained the bed, drew the covers up, and lay still.

It was as well she had done this, for almost at once her door opened stealthily, and though her own eyes remained closed she could sense other eyes straining into the darkness, examining her motionless figure.

A full minute passed. The door closed as quietly as it had opened, but not before her nostrils had caught a whiff of familiar scent. It was her hostess who, well able to walk, had been spying on her—a woman not drugged at all, alert, expectant, at this moment creeping downstairs, for the obvious purpose of letting her lover in. Quick, or it would be too late.

Teeth chattering with nervousness, she drew on the pair of dark stockings laid ready on a chair, covering her pyjama-legs to the knees, bundled round her a coat also dark, and in a trice was outside her closed door and hanging over the balustrade to listen. At first nothing—and then the anticipated sound—the faint grating of a latch furtively withdrawn. She thought it came from the library, where the Baron's body lay. Another pause. If the interview was to be on the lower floor, she would have to go down—a frightful risk. But were these muffled footsteps she now heard coming her way? They were! Already two persons were on the stairs. The bathroom—and she must avoid that creaking board.

Three long steps and she had reached her goal, only to find the door locked, the key removed! Oh God, she had been foiled, and now she would be caught in the open! The couple were at the head of the steps. What was she to do? With a sigh of thanksgiving she saw the Baroness' door standing ajar. In there! The thick carpet deadened her footfalls as, darting past the tumbled emptiness of the bed, she made straight for the first pair of window-curtains and got behind them. The embrasure was just deep enough to allow her to stand completely concealed, with heavy folds of damask falling to the floor. Once here she congratulated herself. How much better this was for hearing—and it would be a simple matter to slip out again while the Baroness went down to refasten the window after her visitor had gone. Really, things were turning out unexpectedly well.

Nevertheless she grew tense with fright when the door softly closed, the key turned in the lock, and she knew herself shut in with these two whose eyes, accustomed to darkness, would be quick to notice the least movement or bulge of the curtains. Was she standing too far forward? She dared not retreat lest the open casement squeak on its hinges. Thank God there was no wind to stir the curtains—but were they looking this way? Her doubt was removed by the stuffless sound of the bed squashing under a sudden weight, but as her ear caught other vague sounds—rustlings, breathings, the impact of lips upon bare flesh—her whole body turned fiery hot. Not for this had she run herself into grave danger. Bad enough to think of these embraces, but to have to stand in close proximity, hear them going on . . .

The woman was speaking, her contralto whisper strangely surcharged with impatience.

"No, no, stupid one, that will do! Don't you realise how insane it is to come here, and with her in the house? The one *bêtise* which could bring ruin upon us. You might have trusted your Bimi to know what is wise. Yes, she is asleep—but she might have been awake. Quick! What is troubling your silly mind?"

"Her—Sarah. The bloody funk I've been in. What's it all about? Have we struck some snag? Why in God's name did you get hold of her like this without warning me? I tell you, I can't leave till I know the facts."

Was she dreaming? This was not Gilcrest's voice. It was Harry's. The midnight gloom splintered into a million dazzling fragments, the shock of the revelation rendering the listener faint. Oh, the incredible joy of it. But how, why—

A low, hard laugh. "Sarah! So that is it! But for what reason? Can it matter to you that she is here?"

More light in the dark places. That sharp tone could mean but one thing—jealousy. Was it possible, though? The Baroness so jealous of her and Harry that she was determined to keep them apart? It must be so. In a flash the puzzle refitted its parts into a totally new pattern. It had been Harry all along. But what was he saying? He sounded worried, sulky.

"Not the way you mean, only how was I to know something fresh hadn't cropped up? You said yourself she was harmless. Well, isn't she?"

"Not now. On the contrary, she could be extremely dangerous, because, though she cannot prove anything—no one can do that—she is certain to spread ugly tales, here, there, everywhere. Darling imbecile, she has fooled you, but I read her as a book, yes, since she began to treat me so coldly. Her snake's eyes have seen through those verdicts. What more they may have seen I cannot tell, but I shall draw her fangs by turning her into a friend. I can do that, you know. For our future happiness it was necessary to get her under my influence. Was I not clever to manage it?"

It was a thin answer, glibly given. Sarah was not taken in by it, nor, it seemed, was the man for whom it was intended wholly satisfied. Uncertainly he remarked, "Oh—so that's why you got ill?"

"Naturally. Did my poor boy think I was frightened over his wild story about the dogs? *Jamais!*" with vibrant scorn. "Only by being ill unto death could I persuade her to come. I thought you would understand."

"Well, I didn't—and I still think . . . dash it, I can swear to you I'd worked her round to believing the whole blasted business was a wash-out, letters and—have I burned them? God, yes! What do you take me for? And per agreement I was going to cart her back to London and lose her. It would have been the end, wouldn't it?"

"The end—of her? Ah, my own, how little you know these man-starved creatures! You really believe it would have been possible to lose a girl who would give the eyes out of her head for someone like you? You would never have shaken her off—and if you were less modest you would know it. That is why I stepped in, to save you from being pursued, blackmailed. Only a woman can deal with her kind—and I shall deal with her, never fear."

"How?" he demanded, startled. "I say, Bimi, you're not planning another of these—" there was a nervous gulp. "Besides, you've just admitted she can't prove—"

"Prove! No—but she is a mischief-maker, that you have seen. It is true we had nothing to fear from post mortems, but we did not invite them, did we? It was her meddling that forced them on us. That will show you what she is capable of."

"Blast it, what choice had she, with all that shout about poison? She'd seen the letters, too. Oh yes, I realise that was another case of a cleft stick, but I always said they might start trouble. In a way, you're right. The girl's been mixed up in things from the day she came. Just one damned mess after another. God, I wish it was over."

"But, darling, it is over. Why do you complain? There has been only one tiny little mistake—Mees Tomlins!" The smothered ripple of mirth turned Sarah's blood cold. "And surely, when you consider the great risk I ran you cannot blame me for that? It did not matter. Again Gilcrest is what you call the goat."

"Bimi!" Harry cleared his throat which seemed suddenly to have gone dry. "I am trusting you about the girl. You see, I don't want any more of these shocks. How I've got through the last the Lord alone knows—and even now . . . are you quite positive that business is completely okay? Your cousin's gone, but what about Gilcrest? Will he start anything?"

"He! And if he tried, who would listen to him?"

"That's so—but why didn't you wait till you'd got up to Arles, or at least till I was out of the way? I know he turned nasty about leaving home, but—"

"Listen, 'Arree! It had to be done quickly, at once. I had a reason—"

"Bimi, you're holding out on me. God, I've known there was something. Do you mean he's guessed about—us?"

"Demo knew, and was going to tell him. He came first to me, demanding money, but I laughed in his face. You remember the one night you came to meet me in the grounds?"

"To tell you about Tomlins. That swine heard?"

"No—only saw us together. If Henri had learned, I might never have got my chance. There, stupid boy, did I frighten you? Do you imagine that *sale bête* can harm us now? Never in this world! Try to get this through your darling head. If we both were arrested this instant and put into the dock, there would not be one shred of evidence which could convict either you or me—no, not one."

"Nor Gilcrest, what?"

"Nor Gilcrest!" The two words were snapped in a singularly vindictive tone. "He, too, is quite safe. He is also muzzled, and if no one will have him again as a doctor, why, let him count himself lucky to have got the money your old aunt was mad enough to leave him—money that should have been ours. Ah, how I boil to think that after all my hard work to put people so nicely off the scent—but what does it matter? That little affair will soon be forgotten. So will everything else, as far as it touches you and me, *n'est-ce pas, mon enfant*?"

"Just one more thing, Bimi. There's no more of the stuff lying about? What you gave me was the last?"

"The very last. And now, my 'Arree, it is time you went. I hope that no one has seen your car, or—but what is wrong? Why do you stare like that?"

"I . . . listen! Down in the garden. Did you hear a noise?"

To Sarah, spellbound in her narrow retreat, these words and the ensuing pause struck terror. Never had life seemed more precious than at this moment when by the horrible unfoldment of guilt in a wholly unexpected quarter the master-key of a situation had been put into her hand. Gilcrest could be saved from a lifetime of calamity—if only she were not caught; but suppose it had been some movement of hers Harry had heard? Icy with fear she stood still, not daring to breathe.

Harry's dry whisper resumed. "My nerves are all jumpy, but I did think . . . that Greek—would it be him?"

"Maybe. I have sent him away, but it would be like him to break in and burgle. Keep calm, stay where you are, while I look out."

Trapped. Paralyzed though she was, Sarah thought with lightning speed. The door was locked, before she could open it Harry would be upon her. The open casement behind her was her one hope, a frail hope, since the drop to the ground beneath would inevitably fracture head or limb. All at once she recalled the thick stem of the wisteria which climbed to the adjacent balcony and on to the roof. She might reach that, and by clinging fast at least break her fall. Not yet, though, for she had heard the rear window cautiously opened, and there was a chance that operations would cease with that. "Stupid! No one is there."

"Better try the side one to make sure."

Soft footfalls, like a cat creeping. The curtains drew back—but by now Sarah had flung wide the casement and with feet dangling into space was hurling herself headlong into the wisteria. A stifled shriek rang in her ear.

"'Arree! It is she."

"Sarah? The bitch! Hold on to her."

An arm shot out, sharp nails clawed at her cheek as she slid beyond reach and gripping the tough stem with both hands swayed perilously in mid-air. The ground below seemed lost in cavernous darkness the mere thought of which made her head swim, but far more terrifying was the hissed command from the room above: "Take this! Do you hear? Quietly now, get below to catch her. I'll drive her down."

The curtains had fallen, blotting out the single glimpse of two fear-blanched faces. Pitch-gloom now, as twixt sky and earth she hung, while tendrils stiff as wires fastened her tightly by the hair. Imprisoned, like Absalom—and meanwhile a murderer on his way, and her slim strength almost gone. One desperate wrench freed her. At the same instant she shifted her whole weight to her good left hand in order to grope with the other for a lower hold. She had just got it when *swish!* From above a steel blade, razor-sharp, launched towards her, slashing her knuckles to the bone. Her right-hand fingers, unequal to the sudden strain put upon them, gave limply, and down she hurtled, six feet, to fall in a heap on the rough gravel.

Bruised, half-stunned, she had wit enough to leap up and run—run like mad, with the sound of Harry's strides in her ears to goad her onward. Blindly, stumbling over flowerbeds, she fled, past the first clump of euca-lyptus trees, through the iron gates of the drive, and out into the lane.

CHAPTER THIRTY-SEVEN

Had she a dog's chance? The ribbon-straight lane offered no cover, while in the whole starlit darkness not a human creature was in sight or call. When in the gateway behind her she heard her pursuer pause to recon-noitre, all her frantic running had brought her only abreast of the gap where the char-a-banc had smashed in the palings. Into it she plunged, her spent breath sobbing in her throat. Not daring to venture far, she wormed her way under the shelving boughs of a tamarisk, cowered against the trunk, and lay still.

Long legs sprinted in her direction, reached the opening, and stopped. Reason must declare she could have got no farther afield than this, yet when long minutes had passed and still the hesitation continued, hope reared a pathetic head. Possibly Harry would press on and give her time to crawl to some safer spot. Indeed, she had begun to plan her next move when *plonk!*—a fallen board resounded under an approaching foot, and without more ado the luminous beam of a torch swept an arc over her head.

Long ago, in London—a child of six she had been then—she had watched grim search-lights in their quest of marauding aeroplanes, slanting, shifting, hounding out the dim speck in a waste of night-sky. Now she was that enemy, only instead of being able to dodge and flee she must lie motionless, craven wretch that she was, and wait for certain capture. Around and above the dazzling ray played, turning first one then another section of the feathery foliage-screen to brilliant emerald. Not yet had it touched her, but at any moment it would. To silence her breathing she had crammed her cut knuckles into her mouth. Blood welled into her throat, but she was not aware of it.

Close, so close that she shivered, a strained and callous voice she would not have known spoke to her.

"You're in there," it said. "Come out, get it over."

She might as well . . . but was that the throb of a motor-engine? Heading for the lane, or so for a wild instant she fancied. Alas, no! It had died to stillness along the coast. The torch-beam grazed her elbow. One more try, and it would hit its mark. She shut her eyes, but no kaleidoscopic vision of past life flashed before her. All she saw was Brian Gilcrest's misunderstood features. She could have put things right, if only . . . and then, slicing across the reflection, "It can't end like this! It's silly, it's ignominious! Why, this is only Harry Venables! How can I be frightened of him?"

The white ray swung back, cutting the gloom like a knife. It rested full on her face—and even as she leapt to her feet brute strength closed upon her. Struggling wildly she had one glimpse of the face looming above hers and saw not the Harry she had known—easy-going, carelessly good-natured—but a being so devoid of sensitiveness to any suffering but his own that no appeal could reach him. Unimaginative, shifty, self-indulgent, and now with his back to the wall—what remained save sheer animal determination to quell what menaced his safety? She had seen the real Harry, and knew that however she might plead, weep, bargain, she would find no response.

None of these things did she do, but summoning all her force she dug her nails straight into the small, blood-suffused eyes. He swore foully, clamping one hot palm tight over her mouth. That was all, for something heavy and metallic crashed down upon her skull, and amidst blinding pain the stars blacked out.

She had fought her way back through midnight jungles, stumbling because her legs were bound, while each time she rose to hobble onward a black ape clutched at her hair. Sweating she woke, weak with relief to know that it had been only a nightmare, and that now she would open her eyes on sunlight, blue mountains, a peach orchard pink with bloom. She did open them—on musty smelling darkness. She tried to move—and a wave of sickness engulfed her, to be followed by horrible panic.

Good God, it was true! Her legs were bound, arms as well, in coils of hard cord that bit into her flesh. Worse still, her mouth was clogged with wet silk she could not dislodge so tightly was it tied behind her head. Throat parched, body bruised as though beaten—she remembered now. But where was she? She heaved herself upright and struck her temple so violent a blow that she fell back, dazed with excruciating pain.

What was this airless place? Gradually she became aware of a soft, irregular, slapping sound, like waves against the side of a boat. It was waves. Of course! She was in the tiny, stuffy cabin of the de Bellesnaves' yacht—and as she felt no movement, the yacht must still be anchored. Dead silence—so she was alone, but would it be for long? Common-sense told her that if she wished to put up a last battle for existence it must be instantly, without a moment's delay. Better to drown in the effort to swim ashore than wait for forcible extinction. Was there any chance of loosening these cords?

Only faintness came of her wriggling. At last, lying still to recover, she tried desperately to picture the little cabin as she had once seen it. Two narrow bunks—it was on the floor between that she was stretched—a cupboard, heaps of cushions—and no more. If only she could recall some bit of metal with a jagged edge—had there been anything of the kind? She seemed to remember that the ladder-like treads of the companion-way had strips of iron nailed on to them. She touched the lowest step with her stockinged feet and felt something hard. One of these might do the trick, if she could shift around and bring the arm-cords up against. . . .

Too late. At her first tortuous movement she stopped, chained by the sound of rusty oar-locks coming across the water. Louder they grew till the impact of a floating body jarred through the cabin, and she knew that the dinghy had been pulled alongside. Her respite was ended—and to settle the matter beyond a doubt she caught the hiss of voices together with clambering feet and the thump of something ponderous being loaded on to the deck. Rapid whispers reached her. The night was so still she could make out the words.

First Harry—and how terrified he sounded! "God, what a rotten break! Let alone she'd have done no harm, but now—"

"Now it is certain she will not!" It was the Baroness' voice, harsh, triumphant. "Inconvenient, yes, but—what is the time? Two o'clock. Well, then, by three I shall be back in my bed, and you on your way to Toulon."

"I daresay, but how the hell can you explain?"

"To the servants? Listen!" The gabble was now in French, sharp, decisive. "She adored you—understand? She had made you promise to wait till the morning train in case she changed her mind about going. To learn her decision you returned, quite late, after everyone else was asleep, found her ready to leave, and carried down her luggage. She will have left a note for me, and a hundred francs on her dressing-table—and she will have told me what to expect, so I shall show no astonishment, only annoyance. There! What is wrong about that? No one will miss her till it is far too late to matter. I made sure of that, for Bimi leaves little to chance."

"Bimi! The way you tell it, it may work!"

"It will work!"—impatiently. "Now, be quick! The biggest stones you can find . . ."

Stones! It was clear now what was to be done with her. Far out to sea, her body, heavily weighted, would be dropped overboard . . .

The dinghy plunged, the rasping oar-locks receded—and then the small square of night-sky at the top of the companion vanished as though a black curtain had been drawn over it. The woman was coming down the ladder.

She was inside the cabin. Sarah, unable to stir hand or foot, lay like a log, staring into darkness which at first showed only one blurred patch denser than the rest. Her ankles were trodden on. The weight removed itself to sink at her side, and, the stars above reappearing, she saw within a few inches of her face two hate-filled eyes blazing into hers.

"So!" came the venomous whisper close to her muffled mouth. "You really believed you could take him from me, did you? Money and all—the rich young idiot, so easy for a clever woman to entrap? I saw it all—yes, from the beginning—and I saw, too, that like other clever women you wanted love as well as money, and that given the chance you would stay behind, yes, even with me, to have one more try for your doctor. That was your reason for remaining, was it not? You thought that if you failed with one you would still return to lay siege to the other. Ah, yes you would have taken them both—and for your greed you shall be punished, because with all your cleverness you overlooked the fact that I was Bimi. Yes, Bimi!"

She beat her breasts in a strange fury of exultation.

"I, I am Bimi! Bertrand's Bimi, you know, who tore into little shreds the woman who stood in the way. When Bimi had done with her nothing was left except some rags of hair and blood. Listen! Do you realise who set you on fire? Bimi did it! For one little minute she slipped away to search for string, and no one guessed that in that minute she dropped—not a match, ah no, that would have been too crude—but something which would light itself and be gone before the flames reached your waist. She left you to burn—as you would have burned, to a black crisp, if that fool had not saved you. Ah, well, you shall burn now, only it will be from the inside. For twenty minutes, longer perhaps, you will know the meaning of hell, till you will pray to be dropped into the sea. You have wanted to learn how those three old women died, hein? Look! I will show you what killed them. I have it here, in this bottle."

A small object was thrust before Sarah's starting eyes. The Baroness fumbled with it, and a few drops of what smelt like some sort of oil splashed on her upturned face. The voice resumed, now in a low, purring patter.

"You cannot see what I hold in my hand, no? It is a little, grey pea. This time it is uncovered, so you will feel it scorching all the way down your throat. I kept a tiny bit back, for one never knows, does one, when it may be wanted? A thing so safe, so sure—and who would think to find in a bottle of anti-wrinkle oil a fine means of killing? When you have swallowed, I will tell you what it is that burns holes in the stomach and leaves behind it no trace—and I, Bimi, shall sit here and watch what happens. Your description was good, but to see for one's self is more amusing, is it not? Now! I loosen the gag just enough so that I can push my little grey pea far down into your throat. And then—"

Deft fingers were busy with the knot behind the victim's head. The silk handkerchief slipped—and Sarah screamed. Once only, for before the echoes had ceased to rebound from the cabin walls an oily hand was slapped over her mouth.

"Quiet, you bitch! You will not be heard, but if you scream again I will stick this knife into your eyes. Here, I am ready. Swallow, swallow!"

She managed to throw herself on her face, but rough hands righted her, and for perhaps two minutes a fierce, unequal battle went on. Once something blistering hot grazed her tongue, but the violent wrench she gave sent the substance, whatever it was, slithering to the floor. A furious search—then her head was firmly wedged between her captor's knees, her nostrils were clamped between finger and thumb, and for the second time the Baroness' free hand poised just above her tightly closed lips.

"Shall it be the knife? No? Then open!"

If she gasped for breath, she was lost—yet gasp she must, for she was suffocating. All the blood in her body hammered and sang in her head, the stuffy darkness spun round. Choking, weakening fast—what was the good. One last, despairing effort, and her lips burst apart.

Why did the hand not pounce upon her? The shadowy face suspended in gloom was upturned with a new and watchful tenseness, eyes staring at—what? Oh, yes. This sudden careen of the boat and the two heavy feet overhead meant Harry had returned. There would be two to master her now. That was why the clutch on her nostrils had relaxed—but she scarcely took in the scurrying retreat up the companion, or realised that if she wished to scream again she was free to do so. The struggle had finished her. She slumped back into stupor.

She roused at the sound of descending footsteps. Harry it was—coming to finish her, but the woman would be close behind. Something clammy and cold brushed her prostrate body, hard breathing broke on her ear, and with waves of sick horror washing over her she cringed from the groping fingers which explored her eyes and slid downward to her throat. They were closing in to strangle her. Well knowing the uselessness of further protest, she threw all that was left of her into one final shriek—and it came forth a husky croak.

"*Sarah!*" gasped a voice which ran through her like a galvanic shock—a voice dry as her own, but with a break in it.

Her heart stopped beating. Who was this who had spoken her name? Not—but no, that was inconceivable. Delirium again, more torture before . . . but the bitter thought was checked, for her bound, bruised body was caught up in a fierce embrace, a man's arms with hard muscles strained her close while a man's kisses, equally hard and frantic, rained upon her face, her mouth. Hungry, inescapable kisses submerging her whole being—kisses she had dreamed about, kisses which if she died of them now would send her into the other world transported with rapture. She had been primed for death, and instead—"But this is life!" whispered the voice within her brain. "Life as you've wanted it—like as you've always known it could be. . . ."

Crash! The yacht reeled with a double shock, the tiny cabin reverberated to the deafening sound just burst inside it, and acrid fumes, uprising in the darkness, blotted out consciousness. The curtain fell on the drama, and Sarah MacNeil, with the taste of joy on her lips, slipped into the unknown.

CHAPTER THIRTY-EIGHT

GILCREST charged up the narrow companion to find Venables, blanched and bestial of face, blocking the way. A smoking revolver took aim as its owner cried, "Back! I'm going to blow the two of you to hell!"

A third shot rang out, but deflected in time, splintered the mainmast. Gilcrest, still on the ladder, dodged the terrific kick directed at his middle, and tackling his opponent's legs in a grip of steel sent the young athlete's body hurtling to the deck. He was out now, but already the man was up and making for him head lowered, chin out-thrust, with fear and hatred in his small, reddened eyes. The full weight of thirteen stone was behind the punch which landed on space. In another second the two were locked in a tight embrace, first swaying and toppling, then crashing to the wet boards to roll and grapple, each seeking a hold on the other's throat. Under the night-sky with its bright peppering of stars they fought without words, only the breath bursting from constricted lungs to tell of the savage force underlying the contest.

What had become of the woman Gilcrest neither knew nor cared. Blood poured from the shoulder-wound she had managed to inflict in her wild-cat rush three minutes ago, but what of that? Murderess and knife had been hurled overboard into deep water, and now if he could send this revolver after them he would have nothing further to fear. Still clutched, it kept lifting to take aim. He had parried it so far, but had not succeeded in wrenching it free. What he wanted was a weapon to use for one smashing blow. Those knuckles must be broken.

Small objects had rained from their pockets to roll about the deck— loose silver, a watch, a box of matches, and—yes, an electric torch, long and fairly massive. Towards it Gilcrest edged, and at last caught it up to bring it down hard on his adversary's right hand. The revolver fell. He sent it sliding under the rail, and simultaneously received an uppercut which drove him dazed against the ruined mast.

They were apart, and Gilcrest was just brushing the sweat from his eyes when across his line of vision slunk a small, dripping form, low-bent, keeping close to the rail. Its coat was gone, and wet, black hair, Medusa-stranded, clung to the plastered nightdress. As he closed with Venables again he was dimly aware of a face greenish-white from the sea-water in the midst of which glared two dark eyes avid with purpose—but what? The question did not trouble him. Out of the tail of his eye he could still see the rise and fall of the low breasts under their covering of drenched fabric, but not until a bare arm shot out and a hand swift as an adder's tongue caught up something from under his stumbling feet did he wonder what move was contemplated. She was gone, melting into the shadows of the stern. He forgot her, and maddened to find he was gaining no ground gave his full attention to the job in hand.

Tearing himself free, he struck, heard the crunch of loosened teeth, and heartened by the sound drew back to strike again. Then he paused, sniffing the air. What were these fumes stealing to his nostrils? Another sniff, and he knew. Petrol! Too late he wheeled to see red pennants of flame mounting the furled mast, licking at the boards, galloping along the rail in both directions. The truth flashed on him in horror, and even as he realised that the aged hulk, sun-baked for weeks, was so much tinder, a steady hum throbbed on his ear.

The engine was going!

Venables, feeling his jaw, stared stupidly at the rosy glare. As Gilcrest plunged towards the companion he heard the woman's rapid hiss in the rear, "Quick, you fool! Don't you see the anchor is up and we're heading to sea? Into the dinghy, leave them to roast!"

There was a scrambling retreat which Gilcrest did not stop to watch. Torch in hand he had cleared the steep ladder in a bound, and not daring to ascertain what harm the first shots might have done gathered the inert Sarah into his arms. His own wet coat he ripped off to wrap around her, then, though the yacht was moving fast and the distance to shore widening every second, he played the torch-beam about the floor.

When he staggered to the deck, heavily laden, his eyeballs were seared by a roaring furnace. The railing was ringed with flame, while fiery sparks filled the air to fall, hissing, into the sea. All about the swift-heading boat the water rippled in a pool of roseate light. The dinghy had disappeared from view, the beach and landing-stage were small, receding specks—

and, supposing he had the luck to reach the water at all, he would have to swim hampered by a helpless burden. . . .

There was no time to dwell on these things. Filling his lungs with a deep breath, he dashed through fire which singed the hair on his scalp, slid over the blazing rail, and with the girl's limp body clasped to his breast, jumped clear.

CHAPTER THIRTY-NINE

"THEY will be captured? Oh, don't say they'll escape!"

"They can't. Don't worry about that."

Sarah, for the first time allowed to discuss matters, sank back with a tremulous sigh. She still lay in Gilcrest's own bed, whither she had been brought straight from her immersion in the sea. The dark limbo of delirium was a thing of the past, keen interest had returned, and Gilcrest, at her side, was doing his best to satisfy her curiosity concerning the blank spaces in events. Only half had been told, she clamoured for more, but now her informant was holding back with a trace of reticence. If she had been less intent on her mental picture of the blazing yacht and the tough fight to haul her ashore she would have detected just a slight evasion in his answers.

"Were they watching us?" she persisted. "Come to think of it, why didn't they make another attack when they saw us land?"

"No weapons," was the terse reply. "Then, too, I managed to pull in almost abreast of my car. It wasn't the moment for bothering about their movements. I had to look after you."

A cloud dimmed the dear brilliance of her eyes.

"I see," she whispered. "But if we had burned up with the boat? We might easily have done it, mightn't we? In that case, I suppose there'd have been no need for a get-away. The Baroness would have gone calmly back to bed, he'd have driven off, and in the morning—"

"In the morning," said Gilcrest, "there'd have been just two puzzling disappearances and a yacht napoo. Later on some charred remains and wreckage might have washed ashore. I leave you to guess what would have been the idea then—and who'd have been able to deny it? But see here, don't forget you're just getting over a mild concussion. Lie back, I'm going to take your temperature, and leave you to quiet down."

"You're hard, hard as nails," she mumbled reproachfully, the thermometer waggling in her mouth. "But I always knew that . . . I'm all right. Why don't you let me talk?"

For answer firm fingers closed on her pulse. He did nothing by halves, this man, and at the realisation of what this intense concentration could mean a thrill of elation left her weak. Then she caught sight of his eyes, faintly-smiling, but for all that inscrutable, and the doubt which for two days had been troubling her reinserted its barb into her mind. She knew he had risked his own life for hers, that the horror of certain moments had not yet left him; but—had she dreamed those kisses? Or if not, did they embody a wild lapse he wished to ignore? He might have kissed her for no other reason than sheer, uncontrollable relief over finding her still alive. Why should she think she meant anything to him? Pampered and spoiled though she had been, she had seen no direct sign to reassure her—and she certainly could not ask.

"Normal? I could have told you that," she declared scornfully. "I've a thick skull, you see. Please, please tell me more! Is it fair to let me pour out all my story and hold back the best part of yours? For instance, what brought you to the beach at that ungodly hour? Why were you prowling round the villa? I simply must know everything, from the beginning, and I can't rest till I do."

"Well," he consented hesitatingly, "though it starts rather far back. I'll make it as brief as I can."

As he spoke, she was acutely conscious of the shabby comfort about her, of the big bunch of blush roses with dew on their petals beside her bed, of the blue forget-me-nots in a bowl, and the dish heaped high with peaches and grapes. He bore her no malice, that at least was certain; yet after what had happened it was hard to lie here and pretend. . . .

She learned how he had not once considered the possibility of foul play in connection with either of his patients till advance information obtained by telephone sent him headlong to Nice to see for himself just what the analyst had found.

"I took a good look—and I got the shock of my life. The perforation in Miss Venables' stomach might pass muster, atypical though it was, but what was one to say about the same sort of puncture in Miss Tomlins' duodenum where I'd never expend anything of the kind? Thrombosis means coagulation of blood. Well, there was plenty of that, but it came from a big clean hole drilled bang through the duodenal wall and into the big portal vein that lies directly at the back, eight or nine inches below the stomach. Collapse from this cause would be as quick as in thrombosis and could—in fact did—give the same outward appearances, except that the patient would turn ghastly pale from the internal hemorrhage. I had noticed Miss Tomlins' pallor. You must have done so, too—but she was very swarthy, you remember, and so it was less striking than it might have been."

"I thought you hesitated just a fraction of a second when I asked why she died—but never mind that now. What did you think when you saw this hole?"

He had shot her a queer glance, but without comment he continued. "Nothing. There was simply no accounting for it—and if I'd made a hell of a bloomer over my diagnosis, all I or anyone could say was that here was an ulcer of a peculiar kind, sufficiently acute to erode two juxtaposed tissue-walls and cause almost instantaneous death. In the complete absence of poison or corrosive substance you couldn't call it murder. Technically, therefore, I was safe—and the Médecin Légiste himself never criticised my diagnosis, perfectly justified in the circumstances. At the same time his manner amounted to accusation. I knew to a dead certainty what he was thinking. It was as though he had caught me with the goods, only couldn't say what the goods were. In his opinion I'd discovered some undetectable way of killing and had got away with two murders."

"He really believed that?" whispered Sarah, her eyes dilated with horror. "Oh, how terrible for you!"

"Every intelligent person who studied the verdicts must have agreed with him," said Gilcrest stoically. "You did, didn't you? Oh, it won't hurt my feelings—now. It would have mattered very little if I'd not inherited money by one of these deaths, but with a thing like that staring the whole world in the face . . . the irony, of course, was that it was a penniless woman's condition which made the real trouble. I couldn't for the life of me see how they'd find a motive for getting rid of Miss Tomlins, though I was certain they would. I daresay you can tell me what my excuse was?"

Blushing red she murmured, "Go on with your story."

"Well, then! Having viewed these odd appearances, I was every bit as positive as I am now that both victims had been murdered—and when I'd reasoned a little I knew that in each instance my medicine was responsible. I'll go into that later on. Now as to Henri's death." He paused, moistening dry lips. "Murder again—or so I believed, but as in the other cases it couldn't be proved. Not possibly. It was too cleverly done . . . from then on I went a trifle mad, I think. Anyhow—but can you bear any more? It's rather horrible. You see, it concerns the two dogs . . ."

A minute's spellbound attention, and Sarah was eyeing him, thunderstruck:

"Stop!" she whispered. "Do you mean to tell me that fiend killed her own little dog just by way of experiment?"

"It may have been that," he answered, shrugging. "In the bulldog's case—but perhaps you can see why that was done?"

She nodded. "I can. Do you know I had a feeling all along that the end wouldn't be reached till the Baron, too, was dead? Not that I had any idea—" she broke off, not wishing to specify her exact conjectures on this point. "What," she resumed quickly, "made you first connect Harry with these affairs?"

"His scared look when he saw the dog-collars. Till that moment he'd never entered my calculations, simply because—" Here Gilcrest showed noticeable embarrassment. "Well, I had the best of reasons for supposing the woman herself had no sort of use for him. The impression, it appears, was deliberately fostered, one needn't ask why."

"And yet," said Sarah, "it couldn't have been hard to give that idea, for you see it was quite true. She does despise Harry from the bottom of her soul—so bitterly that she can't cover it up. If he weren't a hopeless fool he'd have seen it was only his money she was after, and that once she'd made sure of that, his life wouldn't have been worth tuppence. It's odd, isn't it? Because Harry is attractive, at first, that is, and in a purely physical way."

"You think so, do you?"

The swift demand gave her secret pleasure.

"Oh, decidedly!" she declared coolly. "I was quite drawn to him for a bit, till I found out how dull he was. Perhaps it was the same with her. She got bored, lost interest, and found someone who—"

Dangerous ground again! Gilcrest had turned an uncomfortable red, seeing which she adroitly changed the subject.

"What was this illness of hers? I know she did it on purpose to get me there, but how was it managed?"

"I can't tell you that, though at the moment she was sick I tumbled to the conclusion that she had taken something. Can you picture the scene? The two excitable Italians, the deluded old French doctor and a fat slug of a priest all hovering around the bed, herself the centre of attraction—and me guessing what had happened and unable to say a word! I knew that whatever she'd been told about the dogs—and Venables must certainly have rushed straight to her with his information—she was not one whit alarmed for her safety. Why should she be? That being so, I failed to understand why she was doing all this—and I'd still be in the dark but for your explanation. So she was jealous of you, was she? I don't wonder—and in her type jealousy amounts almost to madness. Only an emotion as unbalanced as that could account for her trying to get rid of you at a period when you could scarcely have represented a serious menace to her plan. But possibly you did, even then. Who knows?"

Sarah forbore to interrupt, deriving a smug satisfaction from his remarks. After all, was it not something to know that Harry's attentions to her had not passed unobserved?

"She was badly hampered, you see, well aware the fellow must be making up to you, but unable to stop it. He was losing his nerve, too, and what was to prevent him sliding out of the whole business and leaving her high and dry? She'd no hold on him, for to denounce him was to denounce herself—and she'd argue that you, like herself, were after his money. Wasn't that her notion?"

Sarah admitted it, suppressing the fact that the Baroness' keen eyes had seen where her heart-interest lay, and that herein lay another cause for jealousy.

"That being so, her only means of re-attaching him to herself was to remove your influence. It must have driven her frantic to see the two of you about to go away in each other's company . . . only,"—with a perplexed frown—"how, thinking as she did, could she expect to separate you from him?"

Said Sarah sedately, "I suppose she banked on my kind and gullible nature, in which case she slipped up; but anyway, how right it is for her to be wrecked by her own mistake! She told you, of course, that I was there?"

"Told me? Not a word. Nor did the old woman mention it. Probably ordered to say nothing. No, I should never have known you hadn't left with Venables—I saw you, in the distance, with your luggage on the car—but for Demosthenes too hurriedly getting the sack. It was he—"

"Demosthenes!" She laughed shakily. "Oh, how funny that is! He told you? When? Why?"

"That same evening, very late. I was here, sorting out papers, preparatory to clearing out. What was the use of hanging on with my entire practise gone to pot? Oh, I might have stuck it for a bit, but at the moment . . . here, what's this? For God's sake, my dear child, you're not taking that part of it to heart, are you? It wasn't your doing. Take my handkerchief."

She accepted the offering, gulping back her tears.

"Never mind me. Go on. Demosthenes—?"

"Blundered in on me, drunk as a lord, spinning a wild yarn about paying the Baroness back in her own coin. I was about to boot him out when almost by accident he mentioned your name, and I began to take notice. What were you doing up there? Ought I to drop you a word of warning? I was worried, naturally—more so because I was afraid you wouldn't listen to anything I said. And then something the filthy Greek said made me prick up my ears again. It was hush-money he was after—and Venables was the person he meant to fleece—Venables, whom he'd seen only the week before conducting a secret rendezvous with the Baroness, at midnight, in the grounds! All at once I realised that just possibly this fellow might hold the key to what otherwise was locked and sealed, and if he did . . . I questioned him, and here is all I got: Venables hadn't gone by the evening train. He couldn't have done, because the Greek himself had just spotted his car outside a café in Hyères, and jumped to the conclusion that its owner had missed his train in order to steal back for a last private word with his mistress. If Demo had been less drunk he'd have kept this to himself. As it was, he solicited my aid in an enterprise which, quite simply, meant lying in wait near the villa and catching the lovers red-handed. Two witnesses were better than one was the way he put it. He had just wit enough to see his statements mightn't carry much weight."

"But you—! He really expected you to—"

"Evidently." Gilcrest looked away. "You see, he was assuming I, too, might be feeling revengeful. Well, I got rid of him by means of a hundred francs and half a bottle of whiskey, and just as soon as I'd satisfied myself he was in no state for activity I pushed quietly off to do a little snooping on my own account. Like you, I perceived how hopeless it was to get the truth of this affair except by trapping the two accomplices together. Even then I might not hear anything incriminating, but as it was my last and only chance I didn't dare let it slip.

"I left my two-seater behind the clump of palm-trees at this end of the beach, and making my way through the grounds toured the whole outside of the villa. Not a sound—nothing amiss. I began to fear the visit had already been concluded, or else that Demo had mistaken another Fiat for Venables'. If at the end of an hour I didn't give up and go home it was only because so much was at stake—and it was good I held on, for finally, exploring the roads, I came upon the Fiat, far back in a field, the lights out, the engine warm.

"That proved it. Back I dashed, to find one of the library windows unlatched. Henri's body lay inside. I crept past it, went all over the house listening at doors, and still drew a blank. If an interview was in progress, it must be outside. As I stole into the open again I noticed the creeper badly torn away from the wall—and on the ground I found—what do you think? This—and if I hadn't been looking closely, with a lighted match, I'd never have seen it."

It was a small grip-slide he had taken from his pocket—one of several used by Sarah to hold her hair in place during the night.

"Oh!" she cried. "You knew it was mine?"

"I felt sure the Baroness didn't need them. She hasn't got waves. It must be yours—and I was horribly frightened. I raced about, heading in the main towards the water—for obvious reasons—and about the middle of the grounds I fancied I heard something. Oar-locks. Someone was rowing to or from the yacht; but when I reached the boat-house all I saw was the dinghy, moored to the landing-steps. Venables couldn't have been far off, as he climbed aboard the yacht about a couple of minutes after I'd chucked the woman over the side; but I didn't see him, nor any sign that the yacht was occupied. And then, thank God, you screamed. Just once. If I'd stopped even to throw off my coat before diving in—but we won't speak of that."

Their eyes met consciously, drifted apart. The silence between them lengthened, and Sarah, longing for something more, felt a lump swell in her throat. Was this all he meant to say? He was hoping, no doubt, that she had not been fully conscious when he found her. A fortunate solution—for him.

"And the Baron?" she began anew. "Why did you know he was murdered?"

"By the message he was supposed to have left. Oh, it wasn't forged! That would have been easy; but those two short sentences you recall them?—*L'affaire se termine. Inutile continuer*—had a strangely familiar ring. I could have sworn they had occurred in a letter I'd received from him while I was in England, and that they referred to his futile attempt to find a serum for the bulldog's asthma. I was also struck by the placing of the line—high on the paper, straight across—in fact, more like a continuation of something else than a detached fragment scrawled by a man about to end his life. Last, the ink-blot—which in my judgment clinched it. Henri, you see, was the sort of person who, having spoiled a sheet, would throw it away and take another. His letters were marvels of neatness. Putting all this together, I felt convinced as to how this 'message' had been obtained. It had been salvaged from the waste-basket because its double-reading significance would lend colour to a suicide hoax."

"And only you saw these things!"

"Only I had seen the original letter—and that, worse luck, had been destroyed. No, here again I had no proof—none. And don't forget, I wasn't in a very strong position myself just then. If I'd risked mentioning my suspicions, I'd have incurred severe censure and maybe a libel action into the bargain. Even with what you've told me I should very much doubt if we shall be able to establish this one crime." He was speaking to himself. "It's our word against theirs," he muttered. "Have you thought what that may mean?"

She gazed at him for a moment, her face falling. Was it possible those two might yet skin through?

"But—isn't their running away and hiding an open admission of guilt? I should have supposed—aren't they going to be arrested?"

He examined her face with a keen, professional eye.

"There's something I haven't told you," he said quietly. "But first, remember this: you're safe, it can't touch you, whatever happens. You see, they haven't tried to escape. They're under arrest now, but Venables was halted at Calais, and the Baroness—"

"Oh, where?"

"At a private mental asylum in Toulon. She made no resistance. It is generally believed she was quite out of her mind."

Sarah's eyes flashed. "Do you believe it?" she demanded.

"Certainly not—but she's an excellent actress. Do you want to hear the story Venables and the two servants are giving out?"

"The servants too! They must have been bought . . . what is it?"

"To begin with," said Gilcrest slowly, keeping watch on her reactions, "All you overheard is categorically denied. It's your own malicious invention. Their version—well, here it is."

CHAPTER FORTY

Two minutes later Sarah's eyes were blazing. "Oh, how absurd! How devilish! Surely we can prove it's a lie?"

"Certainly," he soothed her. "Why not?"

"It's so fiendishly clever," she mused. "Why, it almost looks as though . . . see here,"—in sudden dismay, "if we still can't prove these were murders, how can we convict them? We don't yet know what it was they used."

"What's that?" He had been staring at her abstractedly, and came out of his reverie with a start. "Oh, but we do! I found the answer days ago. Haven't I told you?"

"You know? Oh, how cruel to keep me guessing. Tell me, tell me this instant! What is it?"

He smiled at her impatience. "Wait. I want you to hear just how I worked it out. Incidentally, it may gratify you to learn that it was the capsules—or to be exact one capsule, in each bottle. That fact's all-important. Here, if you'll bear with me, are the steps in my argument: first, take the two Venables women. Their medicine was valerian, which acts on the stomach, and is therefore encased in a gelatine, or quick-dissolving covering. Well, both these victims succumbed very soon after the last dose was swallowed, and both from perforations in the stomach-lining. Keep that in mind.

"Next, Miss Tomlins. Her prescription, being designed to act on the intestinal tract, was put into kerotin capsules, because kerotin is much harder than gelatine and won't melt till it has passed through the stomach and reached the duodenum. It may, in fact, take a couple of hours to dissolve. From what you told me, it was about that length of time before Miss Tomlins felt the pain, and the perforation in her case was located not in the stomach but in the duodenum. You see how neatly it all fits? And yet, since Miss Venables and Miss Tomlins died from complaints differently situated it was manifestly absurd to suppose a common cause. Naturally I was badly upset. Any doctor would have been, to have two of his patients dying off like this, one after the other, both in rapid and violent fashion. There seemed something diabolical about it, in spite of which, to judge by the evident symptoms, one couldn't call it other than coincidence. Only when I had examined the organs and seen the precise injuries involved—similar, and in each case atypical—did it seem worth while to weigh the facts just mentioned. Once I did consider them, the deduction was inevitable. *In each bottle of medicine there must have been one altered capsule—a capsule containing a substance which had eliminated itself.*

"Having got thus far, I wired the house-surgeon of Charing Cross Hospital for full particulars of the post mortem on Mrs. Venables—and I got back a night-letter telegram giving me details not considered necessary to mention to the family. It seems there had been a slight peculiarity about the perforation. It was not indurated—that means hardened at the outer rim—though the edges were approximated and sutured, the perforation itself partially blocked with clotted blood, and the stomach-contents found free in the peritonile cavity. Is that too technical? No matter, I'll sum it up by saying that here again I was confronted by the self-same atypical appearances, amply confirming the theory I'd begun to form. I hadn't bothered much about motives, and I can't yet say just why this first woman was murdered; but what the Baroness said about Miss Tomlins' death being a mistake bears out my own idea. Leave that. I want to stick to the main thread.

"Now, then! What was this mysterious substance which tore great holes in its victims but left nothing behind? For obvious reasons I was forced to tackle the problem on purely theoretical lines—and I sat here till two in the morning, trying first one chemical equation then another, and getting failure after failure. My object was to discover what in combination with the weak hydrochloric acid of the stomach would give a non-suspicious reaction. It was self-evident that something would do this—but what? Well, at last I got my answer—on paper—and instantly I saw I was no better off than before. The very absence of detectable residue in the system made the thing for practical purposes unprovable—which was the beauty of it, of course. It explained why the murderer had nothing to fear from post mortems, and why I, for all my certain knowledge, was sewn up in a bag."

Sarah groaned. "Then it's all no good!" she lamented. "What's the use of knowing if it can't be proved? Oh, if only that boat hadn't burned! Why, the stuff was there, in the cabin! Now it's lost, and—"

"Oh, no!" He smiled again, enjoying his triumph. "I can't say how much good it will do, but actually I looked about for something of the kind and found it—bottle and all, lying in a little pool of oil. I corked it tight to keep out the water, jammed it deep down in my trousers-pocket, and got it ashore. No, I can't show it to you, because the police have got it; but I ordered some of the same on purpose for a little demonstration I now propose to make."

"Had you any before?"

"Yes, for experiments—and if it hadn't been used up the actual sight of it might have helped me to a quicker solution. The Baroness must certainly have filched hers from our jar, but she would have wanted only a tiny amount, and as it's in no sense a poison it's not locked up or the exact quantities checked. The difficulty in most cases is to get hold of it. Chemists, even wholesale ones, don't stock the raw article, only its compounds, so it has to be obtained from a laboratory supply. There's even a regulation against sending it by post—and yet it's quite an ordinary thing, familiar to all students of chemistry. Have you ever studied chemistry, by the way?"

"Now you're laughing at me. Let me inform you, Dr. Gilcrest, that I once took chemistry for nearly three months!"

"Splendid! That makes it easier."

He was moving towards the door, but turning he spoke again with an odd expression in his eyes.

"Keep away from water" he quoted. "You wondered what that meant? One second and you'll see."

With a strange prickle all along her skin, Sarah watched him return laden with a large glass jar and a basin of water. At the bottom of the jar, submerged in pale, slightly opalescent fluid, lay a lump of dull, grey matter which he now fished out with a pair of forceps, wiped on a towel, and held up for her inspection. It looked like lead, but seemed much softer. When, with a sharp penknife, he hacked off a small portion, the cut edges shone silver-bright.

"It has to be kept in oil," he explained. "Even the moisture from the atmosphere will—but look, see what happens!" He dropped the small lump into the basin. As it touched the water it floated and instantly burst into a clear, pale flame! From it rose a tiny jet of steam, hissing like a miniature teakettle! The girl leant on her elbow, staring transfixed and astounded.

"It burns—in water?" she gasped. "But how positively uncanny! And yet I feel I ought to know. Is it—?"

"Just sodium—the pure element. Its symbol is Na. Potassium does the same, but sodium possesses this unique advantage: in union with hydrochloric acid it ultimately forms—what do you think? NaCl—in other words, common table-salt."

"Only that?"

"Only that—and now you see why a bit of sodium no bigger than a pea would first of all burn a deep hole in whatever moist surface it touched, and then simply vanish, leaving nothing to show how the pseudo-ulcer had been caused. Who would notice a minute quantity of saline solution? It's normal, negligible. There's just one crab: the stuff must be kept dry till it reaches the interior of the system, otherwise it would burn the mouth and be ejected. For this reason the victim must be already taking some sort of capsules, or else induced to take a capsule, though possibly a cachet might serve. I've found by tests that the sodium capsule can be made to look like any other capsule, consequently there's nothing to prevent its being swallowed without suspicion. The murderer, having hidden his dose in the bottle, can go miles away if he wishes, comfortably certain his result will be achieved. In ninety-nine out of a hundred chances the death will be diagnosed as natural. If it is queried, he's still perfectly safe."

"With me, of course, it was to be a matter of brute force." Sarah touched her throat, shuddering slightly. "But what about the dogs? Would they swallow capsules?"

"Oh, with them I imagine it was merely wrapped in raw meat and wolfed down so quickly it had scarcely begun to sizzle. A coating of powder would be sufficient. In our three human cases, I should think the method was prompted by the fact that capsules were being used, though the amazing thing is, how could either of these people have known enough to—hello, what's this?"

Marjory stood in the open door, her arms filled with flowers. Her brown eyes were very lustrous as they turned apologetically from one face to the other, and she hastened to excuse her entrance.

"I'm so sorry! Miss Whittaker and Mrs. Bulstrode brought these, and I thought—but shall I run away and put them in water?"

Gilcrest, suddenly more formal, had risen.

"The session's closed, Miss Barrows. Our patient's had enough excitement, and we're going to draw the curtains and clear out."

While Marjory, all beaming solicitude, patted Sarah's cheek and tidied her covers, he hung about in an aimless, preoccupied manner, not seeming aware of the girl's presence till, with a meaning glance, she slipped from the room. He appeared curiously downcast, sombre even, as though all his late triumph had evaporated. Sarah, from her pillows, watched him, desperately hoping for some signal to settle her doubt. He moved the lamp so it should not shine full upon her, and as his own face, briefly illumined, turned in her direction she suddenly woke to an appalling fact hitherto overlooked. What a fatuous idiot she must be! Devil though this woman was, he had loved her—spent days with her in Paris, only a few weeks ago, never dreaming the black infamy in her heart. Shock after shock—and there was far worse to come. . . .

"Don't go" She put out her bandaged hand to stop him. "I won't keep you a moment, but—I simply must speak of one thing more. The trial—I hadn't thought of it before, but—I can see now it's going to be a most horrible ordeal for you. Isn't it?"

"I understand," he said quietly. "You found that note."

"Yes," she admitted breathlessly. "And—and I knew you hid away her photograph to keep Miss Venables from seeing it. I'm sorry . . ."

He nodded, standing over her with the shut-in look she knew so well. Oh, why wouldn't he speak? If there was a raw wound in his breast, at least she could sympathise. She realised now how little she meant to him, but all the same. . . .

"Listen," he said dryly. "Would it be any good asking you to believe I myself never set eyes on that bit of writing till you'd returned it to me?"

"You never—*what?*" Under knit brows her eyes, grey-green, enormous, trained on him like search-lights. "But I don't see—"

"Naturally not—but the fact remains I didn't leave it in the book. I didn't know it had been written, and not for one moment do I imagine it was intended for me to read. Sounds like a riddle, doesn't it?"

"Then why did she write it?"

He shrugged. "Ask me another. Perhaps out of spite, to punish me for—well, not responding to her charms. Perhaps—and this is my real belief—it was one more Machiavellian move towards establishing me in the public eye as her lover, and thereby making sure no one could connect her with Venables. Anyhow, Miss Barrows will tell you the book, having been borrowed, was brought back in my absence and given into her care. Given to Miss Barrows, mark you—and with the blue notepaper sticking out a good inch."

"Oh! So you think Miss Barrows was expected to take a peep at it?"

"Certainly, and in a day or so the author would have stolen it back and burned it. Unluckily for her, Miss Barrows is strictly honourable. No one looked at it but you."

Strictly honourable! Sarah writhed with shame. What a worm he must think her!

"Then the whole thing was made-up fiction," she murmured weakly.

"Oh, no! As there was always a chance of my seeing it, the actual letter of it was true. I did look her up in Paris—once—because to refuse her urgent request might have hurt Henri. I was there only one evening, but we dined together and went to a theatre. And then, as she'd been dropping pretty broad hints, I bought her something she'd admired and gave it to her when she got home."

"A watch?"

"Watch?" He frowned affrontedly. "No! A new sort of cocktail set. Her pretending she couldn't thank me properly before her husband was just ballyhoo. There was another bit, wasn't there—something about my happening on better times? Nominally that referred to a vague talk with Henri about my landing a fatter practice; but she knew quite well I hadn't cash enough to—" He gave a sudden amused laugh. "What a blow for her when I fell heir to this money! I wondered why she began clawing away the instant she heard of it. I didn't realise then that the trap had sprung on her."

Sarah, too, had noticed the woman's sudden coolness towards the object of her passion, but it was not of this she was thinking. Seething in blushes, she lay gazing up at him, too severely chastened to have complete command of herself. An uncontrollable impulse seized her.

"Oh!" she burst out "Do you terribly despise me? I'm not Marjory Barrows. When I saw that note, I devoured every word of it. I had to— oh, don't you understand?—because I simply couldn't bear not knowing what—you and she were to one another."

Merciful Heavens—had she really said this? She had—and at once she realised it was the test on which all future life would depend. Well, if she had ruined everything, she had only herself to blame. Cowering deep in the bed, holding her breath for sheer panic, she watched fearfully through her lashes to see what happened. The sun-browned face had grown very fixed, the blue eyes narrowed and stern. She began to tremble all over.

"Why?" came the low demand. "Do you mean it mattered to you one way or the other? You—cared?"

She dared not answer. Their glances met, interpenetrated, and still, though he had drawn very close, she remained dumb. His breathing quickened. In another second brusque hands laid hold on her shoulders, shook her hard.

"It did matter?" he muttered roughly. "Tell me at once, or—"

"More than anything!" she gasped. "Oh, didn't you know?"

"Oh, God, darling, I didn't!"

It was an inarticulate groan as his lips closed over hers. They held each other fast, knit into one rapturous being. What more need be said? Sarah, the waif and stray, had found her home.

CHAPTER FORTY-ONE

GILCREST had said that the sodium evidence could cut two ways. He had also pointed out the power of a name, and added that de Bellesnaves stood for what was most awe-inspiring in France. The trial had not advanced far before Sarah had ample cause to remember both these pronouncements.

Full half the public regarded the prisoners as innocent scapegoats. The most famous avocat of the day hammered this view home to a court packed to suffocation, numerous witnesses lent him support, and the accused couple by their very aspect and demeanour made it creditable. What—this fine, open-browed young Englishman, every clean inch of him eloquent of honesty and fair-play, an assassin of the basest type? And that delicately bred woman with her vacant, mournful eyes and her smooth-banded hair the epitome of meekness—could she by the remotest chance be the monster she was painted? Unthinkable! The whole vile rigmarole had been concocted and put upon them by a man who would stop at nothing to arrest his own professional boycott. Hostile murmurs greeted the two informants' arrival in court. The phrase *"Ça se voit!"* was oft-times repeated with significant shrugs.

Sarah had not supposed it possible that her statement and Brian's could be hacked and riddled with contempt, that even their bodily injuries, vouched for by police inspectors, could be set down as results of the sea-disaster and only that. No one had seen them? Well and good! Having come to grief in a stolen yacht, what was to prevent them covering up a shameful escapade as best they could, thereby worming out of a still more compromising hole at other people's expense? Here, in a nutshell, was the interpretation put on their behaviour. Maddalena de Bellesnaves, in the brief interval at her disposal, had done some boldly-ingenious thinking, as the full fiction, told for her by others, will show.

When Harry paid his last respects to the sorrowing widow, Angela, the old cook, followed him out to his car to whisper an agitated confidence. Without the slightest doubt Madame was mentally deranged by the double shock of her husband's suicide and the rumours of foul play concerning her friend. She had already made one almost fatal attempt at self-destruction and gave unmistakable indications of meditating another. *Faute de mieux*, Angela had secured the presence of Miss MacNeil, but would this precaution be sufficient to avert an act of violence? She feared not, for if the young girl were informed of the true facts she would most assuredly take fright and leave. The servants had not dared appeal to either the English or the French doctor lest interference on their part precipitate the very crisis they dreaded. The truth was, Madame had conceived an insane hatred for both these men, possibly because they had foiled her previous attempt, though in the case of one Angela fancied a deeper-lying repugnance. She rebelled stubbornly against a nurse, yet nothing short of constant supervision could prevent her taking her own life. It was a peculiarly distressing situation. Could not Monsieur Venables suggest some remedy?

Harry was startled and nonplussed. He had heard talk of a suicidal attempt, and just now had been struck by the Baroness' odd manner. Appreciating the servants' dilemma and feeling in duty bound to do what he could for his aunt's dearest friend, he promised to postpone his departure till morning, think matters over, and drive back that evening to go into the affair more fully. After dinner in Hyères he consulted a directory and found the address of what appeared to be a respectable sanatorium in Toulon, his idea being to get the physician in charge to come over on the morrow and give an opinion. A puncture delayed his re-arrival at the villa till a fairly late hour, and when he did get there he found the household in wildest confusion. At close on midnight the Baroness had tried to drown herself, having either climbed or thrown herself from her bedroom window, entanglement with the creeper breaking the fall. By the grace of God Sebastiano had heard the noise and pursued her to the edge of the sea, dragging her by main force out of the shallow water and with great difficulty—for she fought like a maniac—getting her back to bed. Horrified, the young man lent his aid towards restraining the poor creature's frantic efforts to rise. A strong dose of sedative was administered, and presently she calmed down.

It was now that Harry thought to inquire for Miss MacNeil. Was it conceivable she had slept through all this disturbance? Then it came out. The young guest was gone, not only from her room, but from the house—when, why, the Italians could not imagine. Sebastiano had found the front door unbolted, and he had noticed that the yacht had vanished, the dinghy being moored to the landing. The girl could scarcely have dared take the boat out by herself. It looked as though she must have arranged to meet some companion.

All this looked decidedly queer, but no time could be wasted on it now. What was to be done about Madame? Harry felt obliged to catch the morning train on account of his aunt's body, yet on the other hand he saw the grave risk of leaving a woman in this condition in the sole charge of well-meaning but ignorant domestics, neither of them young, both half out of their wits. The Baroness, warmed by brandy and hot-water bottles, seemed physically none the worse for her immersion in the sea. Would not the wisest solution be to convey her at once to the sanatorium and leave her in expert hands? At all events, it appeared the lesser of two evils. A hurried consultation, and the plan was executed. Bundling the drowsy patient into a fur coat, they carried her to the car and settled her safely on the back seat with Angela on one side and the butler on the other. All four then set off for Toulon, Angela remaining with her mistress at the Hôpital de St. Jérôme, Harry and Sebastiano snatching a few hours' rest at an hotel.

In the morning Harry boarded the Paris-Calais express, and it was while he was attending to further transportation at Calais that he was approached by officers of the law and taken into custody. He was completely bowled over. It took him some time to grasp the nature of the charge or charges preferred against him, and not till considerably later had he any idea of what had happened to the de Bellesnaves' yacht.

A substantial portion of the foregoing account was upheld by valid testimony. Inspectors searching the abandoned villa found sea-drenched clothing belonging to the Baroness and her butler, evidences of the hurried departure just described, and the wistaria outside the owner's bedroom mangled and broken loose. Medical witnesses from the Hôpital de St. Jérôme swore to the patient's mental confusion and extremely depressed state, and to certain bruises indicative of a fall. It was the head-sister's mingled pity and indignation which wrought sympathy to fever-pitch. The entire packed court became surcharged with emotion. A woman fainted and was carried out.

The defending advocate saw his opportunity and used it. By what right did Gilcrest declare his two English patients victims of foul play when expert inquiry could detect nothing of the sort? The jury might be justified in thinking this exposition concerning the lethal properties of raw sodium a clear revelation of guilty knowledge on the informer's part. Even supposing one could accept what was undemonstrable and visionary, was it easy to credit either Maddalena de Bellesnaves or Henry Venables with cognisance of a method surely unique in the annals of crime? It had been said that Madame had spent considerable time in watching her late husband's experimental work. In other words, she had displayed a wifely desire to encourage an invalid man in a consoling hobby. Sodium had been within reach, but had she been seen to take any of it, heard to ask one question as to its nature? No, nor was there evidence to show she had so much as looked into a single physiological or chemical treatise. The young Englishman with whom her relations had never extended beyond the purely platonic, was equally remote from the world of science—a stock-broker and amateur athlete. Decidedly, if any individual seemed likely to conceive of this recherché method of taking life, one would be inclined to pick a potential bio-chemist—a man who was known to exhume dogs (previously experimented upon or not as the case might be) for the self-confessed purpose of ascertaining what incriminating clues remained in their organs.

There was a vast amount in this strain. The inference throughout was thinly-veiled and extremely difficult to combat, the prosecution's weakness lying in the total absence of direct evidence. It could not be proved that sodium had been administered at all, simply because no one had seen it put into the capsules. The bottle freely identified as having at one time belonged to the Baroness might have been stolen from a medicine-cupboard. One could not come to grips with anything, the charges resting on an alleged admission of guilt and a subsequent attempt to exterminate an eavesdropper whose whole deposition might be a lie. Questions of time arose and were haggled over to no purpose. In short, by the end of the first day it began to look as though the jury must choose which story to believe—and of the two, that sponsored by the prisoners' had the better ring of truth. Gilcrest said little, but Sarah saw her own dread reflected in his set features. Unless something happened to turn the tables, these devils were going to skin through.

Something did happen, though not in court. For days an odd tale had been circulating. Sarah was acquainted with it, but realising it was not evidence had dismissed it with a sigh when lo, out of the blue a bold radical sheet published it under inch-high scare-lines. A libel action would probably ensue, but no matter, the cat was out of the bag, and those who had been asking who, what, was the Baronne de Bellesnaves before her marriage found their question sensationally answered.

Who, indeed? Why, she was none other than a once-popular cabaret artist of Naples, who ten years ago had quitted her native city on account of bitter feeling evoked by an unsubstantiated suspicion of murder! A rich lover—a manufacturing chemist—died under peculiar circumstances, having recently insured his life for her benefit. His family, positive the young mistress had poisoned him, ordered an inquest—*and nothing whatever was found*. Acute gastric ulcer, that was all. The girl could not be touched, but the turmoil had given her a bad name which made her future precarious. She collected her insurance, invented a new history for herself, and two years later, in Paris, became the wife of the Baron, then fairly well off, and in an apparently moribund condition. The mother in Lyons was a myth. The present accused came from the lowest waterfront slums of Naples, where she had been known as La Madonna delle Scimmie—Our Lady of the Monkeys—a title inspired by certain perversely amusing imitations, said to have had a hidden parallel in her nature.

This was the story made known to Beryl Tomlins by a Fascist officer she had met in Nice—a man at one time well-acquainted with the woman, whom he had seen and recognised while motoring through Ste. Brigitte-la-Mer. Beryl had written a full account of her discovery to her sister, posting it the afternoon of her death, but as Mrs. Cripps left Cheltenham before the letter arrived she knew nothing of its contents till, days afterwards, it was forwarded to her. Immediately on its receipt she saw Sarah and Harry driving off, tried to stop them and failed; but Sarah had since read the communication, and one more mystery was cleared up.

In view of the disinterred scandal, the librarian had been ready to think the worst of Mme. de Bellesnaves' flattering attentions to Christine. The creature had an axe to grind, was probably ensnaring Dr. Gilcrest in order to use him as an innocent tool to bring about a death by which she had long schemed to profit. Why had Ian Frampton warned Christine? Look at the wording of his note! If it had been dope-peddlers, he'd have said so. No, it was something he had to approach delicately, therefore in a personal interview. He had just come from the Casa Giallo, hadn't he? Earlier than usual, his game broken up. Didn't that look as though he'd found out something while he was there, accidentally, of course? Something horrifying—something which made him an active menace to a certain person's safety. As for the tall waiter Mr. Vansittart had seen, why couldn't it have been the de Bellesnaves' rascally butler told off and bribed to do a nasty bit of work? Incidentally, it was a bit odd no one had ever duly considered the hotel fire-escape as a likely means of getting into the building. Most nights about eleven there were too many people going up to bed, but a Friday, with every human soul downstairs, wasn't it a very different proposition?

La Madonna delle Scimmie! It gave popular sentiment a tremendous jar, and from now on the heroine in the dock lost much of her glamour. True, no charge had been brought, but the man had died of gastric ulcer, don't forget that! A trick that has triumphed once can succeed again; and then, manufacturing chemist! Those two words might contain the solution to one mighty puzzle.

The prosecution had other cards to play. A mass of small evidence began to emerge, not touching the crimes, but shedding light in other dark places. Platonic relations? Well . . . what about the Greek gardener's statement of having seen the couple whispering together in the rhododendrons, their attitude compromising, the hour long past midnight? And the preceding spring there had been more glimpses of the same kind. Less prudence in the earlier stages. Any lingering doubt was squashed by a hotel proprietor of Vichy. (Sarah recalled that one of the anonymous letters was posted in Vichy.) Last October the accused pair had spent a week in each other's company, having registered as Charles Graham and wife, of Liverpool. The signature was shown, the writing undisguisedly Harry's.

And now the young man's private life, different indeed from the side kept for his aunt's delectation. Stock-broking job forfeited eighteen months ago as the result of various misdemeanours, no subsequent occupation, living by his wits, eternally hounded by money-lenders! Harry might not have been existing on the very brink of a precipice, kept from falling over by recurrent donations from his aunt, but it looked extremely like it. His actual income, at no time large, was mortgaged to the last penny, his debts reached into thousands. Not one of these facts need ever have come out if an excuse for prying below the surface had not cropped up. As it was, an understandable motive for removing his aunt was clearly established. Opportunity had never been denied, but still the question whether or not murder had been committed remained unanswered—perhaps unanswerable.

However that might be, the two main witnesses for the defence were not standing up particularly well under cross-examination. Glib and convincing before, they began to waver, trip up, contradict each other in small but important details. Those who suspected the Italians had been bought and coached in their parts nodded with satisfaction. One little incident seemed suggestive. Sebastiano, an old man, had been up virtually the whole night, yet on his surprisingly early return next morning he was found by an inspector energetically engaged in raking over the gravel and tidying the flowerbeds! He explained that his master's funeral service was to be held to-day, and that although his mistress lay ill in a sanatorium he could not bear for the place to be seen in disorder for lack of a gardener. Touching devotion to the family he served—or the carrying out of stern instructions. Which? French and English shrugged in unison. It was not typical of an Italian domestic left on his own to do this sort of job without a pressing reason.

In spite of all, the issue of this annoyingly vague case narrowed steadily down to one point: had or had not Miss MacNeil overheard a conversation between the accused while hidden in the Baroness' bedroom? Unless it could be proved incontrovertibly that she had done so, then the murderous attack on which all else hinged was damned as pure, malicious invention. One more tiny bit of evidence was yet to come. If that carried no weight. . . .

What was this strange object—the trousers portion of a lady's pyjamas? Pale green silk, rough-dry, salt to the taste. The jury examined them and nodded. They examined, also, the rusty stains encircling each leg—marks made by wet ropes. The audience craned their necks, the judge suppressed the ripple of laughter. There was another feature to which attention was directed—a small, triangular nick in the seat, where a bit of material had been snagged cleanly out. The trousers had caught on something? Well?

The prosecuting counsel explained. This garment had been worn by Miss MacNeil on board the yacht. In Mme. de Bellesnaves' whole wardrobe there were neither pyjamas nor any silk fabric of a pale green colour. Now, then! The butler declared he had found the front door barred, although earlier in the evening he himself had barred it. Presumably, then, Miss MacNeil left the house by way of the door. She would naturally choose this means of exit in preference to climbing from an upper window, an unnecessary and dangerous proceeding. Least of all would she select her hostess' bedroom window.

Yet someone had climbed through this particular window, or else climbed from the ground up to it, as the state of the wisteria showed. Close scrutiny had failed to reveal who that person could have been. If there had been footprints in the mould of the flowerbeds, all such had been carefully removed by the butler whose rake was busy long before there had been any reason to examine the ground surrounding the house. Miss MacNeil had been delirious for two days, so a long interval had elapsed before her story was made known to either Dr. Gilcrest or the police. As soon as she was interviewed, a thorough search was made, but nothing was found. And then, towards the back of the villa, a small pile of withered rhododendron blossoms was noticed. They had been raked together but not removed. These were gone over bit by bit, and at long last the searchers discovered something so small that if they had not been looking for it they would never have discerned it at all. No doubt it had been caught on a stiff twig of the creeper, but as there was a breeze it had been blown in among the bushes.

Here it was. The watchers held their breath and saw a piece of white paper unfolded from round—but no, it was too small. What was it? The jury were handing it round, laid on the paper, touching it to their lips. A stout man in the front row rose and shouted, *"C'est vrai, alors!"*

The tiny object was a snippet of green silk, which fitted neatly into the tear. It was freshly laundered, not salt. . . .

In a trice the sublime fiction crumbled to dust. That evening every newspaper in France placarded the denouement which of all things was the last any reader had expected. Henry Venables, pale, sweating, utterly broken in morale, had confessed!

CHAPTER FORTY-TWO

WHEN the sum total of Harry Venables' admissions and other information was dovetailed together, the history of the first four crimes ran as follows:

Very soon after Maddalena de Bellesnaves embarked on her liaison with her friend's nephew she began to envisage a way of laying hands on not only stray pickings from the rich woman's fortune but the actual fortune in toto. She had found a young man whose abject infatuation for her made him her slave. He would marry her if the two obstacles which stood between him and his ample inheritance could be removed, moreover his present financial plight was so desperate that, already conscienceless by nature, he would eagerly agree to her proposals. Actually, of course, there was a third obstacle—her husband; but as Henri had been dying for eight years or more he need present no great difficulty. Where she would require help was with the aunt and stepmother, both ageing, useless women who, though delicate in health, might easily drag on their tiresome existences for another twenty years at least.

It was not hard to bend Harry's weak will to hers, and having won his consent she expounded her plan. Years ago a scientist now dead had told her about a chemical substance, not a poison, which smouldered or burst into flame when in contact with water. Introduced into the system it would cause speedy death and in a few seconds eliminate its own traces. The death itself would most probably be diagnosed as natural, but in the event of suspicion arising there was nothing whatever to fear. A post mortem could be performed, and what would it show? Simply a bad abrasion in the stomach—no residue of any kind. In short, it was a perfectly safe method. Maddalena knew that it had been tried once, with complete success, for the scientist had told her so. If it had not been essayed oftener, that was because almost no one had ever thought of it, although there was certainly an additional reason as well. You see, the substance—pure sodium—could be given only in a capsule, which meant the victim must be taking capsules or be persuaded to take them.

Fortunately, as the plotters both knew, Harry's aunt was taking capsules—had been taking them for a long time. As the sodium could be easily obtained from Brian Gilcrest's laboratory, why not set to work at once? Maddalena herself would prepare a single capsule, Harry would put it with the others in his aunt's bottle, and then in the course of hours or days—it really didn't matter—the dose would be swallowed. Chrissie's death would provide Harry with an excuse to visit the stepmother in Yorkshire, where the funeral would take place. While there he could make an opportunity for getting rid of the other tiresome old hag in the same manner. The stepmother was always ailing, always pleased to try new remedies? Excellent! He would tell her about a prescription which one of his aunt's friends had used with advantage. Maddalena would provide him with one, in capsule form. The stepmother would get it put up at her own chemist, he would have his private dose ready, and *voila!* The thing would be done.

The scheme had advanced thus far when a terrifying slip threatened shipwreck to all their hopes. The famous bridge-game had just broken up, Major Frampton had gone home, and, her husband retired to bed. Maddalena met her accomplice in the lonely boat-house to hold a conference on the approaching murder of Miss Venables. By a stroke of fiendish luck, the Major had not gone home at all. Instead, he had sat down under the seaside of the little building to breathe the cool breeze, and just too late a retreating footstep warned the conspirators of what had happened. They caught one fleeting glimpse of a blanched, goggle-eyed face vanishing along the beach. Harry dashed after it, but the Major, panic lending him speed, had managed to make off. Where he had got to it was impossible to say. Anyhow he was gone, hot-foot to warn Miss Venables of her danger.

Quick! What was to be done? One thing first of all: Christine must be detained till Harry came to fetch her. Maddalena attended to that by telephone, and instantly made a plan to get rid of the would-be informant. They must try the safest way first, and if that failed Harry must take Henri's revolver and use it—but perhaps it need not come to that. It could be confidently assumed that Frampton would not speak of this to anyone save Miss Venables herself. His first action would be to inquire at the desk whether she had returned, and then, finding she had not, he would retreat for safety to his room. Only someone with a message purporting to be from Miss Venables could entice him forth. Harry must get himself up as a waiter and deliver that message, directly afterwards shoving the man through the open shaft of the lift. No one need ever guess how the accident had occurred. Here, this old coat of Sebastiano's would do the trick—and Maddalena had a man's black wig which she had once used for some theatricals. Put it on, smudge a few moles with this eyebrow pencil, rub his face over with the dark cream she used for her lids. There—he was quite transformed! It would easily wipe off. Climb up the fire-escape, if anyone caught him he was doing this for a joke—and above all, be careful where he left his car. . . .

It worked, precisely as hoped, and without a hitch. No, just one: Vansittart saw him. No matter, the old ass was blind as a bat and almost totally deaf. There had been a short wait before Frampton came up. That was because he had stopped on his way back to steady himself with a drink, an advantage in a way, since his brain was none too clear. Harry heard the heavy thump six stories down in the basement, and knew the job was a success. He took the other way round, to avoid a second encounter with Vansittart, reached the fire-escape, and in two minutes was in his car, speeding towards St. Raphael.

All the same, he was on tenterhooks lest Frampton had spilled the beans to a third person. Had he? Apparently not—but he had done what was almost as bad, left a note, behind Chrissie's locked door, where no one could get at it before she did. Harry experienced a paralysis of terror till he had seen the contents. If anything definite were said, he would be forced to strike a second death-blow at once and chance the consequences. Unutterable relief! Only vague hints of a peril unnamed—and better still, while Harry was mumbling that Frampton was drunk, his aunt gave him her own interpretation. Dope-peddlers? Marvellous. He must encourage the belief.

It was the Baroness who, from talks with her friend, perceived that the danger though circumvented was not crushed. Trusting in some respects, the old maid was exceedingly shrewd in others. Once let her start putting things together and she might arrive dangerously near the truth. Most certainly she would if, as might happen any day, she found out about Harry's lost job and the money scrapes he had been getting into. Once let the smallest germ of doubt get lodged in her mind and future operations would be severely hampered. No, safety lay in fostering this original delusion of hers, fixing her thoughts firmly on dope-peddlers—then all would be plain sailing. The inquest itself, with its verdict of Death by Misadventure, was unsettling enough. Well, it would not hurt and would serve a useful purpose to allow Christine to think otherwise. So arguing, Maddalena composed and dispatched the first of the anonymous threats, taking care to leave none of her finger-prints on the letter. It did the trick—rather too well. The victim, already intensely miserable in her surroundings, left the same day! Left before the sodium could be stolen or the capsule prepared, to begin a wandering existence during which everything was brought to a standstill.

It may have been the strong streak of sadism in the Baroness' nature which made her continue the letters, but, be that as it may, before long a secondary result was noted with satisfaction. Harry, whom she was meeting from time to time, declared that constant terrorization was making heavy inroads on his aunt's health. It was even possible Chrissie might die during one of these gastric attacks, and if she survived it was plain she could not keep up this restless life much longer. He was doing his best to persuade her to settle down. Maddalena, in her affectionate letters, urged the same, and between them they believed that very soon events would again steer in their direction. The long wait was proving a damned nuisance. Harry had been obliged to pinch corners and even sell his car in order to keep afloat. He dared not ask Chrissie for money, for that would betray his real position. She could not break the entail of his father's will, but she could easily lose faith in him and cut him off from personal contact.

He wangled a Christmas visit to Huddersfield, where, with both his female encumbrances together under one roof, he hoped for immediate results. Not at all. His aunt had contracted the annoying habit of carrying her medicine round in her handbag, the latter never out of her sight, his stepmother, disliking him, sniffed so contemptuously at his suggested prescription that he retired in despair. It would not do to antagonize Gracie. She knew about the cheque he had forged and just why his father had tied his inheritance up for years to come. So far she had the decency not to put Chrissie against him, but it was in her power to do so at any moment. All he gained by the week's boredom was his aunt's generous Christmas present—a new car, and a fat cheque. He returned feeling the difficulties of the game were practically insurmountable.

Suddenly luck turned. Chrissie decided to engage a companion and go south. She and Gracie came to London, saw Gilcrest, and Gracie, by all the gods, was ordered capsules! She even entrusted Harry with the prescription. He called for the medicine in person, performed his delicate substitution in the seclusion of a public lavatory, and handed the bottle, wrapped as before, to a messenger to deliver. By morning Gracie was dead. The post mortem demanded by law proved perfectly satisfactory. One obstacle was removed.

Here we must insert a mention of the parts Gilcrest and Sarah MacNeil were expected to play. As the two lovers must not be supposed to take the remotest interest in each other, it was arranged that each should pretend an attraction in a different quarter. In neither case was this hard, for Harry liked his aunt's companion, while Maddalena for some time had nurtured a secret fondness for the man whose supreme indifference whetted her appetite for conquest. There can be no doubt that she hoped to entangle the doctor into an affair, keeping it well hidden from Harry's stupid eyes. She could make Harry believe anything, and there was certainly a good reason for cultivating the physician whose dispensary must be accessible to her on stated occasions. The trouble came when she saw Harry paying what she feared were serious attentions to a potential rival. What came of that fear is already known so with this brief digression we may pass on to Miss Tomlins' case.

Harry had carried his bit of sodium round in a tiny bottle of oil, not knowing when it would be required or how long the stuff could be left in a capsule without catching fire from the moisture in the air. He had, therefore, emptied one of his stepmother's capsules and refilled it; but the Baroness, having to work with the utmost speed, had her capsule previously prepared, ready to slip into the newly filled bottle. As Gilcrest surmised, she knew little or nothing about the different kinds of capsule casings. By pure haphazard she had filched from Miss Barrows' box a kerotin one, but this she did not guess. Learning that the dispenser would be putting up Miss Venables' prescription on a certain Tuesday evening, she hid in the dark garden outside watching till the room was empty. It was a warm night, the door was wide open for air. If no diversion occurred, she would drop in for a call and create one; but it was unnecessary, for the girl was summoned to answer the telephone.

Quick as a flash she darted to the table, and beheld not one but two bottles of capsules, neither as yet labelled! She must decide instantly or else forfeit her opportunity. For understandable reasons her choice fell on the larger capsules which matched her own and the following night, just after she had polished off the detested dog whose death was to plunge Henri into despair, Harry rushed to her with disturbing news. Had she made a bloomer? Another old girl, a Miss Tomlins, had died in agony, soon after swallowing the first capsule out of a new bottle! Worse, Sarah MacNeil had been with her at the time. Here was a pretty kettle of fish and no mistake. What was to be done about it?

What, indeed? Nothing, except to settle one vital point, namely whether or not this death came from natural causes. To plant a second sodium capsule in Miss Venables' bottle would be running into frightful danger. Supposing any question over her death arose, would not the remaining capsules be analysed? On the other hand, a fortnight's delay was risky, too. The medicine in the meantime might be changed or discontinued. To clear up the doubt, Maddalena paid an early visit to the hotel and heard from Sarah quite enough to satisfy her mind. She also learned that owing to the improvement in Christine's health these present capsules were likely to be the last. She took a good look at them to make sure of the size, then, to provide an excuse for returning at a time when both women would be out, she hid her wrist-watch deep down in a crack of the sofa. Stopping at the dispensary for her husband, she secured one of the smaller capsule shells and bore it home to fill with more sodium, coating the stuff with kaolin to keep it perfectly dry.

To her acute annoyance, the watch was found and brought back. She decided that Harry, who was stupidly calling on her at the moment, must undertake this second job in her stead. How maddening for this watch to be seen at close range by Sarah MacNeil! It was Harry's gift, bought with his Newmarket winnings, in Paris, just before they motored together to Marseilles, where she picked up her train. *Tant pis*—but perhaps it was just as well that Harry, now terribly nervous since the Tomlins' débâcle, should go straight off to Monte. She, also, would get away, to Arles, simply to make things more comfortable.

She called Harry back to give him the capsule and to remind him that the final threat was already in the post. Was it wise to have sent it? Certainly—for now there would be real dyspepsia to lead people astray. With the next postal delivery looming ahead, Harry lost no time in getting off. Nor did he have any trouble over the capsule, the bottle lying in full view on Chrissie's table. All he had to do was to get Chrissie into the bathroom to fetch iodine for a small cut on his chin, and the thing was done. He stuck the capsule well down below several others to postpone the event till he had had a little play at the tables. It might be some time before he got to Monte again.

His next and worst shock came when he was told that, on account of his aunt's absurd statement, there was going to be an inquest. Worst? No, for the news about Gilcrest's enormous legacy hit him still harder. He had expected all Chrissie's money, but that was not the real point. Gilcrest was insisting on two post mortems to clear his own name. Two—and the other one, where the trouble was not in the stomach, might upset the whole game. Not able to know what damaging evidence might come to light, he went through the torments of the damned till the verdict came through. He read it, breathed again. There was a doubt, but that doubt, though it left Gilcrest under a cloud, did not touch him. Everything was all right—or would have been if Maddalena had not enticed Sarah MacNeil to the villa. He did not yet know why, if she deemed it advisable to do this thing, she could not have explained matters to him beforehand. Yes, he had been frightened, lost his nerve. He could have sworn the girl never dimly suspected either of them, but it seems he was wrong.

No disclosures regarding the Baron's death could be drawn from Harry, while the woman, from first to last, sat with sealed lips. There was talk of bringing an additional charge, but it came to nothing for lack of evidence. The suicide verdict held.

Not since the Landru sensation had France been so profoundly stirred. A chain of murders, five in all, and each a cold-blooded, calculated affair. Even the accidental one formed no exception. And yet, but for one tiny slip, all these human sacrifices would, like the final death, have been judged purely fortuitous happenings. The public gasped and shook its head. That the arch-criminal was a woman, young, lovely, unmarked by evil passions, lent the crowning touch of horror. La Madonna delle Scimmie. Bimi, also, had been her name. Wasn't there a ghastly story by an English writer, some tale of a monkey who—? Ah, there you are!

On the deck of the steamer bound for Majorca, Sarah and Brian lay in chairs drawn so close that they touched. Midnight blue sea spread before them, stars powdered the dark bowl of the heavens, phosphorescence flashed white amidst the waves. Filled with a deep peace, neither had spoken for many minutes. It was Sarah who resumed conversation where it had been broken off by an embrace.

"Death-sentences! It's just, heaven knows, but somehow I hate thinking about it."

"Hers will be commuted. You'll see." Brian's tone was grim.

"It oughtn't to be. She took the lead. Harry hadn't the brains or the daring, vile though he is. Oh! Shall you ever forget that sickening collapse of his? Or her face, changing instantaneously from a Raphael madonna to Bertrand's Bimi? Once before, when it wasn't intended, I mean—I saw that same transformation. It was when for a moment she thought Harry was after some English girl. How she laughed when she realised it was only a fib he'd told to put me off. He'd been with her, you see. I ought to have guessed . . . By the way, do you think it was sodium she used when she set me alight? She said it was nothing so crude as a match."

"Was there any water nearby?"

She thought a moment. "Yes, of course, there was! Polly's drinking-vessel, under the edge of my skirt. That was why I heard that funny little noise I supposed was a wasp. It was the sodium hissing as it burned. And to think I suspected every conceivable person except her!"

"I wasn't very brilliant myself," he admitted ruefully.

"You were clever about a lot of things. Which reminds me, how do you suppose the Baron actually came to swallow that poison? Have you got a theory to explain it?"

"Yes," he said slowly. "I've worked it out after this fashion: in spite of all bans, Henri never could entirely resist chocolates, and she knew it. What she didn't officially know was that he wasn't supposed to eat them, therefore she could put temptation in his way without rousing suspicion. It was a kind, thoughtful action, you understand. No, he never discussed his health with her, or anything else that really mattered. They were as the poles apart, and had been, I imagine, since he first found out what she was like. Why did he marry her? Impossible to say. In any case, it's no stranger than many marriages. She usually got what she wanted. First and foremost she was an actress. . . .

"She must have known that nothing better can be found than a soft-centred chocolate for getting paste-cyanide down a person's throat. A small pellet of the stuff can be stuck through from the bottom, the hole closed so it will never be noticed, while the entire chocolate will be eaten before anything really wrong has been detected. Cyanide is bitter, but so is chocolate. Henri generally gulped things down. She chose cyanide because of its swift action. Henri probably had some on hand, which he could get without difficulty, on the strength of his old medical degree . . . let's see—weren't there three chocolates left in the box, all exactly alike?"

"Three—and they had all been the same sort."

"Good! Then she must have saved eight in all, poisoning four and keeping four untouched. Each day just before lunch she placed the four poisoned ones in the box, and when Henri had gone for his nap slipped along quietly to hide and watch, we'll say behind that nearest clump of tamarisks. If nothing happened, she would go on watching till he woke, and if he came away without eating a chocolate, she would simply change the poisoned ones for the others and wait till next day to begin all over again."

"Was that done so no outside person would be killed?"

"Certainly. It wasn't safe to chance this sort of stray murder. I should think, though, that she must have been successful about the second try, possibly the third—and when it did happen it was early enough for her to keep her appointment with the masseuse. The whole affair would have been over in twenty minutes at the outside. A man in his condition would never have strength to reach help, or if he tried he'd be speechless in a few minutes. As soon as it was finished, she went in, changed the three remaining chocolates and laid his fountain-pen and the alleged message on the floor. That was all."

"She watched him die!" Sarah whispered with a shudder. "Just as she must have watched the dogs. As she meant to watch me . . ."

"With gloves on," he supplemented coolly. "It completes the picture, don't you think? She was too sharp to leave her fingerprints on that paper, or the pen."

"Gloves . . ." Sarah leant close, her cheek pressed to his. "Brian, do you know what that brings to my mind? Dear Miss Venables. She put on gloves, white ones, when she handled those letters—the letters Harry tried to make me believe she'd written to herself! I remembered those gloves. How guilty it makes me feel to think for one moment I doubted. We owe her so much."

"We owe her everything," he said simply. "But for her stupendous kindness I couldn't have married you or any other girl till I was a middle-aged man, bald, full of crochets."

She held his hand against her lips, thinking of the sore spot in his past which was no longer a secret from her. The events in question had occurred when, at the completion of his hospital term, he had arranged for a London practise, mainly for experience, and under no urgent necessity of making it pay. Just at this time the financial world had been plunged into chaos by a gigantic and disgraceful failure. The senior Gilcrest, caught in the maelstrom, had lost everything, and ill with pneumonia died from shock and despair. Overnight, as it were, Brian, never before troubled about money, found himself confronted with the support of himself, his mother, and a younger brother, unable to earn a living except by medicine.

In the first crushed moments of this disaster, he was approached by one of his father's chief creditors, a company-promoter, who made him a tempting proposal. Why not turn to account a certain serum he had perfected, and of which his dead father had spoken with pride? Capital could be found and a small private company floated for the manufacture and sale of the thing. A product of such high value, placed within reach of the public—why, it might prove a gold-mine! Did not the project promise to solve the present difficulties? It did—but Brian hesitated, doubtful as to the ethics involved, even though his name need not appear. Allowing the formula for the serum to remain in the promoter's possession while he sought competent advice he later reclaimed it, reluctantly vetoed the suggestion, and considered the matter closed. He did, however, very gratefully accept a loan to tide him over the worst period, never supposing his helper's generosity had any other motive than the desire to repay past kindnesses on the part of the elder Gilcrest. No one would ever know how many men Brian's father had assisted. It was certain this man had been one of them.

Hardly had Brian embarked on the new practise when a thunderbolt fell. A prominent physician brought a charge against him before the Medical Council, alleging unprofessional conduct, and producing as evidence not only brochures but press-cuttings in three foreign languages, all extolling the virtues of a new proprietary article of which Dr. Brian Gilcrest was proclaimed as the inventor! "The epoch-making discovery," purchasable at low price from any chemist, was selling like mad throughout Central Europe and Italy. A fortune was in prospect, but Dr. Gilcrest, by entering the ranks of commercial enterprise, had forfeited his right to remain within the sacred precincts of his profession. Could he prove he had not been a consenting party to the venture? If not, there was no hope for him. He would at once be struck off the rolls.

"It was clear what had happened," Brian had explained. "Bowles, over my head and without my knowledge, had formed his company with headquarters in Vienna, running the risk on the assumption that when profits began to roll into my pocket I would be too rejoiced to raise any objection to his betrayal of confidence. The use of my name was for launching the thing on the continent, a clever advertising device which could have been dropped when the English campaign was started. He never expected that literature issued in German and Polish would reach my colleagues' ears, which showed his stupidity—or perhaps he knew it, but took a chance on my complaisance. But here's another item: The doctor who denounced me was hand in glove with a Berlin man who'd got hold of a serum similar but inferior to mine. He was making a lucrative thing out of sending English patients to Berlin for an exclusive and expensive treatment, undoubtedly splitting the huge fees. The inner circle were aware of this, but it didn't refute the charge against me. In fact, at the first hearing it seemed impossible to refute it at all. I lost my case, and was chucked out, neck and crop."

One difficulty, bolstered up by the well-known state of Brian's finances, was the large sum of money lent without obvious security by the promoter backing the company.

Money with which he had made the first payments on his practise—hush-money, it could now be called. How could that be accounted for? The promoter spoke of a verbal agreement. No papers could be produced, but the Council shrugged, not anticipating any. Brian appealed, and this time, mainly because his statements and manner made a better impression than the promoter's, secured a reversal of the decision. He was reinstated, but could get no damages out of Bowles, who took this occasion to go bankrupt. Moreover the extremely unpleasant sensation caused by the trial and the fact that a number of physicians continued to believe the victim guilty had wrought havoc with a career already badly hampered by lack of funds. Brian was forced to cut his losses, avail himself of the Baron's suggestion, and begin afresh in the south of France. Decidedly embittered, heavily burdened with debt, he had held aloof from personal relationships lest his new set of patients discover what might still lead to prejudicial misunderstandings. His defensive shell was fully explained, but for all that Sarah loved to probe back into the period when she had misconstrued its meaning.

"Oh, if you knew how hard I worked to make you notice me!"

"I noticed you too much. That was the rub."

"When? Not surely that first time in London?"

"I shouldn't wonder. You see, I knew straight off not only that you were my kind of girl, but that you were most likely the only girl I was likely to want for a long time to come. Why did I know it? One of life's mysteries. The point is, I couldn't have you, therefore I resented your very existence. Now! Does that fill the bill?"

It did. His arm was around her, his free hand ruffling her hair, when, clinging more closely, she murmured. "And you don't honestly mind if I'm scatter-brained, flippant, American and—well just on occasions dishonourable?"

"Not so long as you keep on being a few other things."

"What, for instance?"

"Kissable—and mine."

Their eyes met, then their lips. His arm tightened about her, and her senses drifted to sea on a tide of joy.

FINIS

www.ingramcontent.com/pod-product-compliance
Lightning Source LLC
Chambersburg PA
CBHW060812190726
48285CB00002B/639